THE MYTHICS

PAPERCUTZ

MORE GREAT GRAPHIC NOVEL SERIES AVAILABLE FROM

PAPERCUTZ™

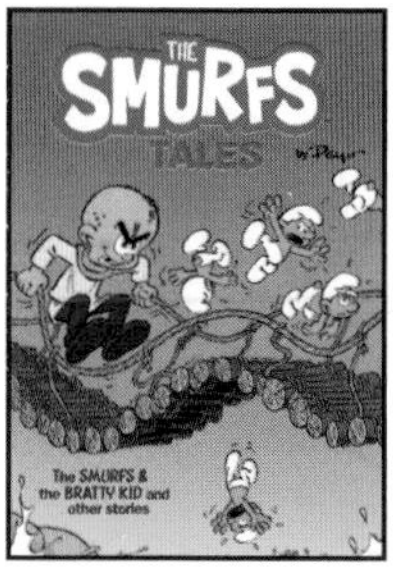
THE SMURFS
TALES
The SMURFS & the BRATTY KID and other stories
THE SMURFS TALES

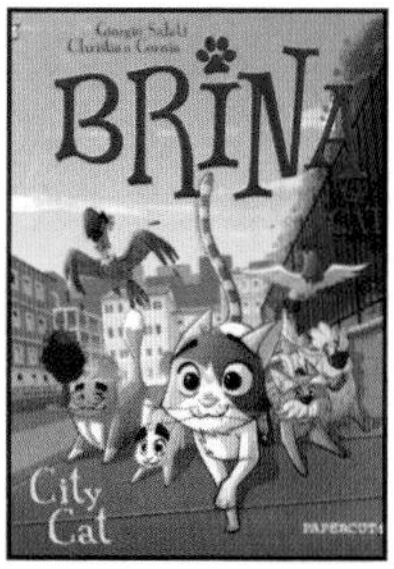
BRINA
City Cat
BRINA THE CAT

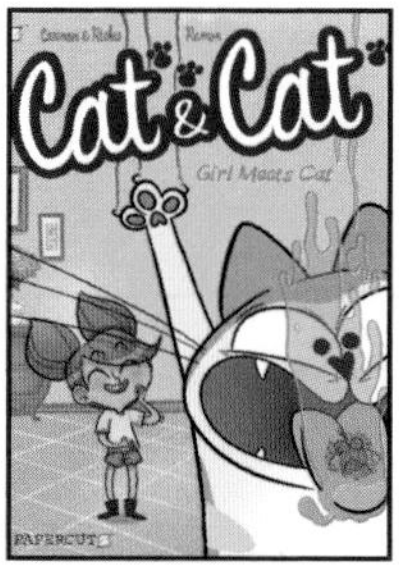
Cat & Cat
Girl Meets Cat
CAT & CAT

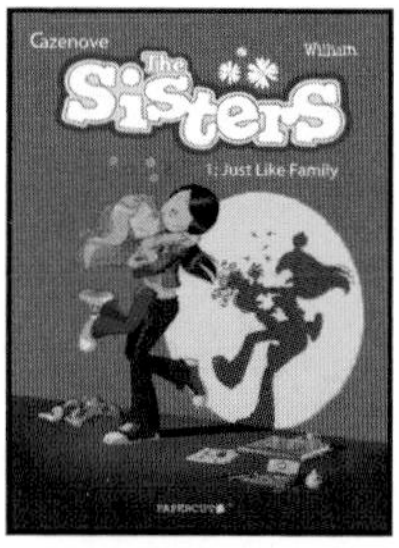
Cazenove
William
The Sisters
1: Just Like Family
THE SISTERS

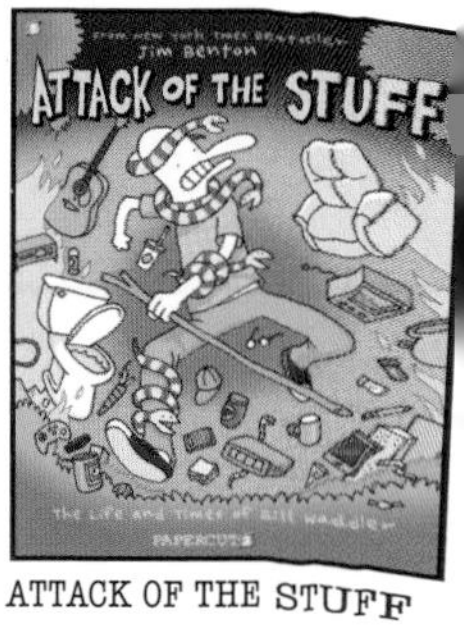
Jim Benton
ATTACK OF THE STUFF
ATTACK OF THE STUFF

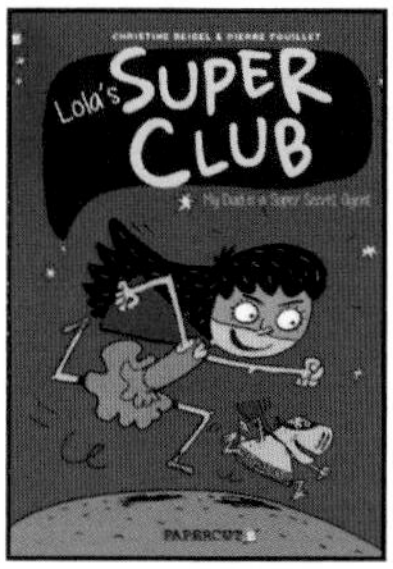
CHRISTINE BEIGEL & PIERRE FOUILLET
Lola's SUPER CLUB
LOLA'S SUPER CLUB

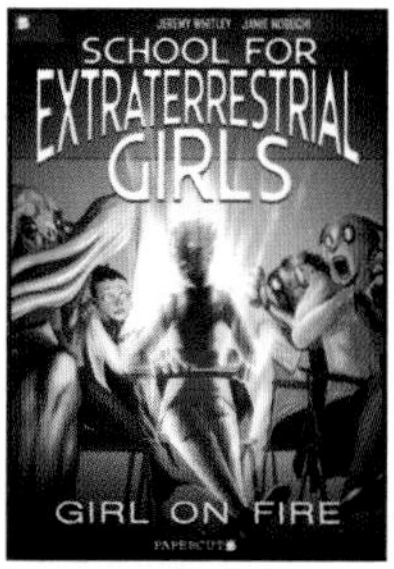
JEREMY WHITLEY · JAMIE NOGUCHI
SCHOOL FOR EXTRATERRESTRIAL GIRLS
GIRL ON FIRE
SCHOOL FOR EXTRATERRESTRIAL GIRLS

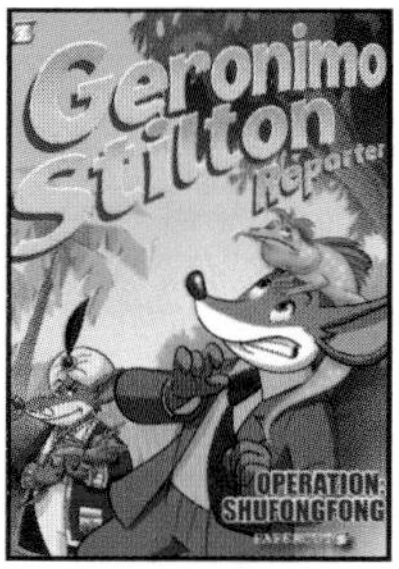
Geronimo Stilton
Reporter
OPERATION: SHUFONGFONG
GERONIMO STILTON REPORTER

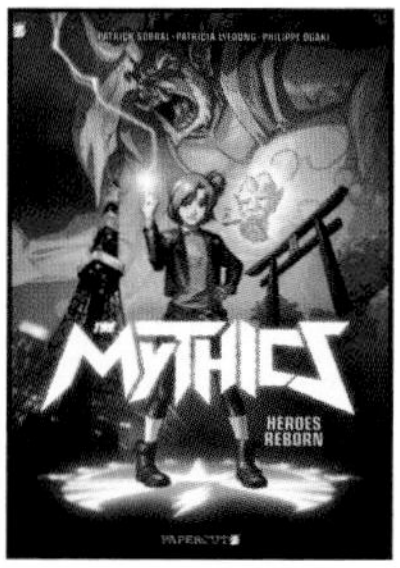
MYTHICS
HEROES REBORN
THE MYTHICS

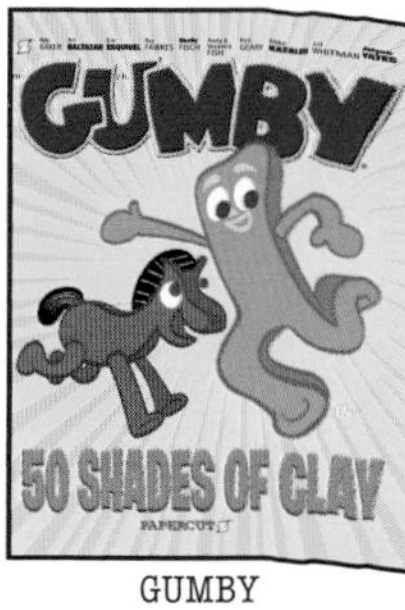
GUMBY
50 SHADES OF CLAY
GUMBY

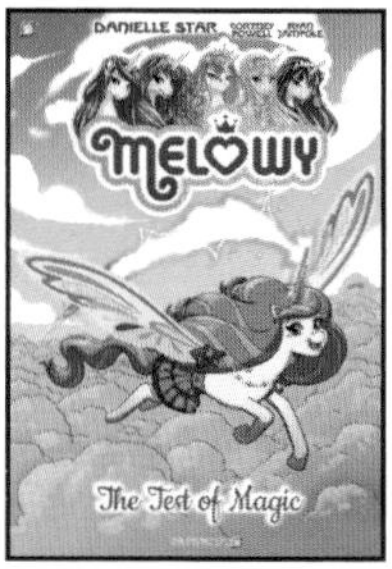
DANIELLE STAR
Melowy
The Test of Magic
MELOWY

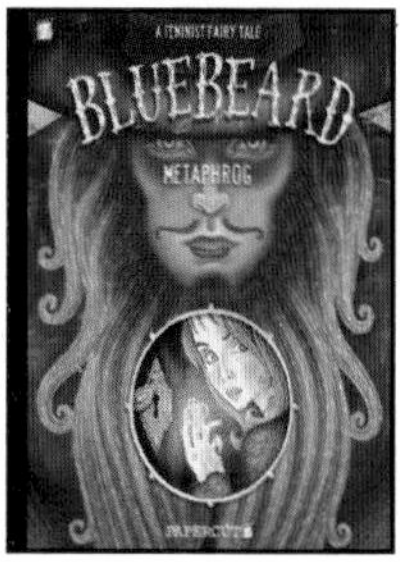
A FEMINIST FAIRY TALE
BLUEBEARD
METAPHROG
BLUEBEARD

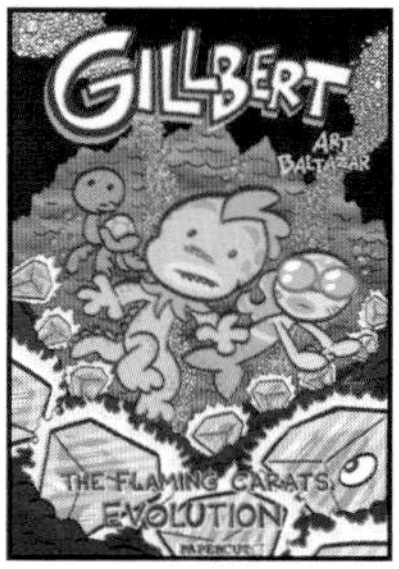
GILLBERT
ART BALTAZAR
THE FLAMING CARATS EVOLUTION
GILLBERT

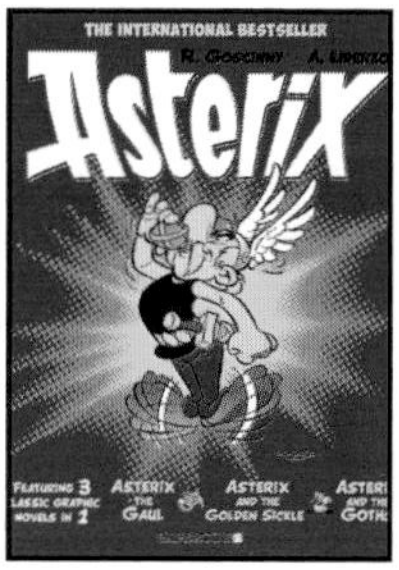
THE INTERNATIONAL BESTSELLER
R. GOSCINNY
A. UDERZO
Asterix
ASTERIX

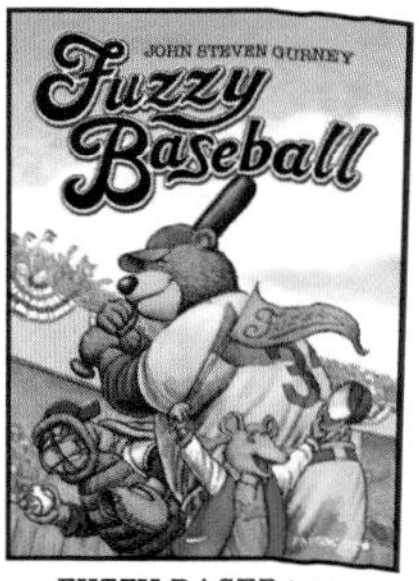
JOHN STEVEN GURNEY
Fuzzy Baseball
FUZZY BASEBALL

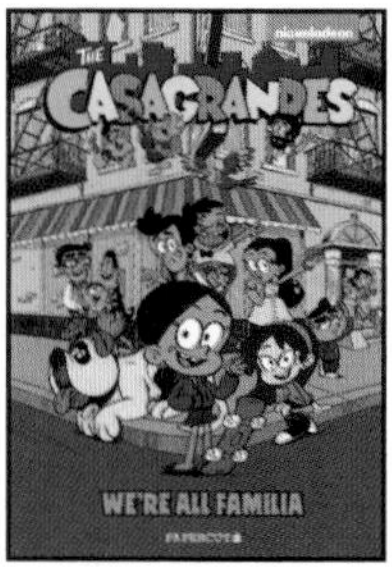
nickelodeon
THE CASAGRANDES
WE'RE ALL FAMILIA
THE CASAGRANDES

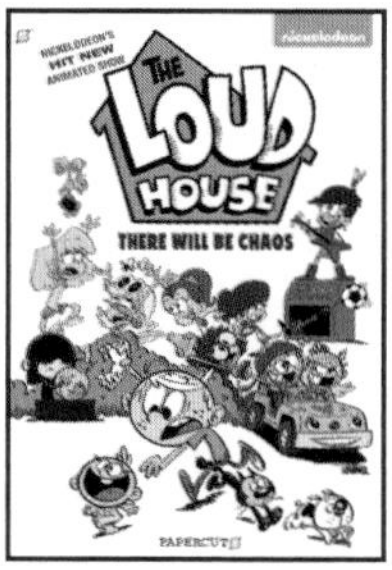
nickelodeon
THE LOUD HOUSE
THERE WILL BE CHAOS
THE LOUD HOUSE

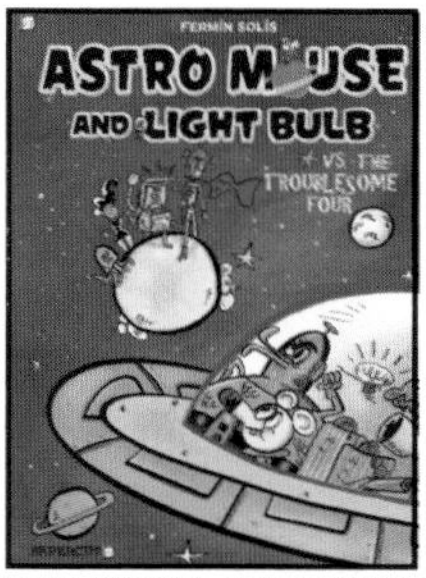
FERMÍN SOLÍS
ASTRO MOUSE AND LIGHT BULB
VS. THE TROUBLESOME FOUR
ASTRO MOUSE AND LIGHT BULB

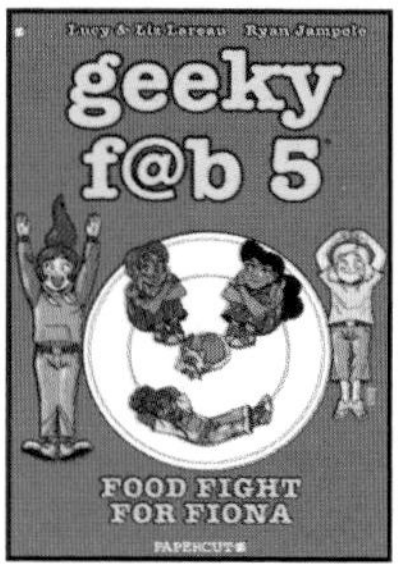
Lucy & Liz Lareau
Ryan Jampole
geeky f@b 5
FOOD FIGHT FOR FIONA
GEEKY F@B 5

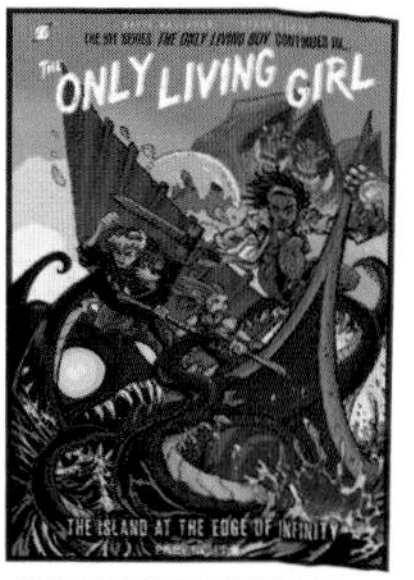
THE ONLY LIVING GIRL
THE ISLAND AT THE EDGE OF INFINITY
THE ONLY LIVING GIRL

papercutz.com

Also available where ebooks are sold.

4. GLOBAL CHAOS

**PATRICK SOBRAL • PATRICIA LYFOUNG
PHILIPPE OGAKI • JENNY • DARA
ALICE PICARD • MAGALI PAILLAT**

New York

Originally published in French under the following titles
Les Mythics, volume 10, by P. Sobral, P. Lyfoung, P. Ogaki, Jenny and Mister Chocoman
Les Mythics, volume 11, by P. Sobral, P. Lyfoung, P. Ogaki, R. Guérin, and Dara
Les Mythics, volume 12, by P. Sobral, P. Lyfoung, P. Ogaki, and A. Picard
©Editions Delcourt, 2020/2021
English Translation and all other editorial material © 2022 Papercutz. All rights reserved.
Created by PATRICK SOBRAL, PATRICIA LYFOUNG, and PHILIPPE OGAKI

Part 10 - Chaos
Script — PHILIPPE OGAKI
Art — JENNY
Color—MAGALI PAILLAT

Part 11 - Lust
Script— PHILIPPE OGAKI
Art — DARA
Color—MAGALI PAILLAT

Part 12 - Envy
Script—PHILIPPE OGAKI
Art — ALICE PICARD
Color—MAGALI PAILLAT

Original editor — THIERRY JOOR

Special thanks to SÉVERINE AUPERT, LUCIE MASSENA, and LINA DI FLAMMINIO

Papercutz books may be purchased for business or promotional use.
For information on bulk purchases please contact Macmillan Corporate and
Premium Sales Department at (800) 221-7945 x5442

Translation — ELIZABETH S. TIERI
Lettering — WILSON RAMOS JR.
Production — MARK McNABB
Editor — JEFF WHITMAN
Editorial Intern — LILY LU
JIM SALICRUP
Editor-in-Chief

PB ISBN: 978-1-5458-0860-3
HC ISBN: 978-1-5458-0861-0

Printed in India
February 2022

Distributed by Macmillan
First Papercutz Printing

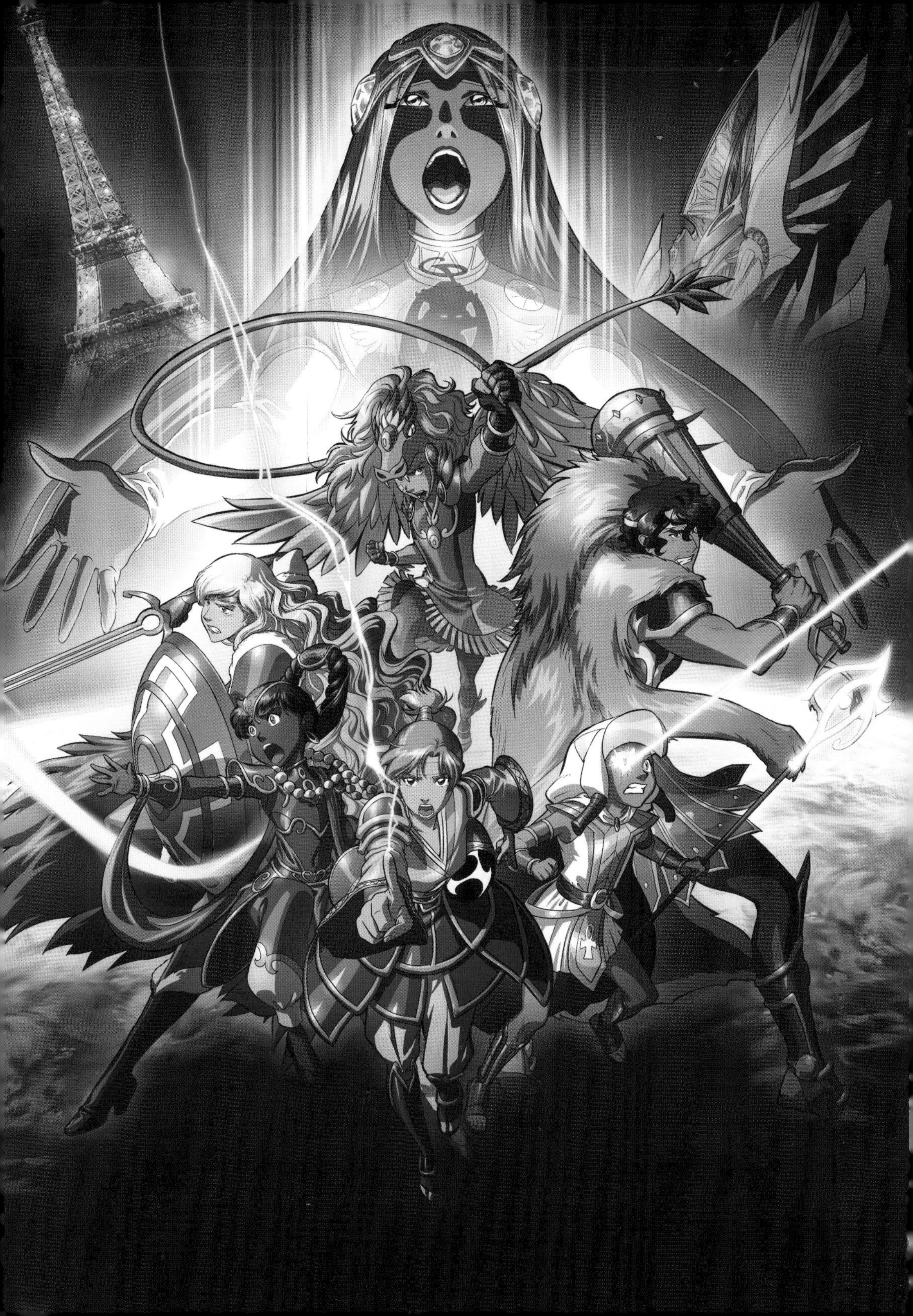

THE MYTHICS

I would like to thank Philippe for the confidence that he granted me with this volume. It was epic to draw. Thanks to the Delcourt team for allowing this book to exist. Thanks to our readers for being here, especially in this overwhelming period through which the world is going through. And thanks to Alexis with whom I could not handle the shock.
–*Jenny*

A great thank you to the entire THE MYTHICS team! The Dream Team to die for! As well as to the Éditions Delcourt and to all the readers! It's thanks to you that THE MYTHICS can continue to live such beautiful adventures! Thanks to Dara for agreeing to continue the adventure of THE MYTHICS with us! Thank you to Alice and Magali! And thank you to all the little Mythics in the world!
–*Patricia Lyfoung*

I would like to thank the wonderful team who gives life to this series, particularly Jenny, who has not spared her efforts on this volume.
–*Philippe Ogaki*

Thank you, readers, for accompanying THE MYTHICS since the start of their adventures.
Thank you to team Mythics!
Thanks for everything to my Cher and Tendre!
–*Alice Picard*

And *voilà* the apotheosis of the first great arc of the Mythics! Thank you to all those who have allowed this saga to get here: the artists, the colorists, my scriptwriting colleagues and friends, not forgetting of course the *Éditions Delcourt*. [And now begins] a completely new adventure with our six heroes. Already [12] chapters of THE MYTHICS? Wow! This series has become so important in so little time… It is without a doubt thanks to everyone on this marvelous team who forged ahead on these volumes, so many artists and colorists to whom we owe the quality of this series, not to mention the team of scriptwriters (Patricia and Philippe, I love you!) and to *Éditions Delcourt*. A great thank you to all!
–*Patrick Sobral*

Thanks to the dream team of THE MYTHICS, for their confidence and their respect, to Thierry and Côme, as well as to the members of my inner circle for their daily support. Thank you to the readers, and thanks to Prune for allowing me to work as needed, who let me finish this volume despite her few months of life.
–*Magali Paillat*

Thanks to Patricia, Philippe, and Patrick for having entrusted this new adventure of THE MYTHICS to me!
Thanks to Marion and my entire family for their support
–*Dara*

Thank you to all those who continue to read our work in this rather peculiar time. ^3^ Thank you to THE MYTHICS team for continuing to keep this beautiful adventure alive and to the *Éditions Delcourt* for their confidence! Thank you to Pierre-Mony and to my family for their support!
–*Alice Picard*

Editor's note: THE MYTHICS was originally published in France by Delcourt, which should explain why they're

PART 10: CHAOS

Story by
PHILIPPE OGAKI

Art by
JENNY
WITH HELP FROM **MISTER CHOCOMAN**

Color by
MAGALI PAILLAT

PREVIOUSLY IN THE MYTHICS

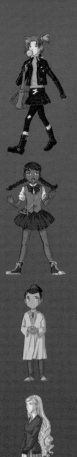

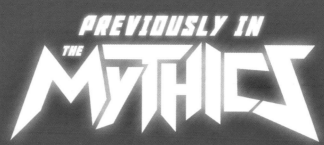

Long ago the old gods – Raijin, the Japanese God of lightning; Horus, the Egyptian Sun and Moon God; Freyja, the Norse Goddess of Beauty; Durga the Hindu Deity; the Aztek God of Wind, Quetzalcoatl; and Hercules, the Ancient Greek Demi-God – banished Evil to Mars. Now, after a space expedition to Mars, Evil returned to plague the Earth. Modern adolescent descendants of these gods inherited their powers, along with guidance from the Gods themselves.

Yuko used the power of electricity to stop Nuclear Warfare from destroying Japan; Parvati gained six arms and a tiger sidekick to vanquish a deadly virus infecting her home country of India; Amir acquired healing abilities to try and save his Egyptian empire; Abigail, already a Opera hopeful, got more powerful lungs with a supersonic scream and helped break the ice storm that plagued Germany; Miguel harnessed the power of the winds as he brought change to his impoverished Mexican neighborhood; and Neo swelled with super strength to strong arm a big business bully and save his mother and triplet siblings.

But Evil wasn't done yet, the entity wants to free Chaos as well, who has been imprisoned in the hands of Gaia, a resting Earth Goddess. To do this, Evil needs to trick each of the Mythics into being its new pawns in this global war.

Parvati and Amir, along with Amir's nanny assistant with spy training, Miss Taylor, stopped terra cotta warfare at the hands of resurrected deranged Emperor Qin Shi Huang. To win this fight, they make a deal with the dragon guardian of the Pearl of Knowledge, at a great price… their courage!

Meanwhile, in Saint Petersburg, Neo and Abigail saw sparks fly as they were manipulated by sorcerer Sergei Ozerov who used their strengths and weaknesses against the two teens, and tricked them into killing his former boss, the Priestess— tribute that Evil needed to get one step closer to unleashing Chaos.

And Yuko and Miguel found themselves at the strange residence of Sir Wallace Wildragon and his living puppet-daughter Alice. Miguel and Yuko "rescue" Alice to show her a normal teenage life which leads them to the mythical remains of Stonehenge. When Wildragon transforms into a dragon to prevent the Earth goddess Gaia from waking, he is overpowered by the Mythics, themselves tricked by Chaos.

Now, all three teams of Mythics are transported to Paris, France, at the base of the Eiffel Tower. Gaia is about to wake… Has Evil awakened a new age of Chaos or do these six young heroes stand a chance now that they are all together?

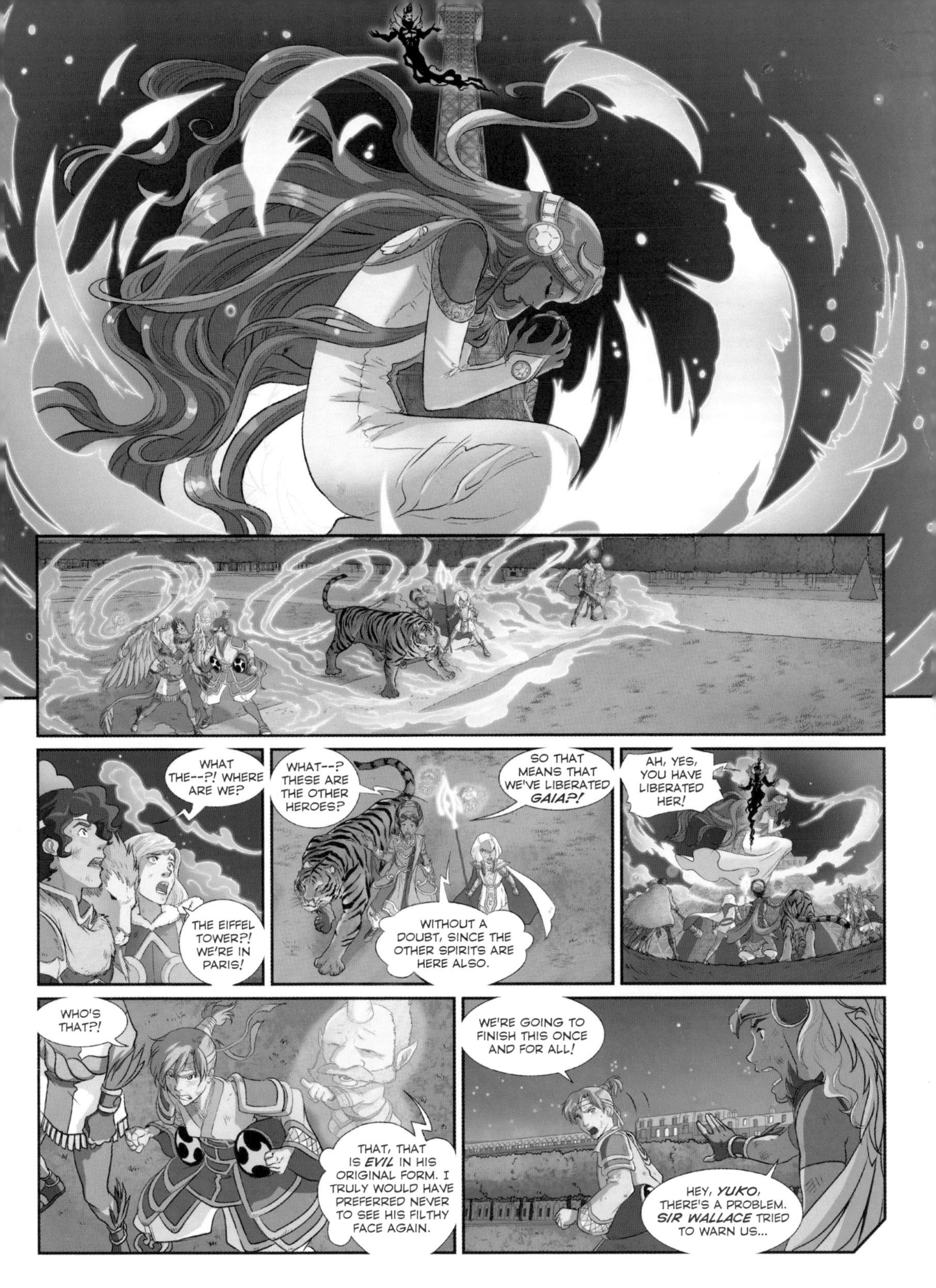
WHAT THE--?! WHERE ARE WE?
THE EIFFEL TOWER?! WE'RE IN PARIS!
WHAT--? THESE ARE THE OTHER HEROES?
SO THAT MEANS THAT WE'VE LIBERATED *GAIA?!*
WITHOUT A DOUBT, SINCE THE OTHER SPIRITS ARE HERE ALSO.
AH, YES, YOU HAVE LIBERATED HER!
WHO'S THAT?!
THAT, THAT IS *EVIL* IN HIS ORIGINAL FORM. I TRULY WOULD HAVE PREFERRED NEVER TO SEE HIS FILTHY FACE AGAIN.
WE'RE GOING TO FINISH THIS ONCE AND FOR ALL!
HEY, *YUKO*, THERE'S A PROBLEM. *SIR WALLACE* TRIED TO WARN US...

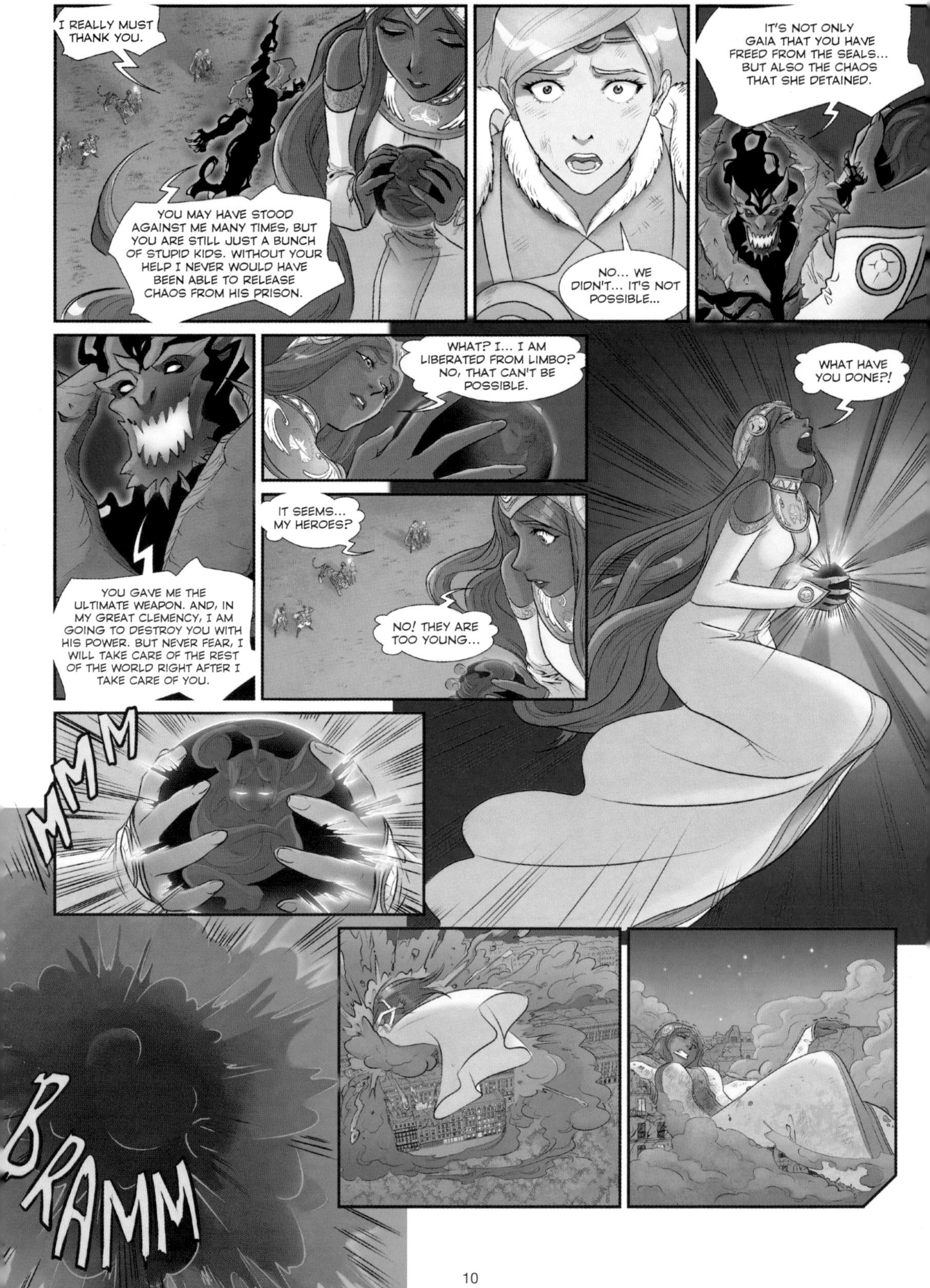
I REALLY MUST THANK YOU.
YOU MAY HAVE STOOD AGAINST ME MANY TIMES, BUT YOU ARE STILL JUST A BUNCH OF STUPID KIDS. WITHOUT YOUR HELP I NEVER WOULD HAVE BEEN ABLE TO RELEASE CHAOS FROM HIS PRISON.
NO... WE DIDN'T... IT'S NOT POSSIBLE...
IT'S NOT ONLY GAIA THAT YOU HAVE FREED FROM THE SEALS... BUT ALSO THE CHAOS THAT SHE DETAINED.
YOU GAVE ME THE ULTIMATE WEAPON. AND, IN MY GREAT CLEMENCY, I AM GOING TO DESTROY YOU WITH HIS POWER. BUT NEVER FEAR, I WILL TAKE CARE OF THE REST OF THE WORLD RIGHT AFTER I TAKE CARE OF YOU.
WHAT? I... I AM LIBERATED FROM LIMBO? NO, THAT CAN'T BE POSSIBLE.
IT SEEMS... MY HEROES?
NO! THEY ARE TOO YOUNG...
WHAT HAVE YOU DONE?!
MMMM
BRAMM

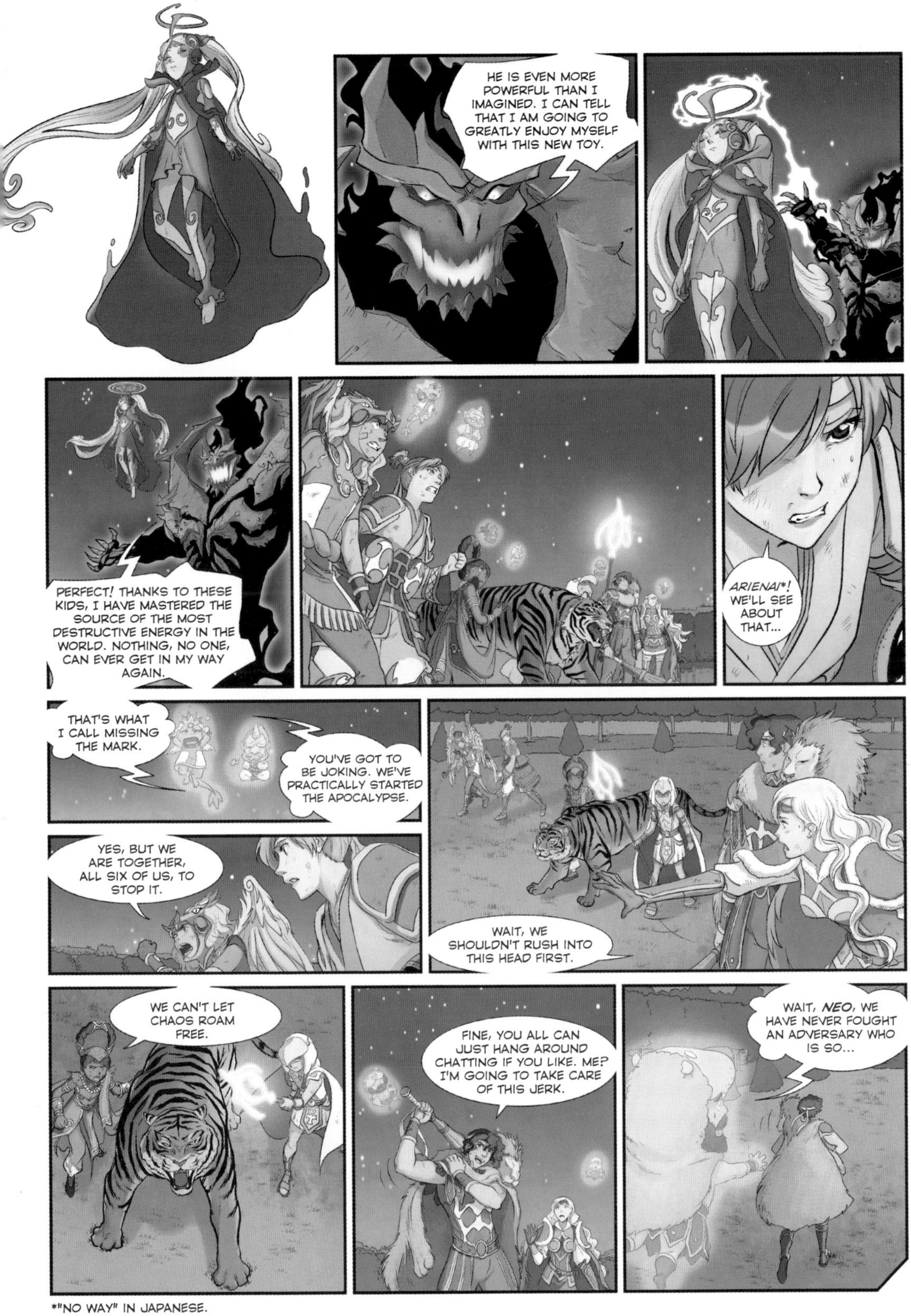
HE IS EVEN MORE POWERFUL THAN I IMAGINED. I CAN TELL THAT I AM GOING TO GREATLY ENJOY MYSELF WITH THIS NEW TOY.
PERFECT! THANKS TO THESE KIDS, I HAVE MASTERED THE SOURCE OF THE MOST DESTRUCTIVE ENERGY IN THE WORLD. NOTHING, NO ONE, CAN EVER GET IN MY WAY AGAIN.
ARIENAI*! WE'LL SEE ABOUT THAT...
THAT'S WHAT I CALL MISSING THE MARK.
YOU'VE GOT TO BE JOKING. WE'VE PRACTICALLY STARTED THE APOCALYPSE.
YES, BUT WE ARE TOGETHER, ALL SIX OF US, TO STOP IT.
WAIT, WE SHOULDN'T RUSH INTO THIS HEAD FIRST.
WE CAN'T LET CHAOS ROAM FREE.
FINE, YOU ALL CAN JUST HANG AROUND CHATTING IF YOU LIKE. ME? I'M GOING TO TAKE CARE OF THIS JERK.
WAIT, NEO, WE HAVE NEVER FOUGHT AN ADVERSARY WHO IS SO...

*"NO WAY" IN JAPANESE.

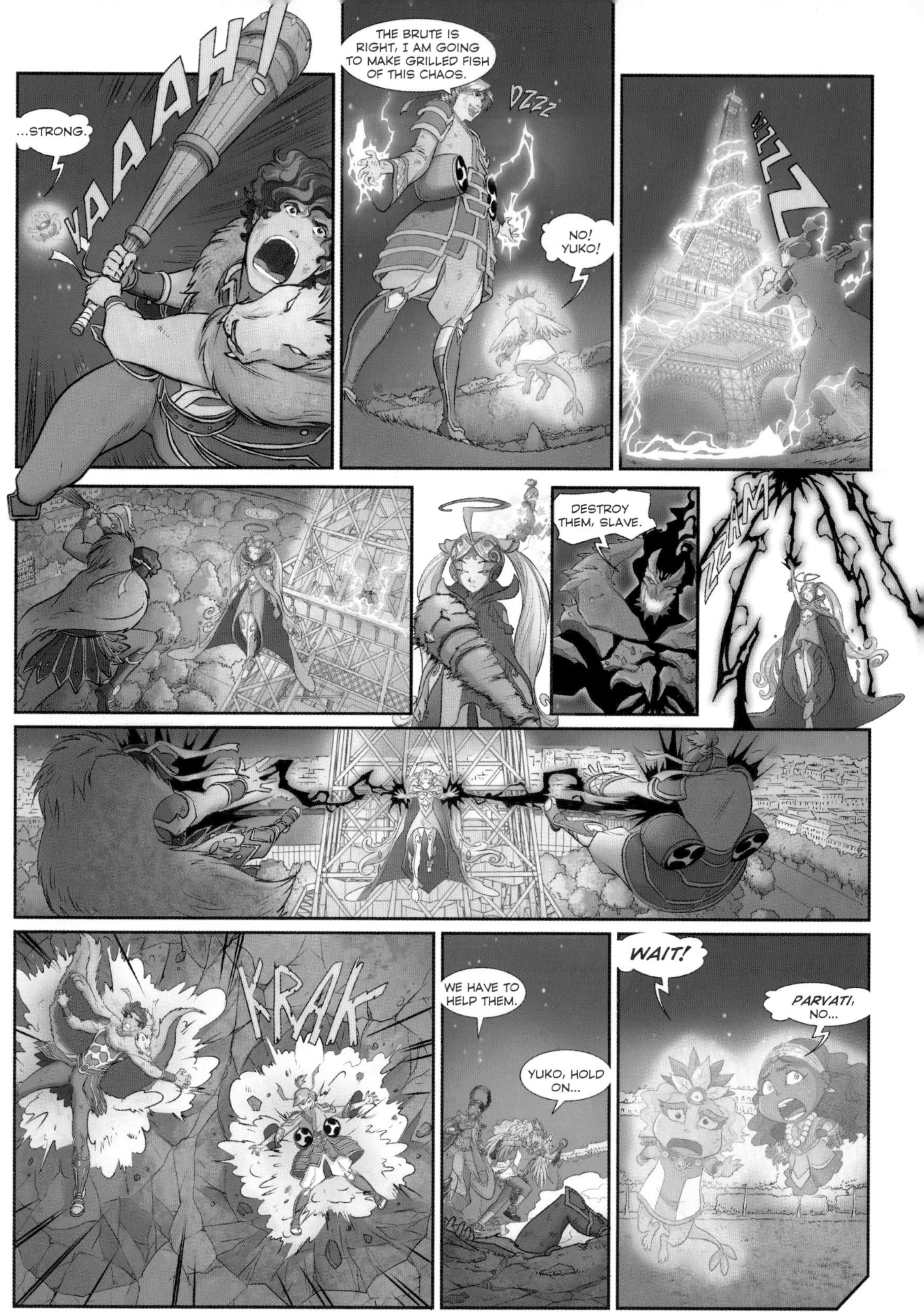
...STRONG.
KAAAAH!
THE BRUTE IS RIGHT, I AM GOING TO MAKE GRILLED FISH OF THIS CHAOS.
DZZZ
NO! YUKO!
DESTROY THEM, SLAVE.
ZZAM
KRAK
WE HAVE TO HELP THEM.
YUKO, HOLD ON...
WAIT!
PARVATI, NO...

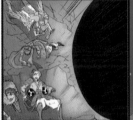

AAAAAH!

WELL PLAYED.

BUT WHERE DID THE BUILDING GO?

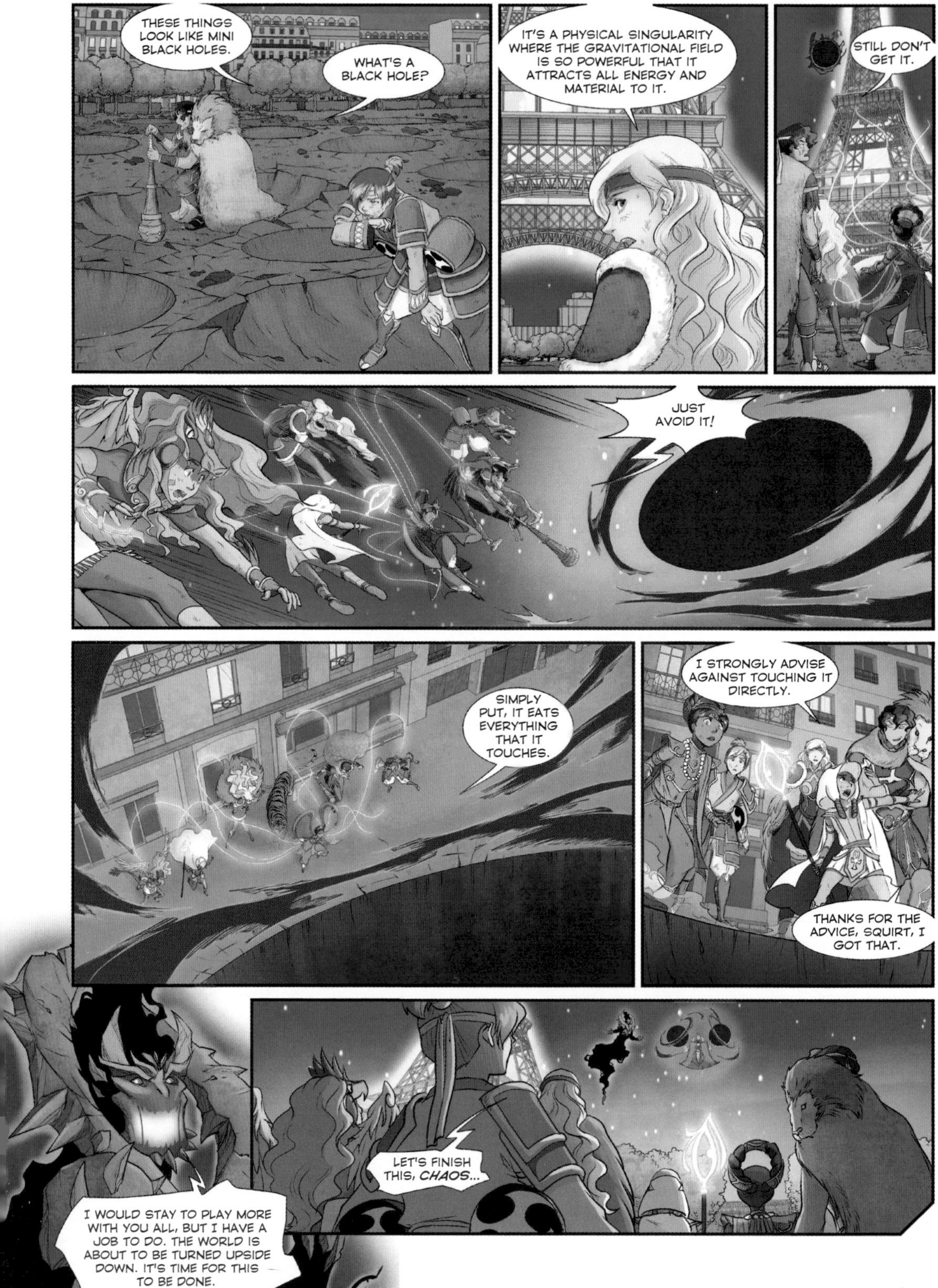

THESE THINGS LOOK LIKE MINI BLACK HOLES.
WHAT'S A BLACK HOLE?
IT'S A PHYSICAL SINGULARITY WHERE THE GRAVITATIONAL FIELD IS SO POWERFUL THAT IT ATTRACTS ALL ENERGY AND MATERIAL TO IT.
STILL DON'T GET IT.
JUST AVOID IT!
SIMPLY PUT, IT EATS EVERYTHING THAT IT TOUCHES.
I STRONGLY ADVISE AGAINST TOUCHING IT DIRECTLY.
THANKS FOR THE ADVICE, SQUIRT, I GOT THAT.
LET'S FINISH THIS, *CHAOS*...
I WOULD STAY TO PLAY MORE WITH YOU ALL, BUT I HAVE A JOB TO DO. THE WORLD IS ABOUT TO BE TURNED UPSIDE DOWN. IT'S TIME FOR THIS TO BE DONE.

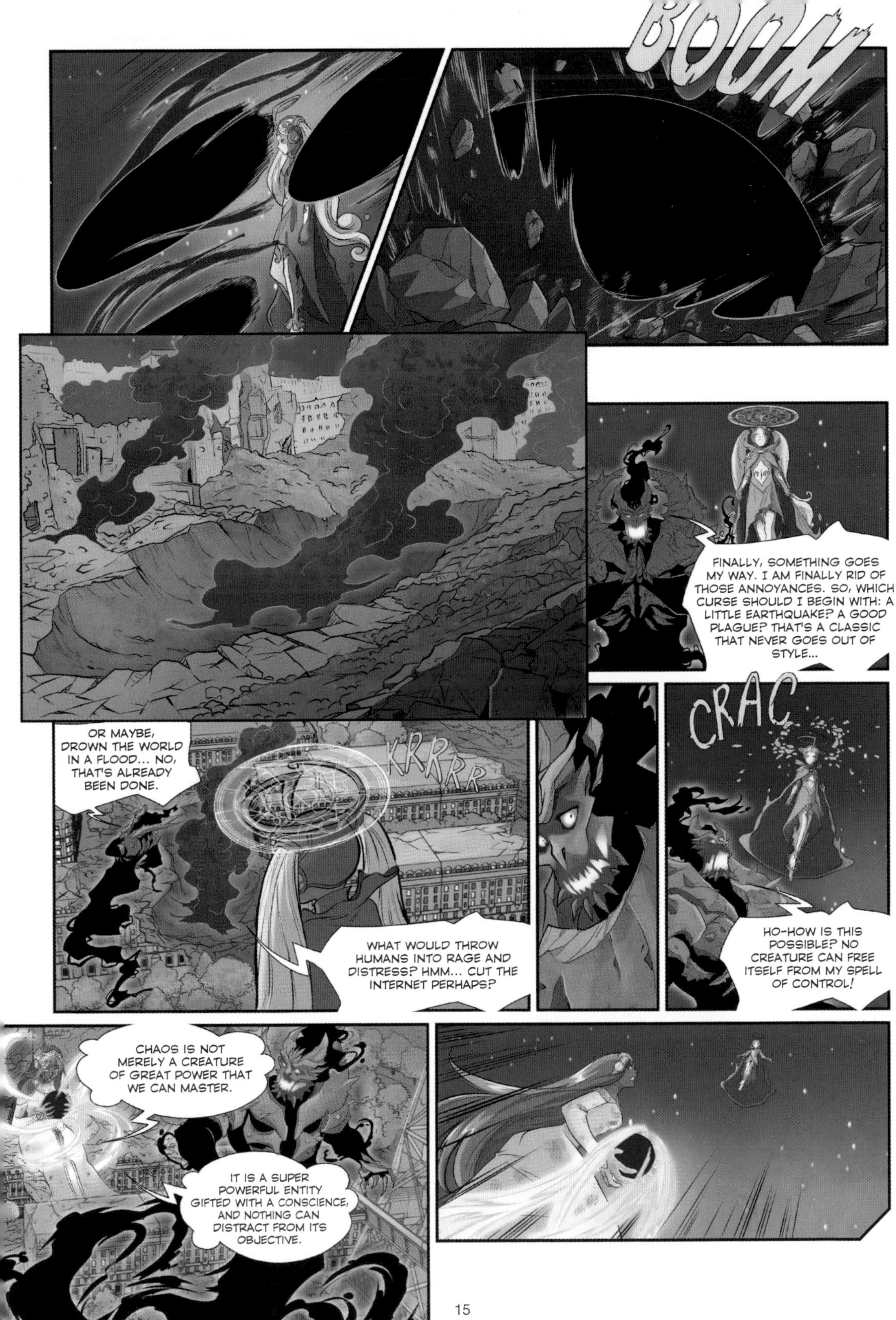
BOOM
FINALLY, SOMETHING GOES MY WAY. I AM FINALLY RID OF THOSE ANNOYANCES. SO, WHICH CURSE SHOULD I BEGIN WITH: A LITTLE EARTHQUAKE? A GOOD PLAGUE? THAT'S A CLASSIC THAT NEVER GOES OUT OF STYLE...
OR MAYBE, DROWN THE WORLD IN A FLOOD... NO, THAT'S ALREADY BEEN DONE.
KRRRR
WHAT WOULD THROW HUMANS INTO RAGE AND DISTRESS? HMM... CUT THE INTERNET PERHAPS?
CRAC
HO-HOW IS THIS POSSIBLE? NO CREATURE CAN FREE ITSELF FROM MY SPELL OF CONTROL!
CHAOS IS NOT MERELY A CREATURE OF GREAT POWER THAT WE CAN MASTER.
IT IS A SUPER POWERFUL ENTITY GIFTED WITH A CONSCIENCE, AND NOTHING CAN DISTRACT FROM ITS OBJECTIVE.

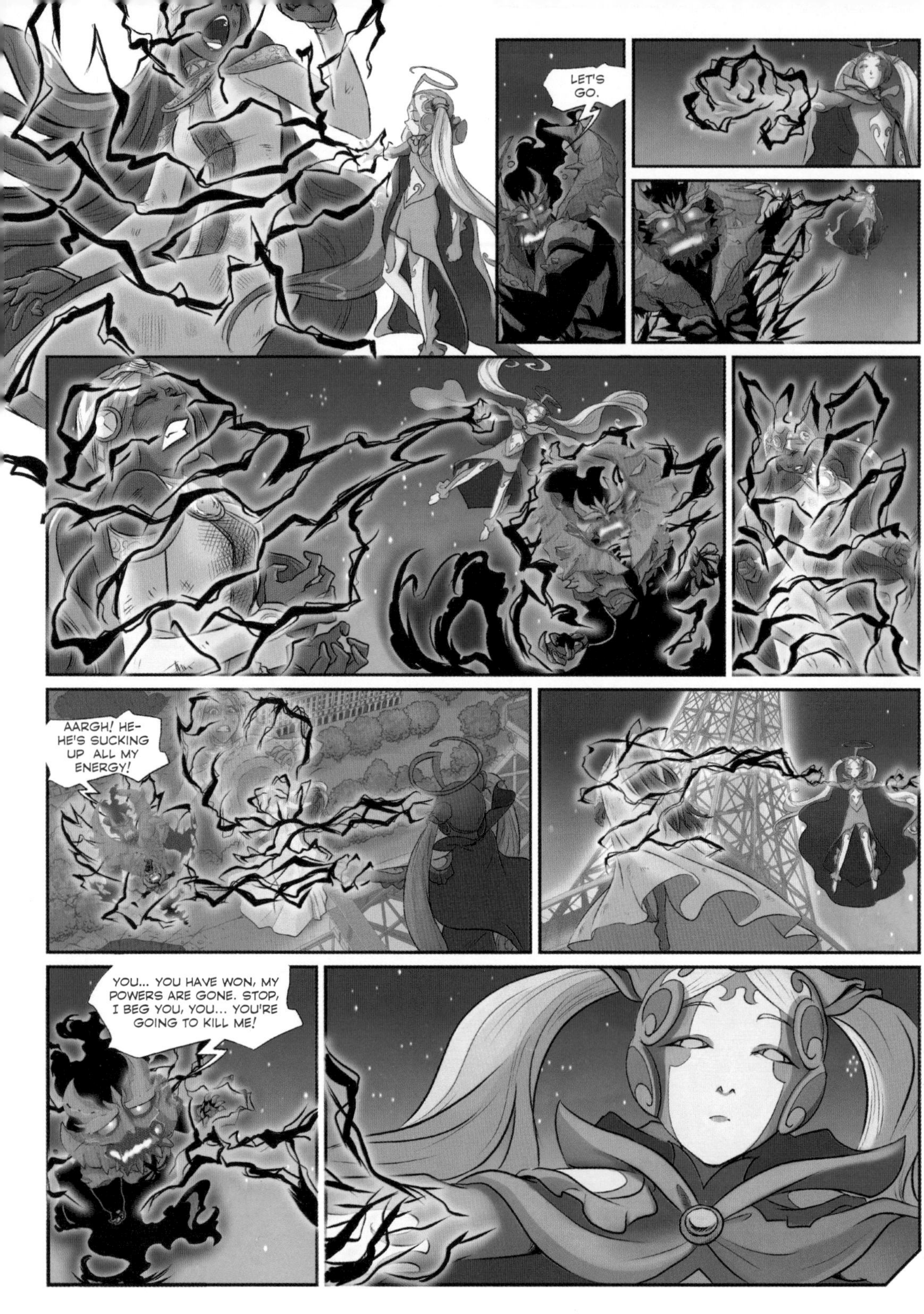
LET'S GO.
AARGH! HE-HE'S SUCKING UP ALL MY ENERGY!
YOU... YOU HAVE WON, MY POWERS ARE GONE. STOP, I BEG YOU, YOU... YOU'RE GOING TO KILL ME!

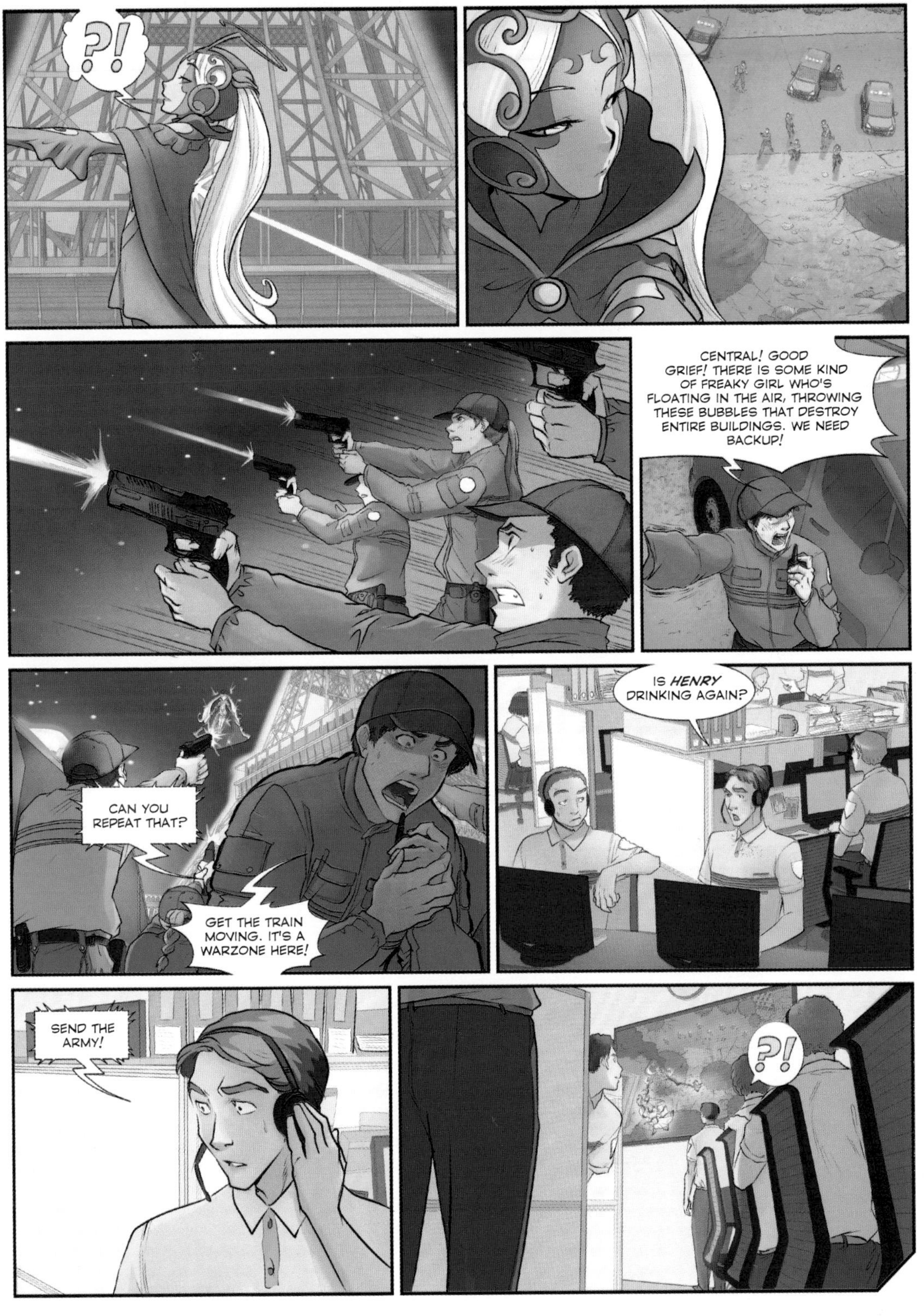
?!
CENTRAL! GOOD GRIEF! THERE IS SOME KIND OF FREAKY GIRL WHO'S FLOATING IN THE AIR, THROWING THESE BUBBLES THAT DESTROY ENTIRE BUILDINGS. WE NEED BACKUP!
CAN YOU REPEAT THAT?
GET THE TRAIN MOVING. IT'S A WARZONE HERE!
IS *HENRY* DRINKING AGAIN?
SEND THE ARMY!
?!

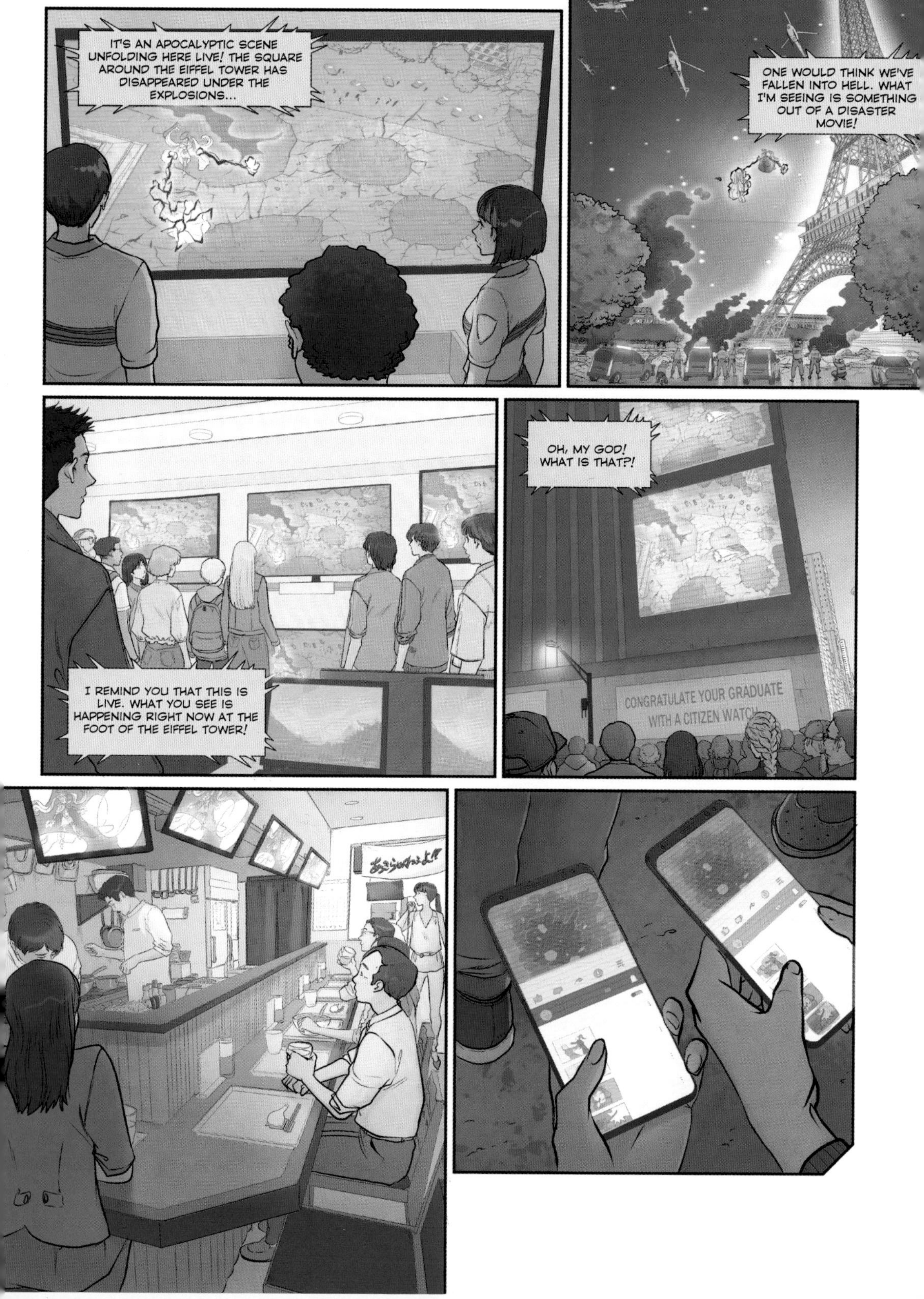
IT'S AN APOCALYPTIC SCENE UNFOLDING HERE LIVE! THE SQUARE AROUND THE EIFFEL TOWER HAS DISAPPEARED UNDER THE EXPLOSIONS...
ONE WOULD THINK WE'VE FALLEN INTO HELL. WHAT I'M SEEING IS SOMETHING OUT OF A DISASTER MOVIE!
I REMIND YOU THAT THIS IS LIVE. WHAT YOU SEE IS HAPPENING RIGHT NOW AT THE FOOT OF THE EIFFEL TOWER!
OH, MY GOD! WHAT IS THAT?!
CONGRATULATE YOUR GRADUATE WITH A CITIZEN WATCH

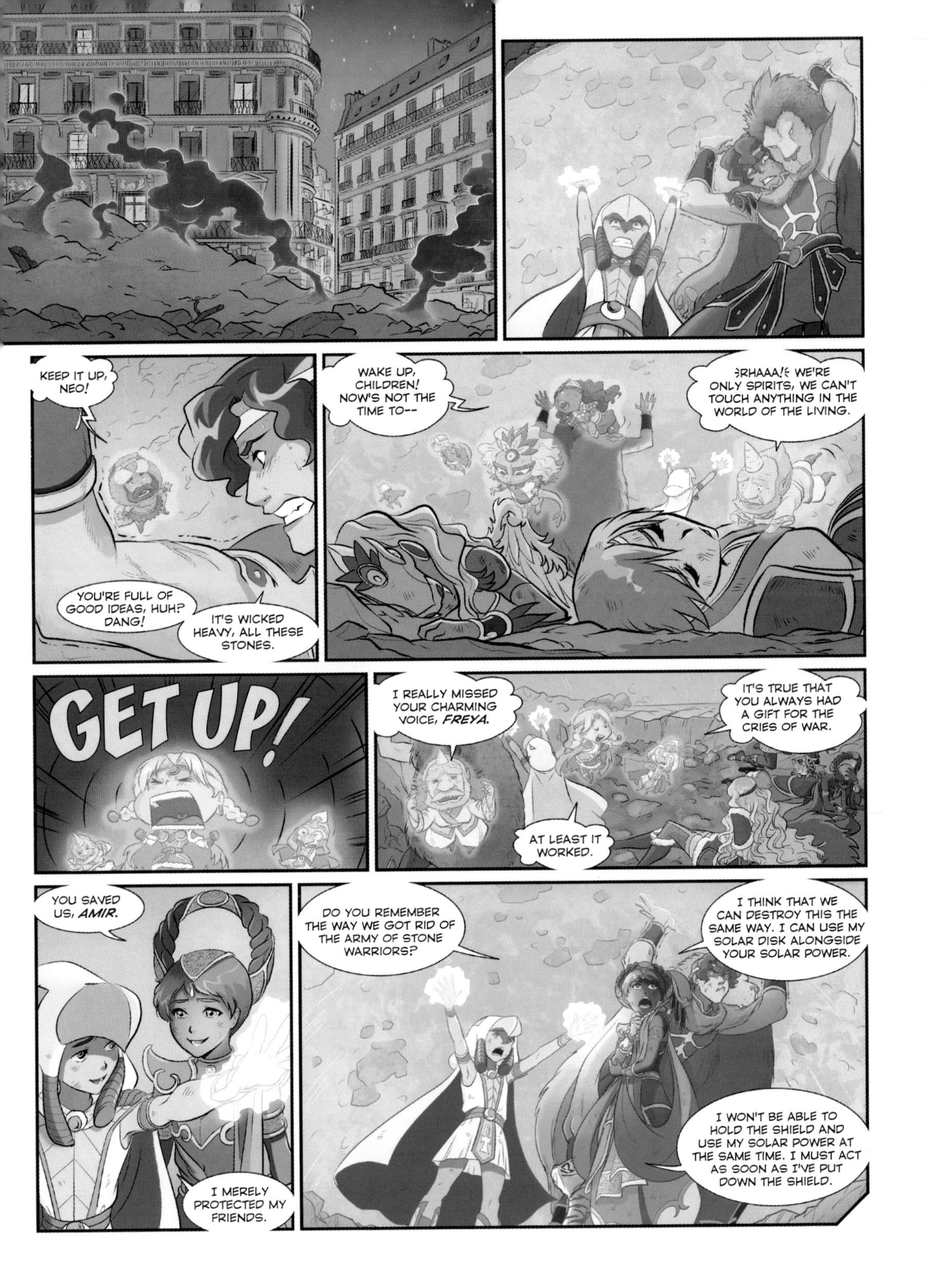
KEEP IT UP, NEO!
YOU'RE FULL OF GOOD IDEAS, HUH? DANG!
IT'S WICKED HEAVY, ALL THESE STONES.
WAKE UP, CHILDREN! NOW'S NOT THE TIME TO--
GRHAAA! WE'RE ONLY SPIRITS, WE CAN'T TOUCH ANYTHING IN THE WORLD OF THE LIVING.
GET UP!
I REALLY MISSED YOUR CHARMING VOICE, FREYA.
IT'S TRUE THAT YOU ALWAYS HAD A GIFT FOR THE CRIES OF WAR.
AT LEAST IT WORKED.
YOU SAVED US, AMIR.
I MERELY PROTECTED MY FRIENDS.
DO YOU REMEMBER THE WAY WE GOT RID OF THE ARMY OF STONE WARRIORS?
I THINK THAT WE CAN DESTROY THIS THE SAME WAY. I CAN USE MY SOLAR DISK ALONGSIDE YOUR SOLAR POWER.
I WON'T BE ABLE TO HOLD THE SHIELD AND USE MY SOLAR POWER AT THE SAME TIME. I MUST ACT AS SOON AS I'VE PUT DOWN THE SHIELD.

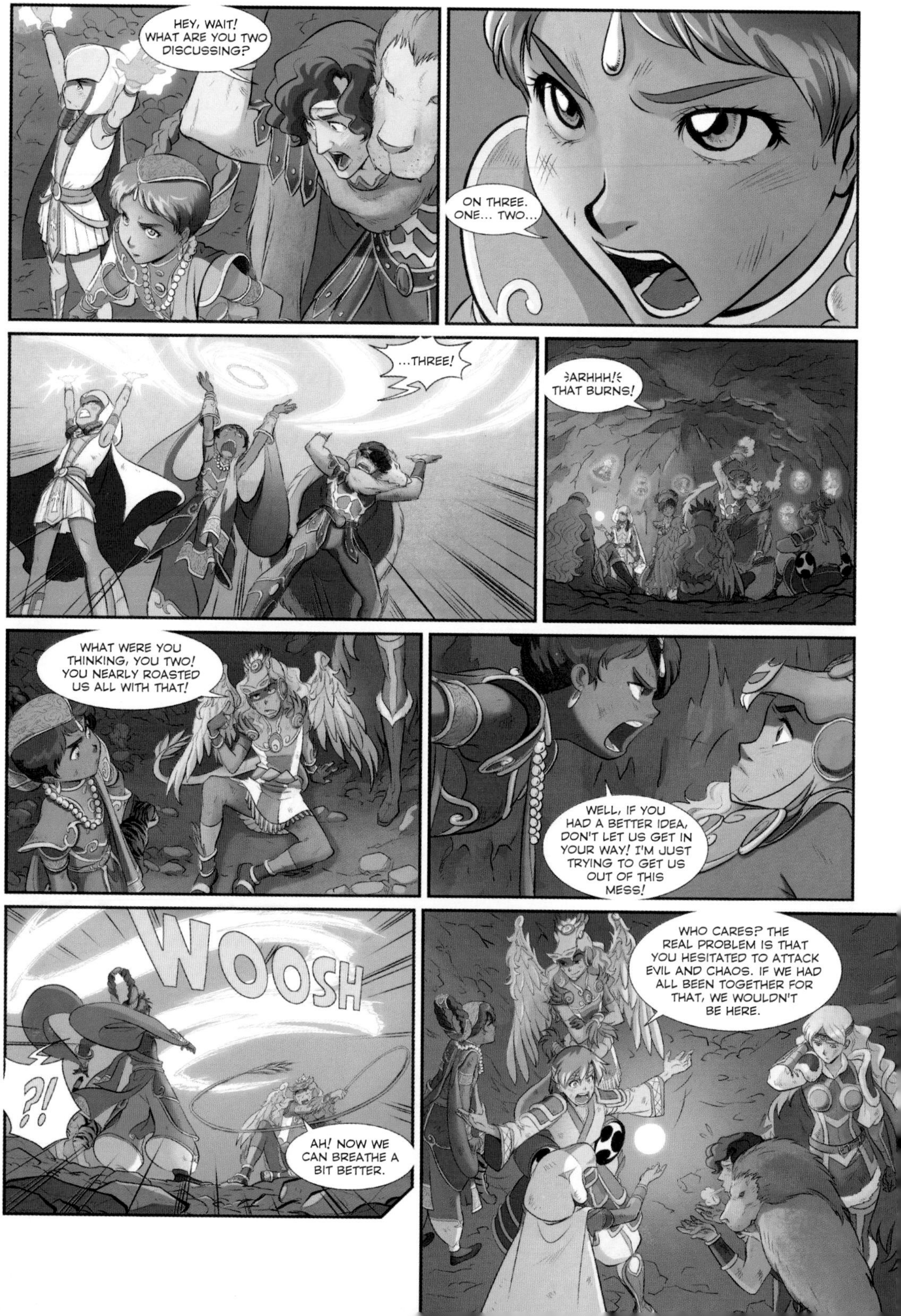
HEY, WAIT! WHAT ARE YOU TWO DISCUSSING?
ON THREE. ONE... TWO...
...THREE!
ARHHH! THAT BURNS!
WHAT WERE YOU THINKING, YOU TWO! YOU NEARLY ROASTED US ALL WITH THAT!
WELL, IF YOU HAD A BETTER IDEA, DON'T LET US GET IN YOUR WAY! I'M JUST TRYING TO GET US OUT OF THIS MESS!
WOOSH
?!
AH! NOW WE CAN BREATHE A BIT BETTER.
WHO CARES? THE REAL PROBLEM IS THAT YOU HESITATED TO ATTACK EVIL AND CHAOS. IF WE HAD ALL BEEN TOGETHER FOR THAT, WE WOULDN'T BE HERE.

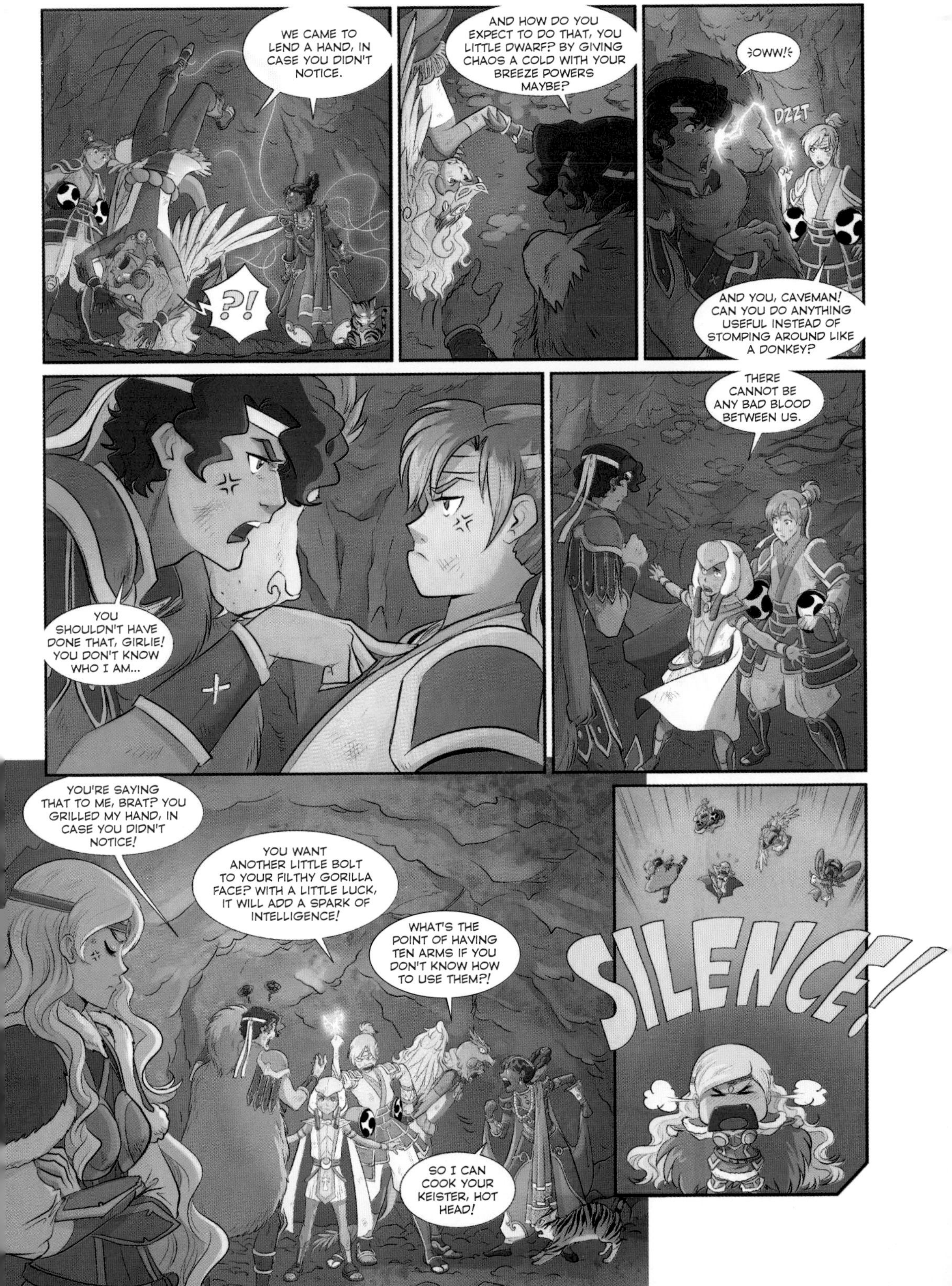
WE CAME TO LEND A HAND, IN CASE YOU DIDN'T NOTICE.
?!
AND HOW DO YOU EXPECT TO DO THAT, YOU LITTLE DWARF? BY GIVING CHAOS A COLD WITH YOUR BREEZE POWERS MAYBE?
OWW!
DZZT
AND YOU, CAVEMAN! CAN YOU DO ANYTHING USEFUL INSTEAD OF STOMPING AROUND LIKE A DONKEY?
YOU SHOULDN'T HAVE DONE THAT, GIRLIE! YOU DON'T KNOW WHO I AM...
THERE CANNOT BE ANY BAD BLOOD BETWEEN US.
YOU'RE SAYING THAT TO ME, BRAT? YOU GRILLED MY HAND, IN CASE YOU DIDN'T NOTICE!
YOU WANT ANOTHER LITTLE BOLT TO YOUR FILTHY GORILLA FACE? WITH A LITTLE LUCK, IT WILL ADD A SPARK OF INTELLIGENCE!
WHAT'S THE POINT OF HAVING TEN ARMS IF YOU DON'T KNOW HOW TO USE THEM?!
SO I CAN COOK YOUR KEISTER, HOT HEAD!
SILENCE!

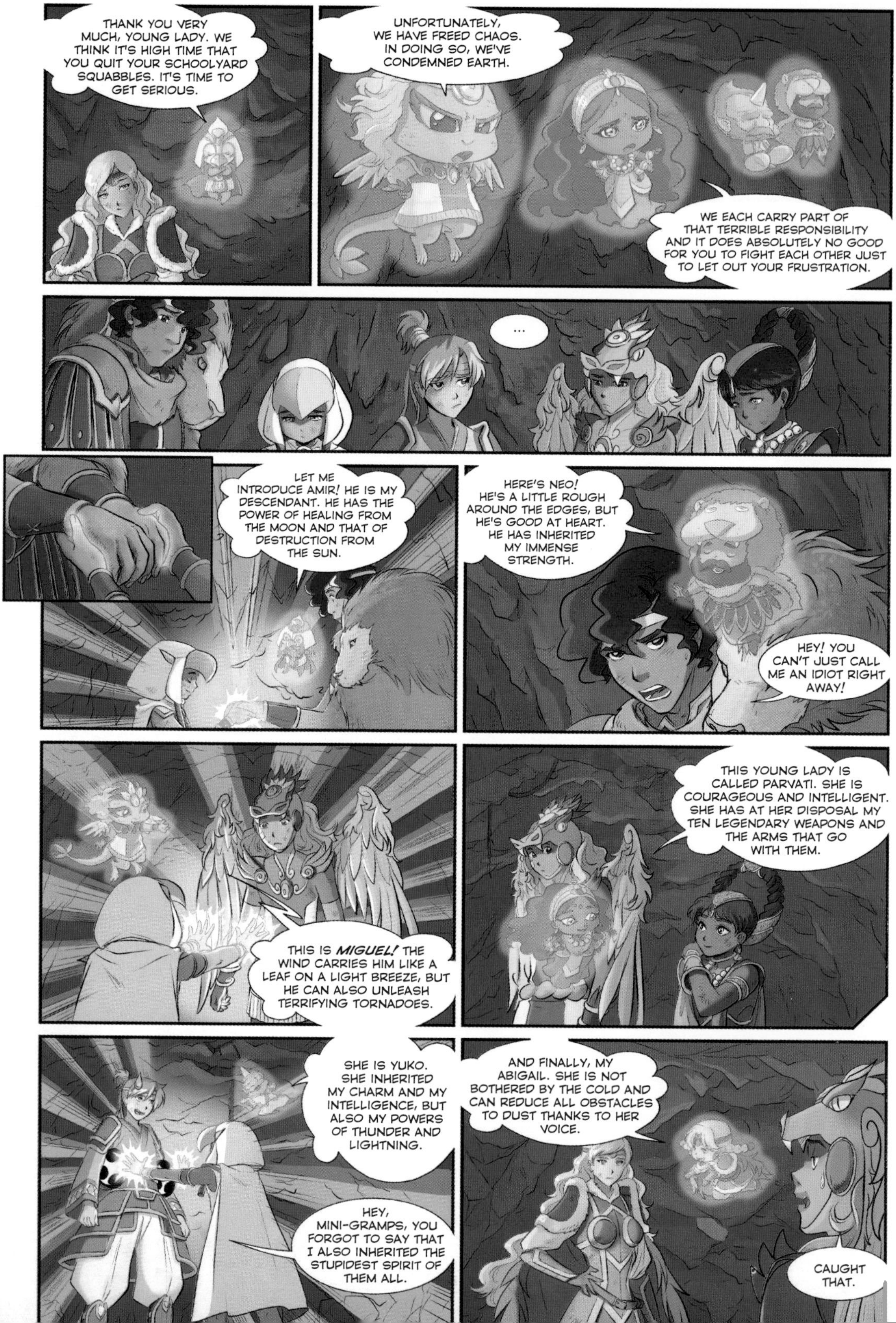
THANK YOU VERY MUCH, YOUNG LADY. WE THINK IT'S HIGH TIME THAT YOU QUIT YOUR SCHOOLYARD SQUABBLES. IT'S TIME TO GET SERIOUS.
UNFORTUNATELY, WE HAVE FREED CHAOS. IN DOING SO, WE'VE CONDEMNED EARTH.
WE EACH CARRY PART OF THAT TERRIBLE RESPONSIBILITY AND IT DOES ABSOLUTELY NO GOOD FOR YOU TO FIGHT EACH OTHER JUST TO LET OUT YOUR FRUSTRATION.
...
LET ME INTRODUCE AMIR! HE IS MY DESCENDANT. HE HAS THE POWER OF HEALING FROM THE MOON AND THAT OF DESTRUCTION FROM THE SUN.
HERE'S NEO! HE'S A LITTLE ROUGH AROUND THE EDGES, BUT HE'S GOOD AT HEART. HE HAS INHERITED MY IMMENSE STRENGTH.
HEY! YOU CAN'T JUST CALL ME AN IDIOT RIGHT AWAY!
THIS IS MIGUEL! THE WIND CARRIES HIM LIKE A LEAF ON A LIGHT BREEZE, BUT HE CAN ALSO UNLEASH TERRIFYING TORNADOES.
THIS YOUNG LADY IS CALLED PARVATI. SHE IS COURAGEOUS AND INTELLIGENT. SHE HAS AT HER DISPOSAL MY TEN LEGENDARY WEAPONS AND THE ARMS THAT GO WITH THEM.
SHE IS YUKO. SHE INHERITED MY CHARM AND MY INTELLIGENCE, BUT ALSO MY POWERS OF THUNDER AND LIGHTNING.
HEY, MINI-GRAMPS, YOU FORGOT TO SAY THAT I ALSO INHERITED THE STUPIDEST SPIRIT OF THEM ALL.
AND FINALLY, MY ABIGAIL. SHE IS NOT BOTHERED BY THE COLD AND CAN REDUCE ALL OBSTACLES TO DUST THANKS TO HER VOICE.
CAUGHT THAT.

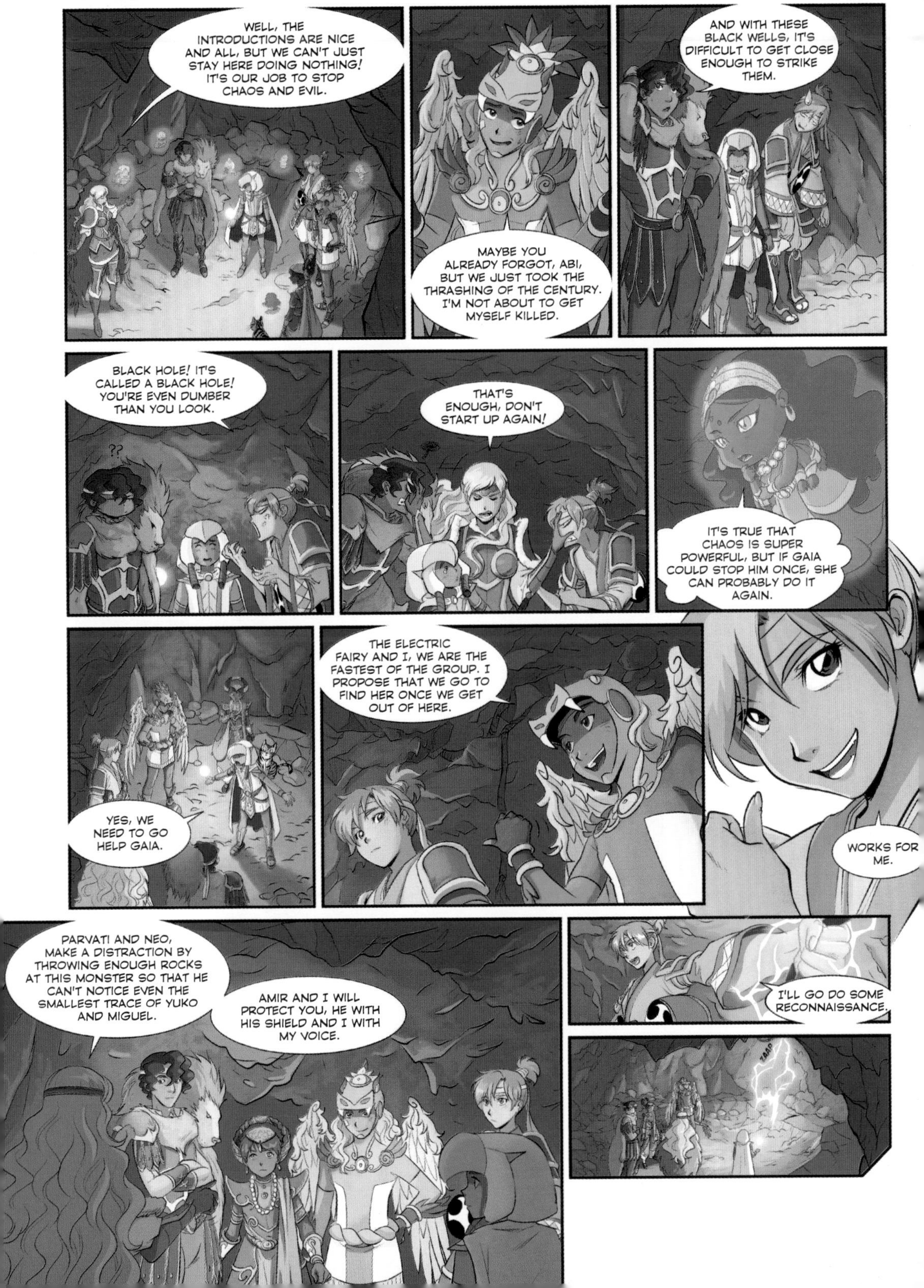
WELL, THE INTRODUCTIONS ARE NICE AND ALL, BUT WE CAN'T JUST STAY HERE DOING NOTHING! IT'S OUR JOB TO STOP CHAOS AND EVIL.
MAYBE YOU ALREADY FORGOT, ABI, BUT WE JUST TOOK THE THRASHING OF THE CENTURY. I'M NOT ABOUT TO GET MYSELF KILLED.
AND WITH THESE BLACK WELLS, IT'S DIFFICULT TO GET CLOSE ENOUGH TO STRIKE THEM.
BLACK HOLE! IT'S CALLED A BLACK HOLE! YOU'RE EVEN DUMBER THAN YOU LOOK.
??
THAT'S ENOUGH, DON'T START UP AGAIN!
IT'S TRUE THAT CHAOS IS SUPER POWERFUL, BUT IF GAIA COULD STOP HIM ONCE, SHE CAN PROBABLY DO IT AGAIN.
YES, WE NEED TO GO HELP GAIA.
THE ELECTRIC FAIRY AND I, WE ARE THE FASTEST OF THE GROUP. I PROPOSE THAT WE GO TO FIND HER ONCE WE GET OUT OF HERE.
WORKS FOR ME.
PARVATI AND NEO, MAKE A DISTRACTION BY THROWING ENOUGH ROCKS AT THIS MONSTER SO THAT HE CAN'T NOTICE EVEN THE SMALLEST TRACE OF YUKO AND MIGUEL.
AMIR AND I WILL PROTECT YOU, HE WITH HIS SHIELD AND I WITH MY VOICE.
I'LL GO DO SOME RECONNAISSANCE.

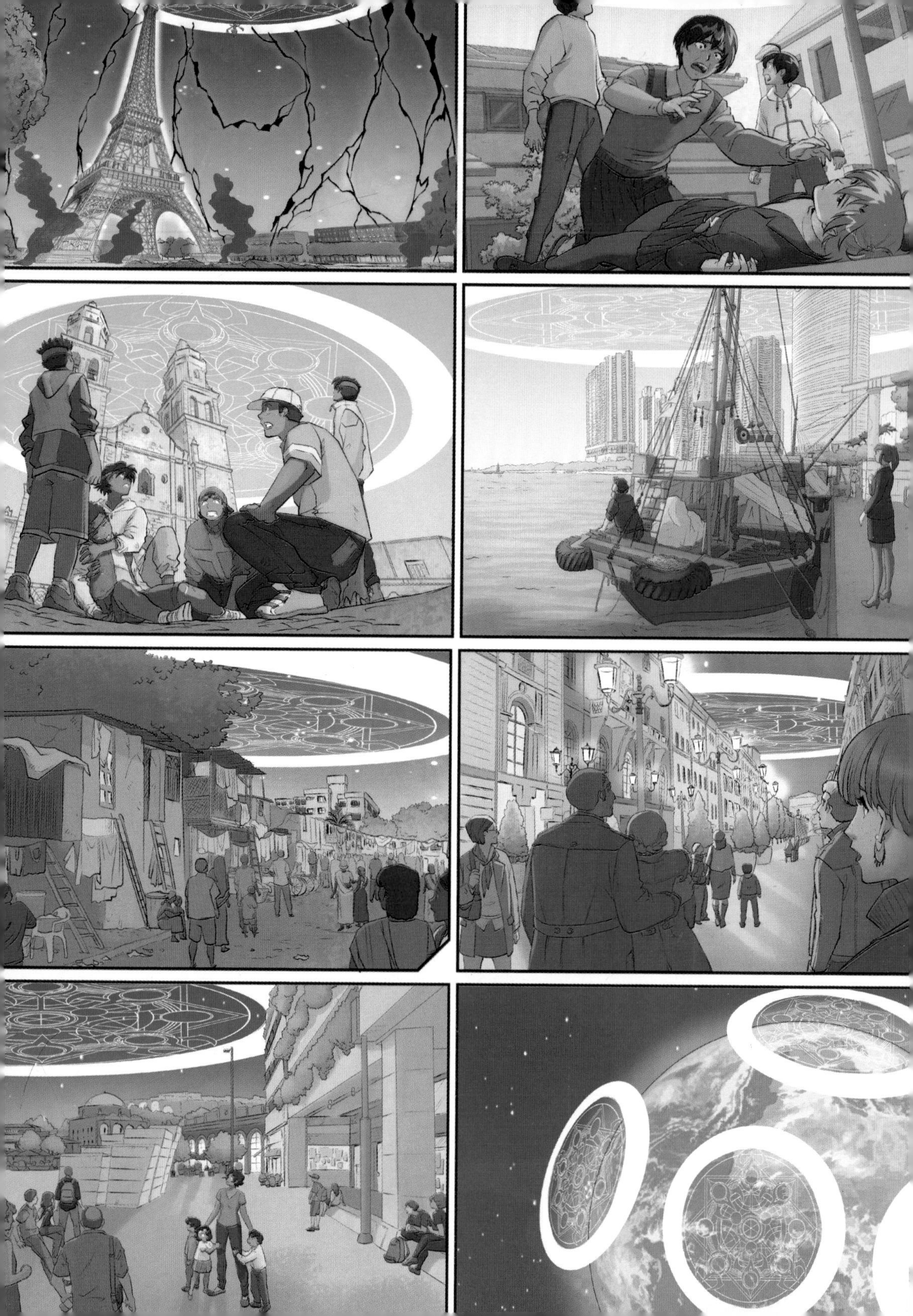

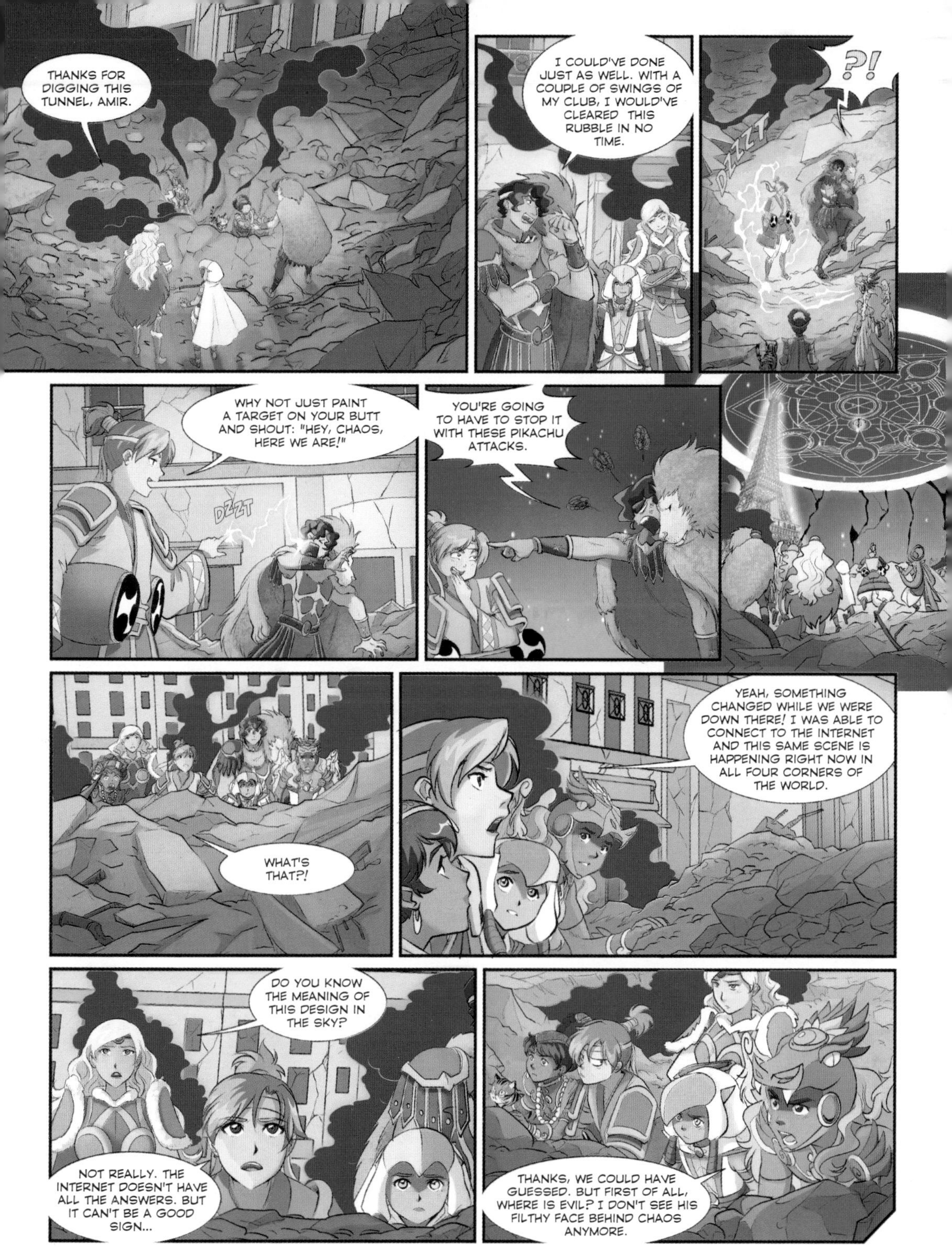
THANKS FOR DIGGING THIS TUNNEL, AMIR.
I COULD'VE DONE JUST AS WELL. WITH A COUPLE OF SWINGS OF MY CLUB, I WOULD'VE CLEARED THIS RUBBLE IN NO TIME.
?!
DZZZT
WHY NOT JUST PAINT A TARGET ON YOUR BUTT AND SHOUT: "HEY, CHAOS, HERE WE ARE!"
DZZT
YOU'RE GOING TO HAVE TO STOP IT WITH THESE PIKACHU ATTACKS.
WHAT'S THAT?!
YEAH, SOMETHING CHANGED WHILE WE WERE DOWN THERE! I WAS ABLE TO CONNECT TO THE INTERNET AND THIS SAME SCENE IS HAPPENING RIGHT NOW IN ALL FOUR CORNERS OF THE WORLD.
DO YOU KNOW THE MEANING OF THIS DESIGN IN THE SKY?
NOT REALLY. THE INTERNET DOESN'T HAVE ALL THE ANSWERS. BUT IT CAN'T BE A GOOD SIGN...
THANKS, WE COULD HAVE GUESSED. BUT FIRST OF ALL, WHERE IS EVIL? I DON'T SEE HIS FILTHY FACE BEHIND CHAOS ANYMORE.

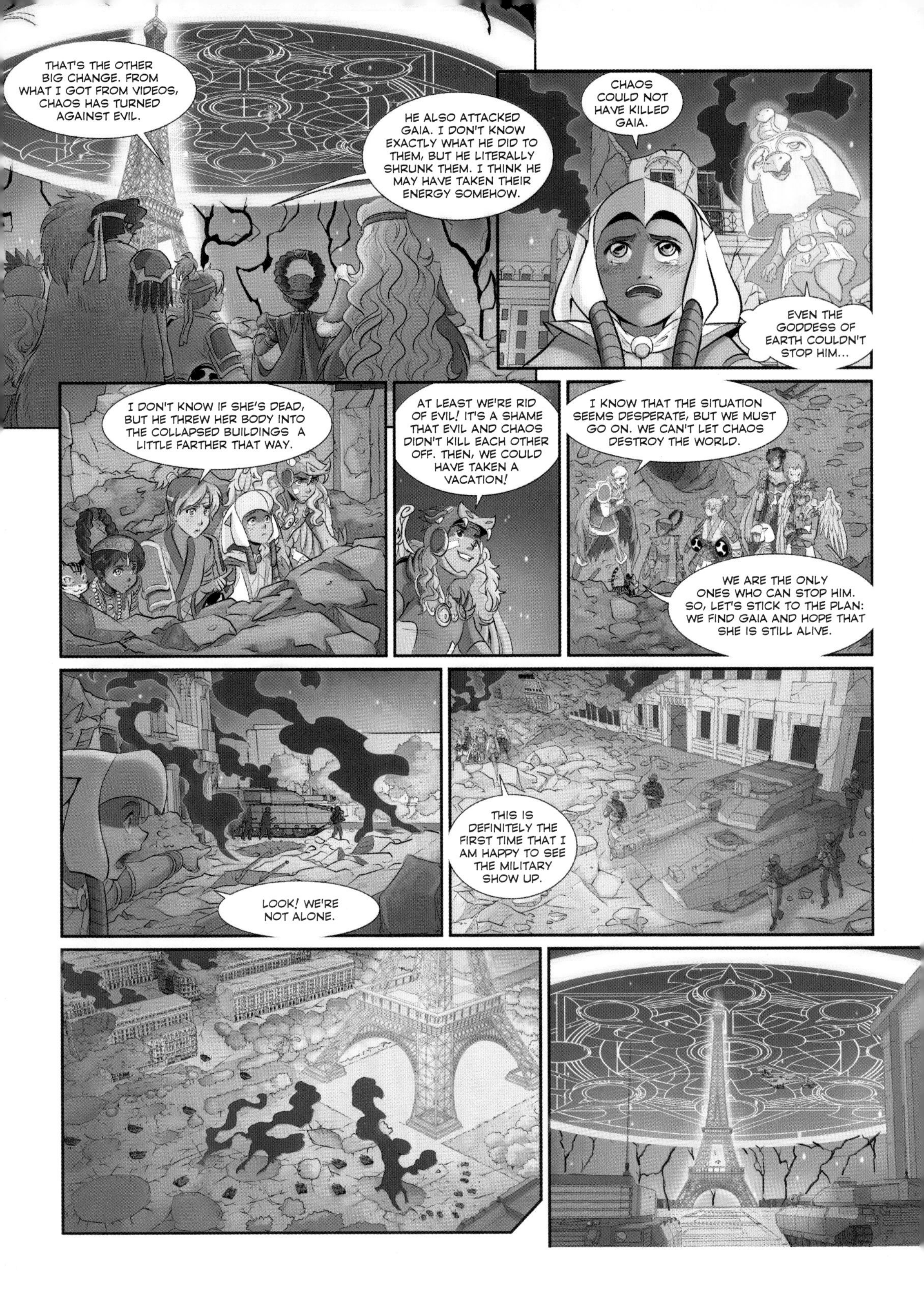
THAT'S THE OTHER BIG CHANGE. FROM WHAT I GOT FROM VIDEOS, CHAOS HAS TURNED AGAINST EVIL.
HE ALSO ATTACKED GAIA. I DON'T KNOW EXACTLY WHAT HE DID TO THEM, BUT HE LITERALLY SHRUNK THEM. I THINK HE MAY HAVE TAKEN THEIR ENERGY SOMEHOW.
CHAOS COULD NOT HAVE KILLED GAIA.
EVEN THE GODDESS OF EARTH COULDN'T STOP HIM...
I DON'T KNOW IF SHE'S DEAD, BUT HE THREW HER BODY INTO THE COLLAPSED BUILDINGS A LITTLE FARTHER THAT WAY.
AT LEAST WE'RE RID OF EVIL! IT'S A SHAME THAT EVIL AND CHAOS DIDN'T KILL EACH OTHER OFF. THEN, WE COULD HAVE TAKEN A VACATION!
I KNOW THAT THE SITUATION SEEMS DESPERATE, BUT WE MUST GO ON. WE CAN'T LET CHAOS DESTROY THE WORLD.
WE ARE THE ONLY ONES WHO CAN STOP HIM. SO, LET'S STICK TO THE PLAN: WE FIND GAIA AND HOPE THAT SHE IS STILL ALIVE.
LOOK! WE'RE NOT ALONE.
THIS IS DEFINITELY THE FIRST TIME THAT I AM HAPPY TO SEE THE MILITARY SHOW UP.

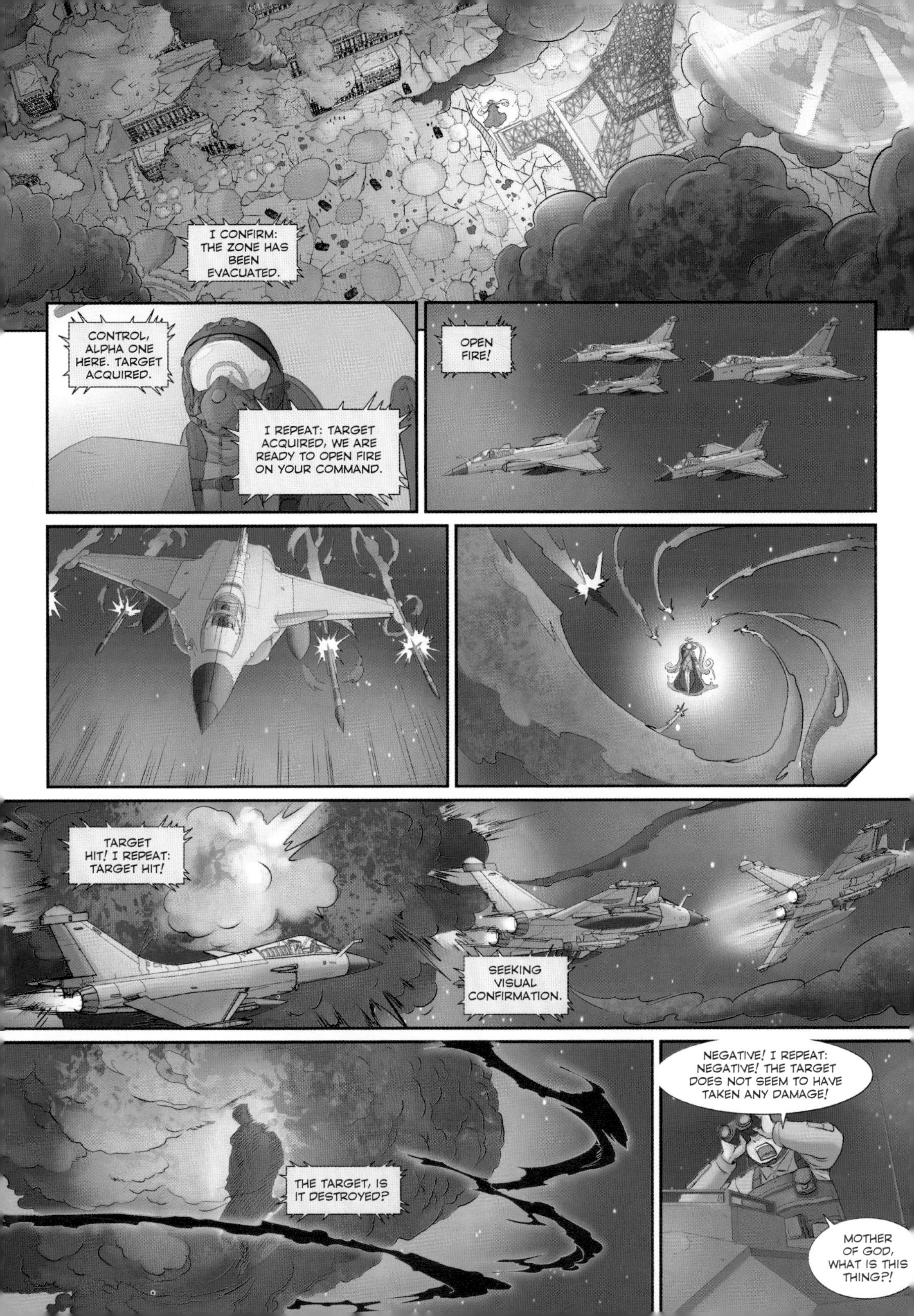
I CONFIRM: THE ZONE HAS BEEN EVACUATED.
CONTROL, ALPHA ONE HERE. TARGET ACQUIRED.
I REPEAT: TARGET ACQUIRED, WE ARE READY TO OPEN FIRE ON YOUR COMMAND.
OPEN FIRE!
TARGET HIT! I REPEAT: TARGET HIT!
SEEKING VISUAL CONFIRMATION.
THE TARGET, IS IT DESTROYED?
NEGATIVE! I REPEAT: NEGATIVE! THE TARGET DOES NOT SEEM TO HAVE TAKEN ANY DAMAGE!
MOTHER OF GOD, WHAT IS THIS THING?!

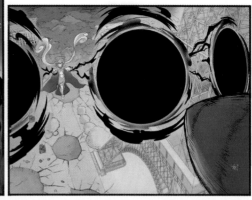

KEEP FORMATION. GIVE HIM EVERYTHING YOU'VE GOT, BOYS!

WHAT'S HAPPENING?! WH-WHERE ARE THE MISSILES?!

WATCH OUT! MISSILES APPROACHING!

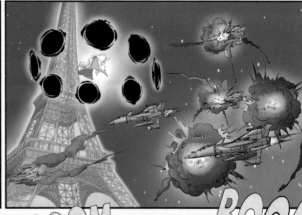

FIRE AT WILL! WE MUST BACK UP OUR PILOTS!

BOOM

BOOM

BOOM

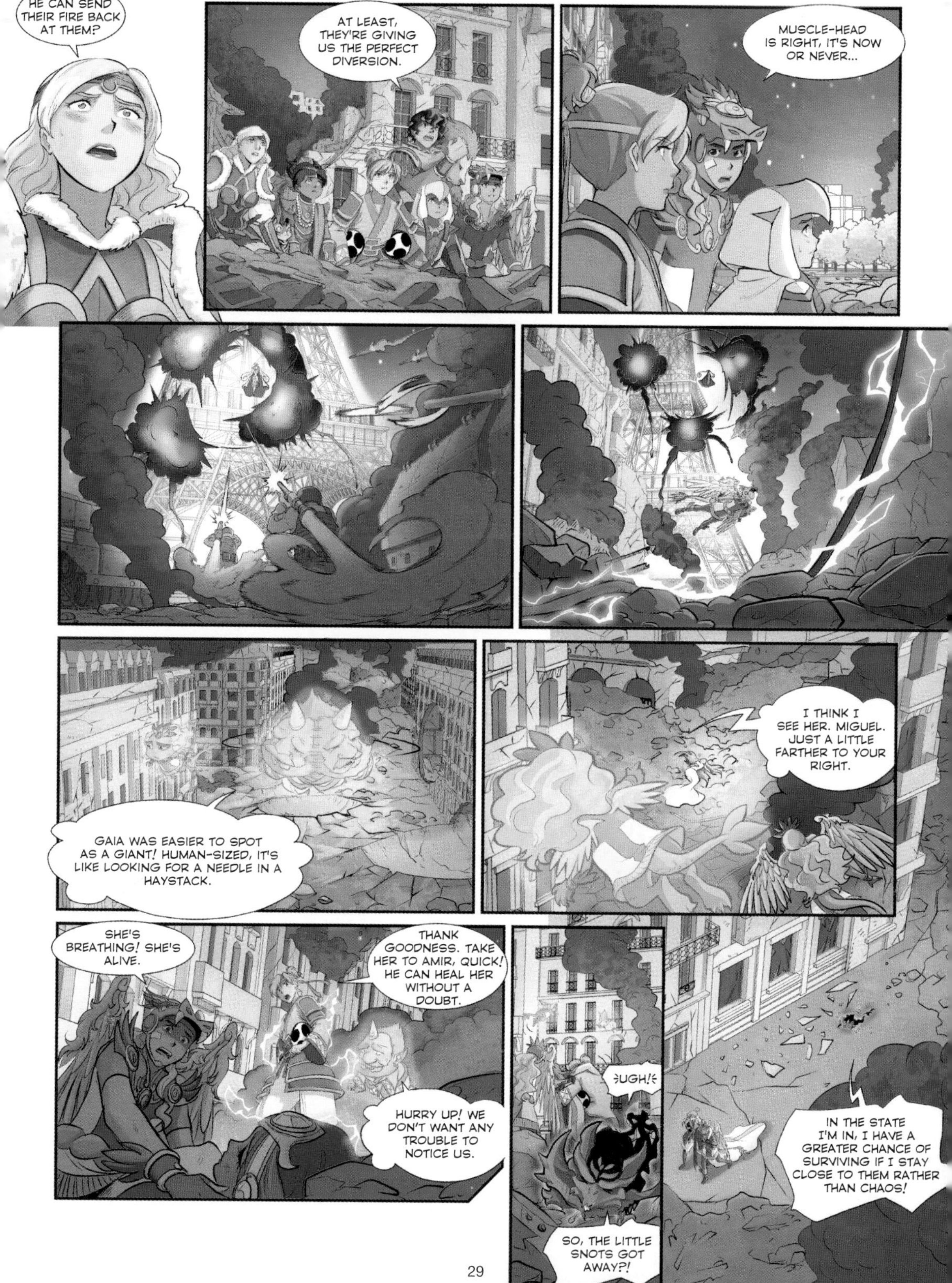
HE CAN SEND THEIR FIRE BACK AT THEM?
AT LEAST, THEY'RE GIVING US THE PERFECT DIVERSION.
MUSCLE-HEAD IS RIGHT, IT'S NOW OR NEVER...
GAIA WAS EASIER TO SPOT AS A GIANT! HUMAN-SIZED, IT'S LIKE LOOKING FOR A NEEDLE IN A HAYSTACK.
I THINK I SEE HER. MIGUEL. JUST A LITTLE FARTHER TO YOUR RIGHT.
SHE'S BREATHING! SHE'S ALIVE.
THANK GOODNESS. TAKE HER TO AMIR, QUICK! HE CAN HEAL HER WITHOUT A DOUBT.
HURRY UP! WE DON'T WANT ANY TROUBLE TO NOTICE US.
UGH!
SO, THE LITTLE SNOTS GOT AWAY?!
IN THE STATE I'M IN, I HAVE A GREATER CHANCE OF SURVIVING IF I STAY CLOSE TO THEM RATHER THAN CHAOS!

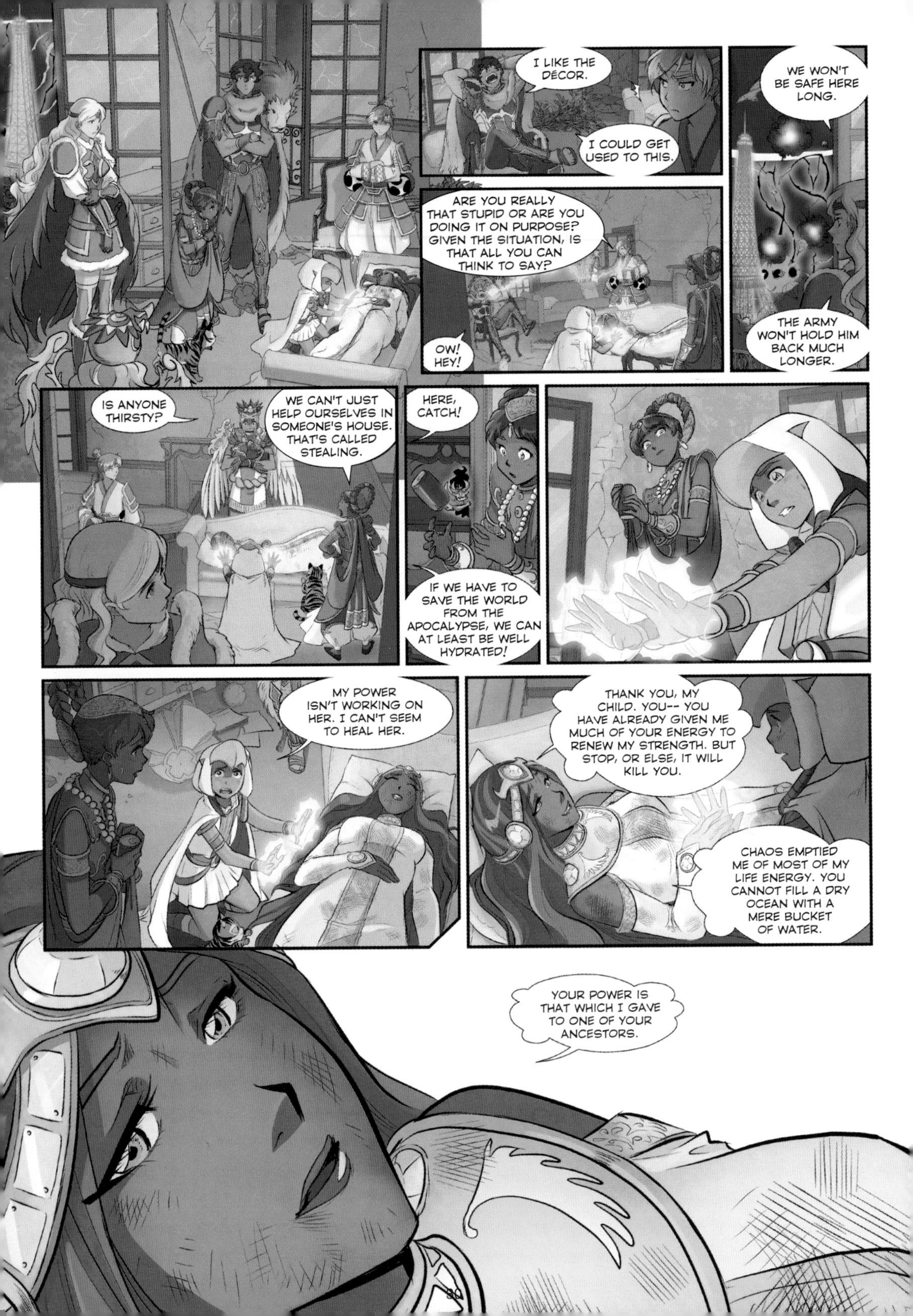

I LIKE THE DÉCOR.
I COULD GET USED TO THIS.
WE WON'T BE SAFE HERE LONG.
ARE YOU REALLY THAT STUPID OR ARE YOU DOING IT ON PURPOSE? GIVEN THE SITUATION, IS THAT ALL YOU CAN THINK TO SAY?
OW! HEY!
THE ARMY WON'T HOLD HIM BACK MUCH LONGER.
IS ANYONE THIRSTY?
WE CAN'T JUST HELP OURSELVES IN SOMEONE'S HOUSE. THAT'S CALLED STEALING.
HERE, CATCH!
IF WE HAVE TO SAVE THE WORLD FROM THE APOCALYPSE, WE CAN AT LEAST BE WELL HYDRATED!
MY POWER ISN'T WORKING ON HER. I CAN'T SEEM TO HEAL HER.
THANK YOU, MY CHILD. YOU-- YOU HAVE ALREADY GIVEN ME MUCH OF YOUR ENERGY TO RENEW MY STRENGTH. BUT STOP, OR ELSE, IT WILL KILL YOU.
CHAOS EMPTIED ME OF MOST OF MY LIFE ENERGY. YOU CANNOT FILL A DRY OCEAN WITH A MERE BUCKET OF WATER.
YOUR POWER IS THAT WHICH I GAVE TO ONE OF YOUR ANCESTORS.

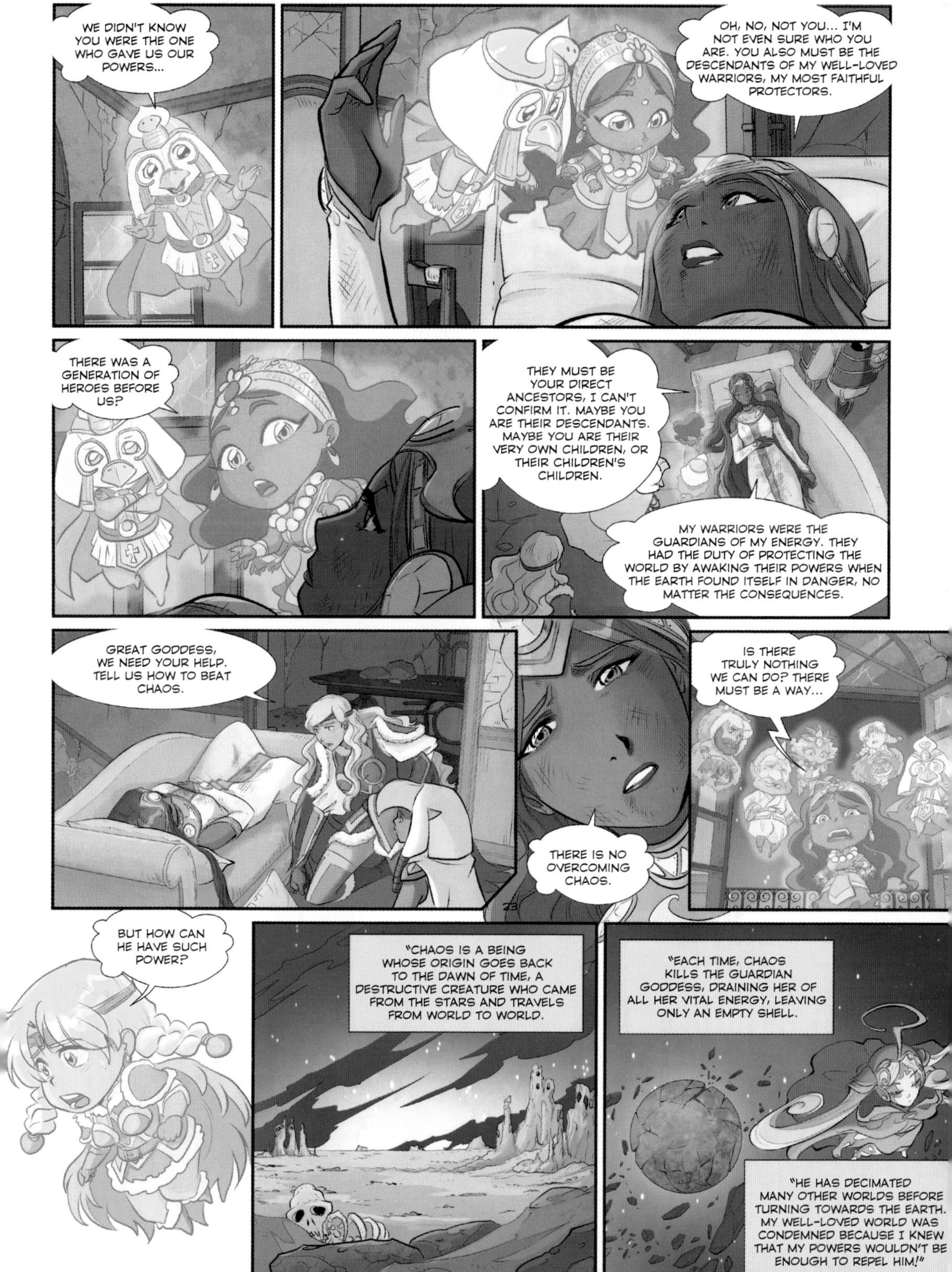
WE DIDN'T KNOW YOU WERE THE ONE WHO GAVE US OUR POWERS...
OH, NO, NOT YOU... I'M NOT EVEN SURE WHO YOU ARE. YOU ALSO MUST BE THE DESCENDANTS OF MY WELL-LOVED WARRIORS, MY MOST FAITHFUL PROTECTORS.
THERE WAS A GENERATION OF HEROES BEFORE US?
THEY MUST BE YOUR DIRECT ANCESTORS, I CAN'T CONFIRM IT. MAYBE YOU ARE THEIR DESCENDANTS. MAYBE YOU ARE THEIR VERY OWN CHILDREN, OR THEIR CHILDREN'S CHILDREN.
MY WARRIORS WERE THE GUARDIANS OF MY ENERGY. THEY HAD THE DUTY OF PROTECTING THE WORLD BY AWAKING THEIR POWERS WHEN THE EARTH FOUND ITSELF IN DANGER, NO MATTER THE CONSEQUENCES.
GREAT GODDESS, WE NEED YOUR HELP. TELL US HOW TO BEAT CHAOS.
THERE IS NO OVERCOMING CHAOS.
IS THERE TRULY NOTHING WE CAN DO? THERE MUST BE A WAY...
BUT HOW CAN HE HAVE SUCH POWER?
"CHAOS IS A BEING WHOSE ORIGIN GOES BACK TO THE DAWN OF TIME, A DESTRUCTIVE CREATURE WHO CAME FROM THE STARS AND TRAVELS FROM WORLD TO WORLD.
"EACH TIME, CHAOS KILLS THE GUARDIAN GODDESS, DRAINING HER OF ALL HER VITAL ENERGY, LEAVING ONLY AN EMPTY SHELL.
"HE HAS DECIMATED MANY OTHER WORLDS BEFORE TURNING TOWARDS THE EARTH. MY WELL-LOVED WORLD WAS CONDEMNED BECAUSE I KNEW THAT MY POWERS WOULDN'T BE ENOUGH TO REPEL HIM!"

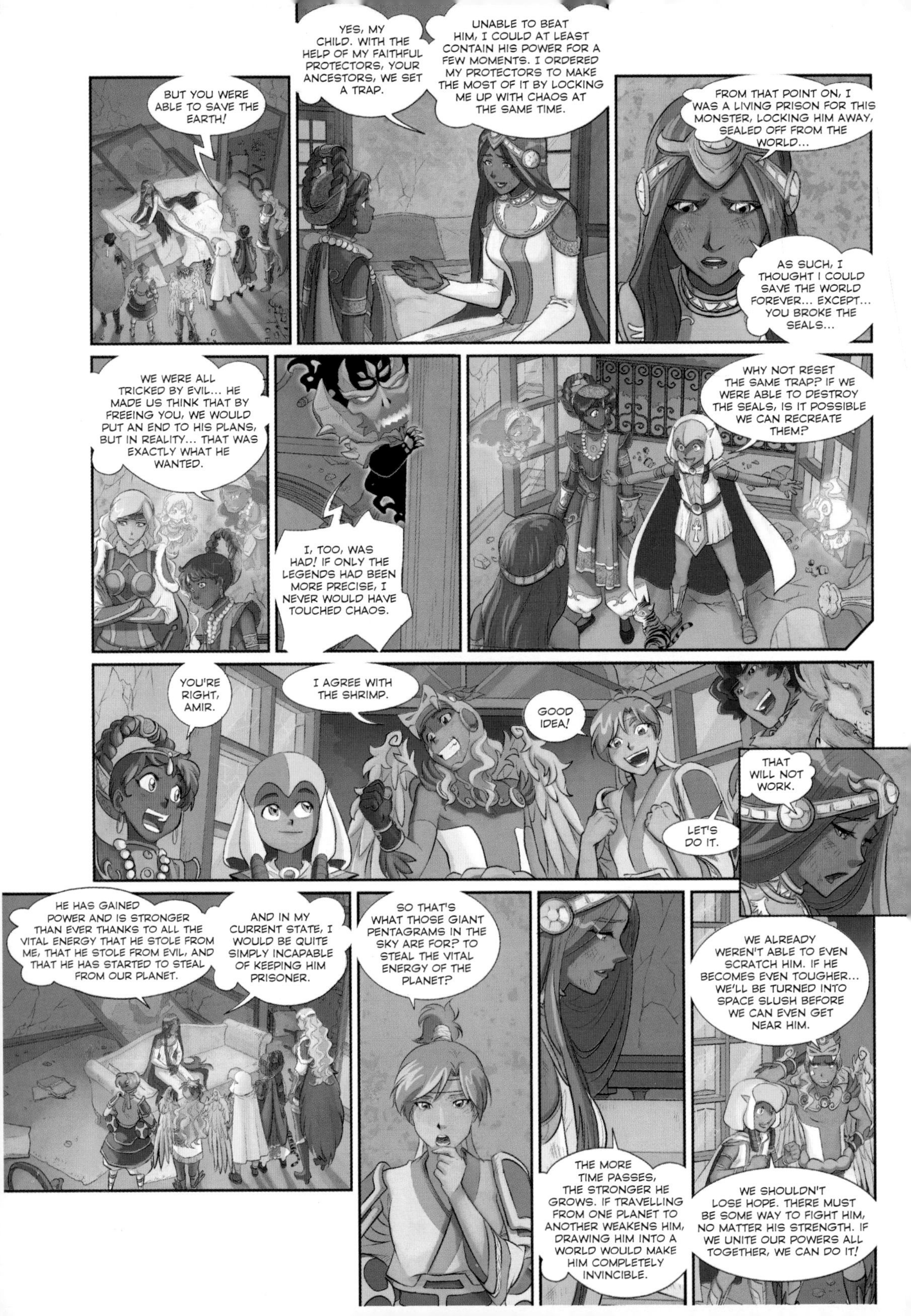
BUT YOU WERE ABLE TO SAVE THE EARTH!
YES, MY CHILD. WITH THE HELP OF MY FAITHFUL PROTECTORS, YOUR ANCESTORS, WE SET A TRAP.
UNABLE TO BEAT HIM, I COULD AT LEAST CONTAIN HIS POWER FOR A FEW MOMENTS. I ORDERED MY PROTECTORS TO MAKE THE MOST OF IT BY LOCKING ME UP WITH CHAOS AT THE SAME TIME.
FROM THAT POINT ON, I WAS A LIVING PRISON FOR THIS MONSTER, LOCKING HIM AWAY, SEALED OFF FROM THE WORLD...
AS SUCH, I THOUGHT I COULD SAVE THE WORLD FOREVER... EXCEPT... YOU BROKE THE SEALS...
WE WERE ALL TRICKED BY EVIL... HE MADE US THINK THAT BY FREEING YOU, WE WOULD PUT AN END TO HIS PLANS, BUT IN REALITY... THAT WAS EXACTLY WHAT HE WANTED.
I, TOO, WAS HAD! IF ONLY THE LEGENDS HAD BEEN MORE PRECISE, I NEVER WOULD HAVE TOUCHED CHAOS.
WHY NOT RESET THE SAME TRAP? IF WE WERE ABLE TO DESTROY THE SEALS, IS IT POSSIBLE WE CAN RECREATE THEM?
YOU'RE RIGHT, AMIR.
I AGREE WITH THE SHRIMP.
GOOD IDEA!
LET'S DO IT.
THAT WILL NOT WORK.
HE HAS GAINED POWER AND IS STRONGER THAN EVER THANKS TO ALL THE VITAL ENERGY THAT HE STOLE FROM ME, THAT HE STOLE FROM EVIL, AND THAT HE HAS STARTED TO STEAL FROM OUR PLANET.
AND IN MY CURRENT STATE, I WOULD BE QUITE SIMPLY INCAPABLE OF KEEPING HIM PRISONER.
SO THAT'S WHAT THOSE GIANT PENTAGRAMS IN THE SKY ARE FOR? TO STEAL THE VITAL ENERGY OF THE PLANET?
THE MORE TIME PASSES, THE STRONGER HE GROWS. IF TRAVELLING FROM ONE PLANET TO ANOTHER WEAKENS HIM, DRAWING HIM INTO A WORLD WOULD MAKE HIM COMPLETELY INVINCIBLE.
WE ALREADY WEREN'T ABLE TO EVEN SCRATCH HIM. IF HE BECOMES EVEN TOUGHER... WE'LL BE TURNED INTO SPACE SLUSH BEFORE WE CAN EVEN GET NEAR HIM.
WE SHOULDN'T LOSE HOPE. THERE MUST BE SOME WAY TO FIGHT HIM, NO MATTER HIS STRENGTH. IF WE UNITE OUR POWERS ALL TOGETHER, WE CAN DO IT!

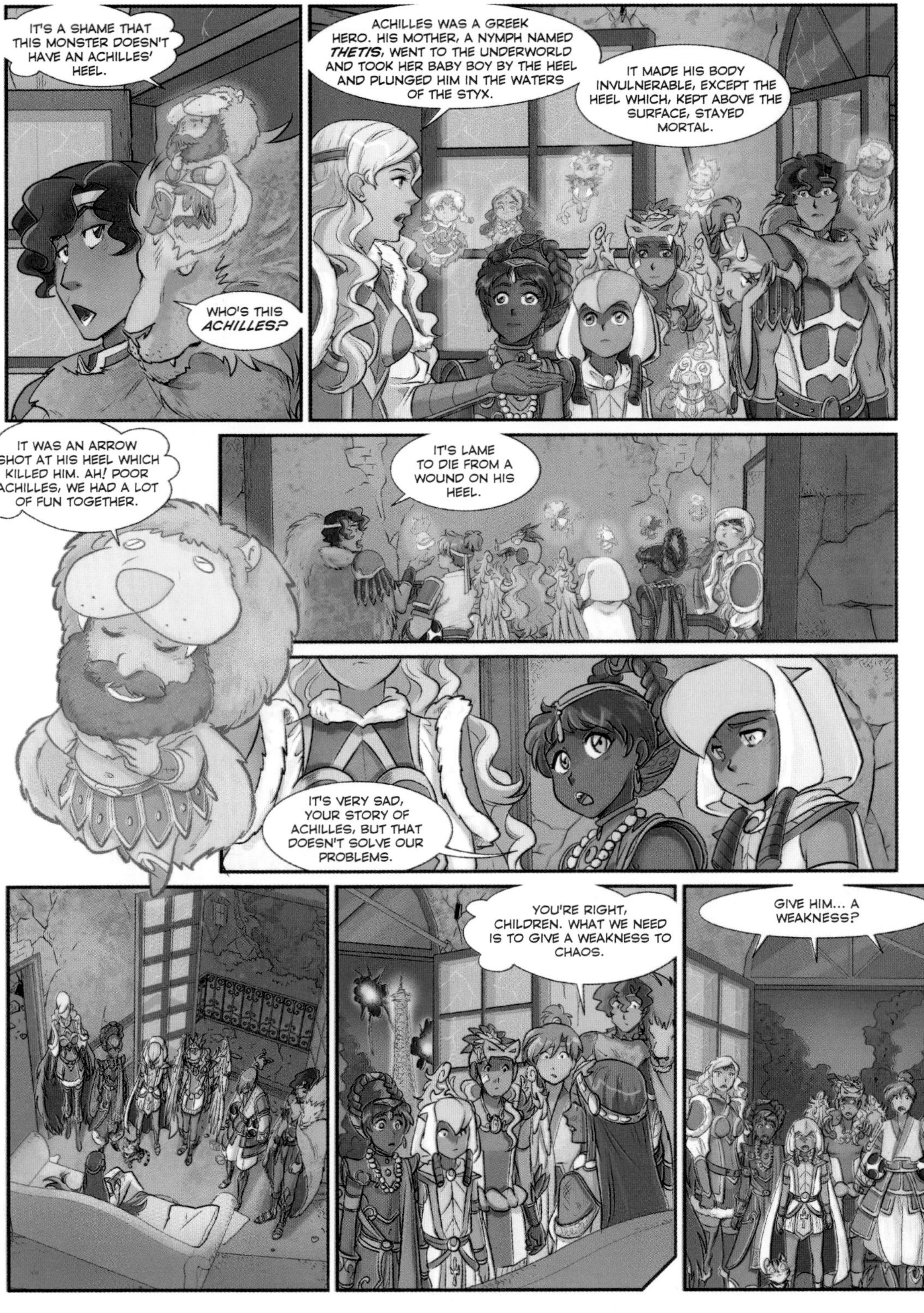
IT'S A SHAME THAT THIS MONSTER DOESN'T HAVE AN ACHILLES' HEEL.
WHO'S THIS *ACHILLES?*
ACHILLES WAS A GREEK HERO. HIS MOTHER, A NYMPH NAMED ***THETIS,*** WENT TO THE UNDERWORLD AND TOOK HER BABY BOY BY THE HEEL AND PLUNGED HIM IN THE WATERS OF THE STYX.
IT MADE HIS BODY INVULNERABLE, EXCEPT THE HEEL WHICH, KEPT ABOVE THE SURFACE, STAYED MORTAL.
IT WAS AN ARROW SHOT AT HIS HEEL WHICH KILLED HIM. AH! POOR ACHILLES, WE HAD A LOT OF FUN TOGETHER.
IT'S LAME TO DIE FROM A WOUND ON HIS HEEL.
IT'S VERY SAD, YOUR STORY OF ACHILLES, BUT THAT DOESN'T SOLVE OUR PROBLEMS.
YOU'RE RIGHT, CHILDREN. WHAT WE NEED IS TO GIVE A WEAKNESS TO CHAOS.
GIVE HIM... A WEAKNESS?

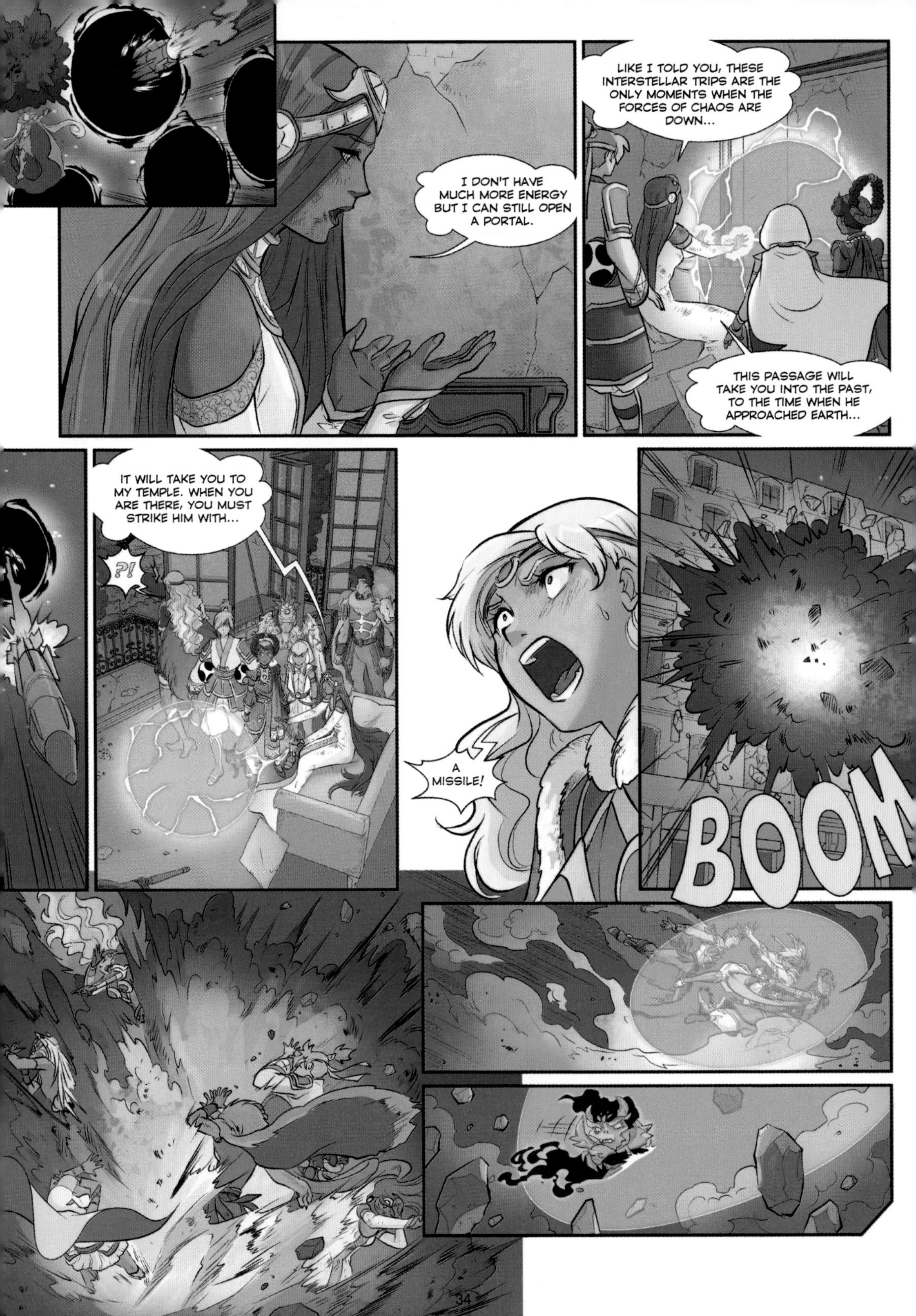
I DON'T HAVE MUCH MORE ENERGY BUT I CAN STILL OPEN A PORTAL.
LIKE I TOLD YOU, THESE INTERSTELLAR TRIPS ARE THE ONLY MOMENTS WHEN THE FORCES OF CHAOS ARE DOWN...
THIS PASSAGE WILL TAKE YOU INTO THE PAST, TO THE TIME WHEN HE APPROACHED EARTH...
IT WILL TAKE YOU TO MY TEMPLE. WHEN YOU ARE THERE, YOU MUST STRIKE HIM WITH...
?!
A MISSILE!
BOOM

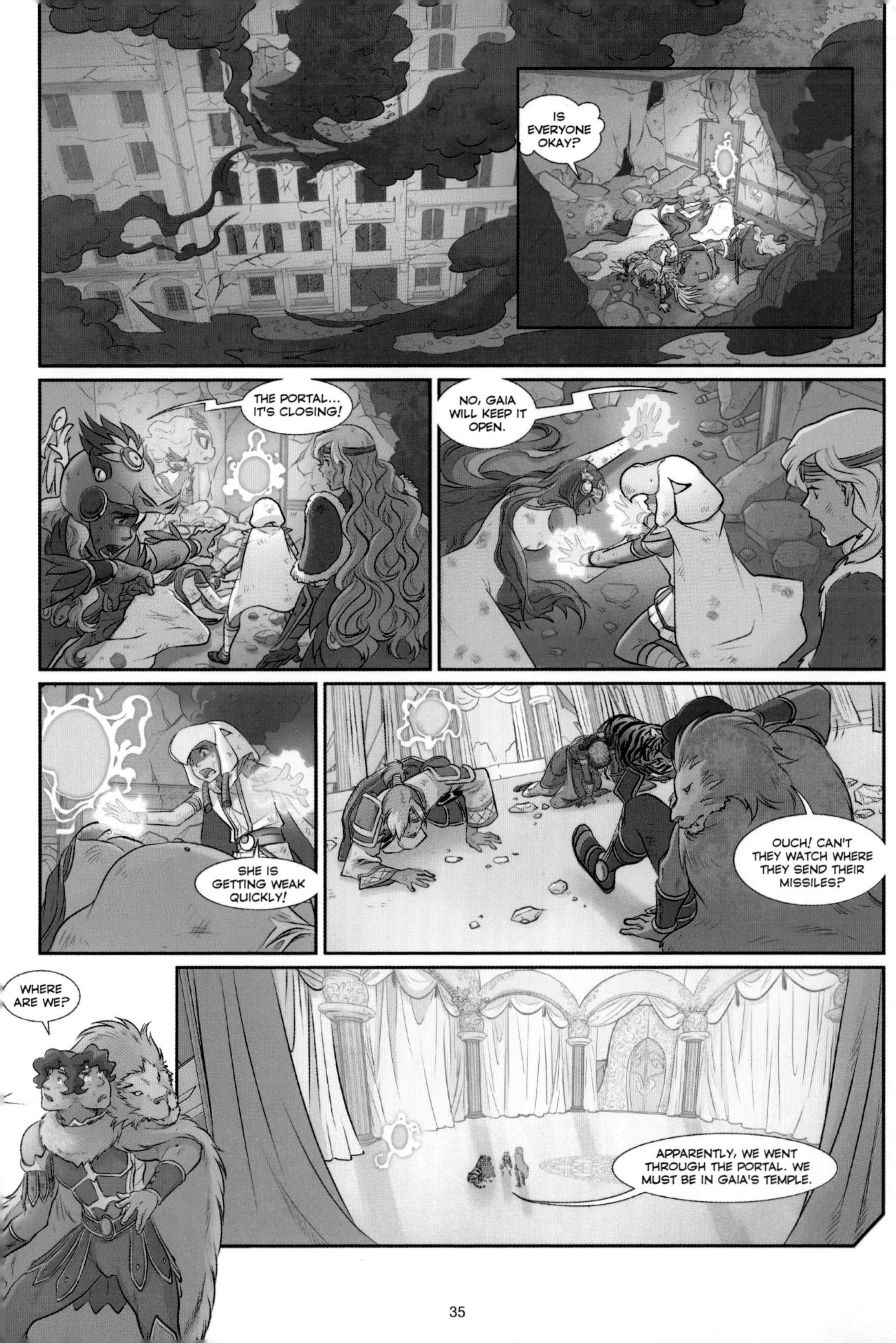

IS EVERYONE OKAY?
THE PORTAL... IT'S CLOSING!
NO, GAIA WILL KEEP IT OPEN.
SHE IS GETTING WEAK QUICKLY!
OUCH! CAN'T THEY WATCH WHERE THEY SEND THEIR MISSILES?
WHERE ARE WE?
APPARENTLY, WE WENT THROUGH THE PORTAL. WE MUST BE IN GAIA'S TEMPLE.

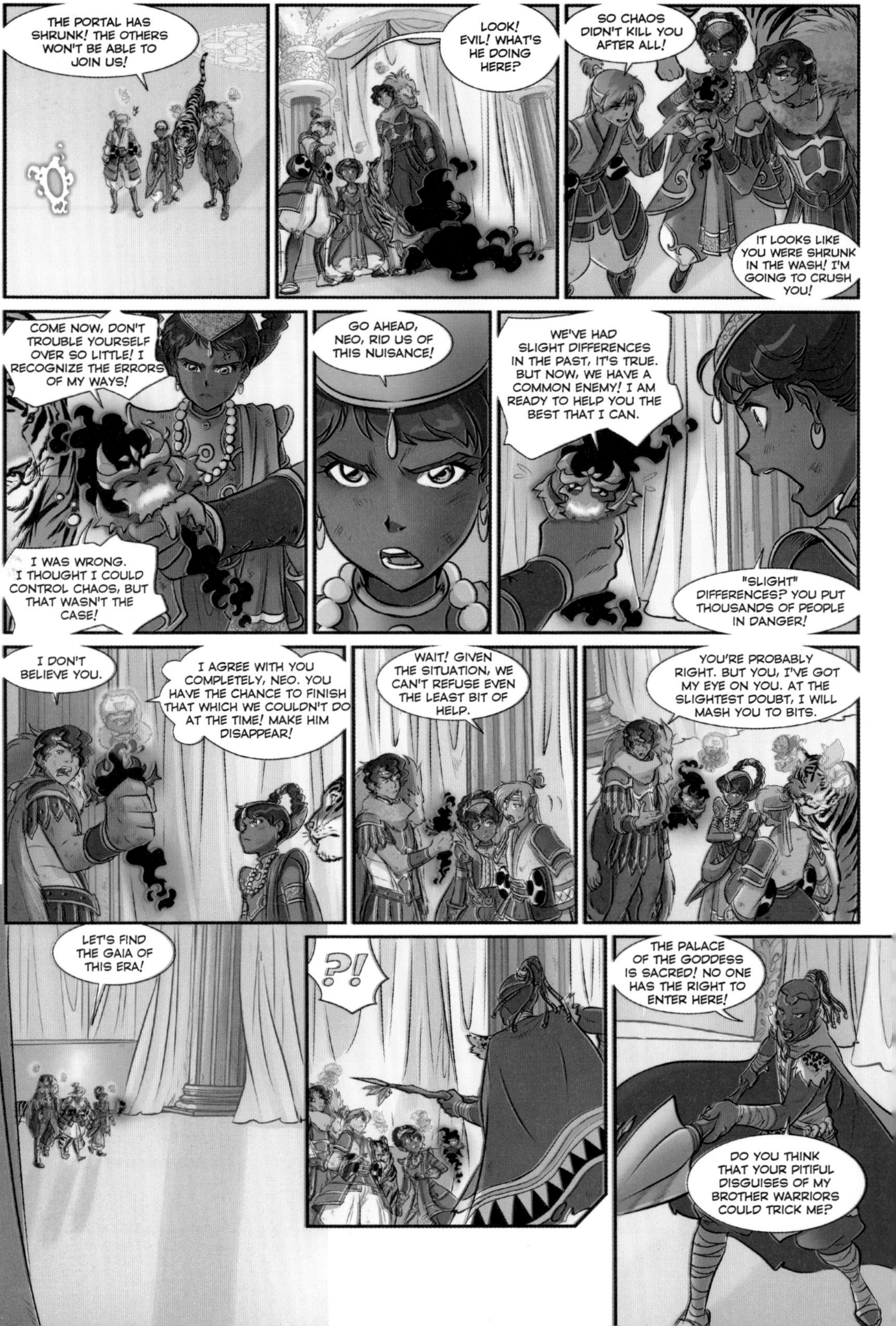
THE PORTAL HAS SHRUNK! THE OTHERS WON'T BE ABLE TO JOIN US!
LOOK! EVIL! WHAT'S HE DOING HERE?
SO CHAOS DIDN'T KILL YOU AFTER ALL!
IT LOOKS LIKE YOU WERE SHRUNK IN THE WASH! I'M GOING TO CRUSH YOU!
COME NOW, DON'T TROUBLE YOURSELF OVER SO LITTLE! I RECOGNIZE THE ERRORS OF MY WAYS!
I WAS WRONG. I THOUGHT I COULD CONTROL CHAOS, BUT THAT WASN'T THE CASE!
GO AHEAD, NEO, RID US OF THIS NUISANCE!
WE'VE HAD SLIGHT DIFFERENCES IN THE PAST, IT'S TRUE. BUT NOW, WE HAVE A COMMON ENEMY! I AM READY TO HELP YOU THE BEST THAT I CAN.
"SLIGHT" DIFFERENCES? YOU PUT THOUSANDS OF PEOPLE IN DANGER!
I DON'T BELIEVE YOU.
I AGREE WITH YOU COMPLETELY, NEO. YOU HAVE THE CHANCE TO FINISH THAT WHICH WE COULDN'T DO AT THE TIME! MAKE HIM DISAPPEAR!
WAIT! GIVEN THE SITUATION, WE CAN'T REFUSE EVEN THE LEAST BIT OF HELP.
YOU'RE PROBABLY RIGHT. BUT YOU, I'VE GOT MY EYE ON YOU. AT THE SLIGHTEST DOUBT, I WILL MASH YOU TO BITS.
LET'S FIND THE GAIA OF THIS ERA!
?!
THE PALACE OF THE GODDESS IS SACRED! NO ONE HAS THE RIGHT TO ENTER HERE!
DO YOU THINK THAT YOUR PITIFUL DISGUISES OF MY BROTHER WARRIORS COULD TRICK ME?

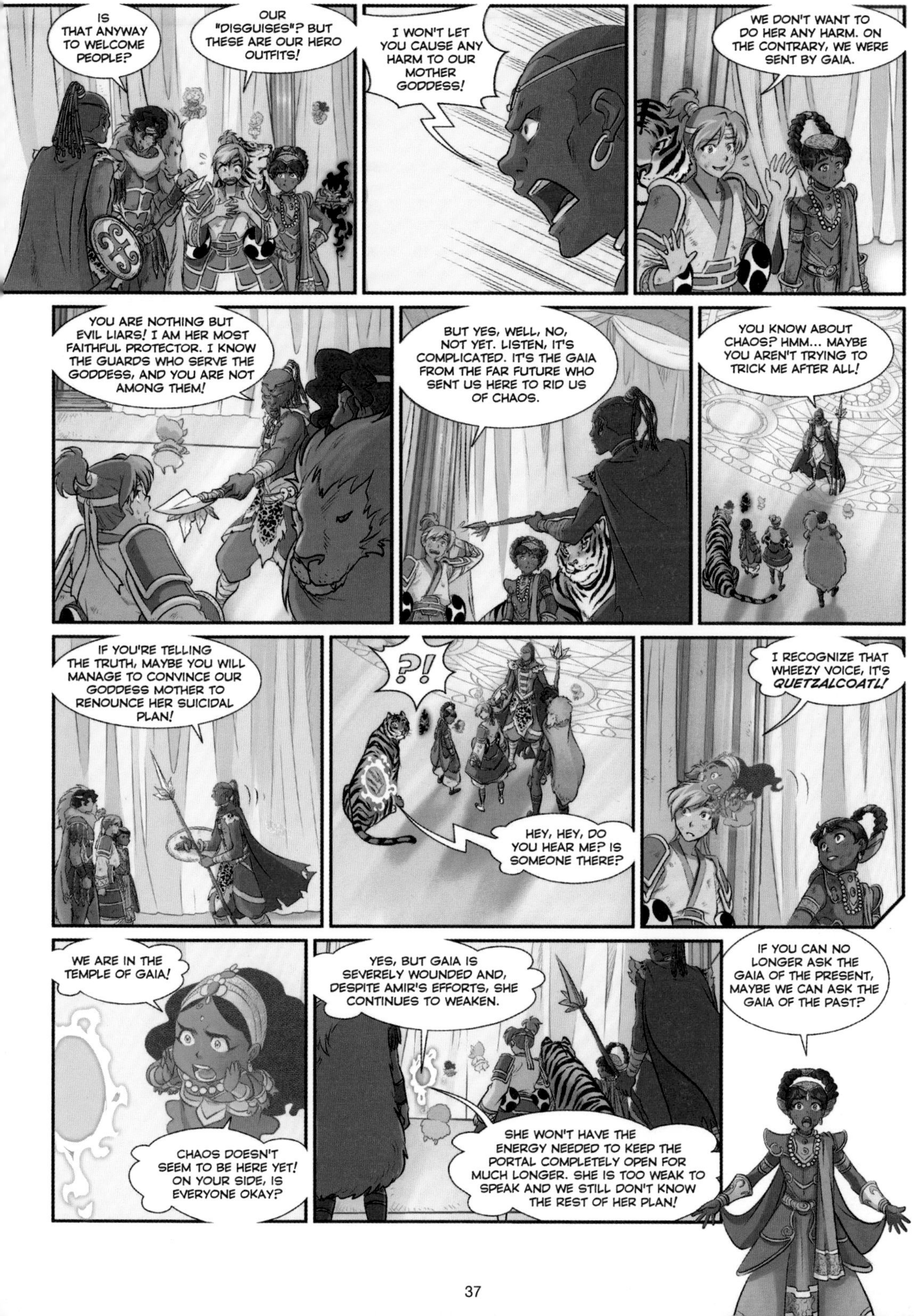
IS THAT ANYWAY TO WELCOME PEOPLE?
OUR "DISGUISES"? BUT THESE ARE OUR HERO OUTFITS!
I WON'T LET YOU CAUSE ANY HARM TO OUR MOTHER GODDESS!
WE DON'T WANT TO DO HER ANY HARM. ON THE CONTRARY, WE WERE SENT BY GAIA.
YOU ARE NOTHING BUT EVIL LIARS! I AM HER MOST FAITHFUL PROTECTOR. I KNOW THE GUARDS WHO SERVE THE GODDESS, AND YOU ARE NOT AMONG THEM!
BUT YES, WELL, NO, NOT YET. LISTEN, IT'S COMPLICATED. IT'S THE GAIA FROM THE FAR FUTURE WHO SENT US HERE TO RID US OF CHAOS.
YOU KNOW ABOUT CHAOS? HMM... MAYBE YOU AREN'T TRYING TO TRICK ME AFTER ALL!
IF YOU'RE TELLING THE TRUTH, MAYBE YOU WILL MANAGE TO CONVINCE OUR GODDESS MOTHER TO RENOUNCE HER SUICIDAL PLAN!
?!
HEY, HEY, DO YOU HEAR ME? IS SOMEONE THERE?
I RECOGNIZE THAT WHEEZY VOICE, IT'S QUETZALCOATL!
WE ARE IN THE TEMPLE OF GAIA!
CHAOS DOESN'T SEEM TO BE HERE YET! ON YOUR SIDE, IS EVERYONE OKAY?
YES, BUT GAIA IS SEVERELY WOUNDED AND, DESPITE AMIR'S EFFORTS, SHE CONTINUES TO WEAKEN.
SHE WON'T HAVE THE ENERGY NEEDED TO KEEP THE PORTAL COMPLETELY OPEN FOR MUCH LONGER. SHE IS TOO WEAK TO SPEAK AND WE STILL DON'T KNOW THE REST OF HER PLAN!
IF YOU CAN NO LONGER ASK THE GAIA OF THE PRESENT, MAYBE WE CAN ASK THE GAIA OF THE PAST?

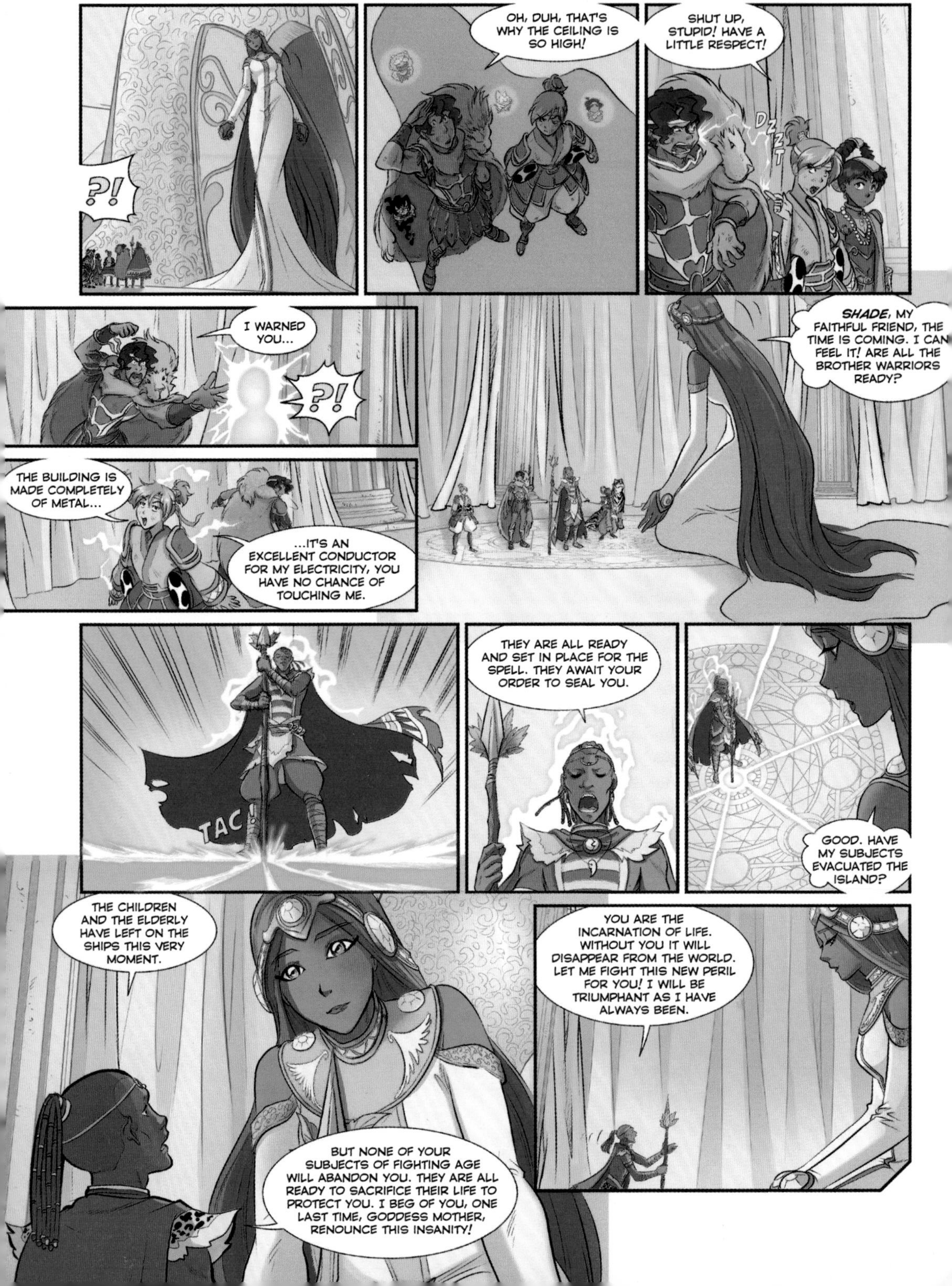
?!
OH, DUH, THAT'S WHY THE CEILING IS SO HIGH!
SHUT UP, STUPID! HAVE A LITTLE RESPECT!
DZZT
I WARNED YOU...
?!
THE BUILDING IS MADE COMPLETELY OF METAL...
...IT'S AN EXCELLENT CONDUCTOR FOR MY ELECTRICITY, YOU HAVE NO CHANCE OF TOUCHING ME.
SHADE, MY FAITHFUL FRIEND, THE TIME IS COMING. I CAN FEEL IT! ARE ALL THE BROTHER WARRIORS READY?
TAC
THEY ARE ALL READY AND SET IN PLACE FOR THE SPELL. THEY AWAIT YOUR ORDER TO SEAL YOU.
GOOD. HAVE MY SUBJECTS EVACUATED THE ISLAND?
THE CHILDREN AND THE ELDERLY HAVE LEFT ON THE SHIPS THIS VERY MOMENT.
BUT NONE OF YOUR SUBJECTS OF FIGHTING AGE WILL ABANDON YOU. THEY ARE ALL READY TO SACRIFICE THEIR LIFE TO PROTECT YOU. I BEG OF YOU, ONE LAST TIME, GODDESS MOTHER, RENOUNCE THIS INSANITY!
YOU ARE THE INCARNATION OF LIFE. WITHOUT YOU IT WILL DISAPPEAR FROM THE WORLD. LET ME FIGHT THIS NEW PERIL FOR YOU! I WILL BE TRIUMPHANT AS I HAVE ALWAYS BEEN.

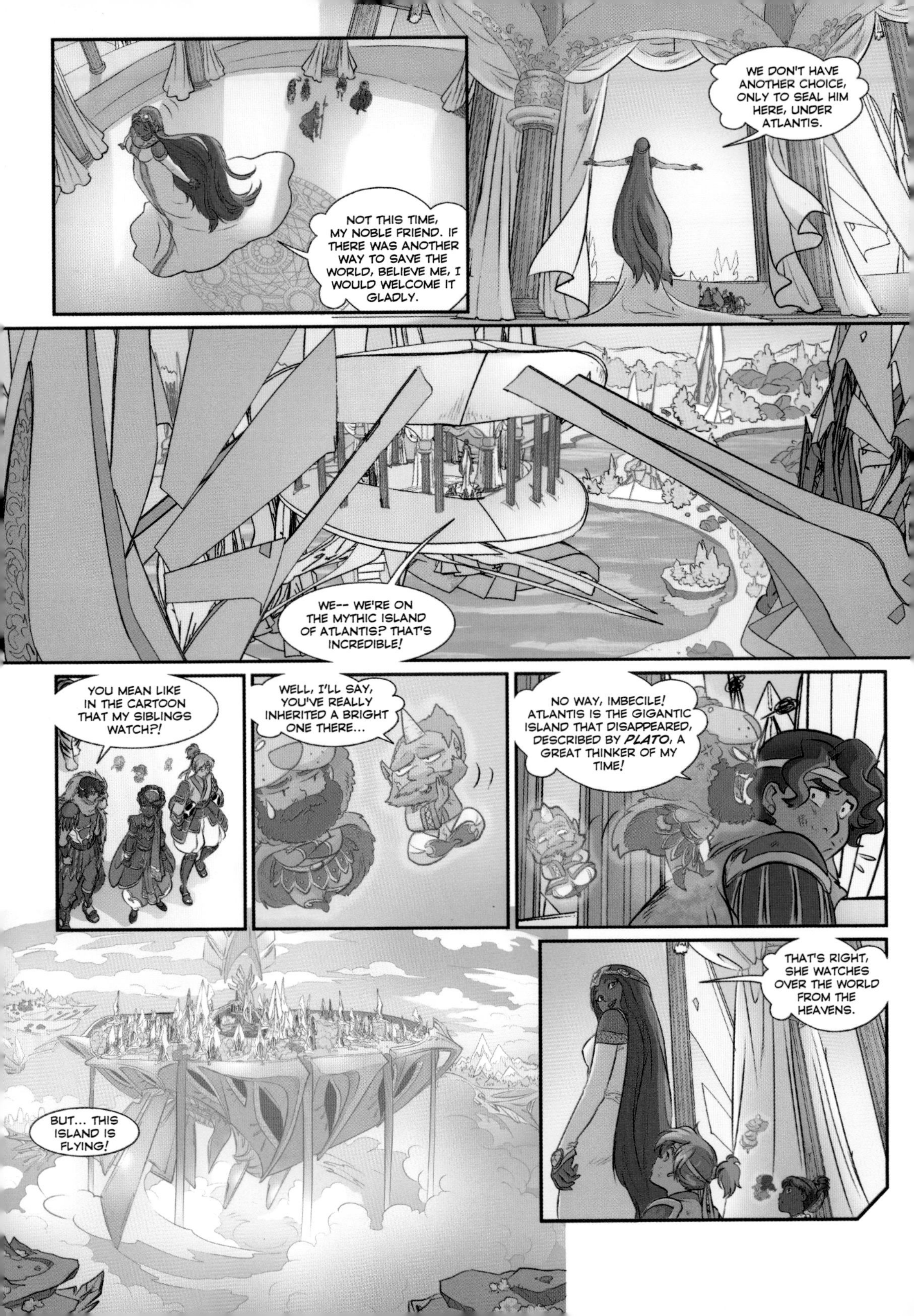

NOT THIS TIME, MY NOBLE FRIEND. IF THERE WAS ANOTHER WAY TO SAVE THE WORLD, BELIEVE ME, I WOULD WELCOME IT GLADLY.
WE DON'T HAVE ANOTHER CHOICE, ONLY TO SEAL HIM HERE, UNDER ATLANTIS.
WE-- WE'RE ON THE MYTHIC ISLAND OF ATLANTIS? THAT'S INCREDIBLE!
YOU MEAN LIKE IN THE CARTOON THAT MY SIBLINGS WATCH?!
WELL, I'LL SAY, YOU'VE REALLY INHERITED A BRIGHT ONE THERE...
NO WAY, IMBECILE! ATLANTIS IS THE GIGANTIC ISLAND THAT DISAPPEARED, DESCRIBED BY PLATO, A GREAT THINKER OF MY TIME!
BUT... THIS ISLAND IS FLYING!
THAT'S RIGHT, SHE WATCHES OVER THE WORLD FROM THE HEAVENS.

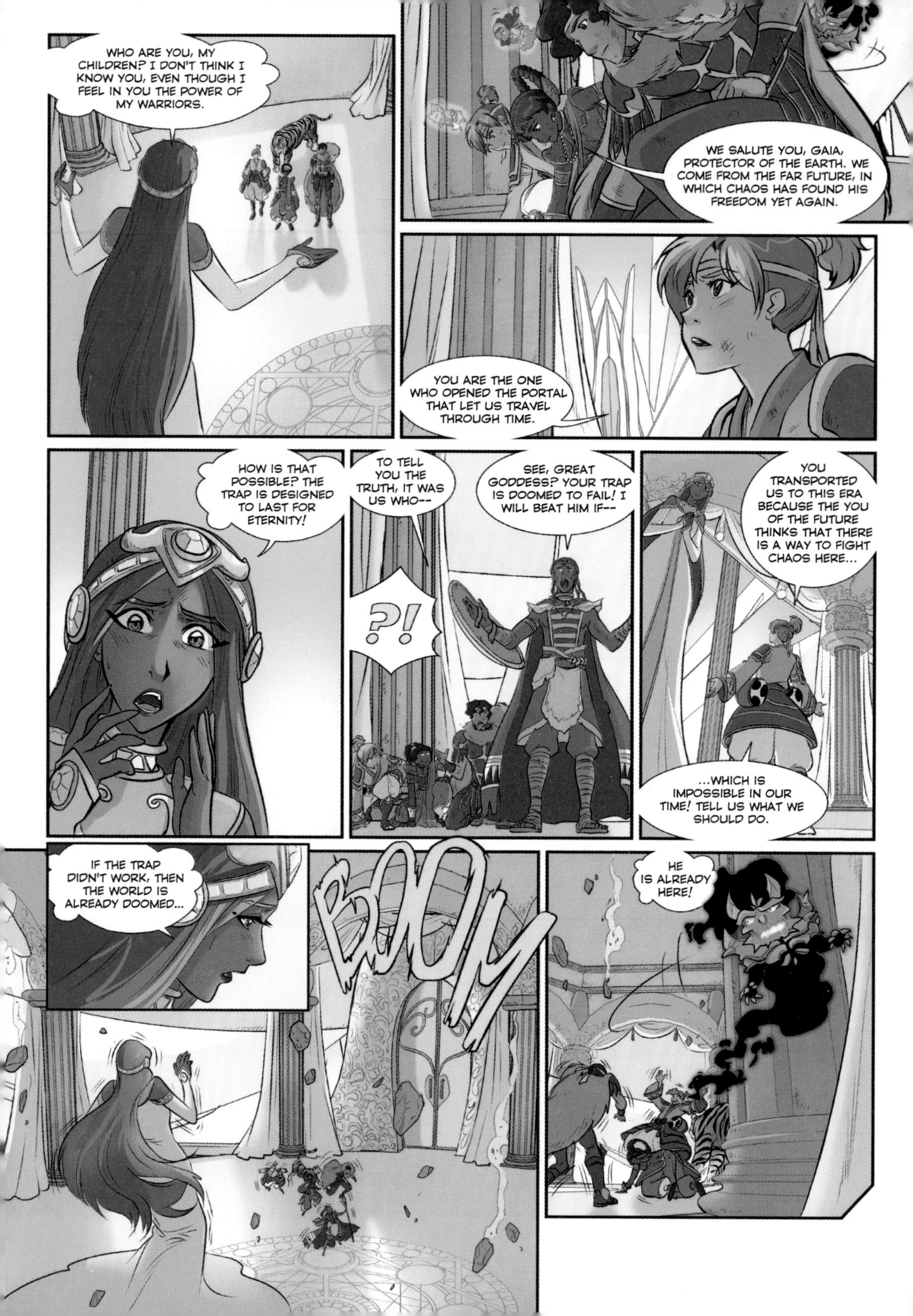
WHO ARE YOU, MY CHILDREN? I DON'T THINK I KNOW YOU, EVEN THOUGH I FEEL IN YOU THE POWER OF MY WARRIORS.
WE SALUTE YOU, GAIA, PROTECTOR OF THE EARTH. WE COME FROM THE FAR FUTURE, IN WHICH CHAOS HAS FOUND HIS FREEDOM YET AGAIN.
YOU ARE THE ONE WHO OPENED THE PORTAL THAT LET US TRAVEL THROUGH TIME.
HOW IS THAT POSSIBLE? THE TRAP IS DESIGNED TO LAST FOR ETERNITY!
TO TELL YOU THE TRUTH, IT WAS US WHO--
SEE, GREAT GODDESS? YOUR TRAP IS DOOMED TO FAIL! I WILL BEAT HIM IF--
?!
YOU TRANSPORTED US TO THIS ERA BECAUSE THE YOU OF THE FUTURE THINKS THAT THERE IS A WAY TO FIGHT CHAOS HERE...
...WHICH IS IMPOSSIBLE IN OUR TIME! TELL US WHAT WE SHOULD DO.
IF THE TRAP DIDN'T WORK, THEN THE WORLD IS ALREADY DOOMED...
BOOM
HE IS ALREADY HERE!

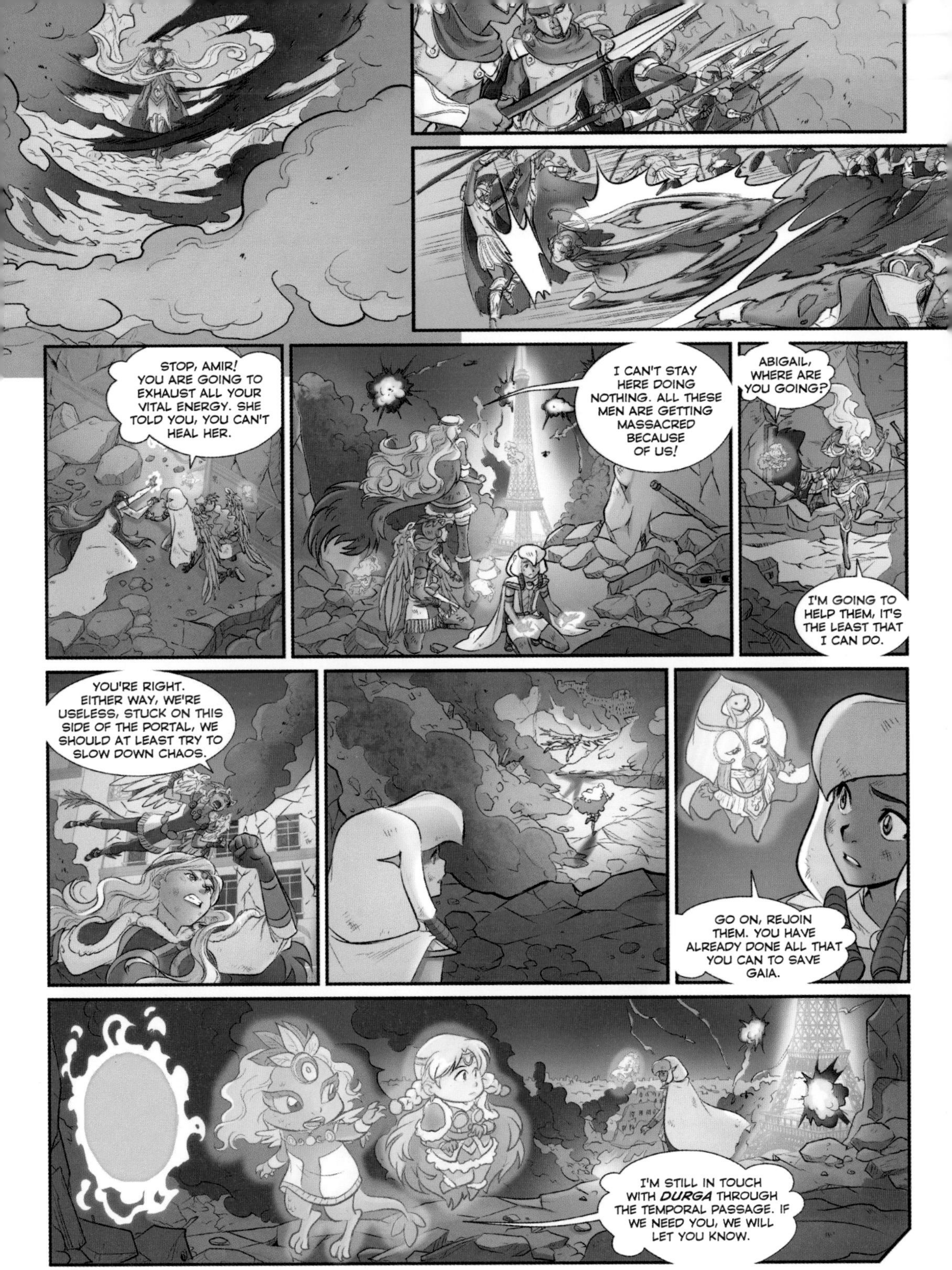
STOP, AMIR! YOU ARE GOING TO EXHAUST ALL YOUR VITAL ENERGY. SHE TOLD YOU, YOU CAN'T HEAL HER.
I CAN'T STAY HERE DOING NOTHING. ALL THESE MEN ARE GETTING MASSACRED BECAUSE OF US!
ABIGAIL, WHERE ARE YOU GOING?
I'M GOING TO HELP THEM, IT'S THE LEAST THAT I CAN DO.
YOU'RE RIGHT. EITHER WAY, WE'RE USELESS, STUCK ON THIS SIDE OF THE PORTAL, WE SHOULD AT LEAST TRY TO SLOW DOWN CHAOS.
GO ON, REJOIN THEM. YOU HAVE ALREADY DONE ALL THAT YOU CAN TO SAVE GAIA.
I'M STILL IN TOUCH WITH ***DURGA*** THROUGH THE TEMPORAL PASSAGE. IF WE NEED YOU, WE WILL LET YOU KNOW.

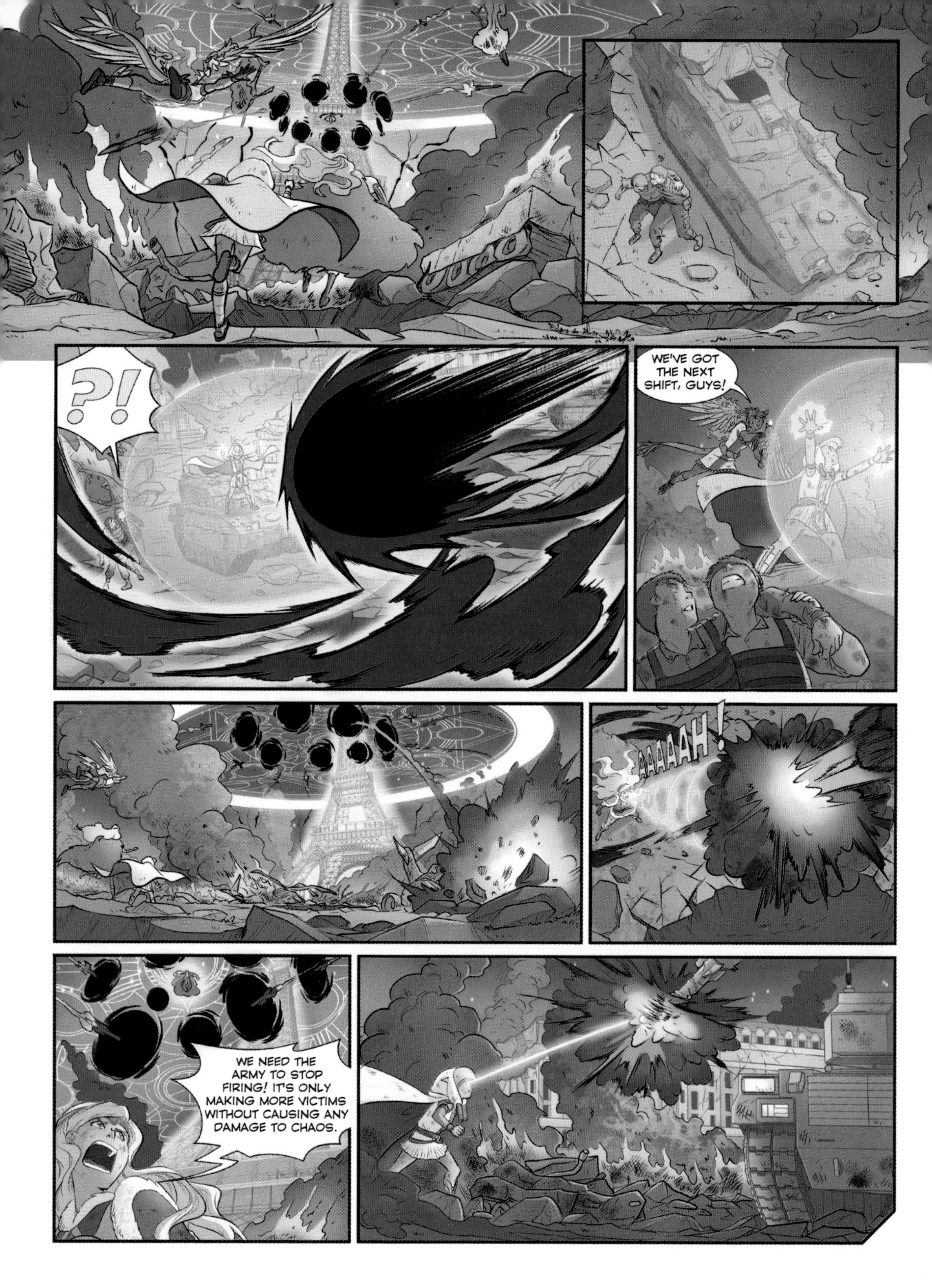
?!
WE'VE GOT THE NEXT SHIFT, GUYS!
AAAAAH!
WE NEED THE ARMY TO STOP FIRING! IT'S ONLY MAKING MORE VICTIMS WITHOUT CAUSING ANY DAMAGE TO CHAOS.

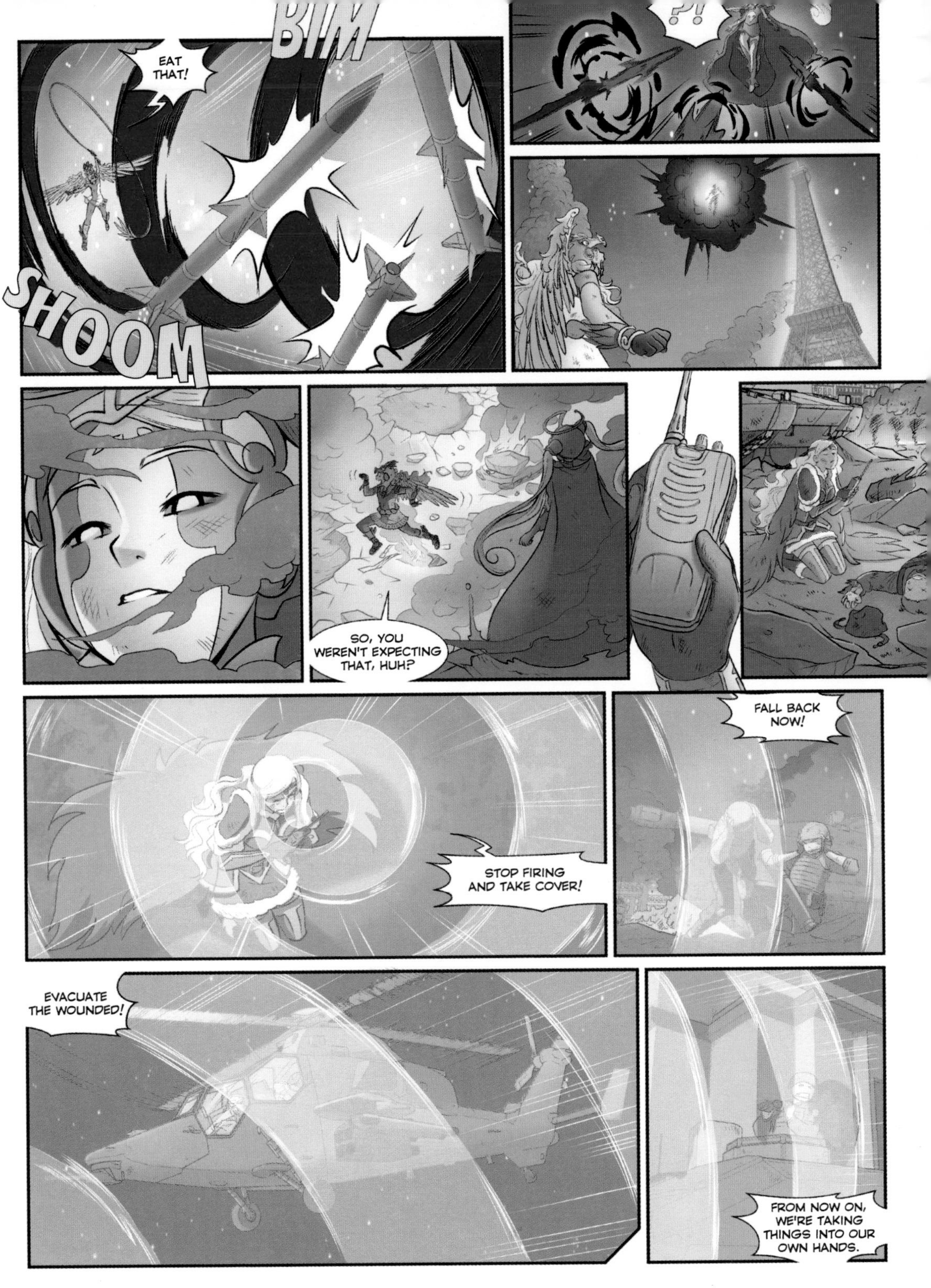
BIM
EAT THAT!
SHOOM
?!
SO, YOU WEREN'T EXPECTING THAT, HUH?
STOP FIRING AND TAKE COVER!
FALL BACK NOW!
EVACUATE THE WOUNDED!
FROM NOW ON, WE'RE TAKING THINGS INTO OUR OWN HANDS.

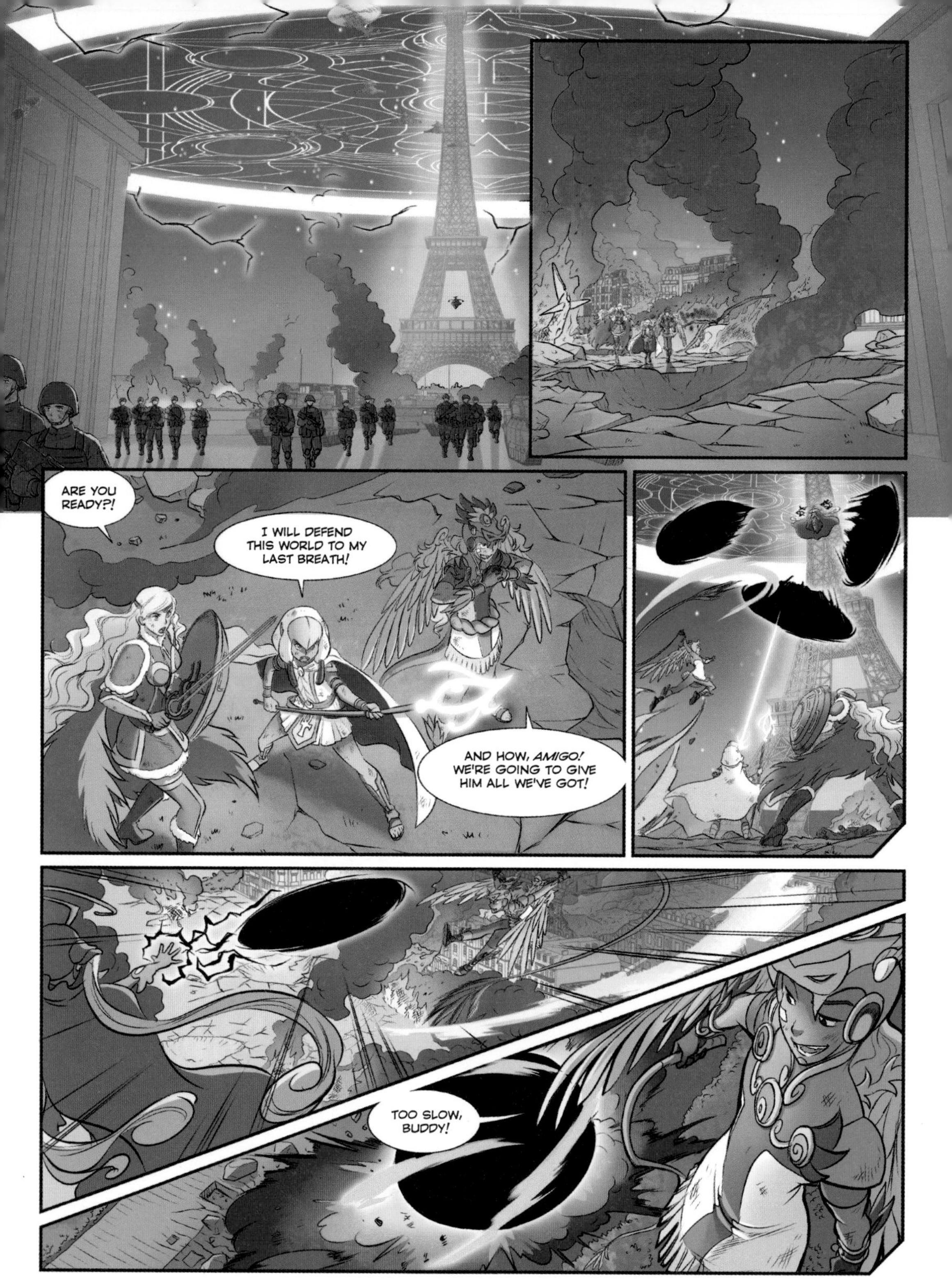
ARE YOU READY?!
I WILL DEFEND THIS WORLD TO MY LAST BREATH!
AND HOW, *AMIGO!* WE'RE GOING TO GIVE HIM ALL WE'VE GOT!
TOO SLOW, BUDDY!

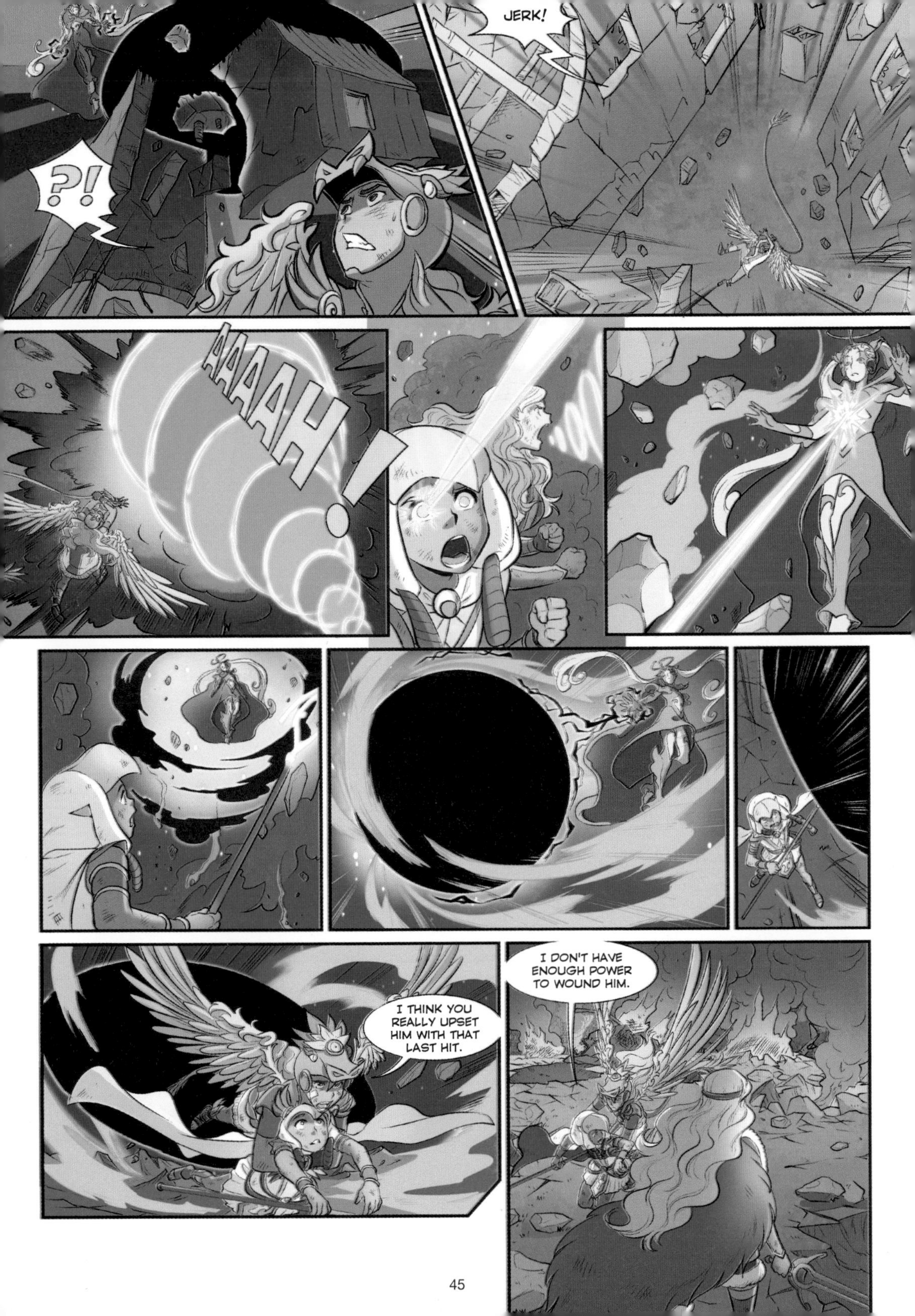
?!
JERK!
AAAAH!
I THINK YOU REALLY UPSET HIM WITH THAT LAST HIT.
I DON'T HAVE ENOUGH POWER TO WOUND HIM.

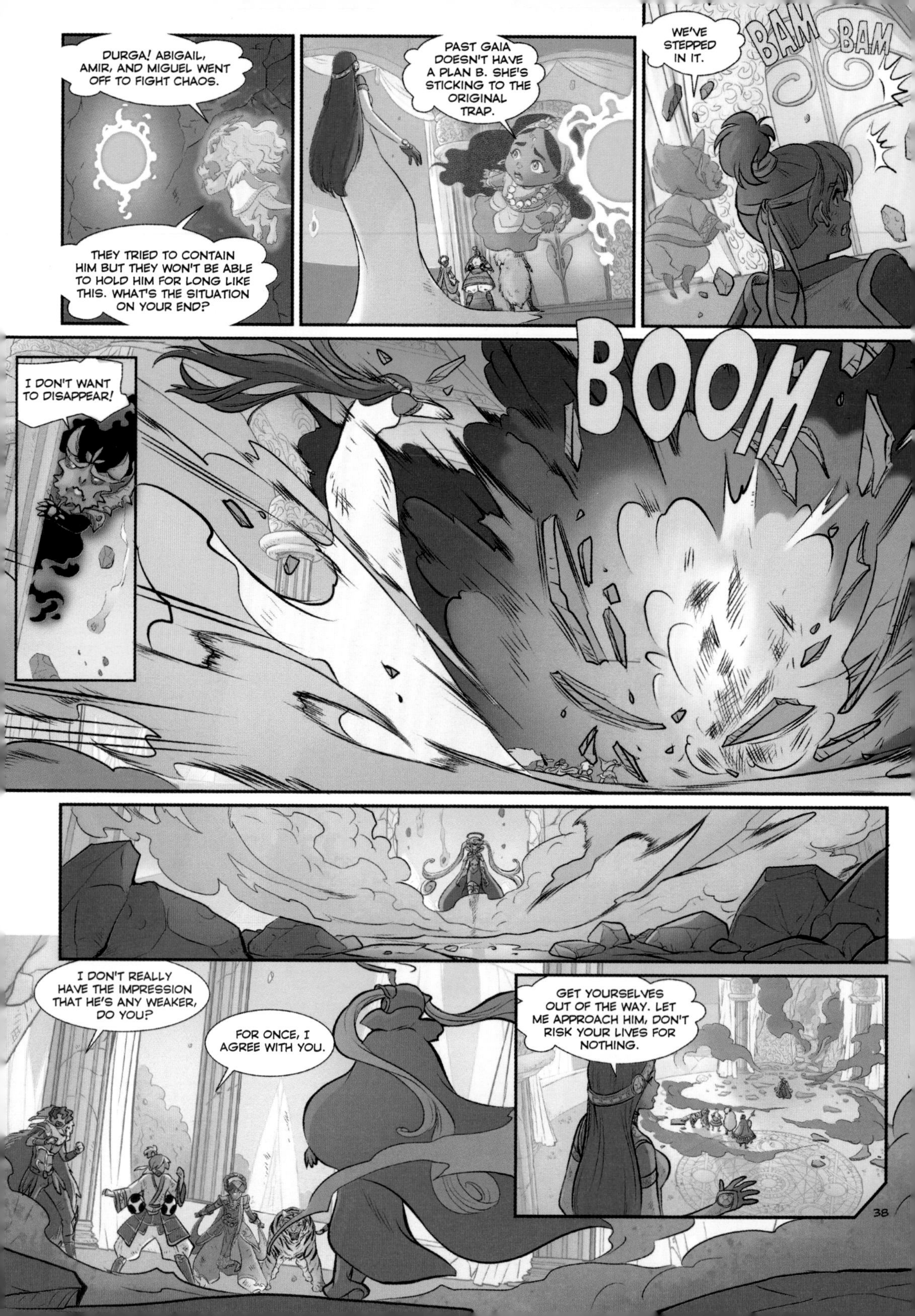
DURGA! ABIGAIL, AMIR, AND MIGUEL WENT OFF TO FIGHT CHAOS.
THEY TRIED TO CONTAIN HIM BUT THEY WON'T BE ABLE TO HOLD HIM FOR LONG LIKE THIS. WHAT'S THE SITUATION ON YOUR END?
PAST GAIA DOESN'T HAVE A PLAN B. SHE'S STICKING TO THE ORIGINAL TRAP.
WE'VE STEPPED IN IT.
BAM
BAM
BOOM
I DON'T WANT TO DISAPPEAR!
I DON'T REALLY HAVE THE IMPRESSION THAT HE'S ANY WEAKER, DO YOU?
FOR ONCE, I AGREE WITH YOU.
GET YOURSELVES OUT OF THE WAY. LET ME APPROACH HIM, DON'T RISK YOUR LIVES FOR NOTHING.

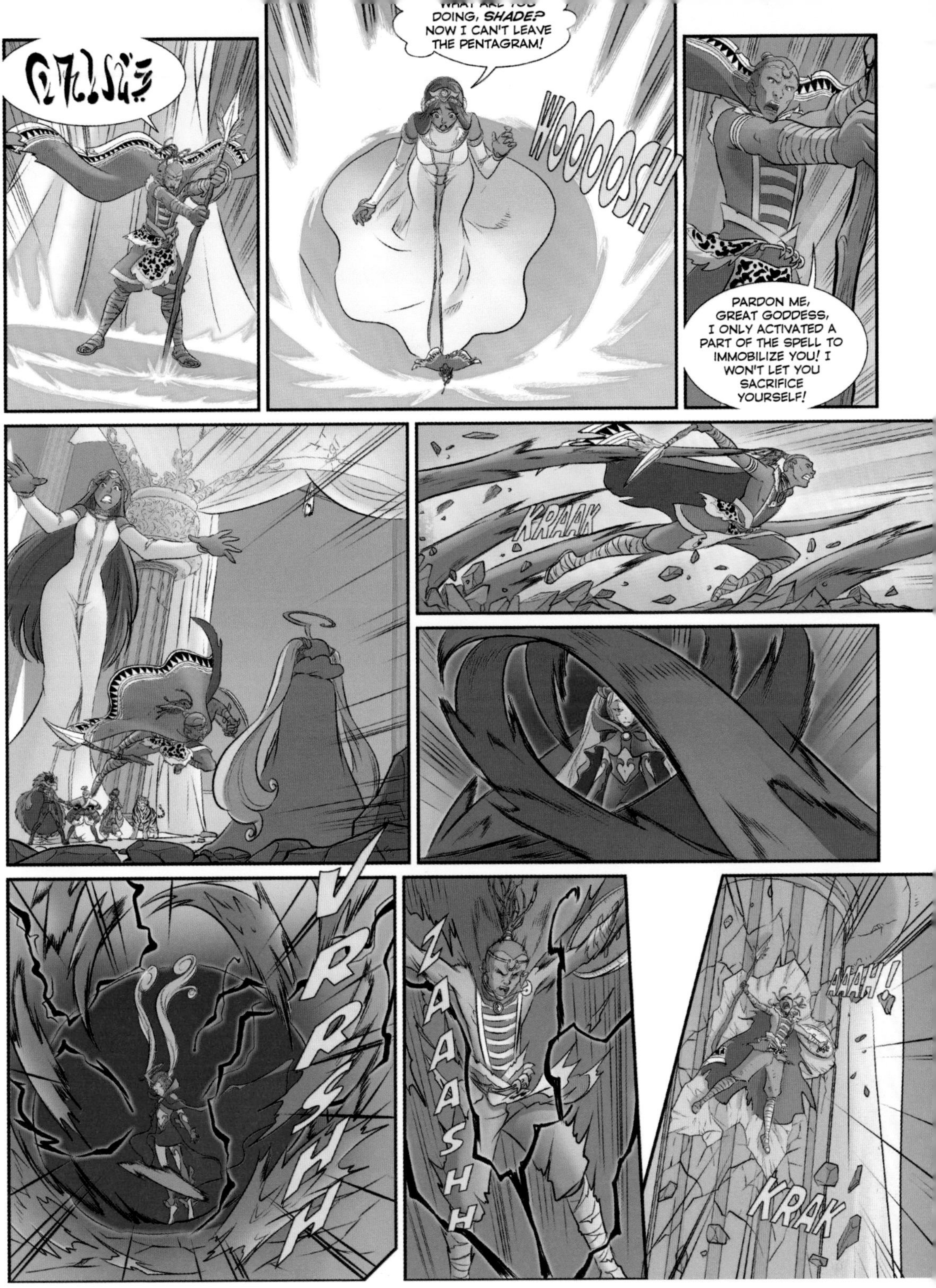
WHAT ARE YOU DOING, SHADE? NOW I CAN'T LEAVE THE PENTAGRAM!
WOOOOSH
PARDON ME, GREAT GODDESS, I ONLY ACTIVATED A PART OF THE SPELL TO IMMOBILIZE YOU! I WON'T LET YOU SACRIFICE YOURSELF!
KRAAK
VRRSHHH
ZAAASHH
AAAH!
KRAK

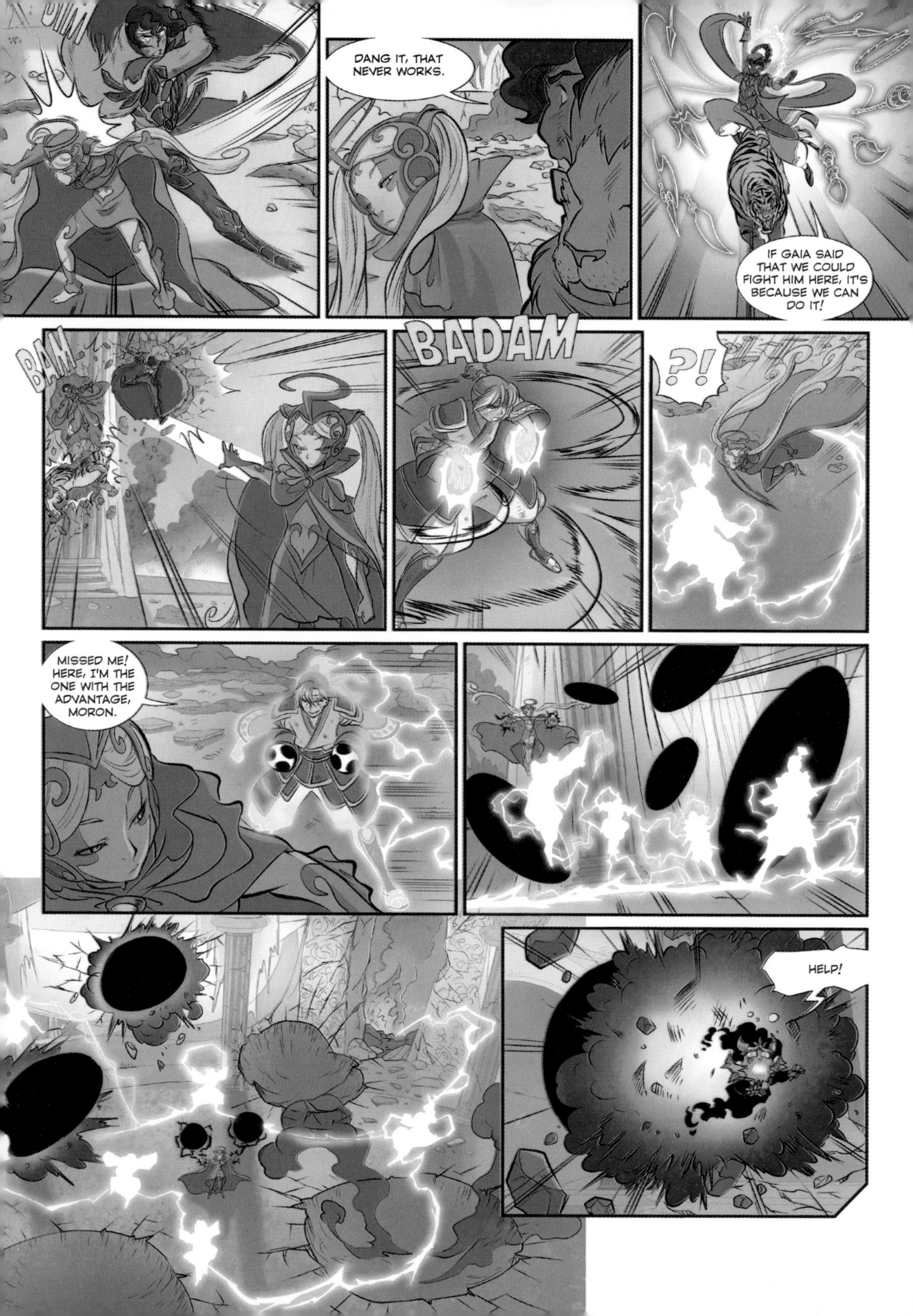
DANG IT, THAT NEVER WORKS.
IF GAIA SAID THAT WE COULD FIGHT HIM HERE, IT'S BECAUSE WE CAN DO IT!
BAM
BADAM
?!
MISSED ME! HERE, I'M THE ONE WITH THE ADVANTAGE, MORON.
HELP!

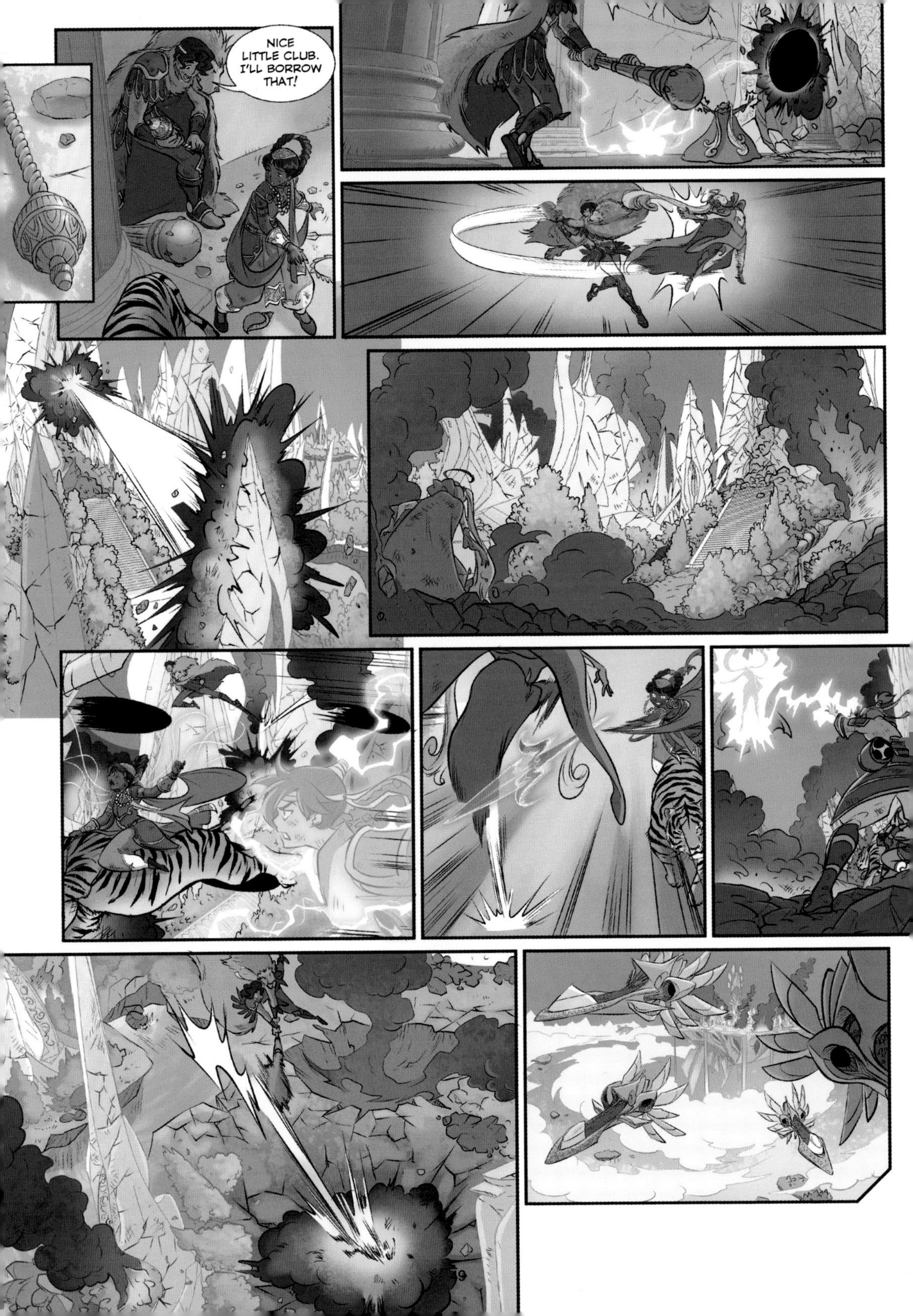
NICE LITTLE CLUB. I'LL BORROW THAT!

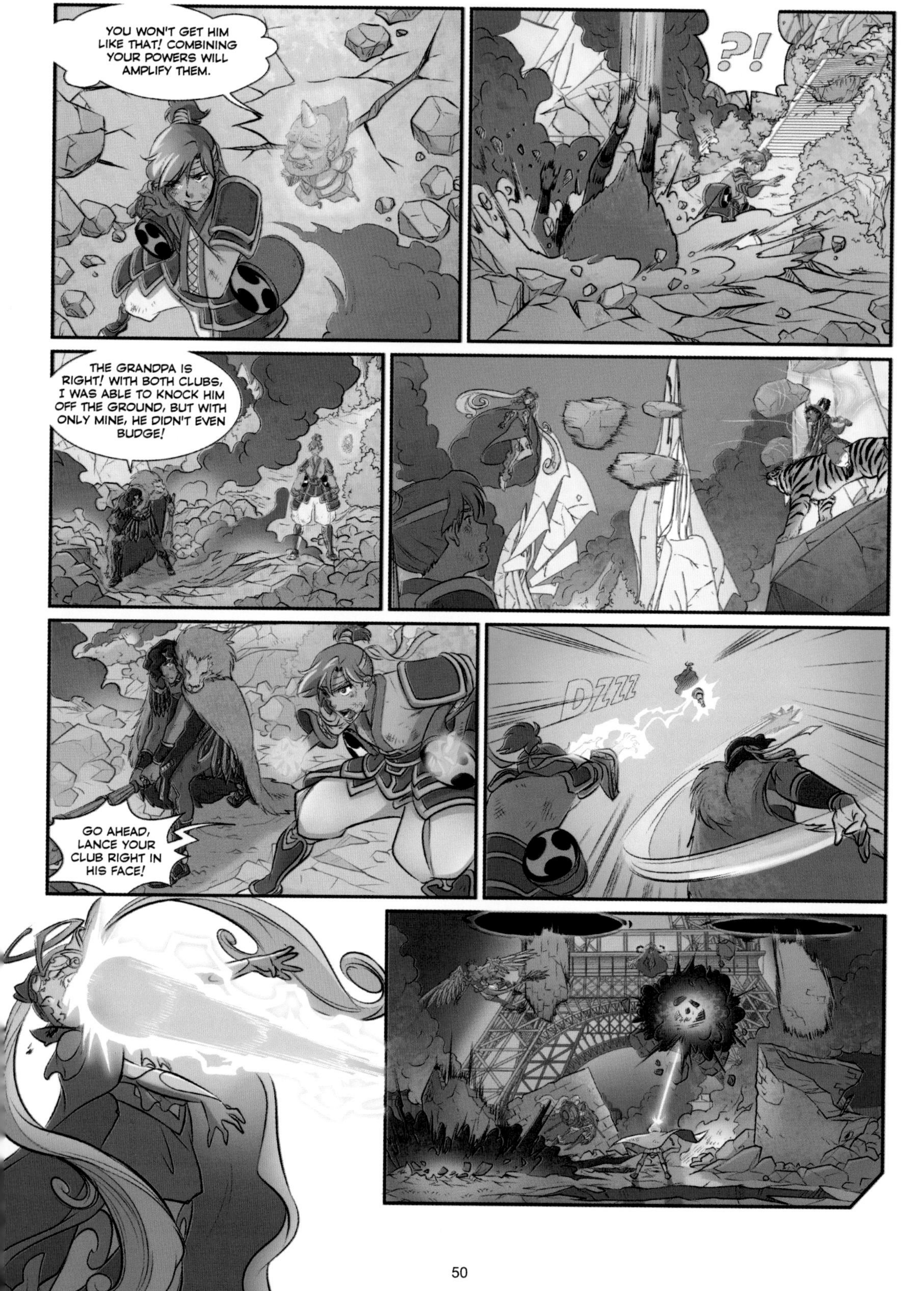
YOU WON'T GET HIM LIKE THAT! COMBINING YOUR POWERS WILL AMPLIFY THEM.
?!
THE GRANDPA IS RIGHT! WITH BOTH CLUBS, I WAS ABLE TO KNOCK HIM OFF THE GROUND, BUT WITH ONLY MINE, HE DIDN'T EVEN BUDGE!
GO AHEAD, LANCE YOUR CLUB RIGHT IN HIS FACE!
DZZZ

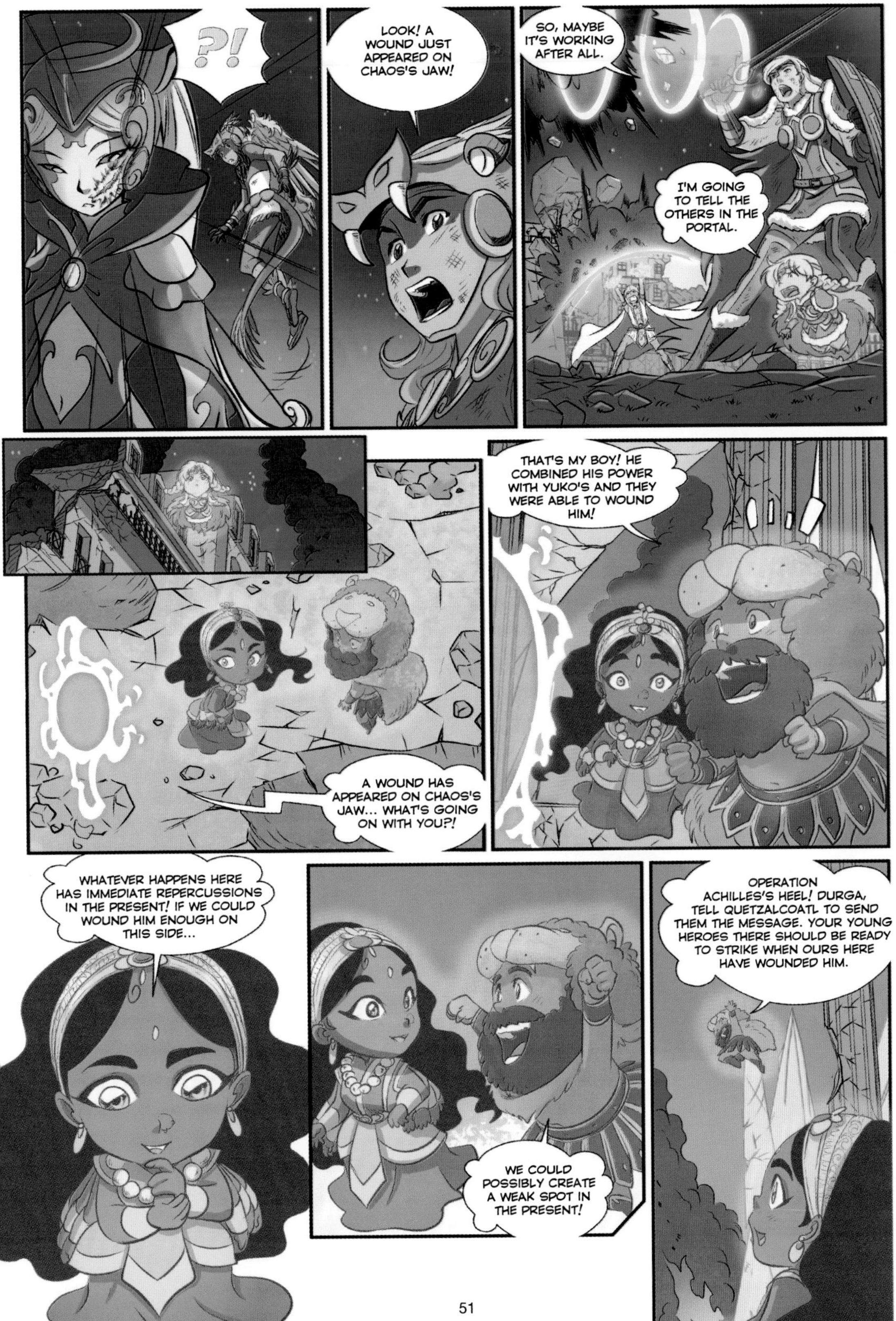
?!
LOOK! A WOUND JUST APPEARED ON CHAOS'S JAW!
SO, MAYBE IT'S WORKING AFTER ALL.
I'M GOING TO TELL THE OTHERS IN THE PORTAL.
THAT'S MY BOY! HE COMBINED HIS POWER WITH YUKO'S AND THEY WERE ABLE TO WOUND HIM!
A WOUND HAS APPEARED ON CHAOS'S JAW... WHAT'S GOING ON WITH YOU?!
WHATEVER HAPPENS HERE HAS IMMEDIATE REPERCUSSIONS IN THE PRESENT! IF WE COULD WOUND HIM ENOUGH ON THIS SIDE...
WE COULD POSSIBLY CREATE A WEAK SPOT IN THE PRESENT!
OPERATION ACHILLES'S HEEL! DURGA, TELL QUETZALCOATL TO SEND THEM THE MESSAGE. YOUR YOUNG HEROES THERE SHOULD BE READY TO STRIKE WHEN OURS HERE HAVE WOUNDED HIM.

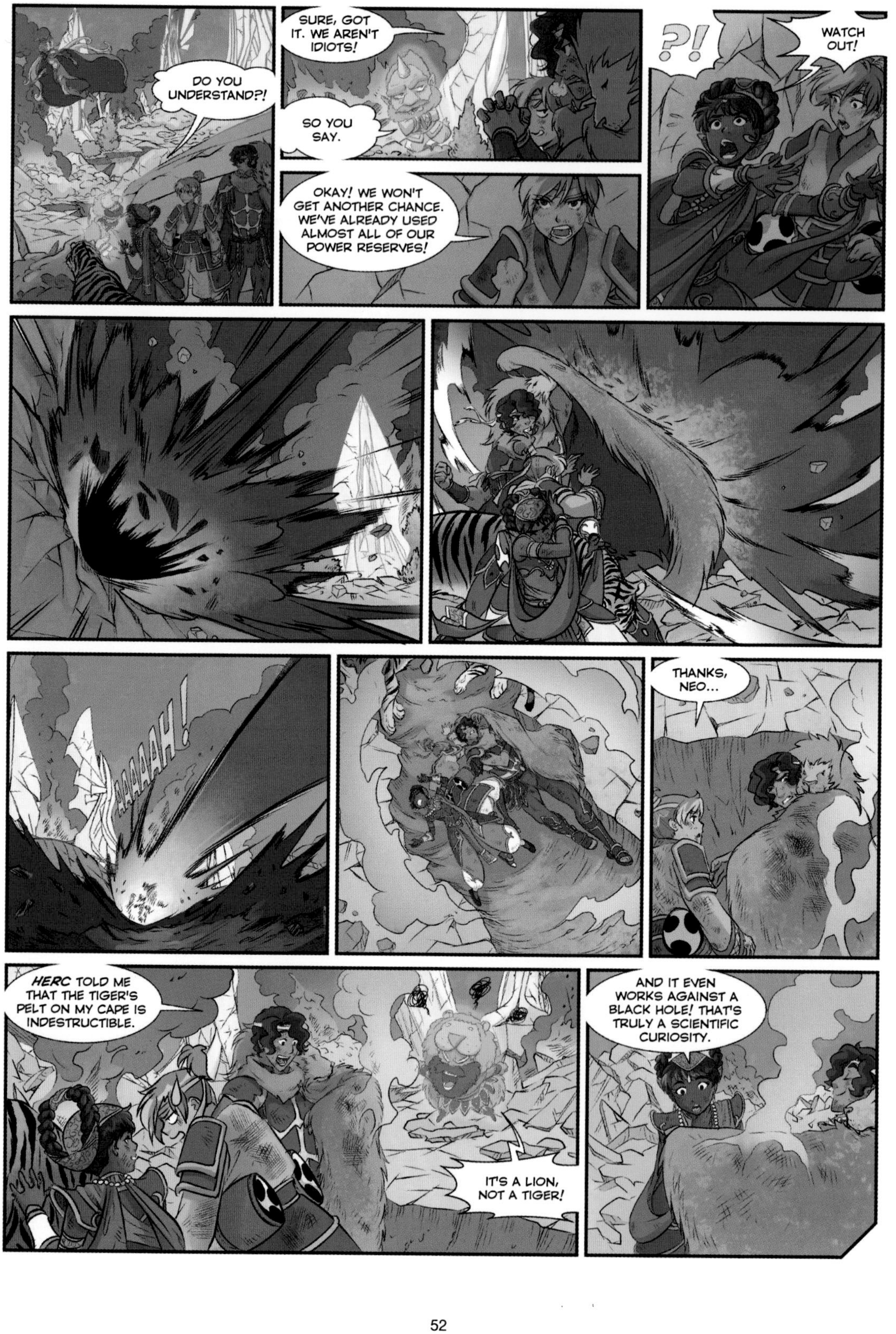
DO YOU UNDERSTAND?!
SURE, GOT IT. WE AREN'T IDIOTS!
SO YOU SAY.
OKAY! WE WON'T GET ANOTHER CHANCE. WE'VE ALREADY USED ALMOST ALL OF OUR POWER RESERVES!
?!
WATCH OUT!
AAAAAAH!
THANKS, NEO...
HERC TOLD ME THAT THE TIGER'S PELT ON MY CAPE IS INDESTRUCTIBLE.
IT'S A LION, NOT A TIGER!
AND IT EVEN WORKS AGAINST A BLACK HOLE! THAT'S TRULY A SCIENTIFIC CURIOSITY.

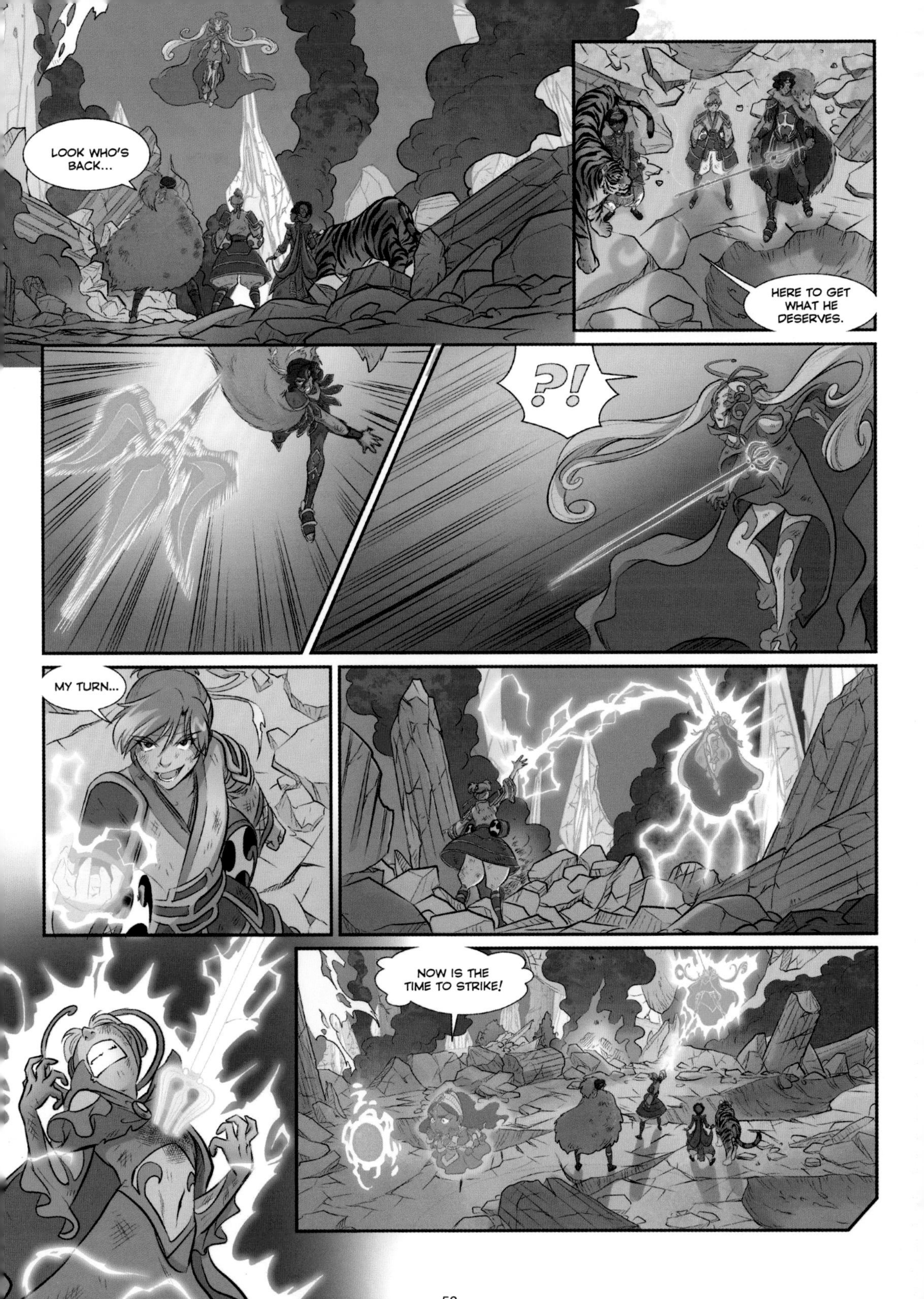
LOOK WHO'S BACK...
HERE TO GET WHAT HE DESERVES.
?!
MY TURN...
NOW IS THE TIME TO STRIKE!

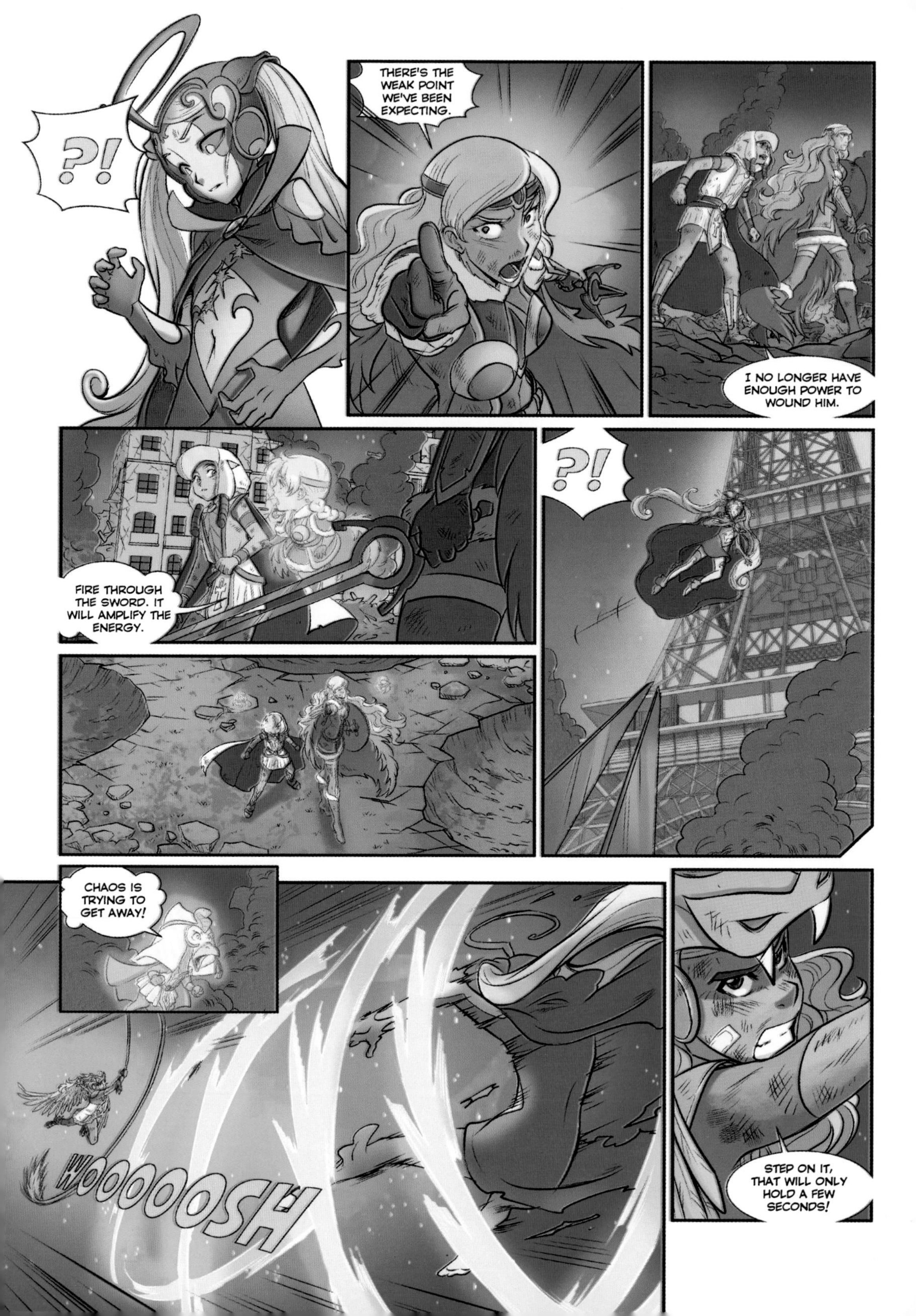
?!
THERE'S THE WEAK POINT WE'VE BEEN EXPECTING.
I NO LONGER HAVE ENOUGH POWER TO WOUND HIM.
FIRE THROUGH THE SWORD. IT WILL AMPLIFY THE ENERGY.
?!
CHAOS IS TRYING TO GET AWAY!
WOOOOOSH
STEP ON IT, THAT WILL ONLY HOLD A FEW SECONDS!

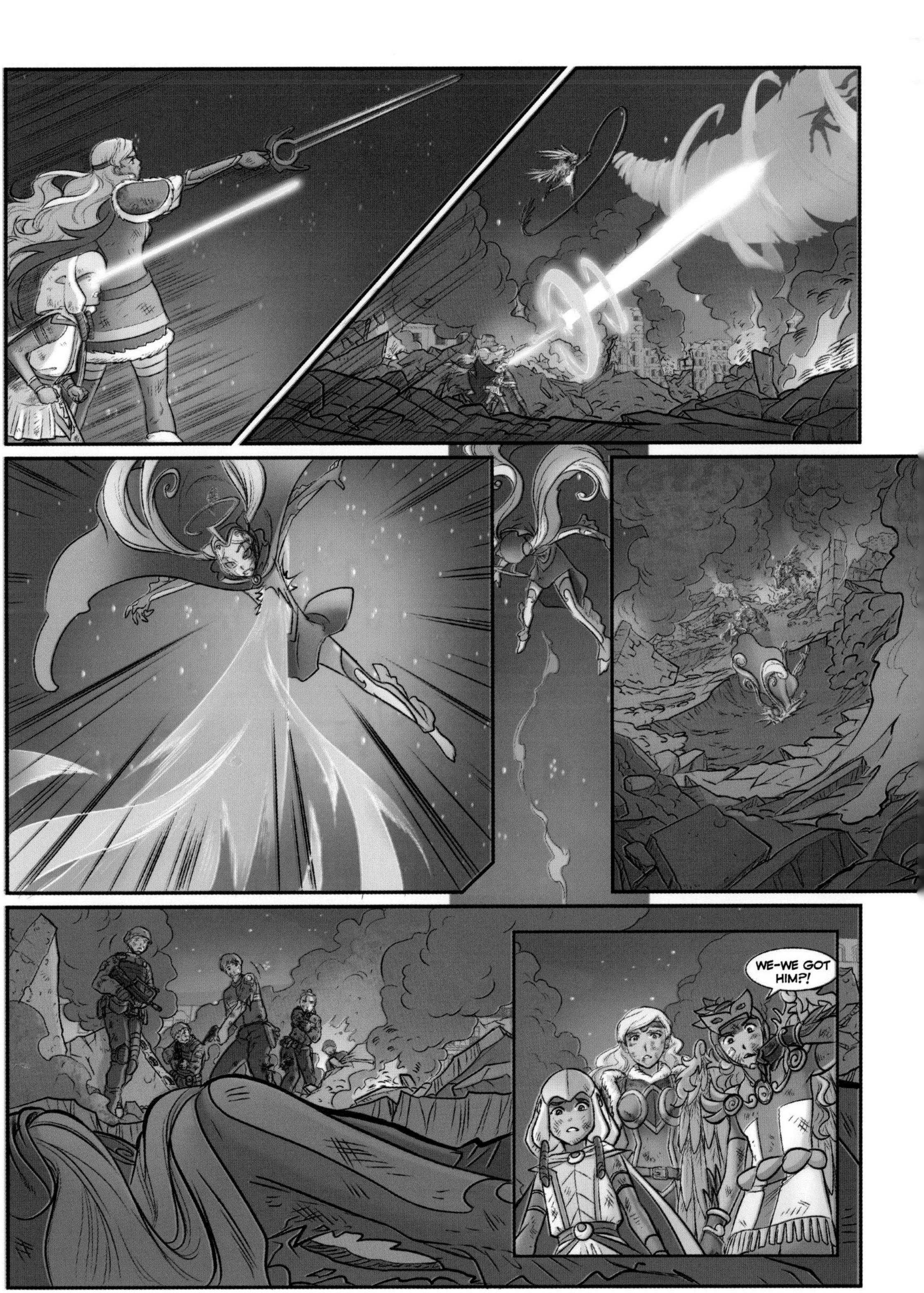
WE-WE GOT HIM?!

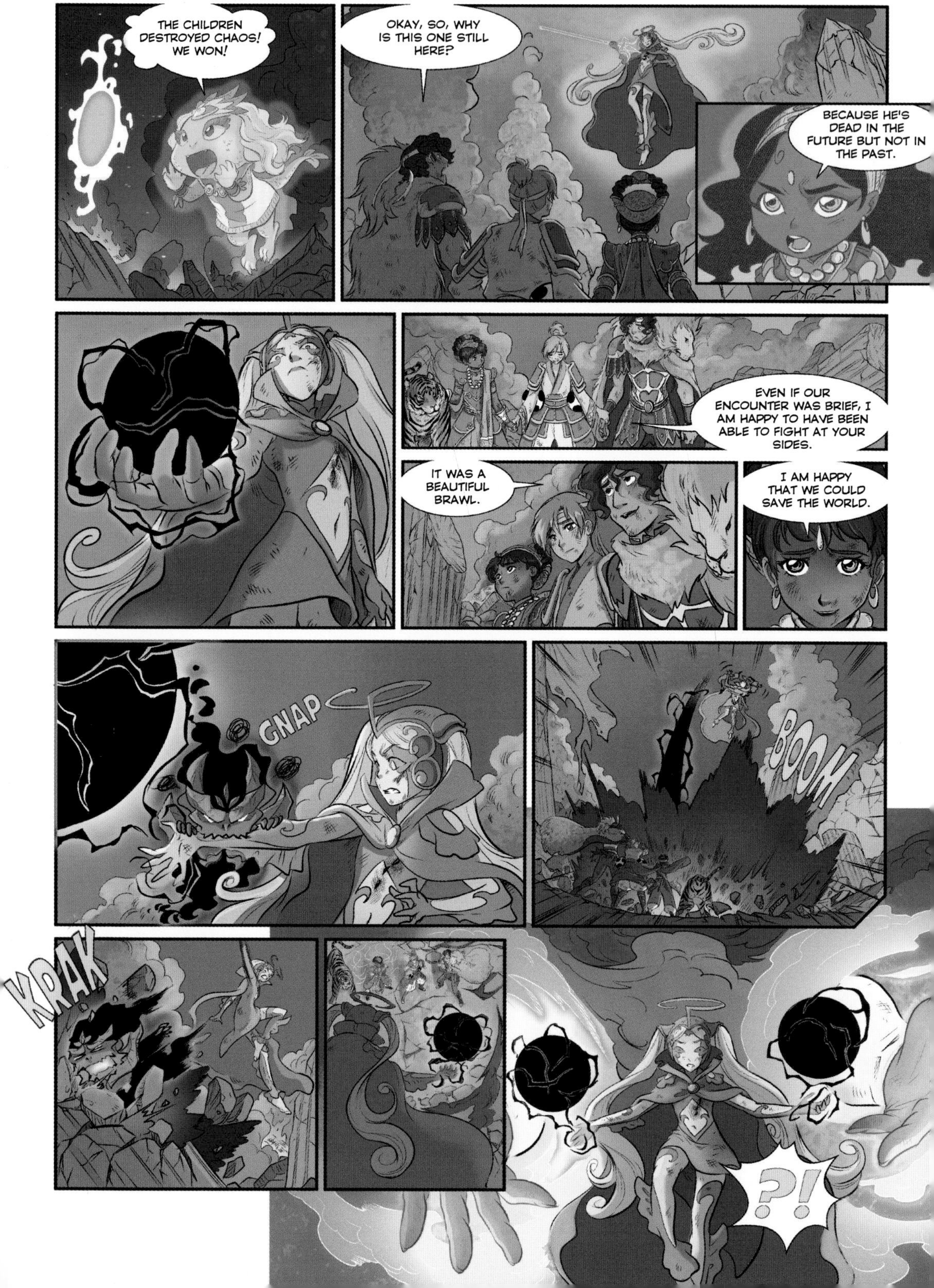
THE CHILDREN DESTROYED CHAOS! WE WON!
OKAY, SO, WHY IS THIS ONE STILL HERE?
BECAUSE HE'S DEAD IN THE FUTURE BUT NOT IN THE PAST.
EVEN IF OUR ENCOUNTER WAS BRIEF, I AM HAPPY TO HAVE BEEN ABLE TO FIGHT AT YOUR SIDES.
IT WAS A BEAUTIFUL BRAWL.
I AM HAPPY THAT WE COULD SAVE THE WORLD.
GNAP
BOOM
KRAK
?!

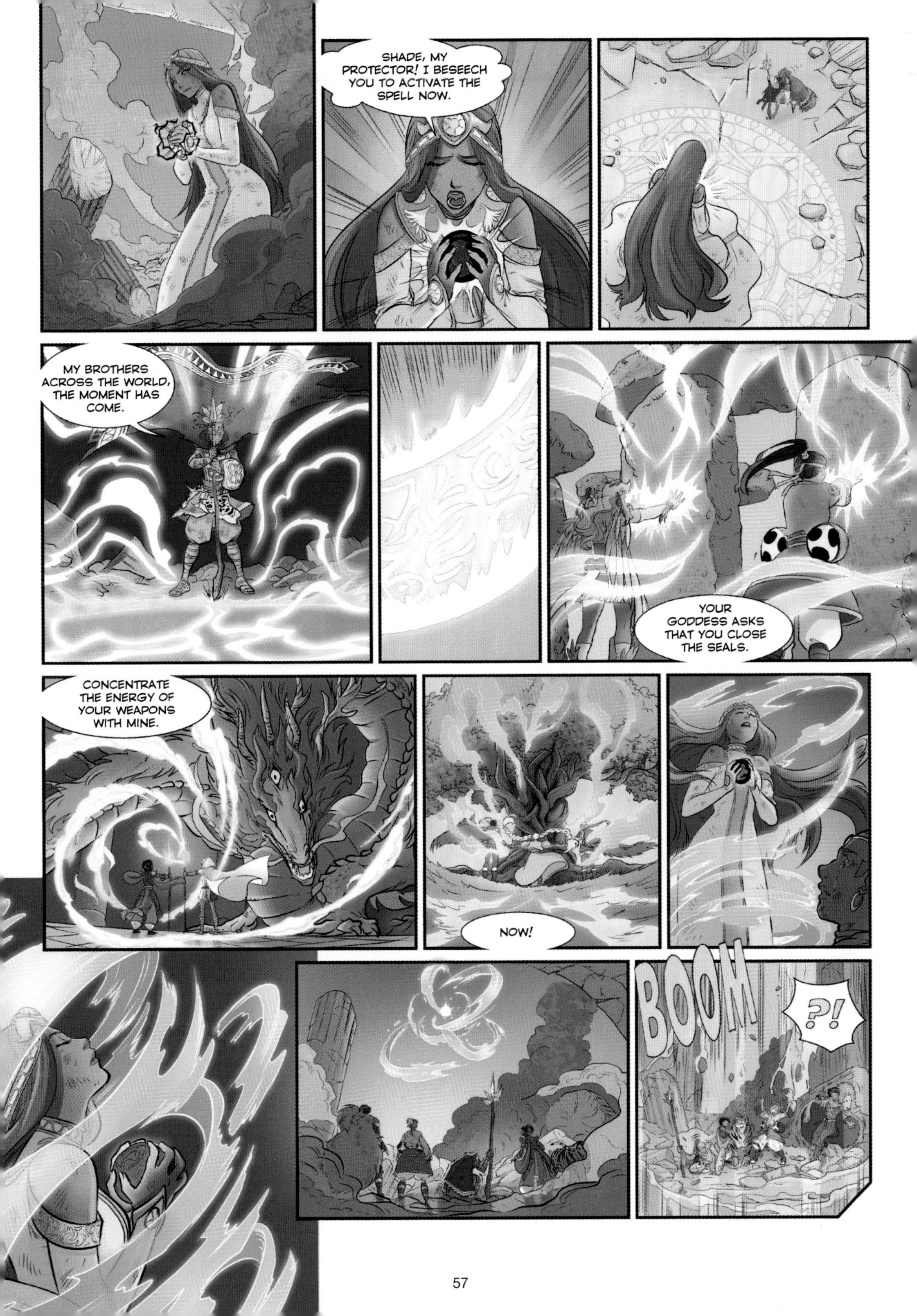
SHADE, MY PROTECTOR! I BESEECH YOU TO ACTIVATE THE SPELL NOW.
MY BROTHERS ACROSS THE WORLD, THE MOMENT HAS COME.
YOUR GODDESS ASKS THAT YOU CLOSE THE SEALS.
CONCENTRATE THE ENERGY OF YOUR WEAPONS WITH MINE.
NOW!
BOOM
?!

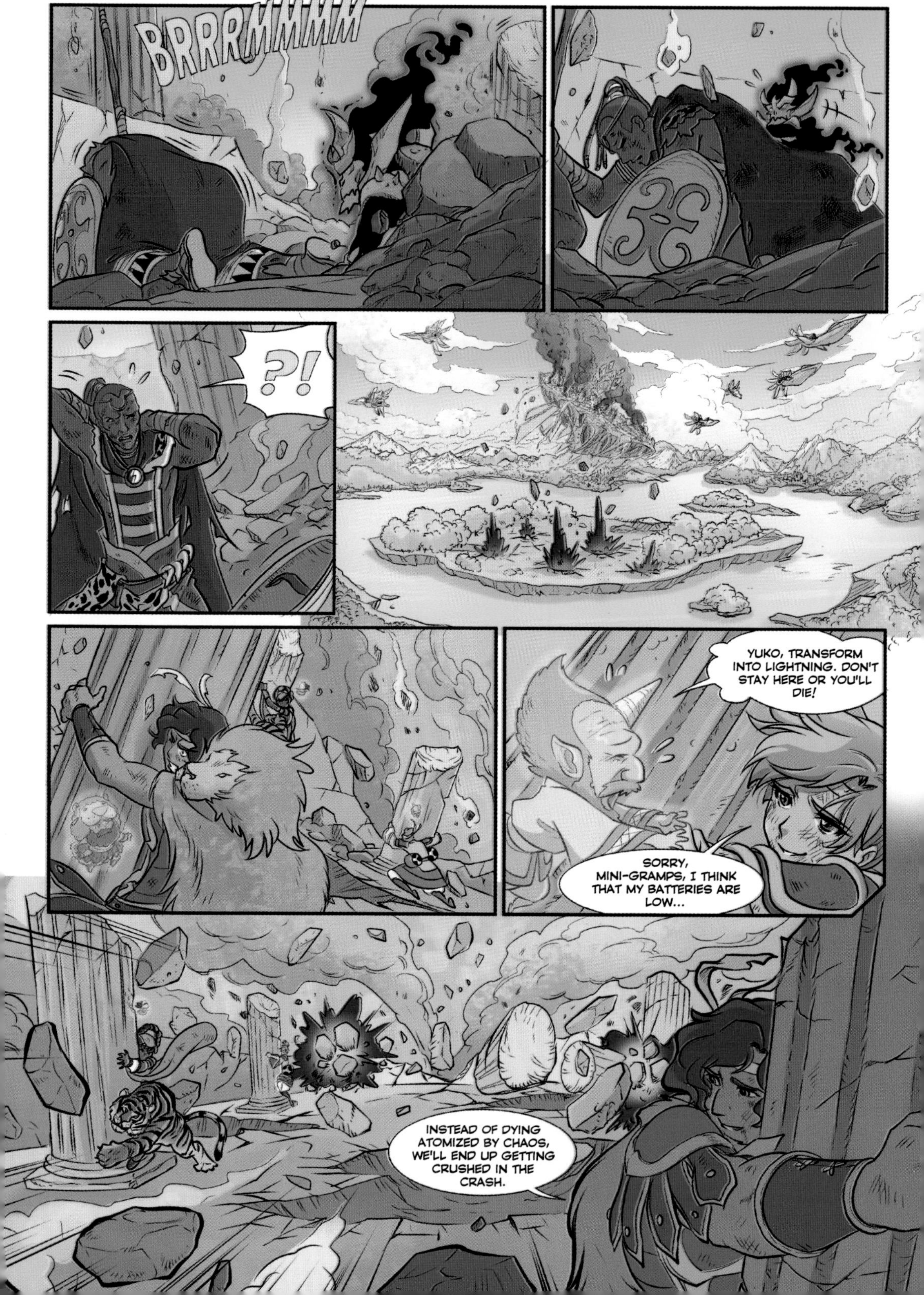
BRRRMMMMM
?!
YUKO, TRANSFORM INTO LIGHTNING. DON'T STAY HERE OR YOU'LL DIE!
SORRY, MINI-GRAMPS, I THINK THAT MY BATTERIES ARE LOW...
INSTEAD OF DYING ATOMIZED BY CHAOS, WE'LL END UP GETTING CRUSHED IN THE CRASH.

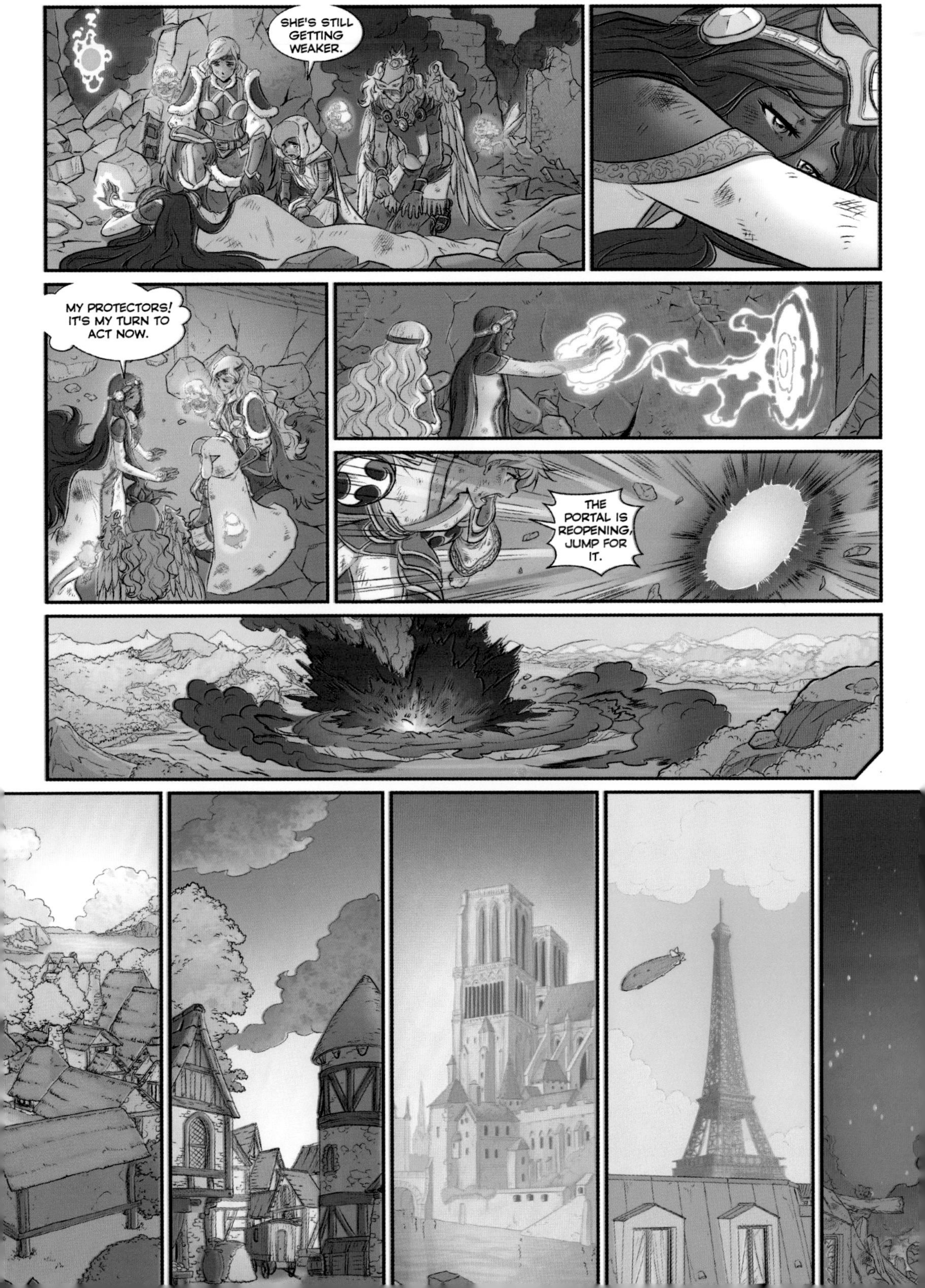
SHE'S STILL GETTING WEAKER.
MY PROTECTORS! IT'S MY TURN TO ACT NOW.
THE PORTAL IS REOPENING, JUMP FOR IT.

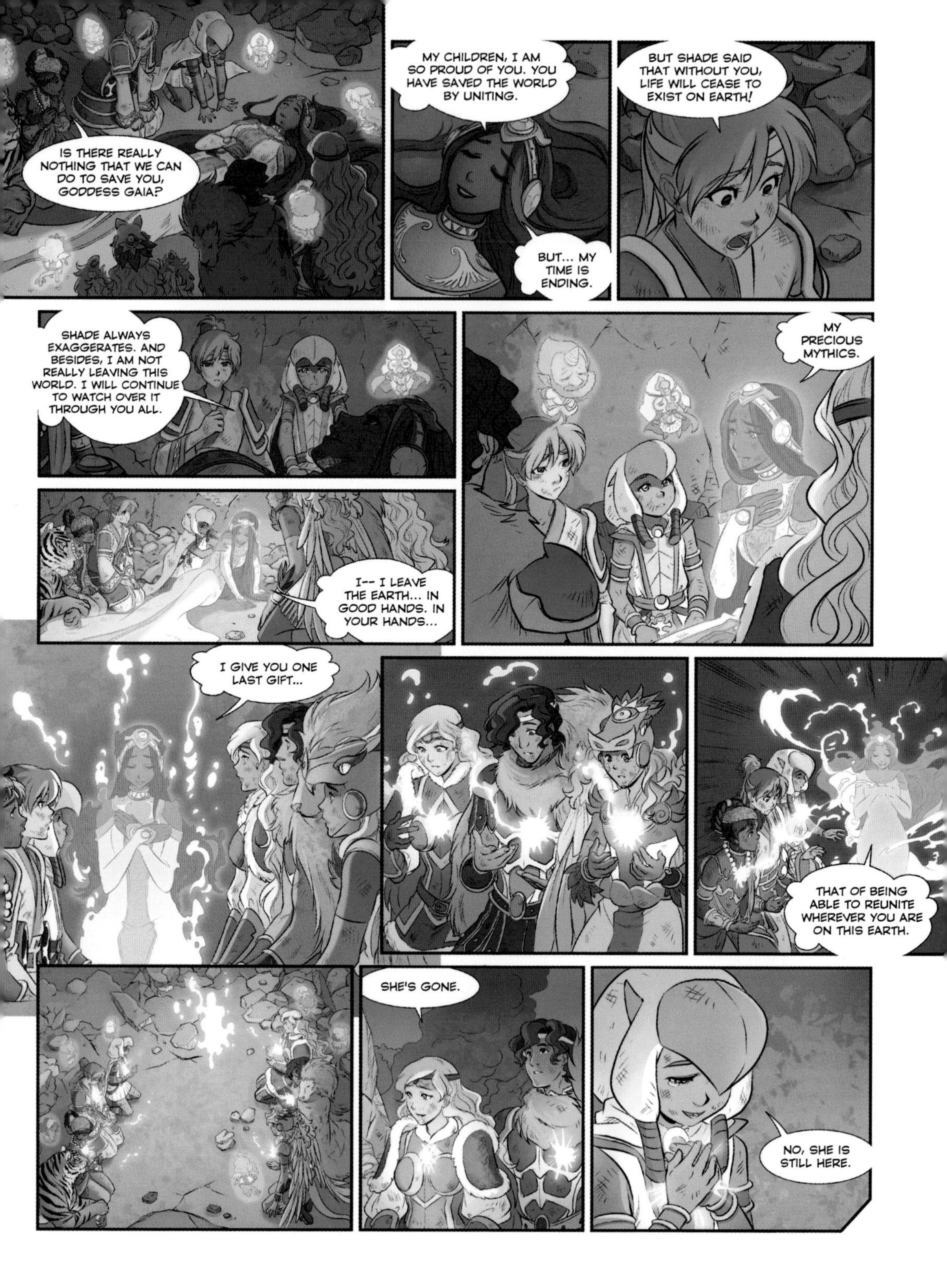
IS THERE REALLY NOTHING THAT WE CAN DO TO SAVE YOU, GODDESS GAIA?
MY CHILDREN, I AM SO PROUD OF YOU. YOU HAVE SAVED THE WORLD BY UNITING.
BUT... MY TIME IS ENDING.
BUT SHADE SAID THAT WITHOUT YOU, LIFE WILL CEASE TO EXIST ON EARTH!
SHADE ALWAYS EXAGGERATES. AND BESIDES, I AM NOT REALLY LEAVING THIS WORLD. I WILL CONTINUE TO WATCH OVER IT THROUGH YOU ALL.
MY PRECIOUS MYTHICS.
I-- I LEAVE THE EARTH... IN GOOD HANDS. IN YOUR HANDS...
I GIVE YOU ONE LAST GIFT...
THAT OF BEING ABLE TO REUNITE WHEREVER YOU ARE ON THIS EARTH.
SHE'S GONE.
NO, SHE IS STILL HERE.

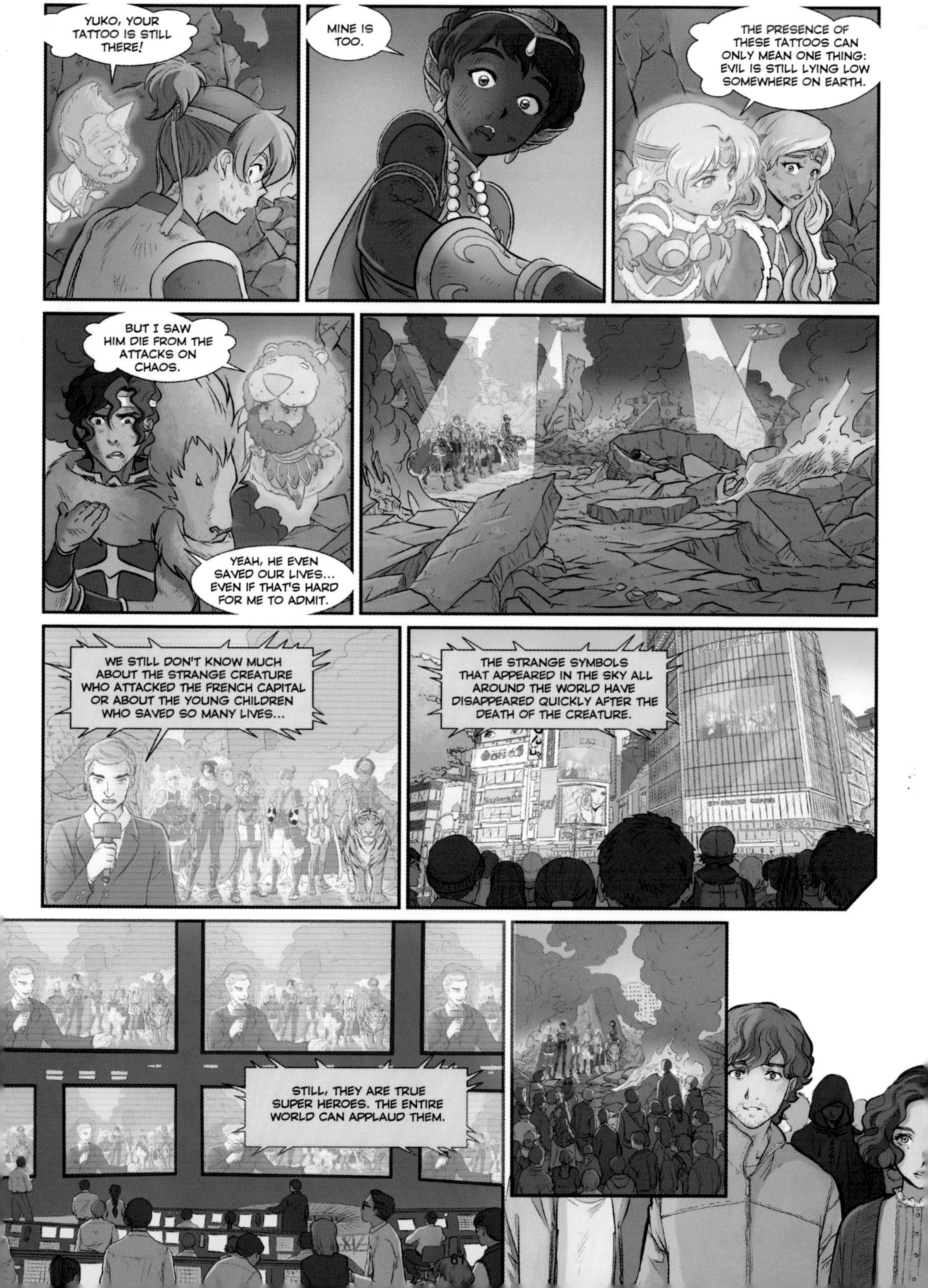
YUKO, YOUR TATTOO IS STILL THERE!
MINE IS TOO.
THE PRESENCE OF THESE TATTOOS CAN ONLY MEAN ONE THING: EVIL IS STILL LYING LOW SOMEWHERE ON EARTH.
BUT I SAW HIM DIE FROM THE ATTACKS ON CHAOS.
YEAH, HE EVEN SAVED OUR LIVES... EVEN IF THAT'S HARD FOR ME TO ADMIT.
WE STILL DON'T KNOW MUCH ABOUT THE STRANGE CREATURE WHO ATTACKED THE FRENCH CAPITAL OR ABOUT THE YOUNG CHILDREN WHO SAVED SO MANY LIVES...
THE STRANGE SYMBOLS THAT APPEARED IN THE SKY ALL AROUND THE WORLD HAVE DISAPPEARED QUICKLY AFTER THE DEATH OF THE CREATURE.
STILL, THEY ARE TRUE SUPER HEROES. THE ENTIRE WORLD CAN APPLAUD THEM.

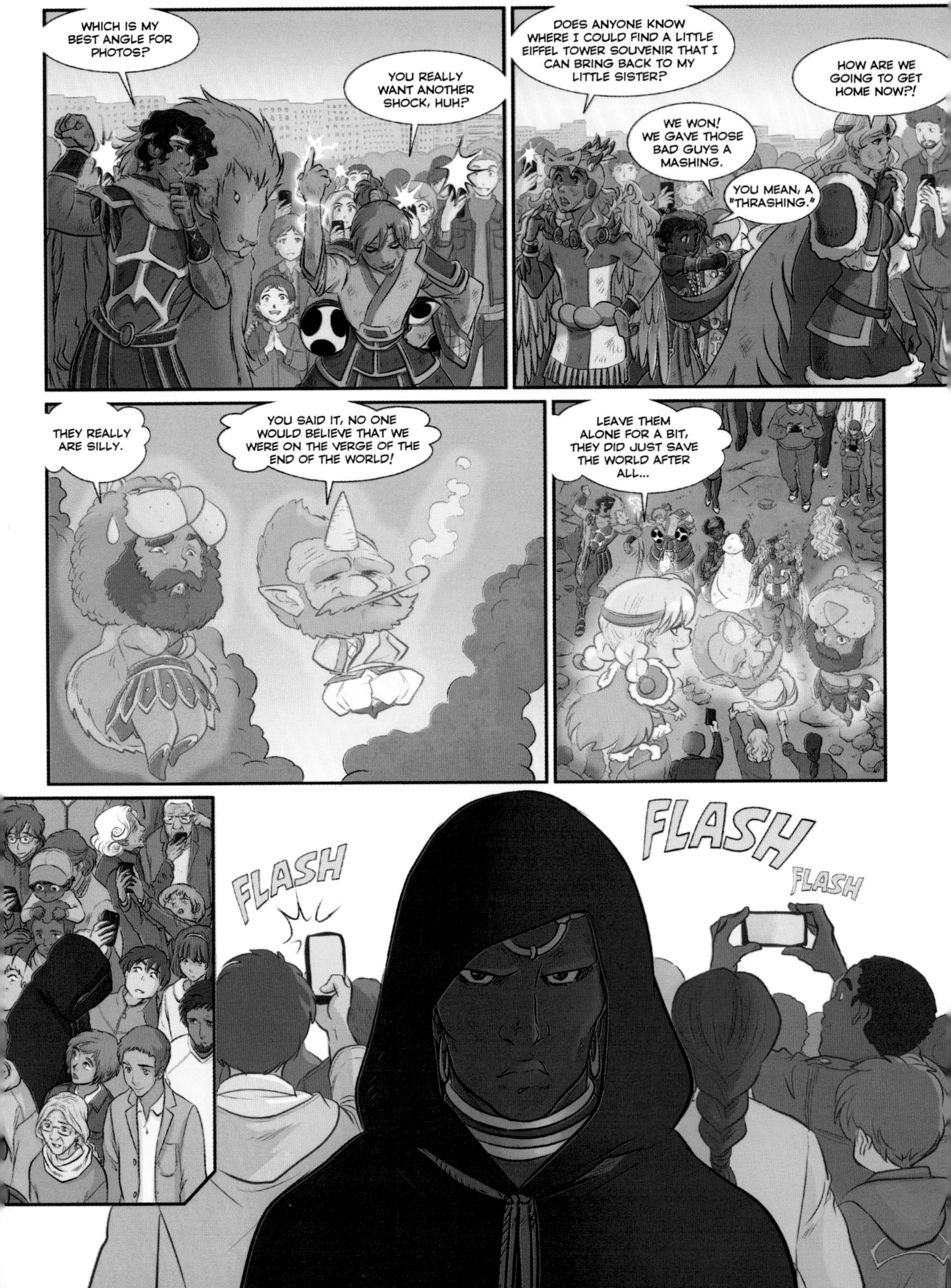
WHICH IS MY BEST ANGLE FOR PHOTOS?
YOU REALLY WANT ANOTHER SHOCK, HUH?
DOES ANYONE KNOW WHERE I COULD FIND A LITTLE EIFFEL TOWER SOUVENIR THAT I CAN BRING BACK TO MY LITTLE SISTER?
WE WON! WE GAVE THOSE BAD GUYS A MASHING.
YOU MEAN, A "THRASHING."
HOW ARE WE GOING TO GET HOME NOW?!
THEY REALLY ARE SILLY.
YOU SAID IT, NO ONE WOULD BELIEVE THAT WE WERE ON THE VERGE OF THE END OF THE WORLD!
LEAVE THEM ALONE FOR A BIT, THEY DID JUST SAVE THE WORLD AFTER ALL...
FLASH
FLASH
FLASH

THE MYTHICS

PART 11 : LUST

Story
PHILIPPE OGAKI
WITH HELP FROM **RÉMI GUÉRIN**

Art
DARA

Color
MAGALI PAILLAT

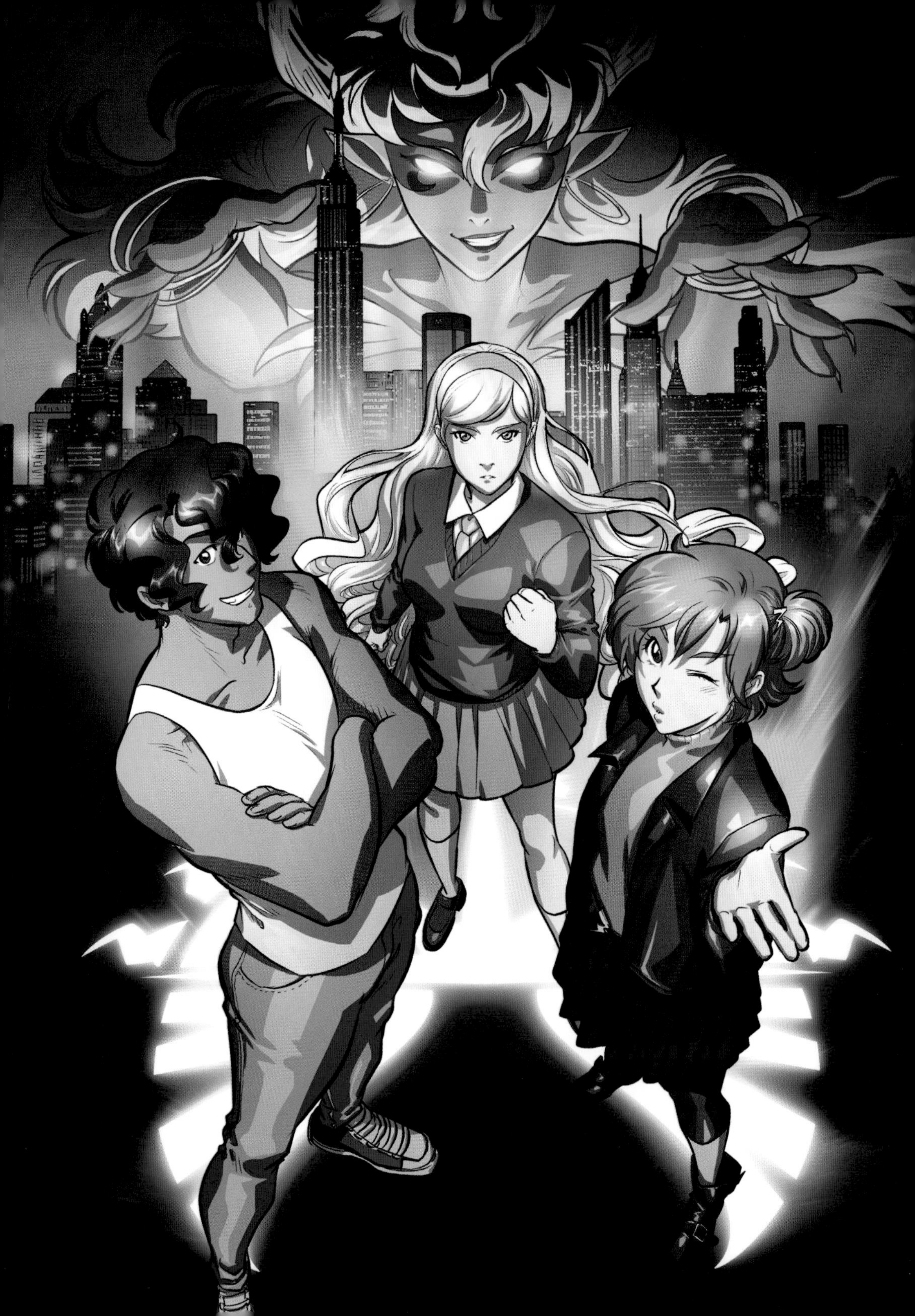

TOKYO, HIGH-SECURITY PRISON...

...THEIR COURAGE DEMANDS RESPECT...

... AND WITHOUT QUESTION, THEY PREVENTED A MAJOR CATASTROPHE!

GIFTED WITH EXTRAORDINARY POWERS, THESE NEW HEROES SEEM TO WANT TO PUT THEMSELVES IN THE SERVICE OF HUMANITY AND...

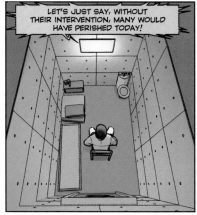

LET'S JUST SAY, WITHOUT THEIR INTERVENTION, MANY WOULD HAVE PERISHED TODAY!

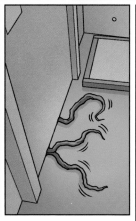

65

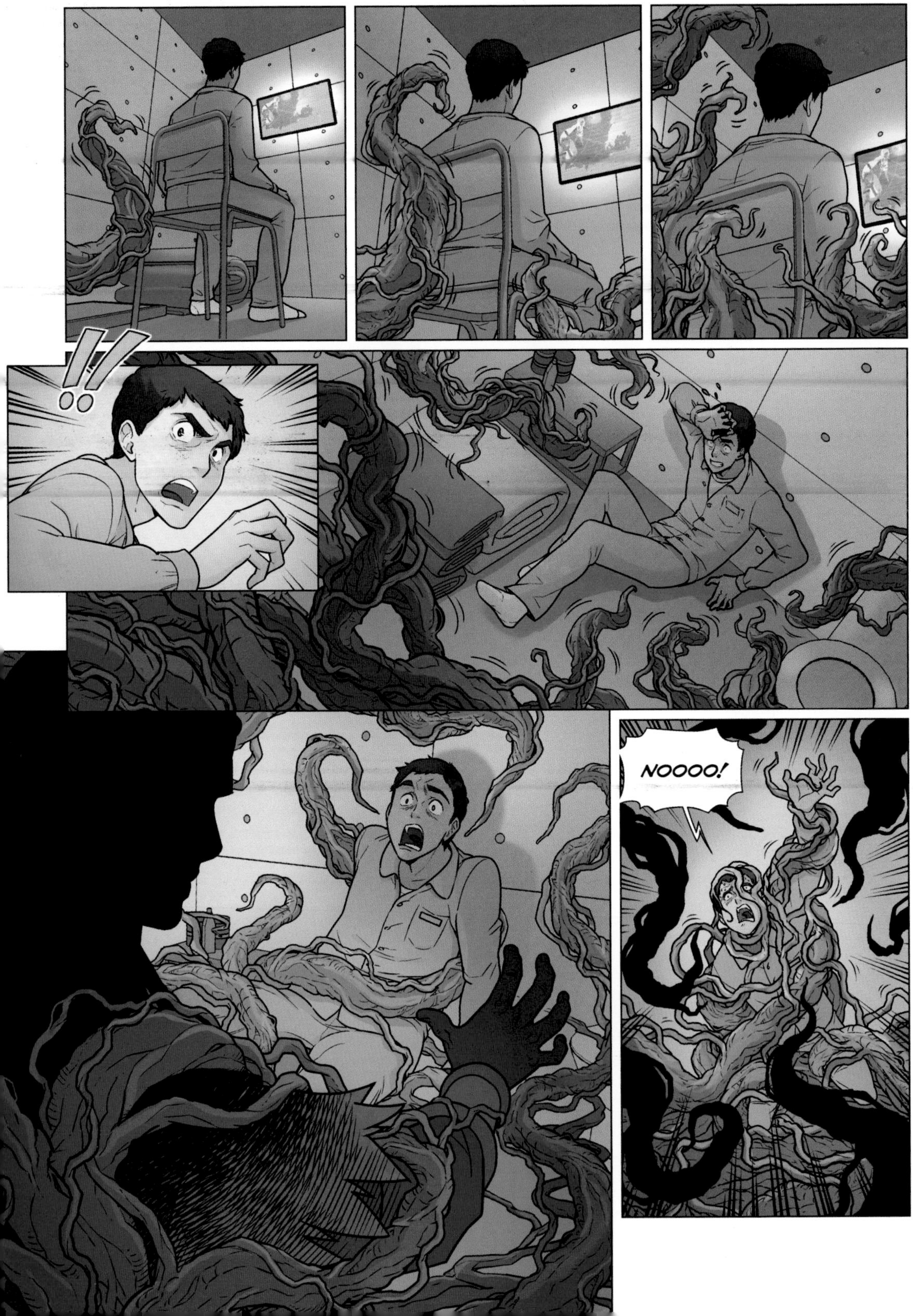
!!
NOOOO!

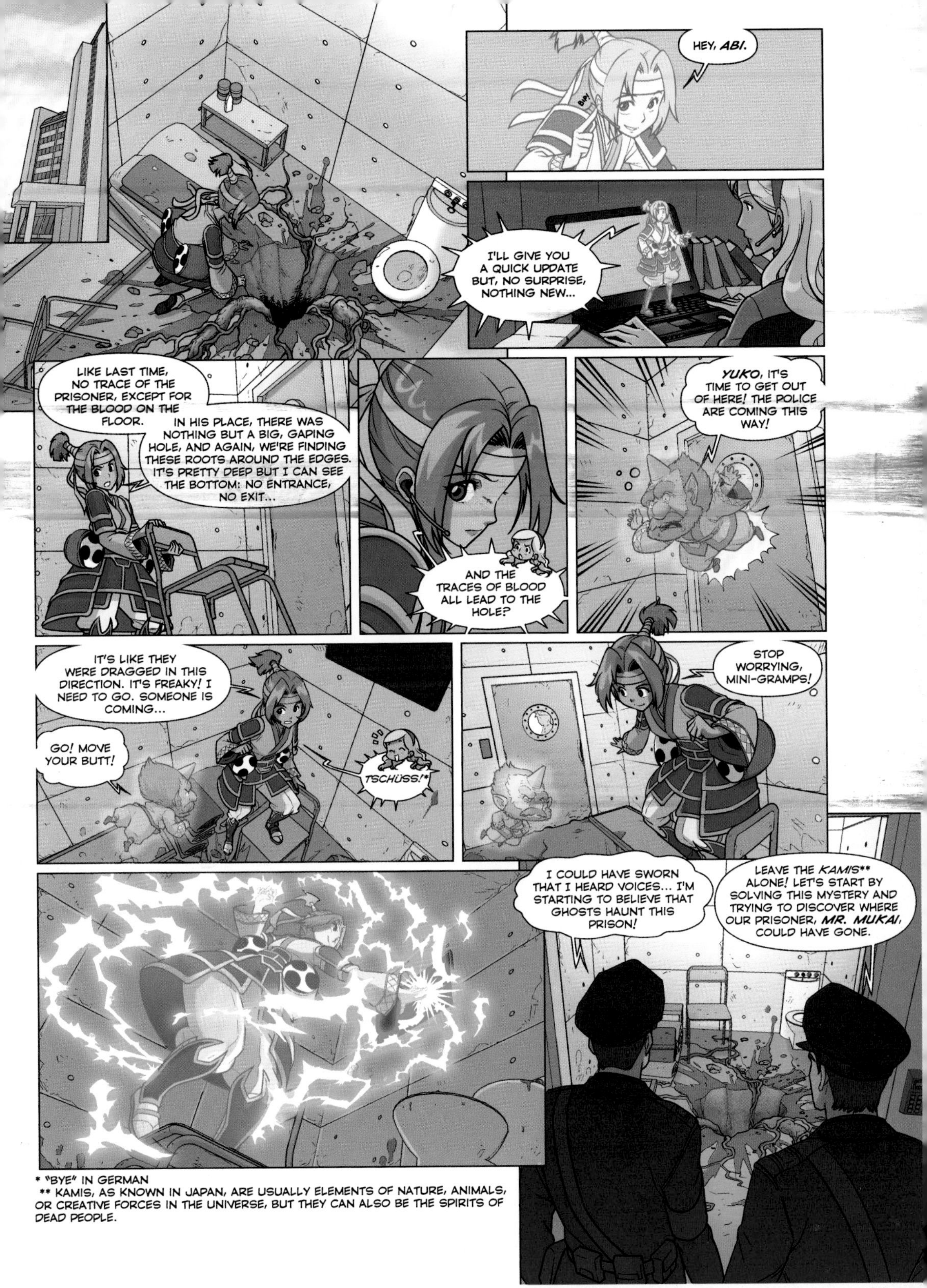
HEY, ABI.
BIP!
I'LL GIVE YOU A QUICK UPDATE BUT, NO SURPRISE, NOTHING NEW...
LIKE LAST TIME, NO TRACE OF THE PRISONER, EXCEPT FOR THE BLOOD ON THE FLOOR.
IN HIS PLACE, THERE WAS NOTHING BUT A BIG, GAPING HOLE, AND AGAIN, WE'RE FINDING THESE ROOTS AROUND THE EDGES. IT'S PRETTY DEEP BUT I CAN SEE THE BOTTOM: NO ENTRANCE, NO EXIT...
AND THE TRACES OF BLOOD ALL LEAD TO THE HOLE?
YUKO, IT'S TIME TO GET OUT OF HERE! THE POLICE ARE COMING THIS WAY!
IT'S LIKE THEY WERE DRAGGED IN THIS DIRECTION. IT'S FREAKY! I NEED TO GO. SOMEONE IS COMING...
GO! MOVE YOUR BUTT!
TSCHÜSS!*
STOP WORRYING, MINI-GRAMPS!
I COULD HAVE SWORN THAT I HEARD VOICES... I'M STARTING TO BELIEVE THAT GHOSTS HAUNT THIS PRISON!
LEAVE THE KAMIS** ALONE! LET'S START BY SOLVING THIS MYSTERY AND TRYING TO DISCOVER WHERE OUR PRISONER, MR. MUKAI, COULD HAVE GONE.

* "BYE" IN GERMAN

** KAMIS, AS KNOWN IN JAPAN, ARE USUALLY ELEMENTS OF NATURE, ANIMALS, OR CREATIVE FORCES IN THE UNIVERSE, BUT THEY CAN ALSO BE THE SPIRITS OF DEAD PEOPLE.

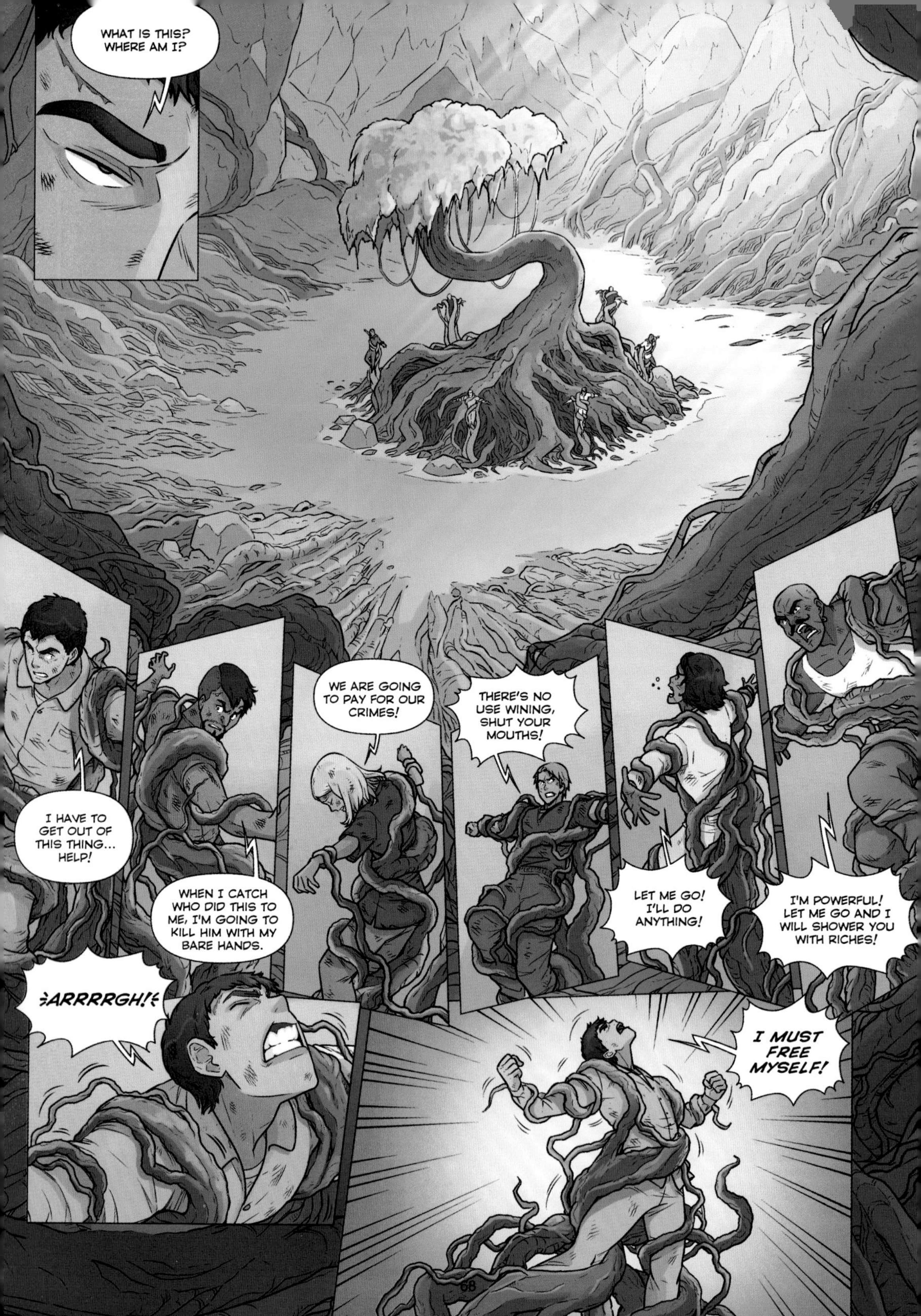

WHAT IS THIS? WHERE AM I?
I HAVE TO GET OUT OF THIS THING... HELP!
WHEN I CATCH WHO DID THIS TO ME, I'M GOING TO KILL HIM WITH MY BARE HANDS.
WE ARE GOING TO PAY FOR OUR CRIMES!
THERE'S NO USE WINING, SHUT YOUR MOUTHS!
LET ME GO! I'LL DO ANYTHING!
I'M POWERFUL! LET ME GO AND I WILL SHOWER YOU WITH RICHES!
ARRRRGH!
I MUST FREE MYSELF!

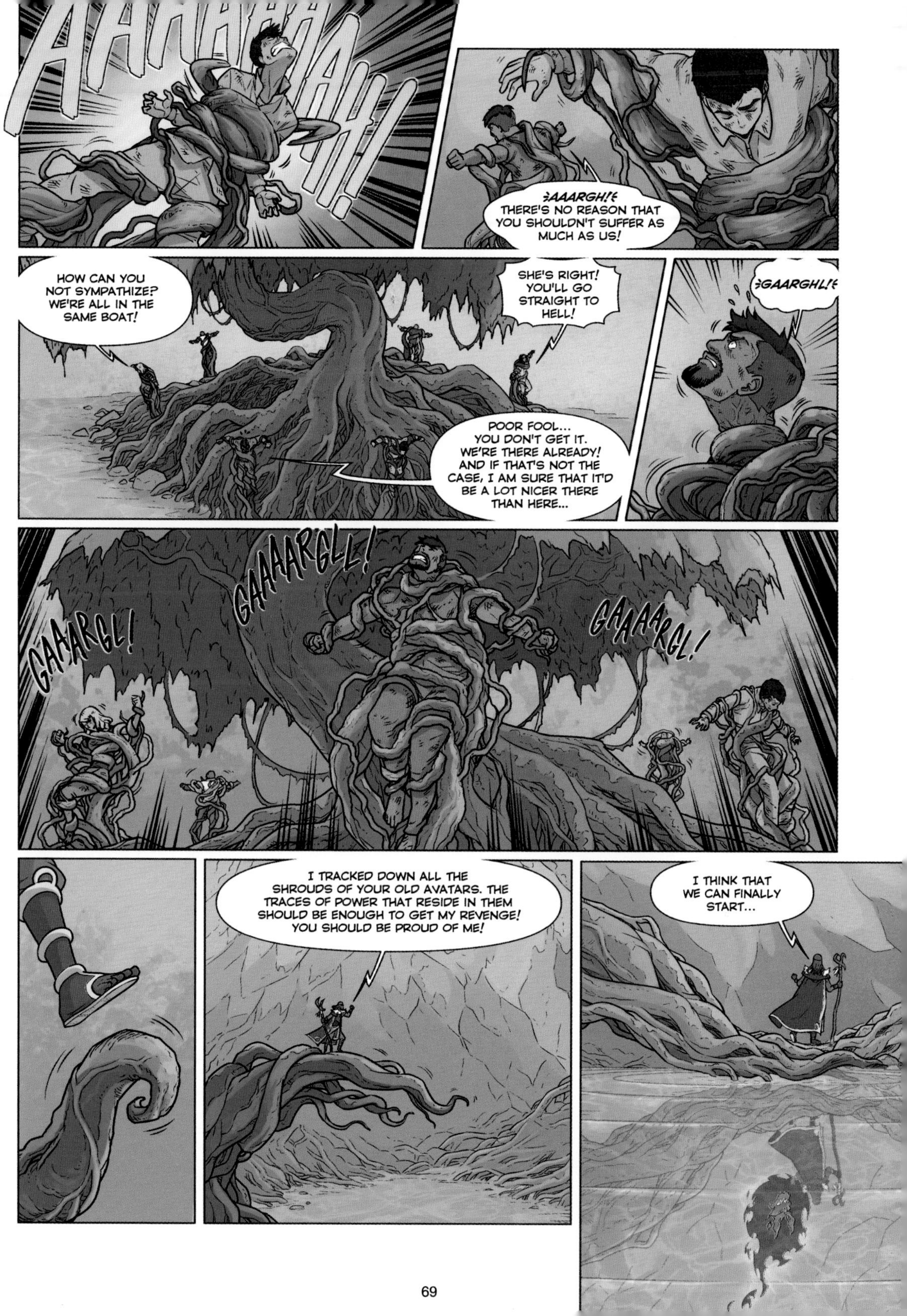
AAAAAAAAAH!
¡AAARGH!
THERE'S NO REASON THAT YOU SHOULDN'T SUFFER AS MUCH AS US!
HOW CAN YOU NOT SYMPATHIZE? WE'RE ALL IN THE SAME BOAT!
SHE'S RIGHT! YOU'LL GO STRAIGHT TO HELL!
POOR FOOL... YOU DON'T GET IT. WE'RE THERE ALREADY! AND IF THAT'S NOT THE CASE, I AM SURE THAT IT'D BE A LOT NICER THERE THAN HERE...
¡GAARGHL!
GAAARGL!
GAAAARGLL!
GAAAARGL!
I TRACKED DOWN ALL THE SHROUDS OF YOUR OLD AVATARS. THE TRACES OF POWER THAT RESIDE IN THEM SHOULD BE ENOUGH TO GET MY REVENGE! YOU SHOULD BE PROUD OF ME!
I THINK THAT WE CAN FINALLY START...

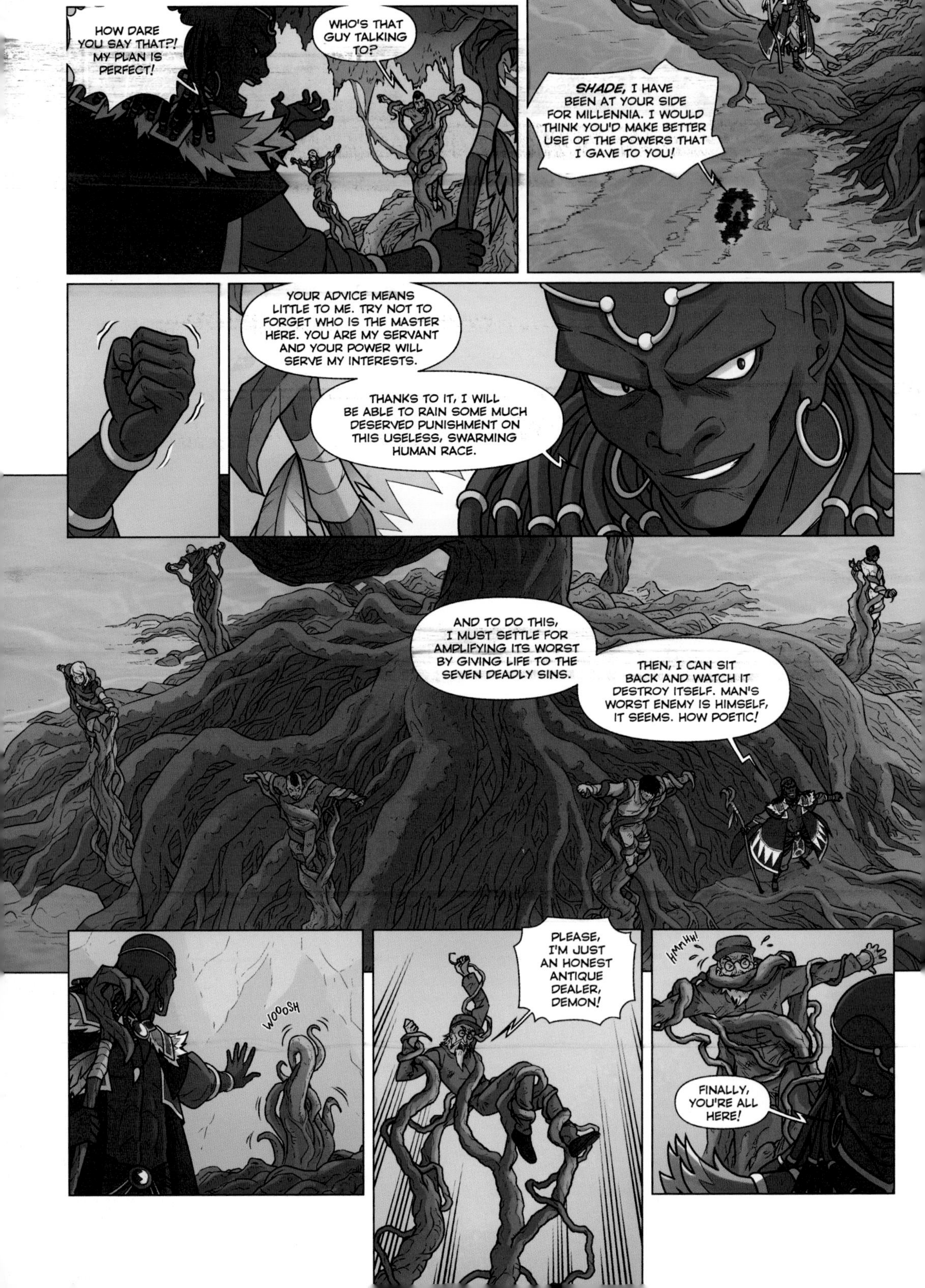
HOW DARE YOU SAY THAT?! MY PLAN IS PERFECT!
WHO'S THAT GUY TALKING TO?
SHADE, I HAVE BEEN AT YOUR SIDE FOR MILLENNIA. I WOULD THINK YOU'D MAKE BETTER USE OF THE POWERS THAT I GAVE TO YOU!
YOUR ADVICE MEANS LITTLE TO ME. TRY NOT TO FORGET WHO IS THE MASTER HERE. YOU ARE MY SERVANT AND YOUR POWER WILL SERVE MY INTERESTS.
THANKS TO IT, I WILL BE ABLE TO RAIN SOME MUCH DESERVED PUNISHMENT ON THIS USELESS, SWARMING HUMAN RACE.
AND TO DO THIS, I MUST SETTLE FOR AMPLIFYING ITS WORST BY GIVING LIFE TO THE SEVEN DEADLY SINS.
THEN, I CAN SIT BACK AND WATCH IT DESTROY ITSELF. MAN'S WORST ENEMY IS HIMSELF, IT SEEMS. HOW POETIC!
WOOOSH
PLEASE, I'M JUST AN HONEST ANTIQUE DEALER, DEMON!
HMMHH!
FINALLY, YOU'RE ALL HERE!

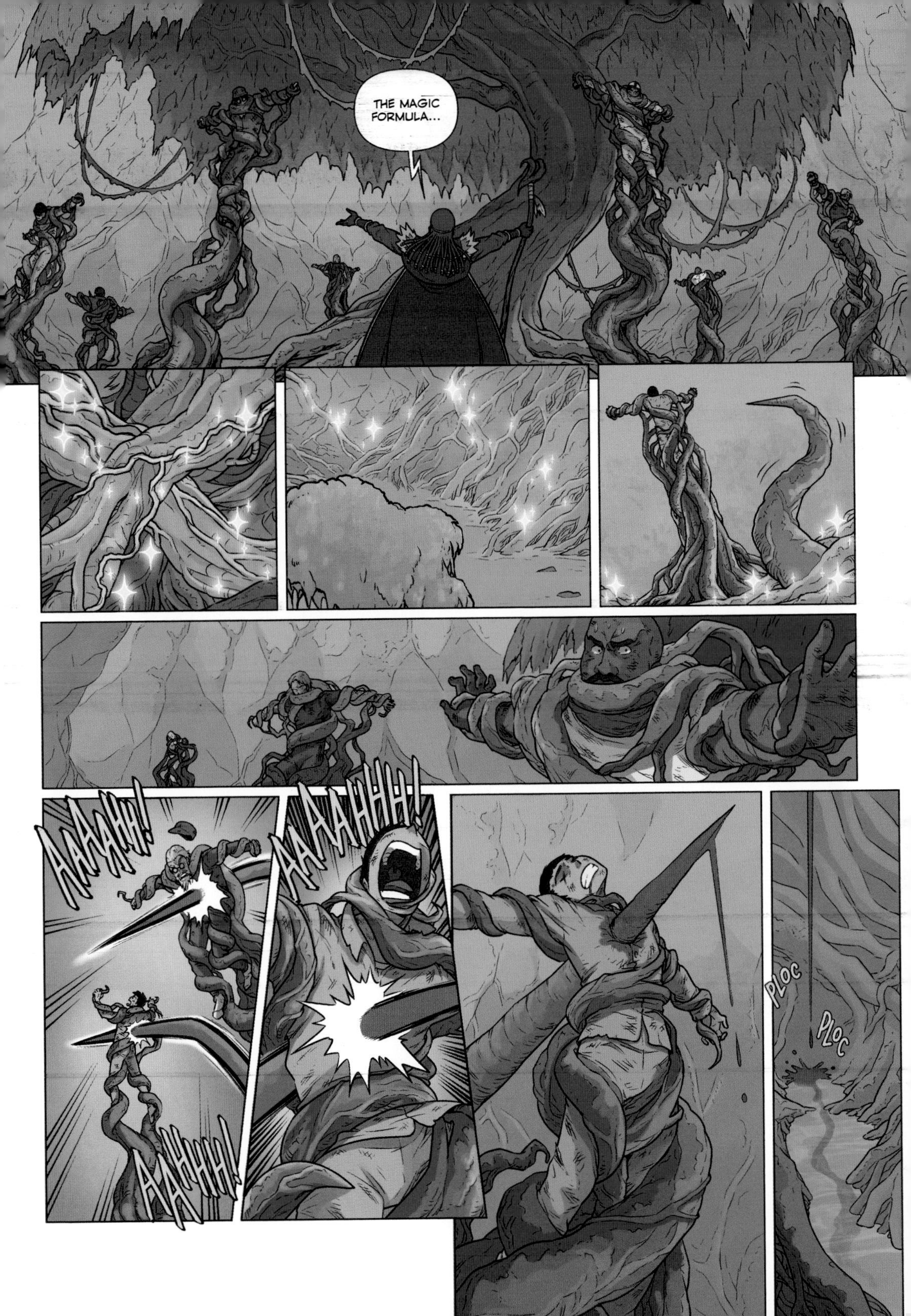
THE MAGIC FORMULA...
AAAHH!
AAAAHHH!
AAHHH!
PLOC
PLOC

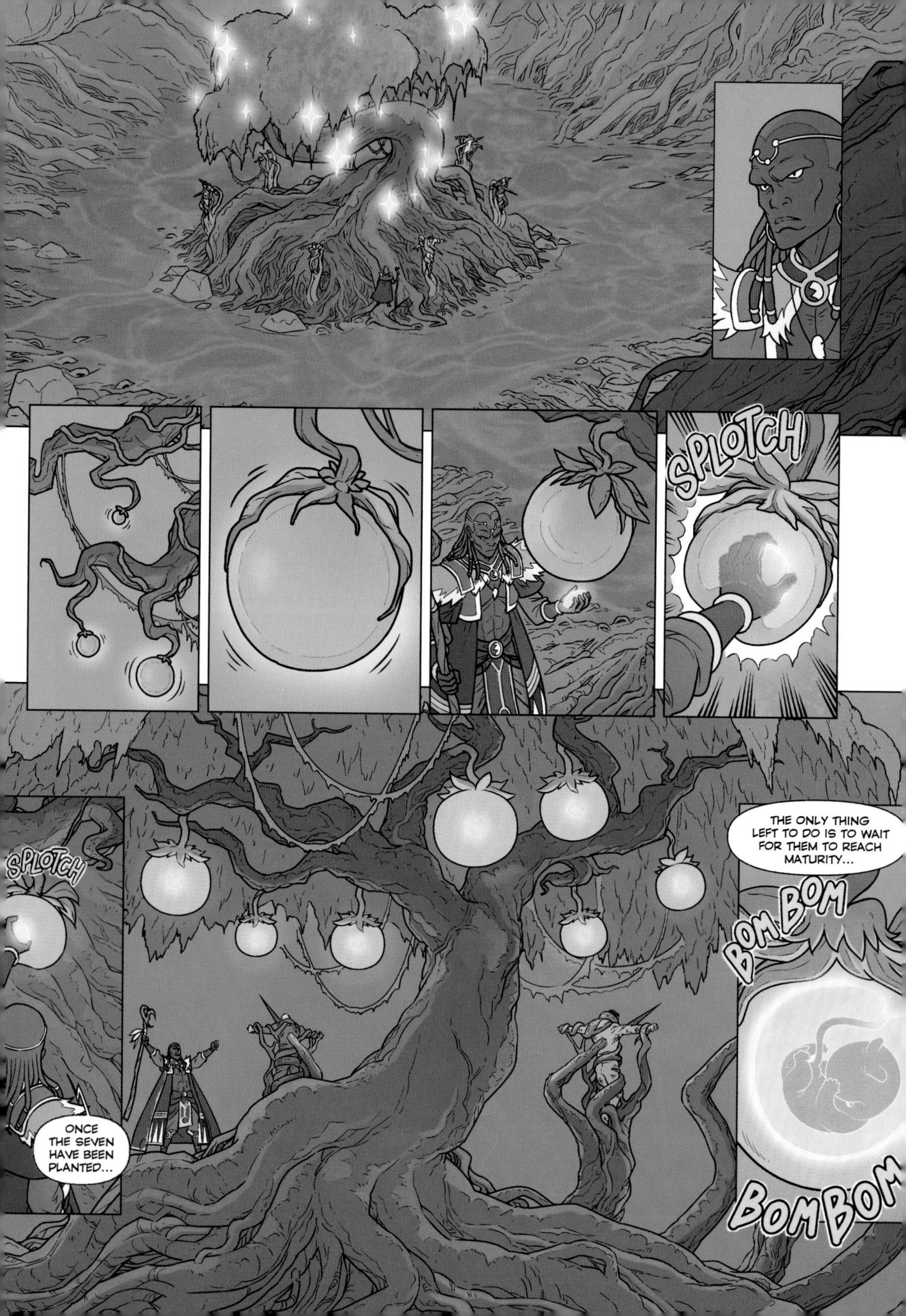
SPLOTCH
SPLOTCH
ONCE THE SEVEN HAVE BEEN PLANTED...
THE ONLY THING LEFT TO DO IS TO WAIT FOR THEM TO REACH MATURITY...
BOM BOM
BOM BOM

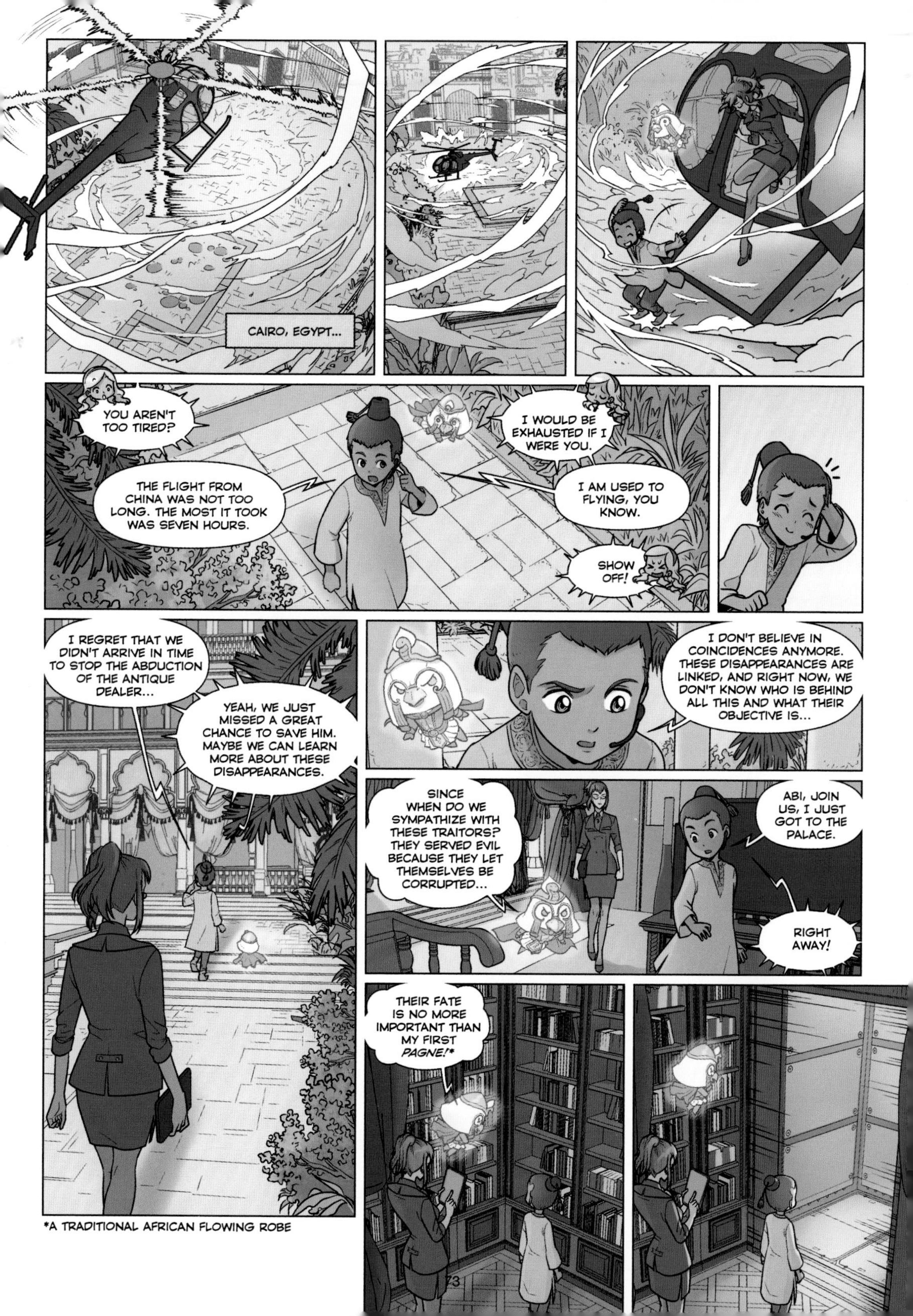
CAIRO, EGYPT...
YOU AREN'T TOO TIRED?
I WOULD BE EXHAUSTED IF I WERE YOU.
THE FLIGHT FROM CHINA WAS NOT TOO LONG. THE MOST IT TOOK WAS SEVEN HOURS.
I AM USED TO FLYING, YOU KNOW.
SHOW OFF!
I REGRET THAT WE DIDN'T ARRIVE IN TIME TO STOP THE ABDUCTION OF THE ANTIQUE DEALER...
YEAH, WE JUST MISSED A GREAT CHANCE TO SAVE HIM. MAYBE WE CAN LEARN MORE ABOUT THESE DISAPPEARANCES.
I DON'T BELIEVE IN COINCIDENCES ANYMORE. THESE DISAPPEARANCES ARE LINKED, AND RIGHT NOW, WE DON'T KNOW WHO IS BEHIND ALL THIS AND WHAT THEIR OBJECTIVE IS...
SINCE WHEN DO WE SYMPATHIZE WITH THESE TRAITORS? THEY SERVED EVIL BECAUSE THEY LET THEMSELVES BE CORRUPTED...
ABI, JOIN US, I JUST GOT TO THE PALACE.
RIGHT AWAY!
THEIR FATE IS NO MORE IMPORTANT THAN MY FIRST *PAGNE!**

*A TRADITIONAL AFRICAN FLOWING ROBE

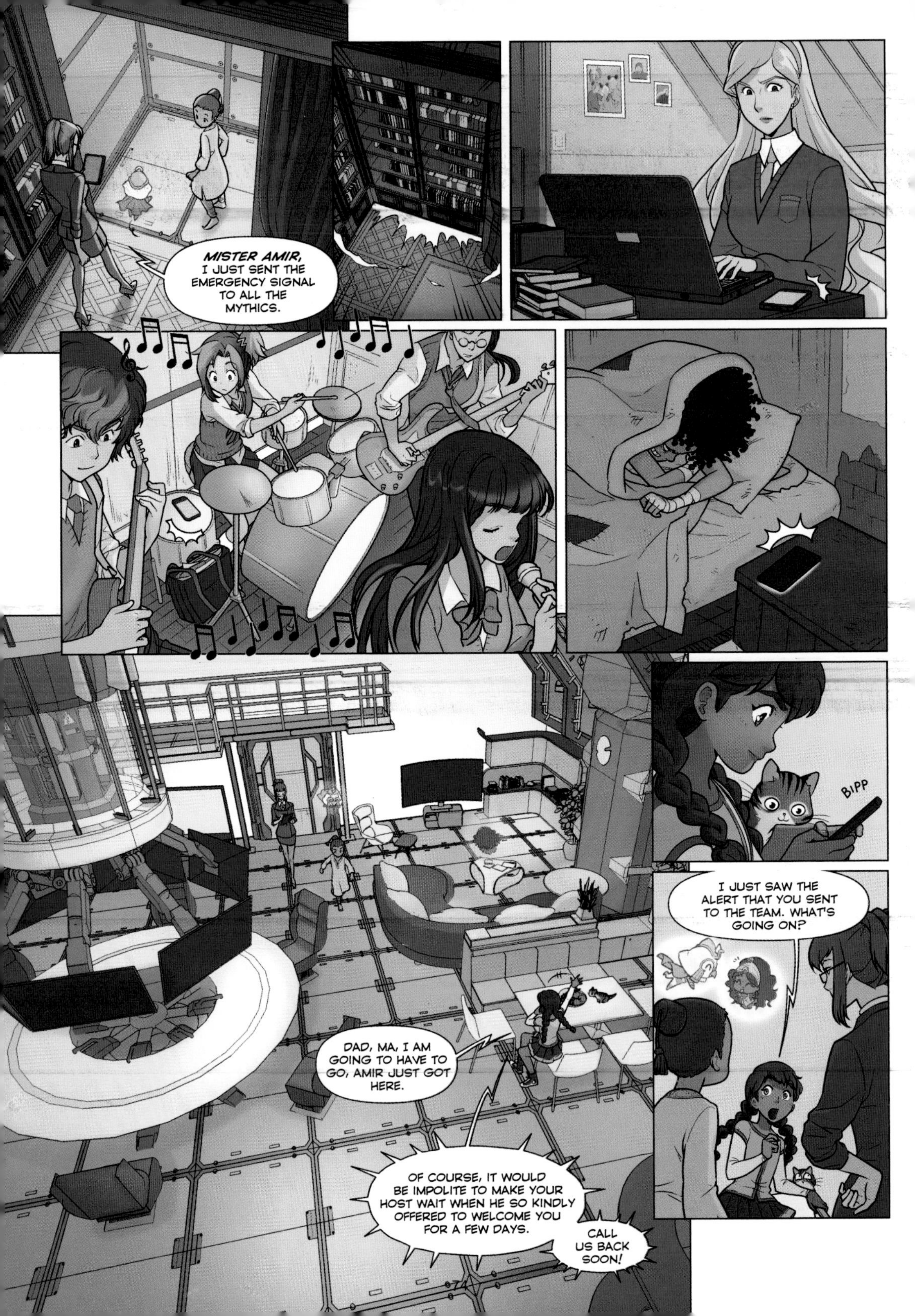
MISTER AMIR, I JUST SENT THE EMERGENCY SIGNAL TO ALL THE MYTHICS.
BIPP
I JUST SAW THE ALERT THAT YOU SENT TO THE TEAM. WHAT'S GOING ON?
DAD, MA, I AM GOING TO HAVE TO GO, AMIR JUST GOT HERE.
OF COURSE, IT WOULD BE IMPOLITE TO MAKE YOUR HOST WAIT WHEN HE SO KINDLY OFFERED TO WELCOME YOU FOR A FEW DAYS.
CALL US BACK SOON!

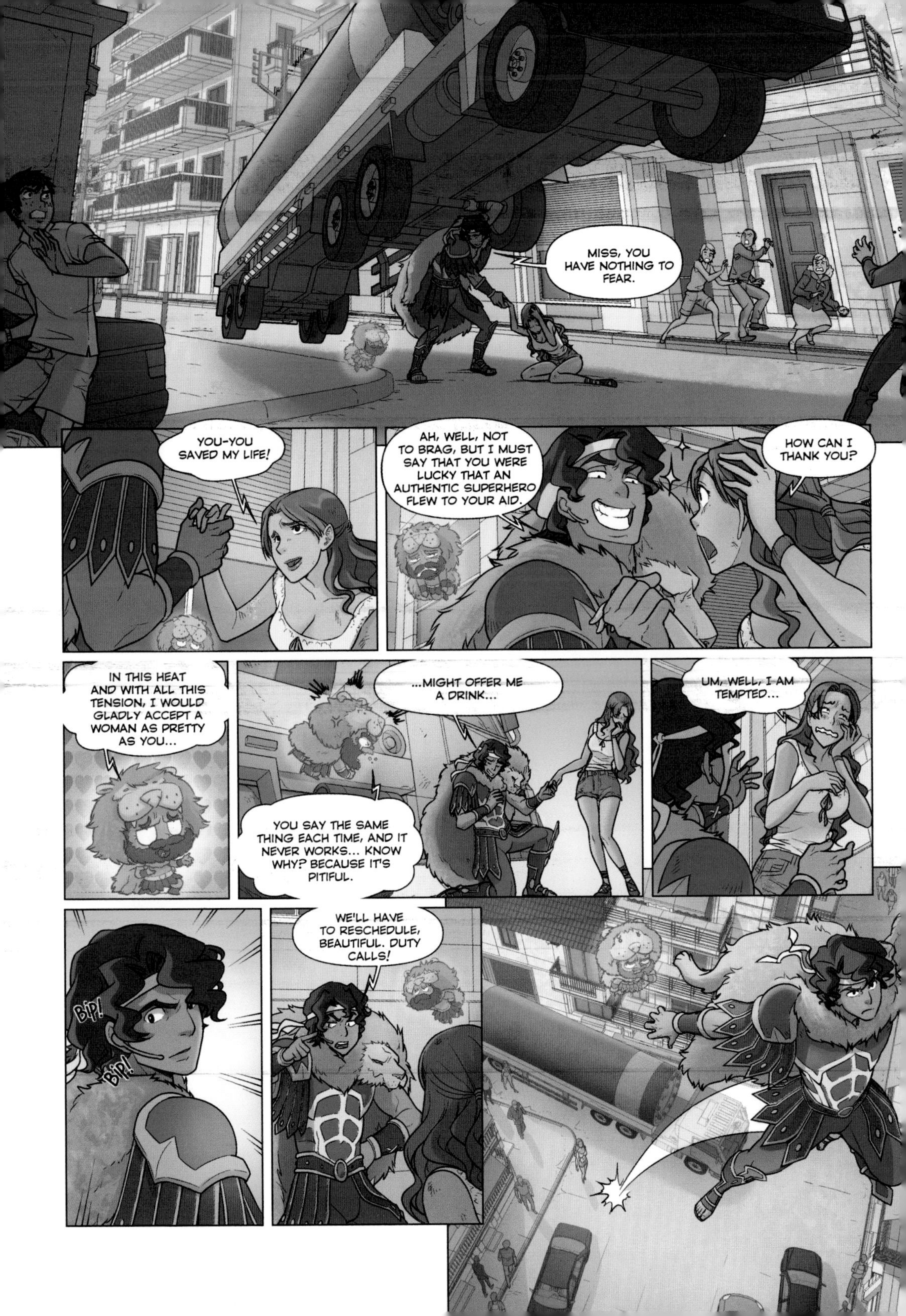
MISS, YOU HAVE NOTHING TO FEAR.
YOU-YOU SAVED MY LIFE!
AH, WELL, NOT TO BRAG, BUT I MUST SAY THAT YOU WERE LUCKY THAT AN AUTHENTIC SUPERHERO FLEW TO YOUR AID.
HOW CAN I THANK YOU?
IN THIS HEAT AND WITH ALL THIS TENSION, I WOULD GLADLY ACCEPT A WOMAN AS PRETTY AS YOU...
...MIGHT OFFER ME A DRINK...
YOU SAY THE SAME THING EACH TIME, AND IT NEVER WORKS... KNOW WHY? BECAUSE IT'S PITIFUL.
UM, WELL, I AM TEMPTED...
BIP!
BIP!
WE'LL HAVE TO RESCHEDULE, BEAUTIFUL. DUTY CALLS!

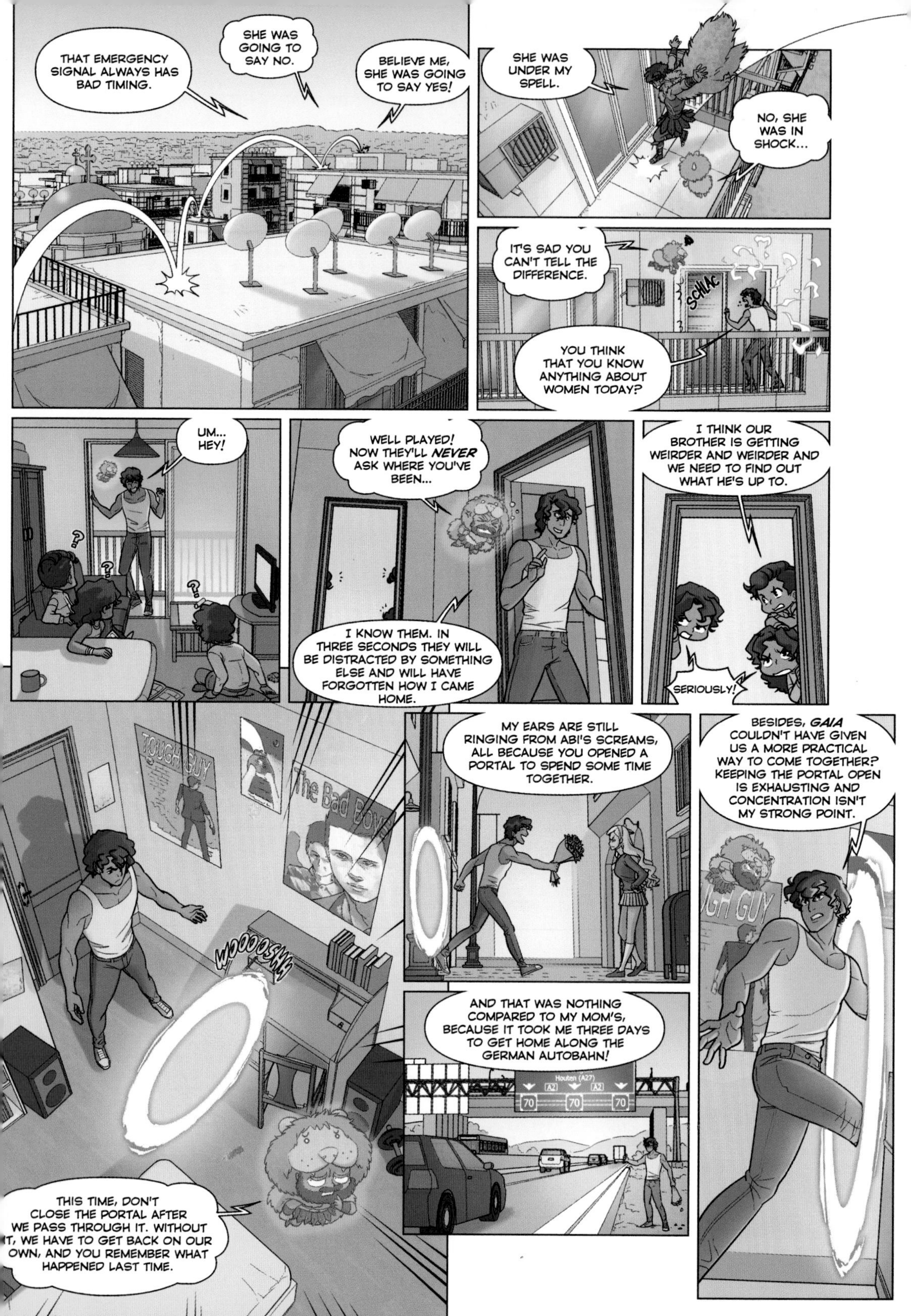

THAT EMERGENCY SIGNAL ALWAYS HAS BAD TIMING.
SHE WAS GOING TO SAY NO.
BELIEVE ME, SHE WAS GOING TO SAY YES!
SHE WAS UNDER MY SPELL.
NO, SHE WAS IN SHOCK...
IT'S SAD YOU CAN'T TELL THE DIFFERENCE.
SCHLAC
YOU THINK THAT YOU KNOW ANYTHING ABOUT WOMEN TODAY?
UM... HEY!
WELL PLAYED! NOW THEY'LL *NEVER* ASK WHERE YOU'VE BEEN...
I KNOW THEM. IN THREE SECONDS THEY WILL BE DISTRACTED BY SOMETHING ELSE AND WILL HAVE FORGOTTEN HOW I CAME HOME.
I THINK OUR BROTHER IS GETTING WEIRDER AND WEIRDER AND WE NEED TO FIND OUT WHAT HE'S UP TO.
SERIOUSLY!
TOUGH GUY
THIS TIME, DON'T CLOSE THE PORTAL AFTER WE PASS THROUGH IT. WITHOUT IT, WE HAVE TO GET BACK ON OUR OWN, AND YOU REMEMBER WHAT HAPPENED LAST TIME.
MY EARS ARE STILL RINGING FROM ABI'S SCREAMS, ALL BECAUSE YOU OPENED A PORTAL TO SPEND SOME TIME TOGETHER.
AND THAT WAS NOTHING COMPARED TO MY MOM'S, BECAUSE IT TOOK ME THREE DAYS TO GET HOME ALONG THE GERMAN AUTOBAHN!
Houten (A27)
A2
70
BESIDES, *GAIA* COULDN'T HAVE GIVEN US A MORE PRACTICAL WAY TO COME TOGETHER? KEEPING THE PORTAL OPEN IS EXHAUSTING AND CONCENTRATION ISN'T MY STRONG POINT.

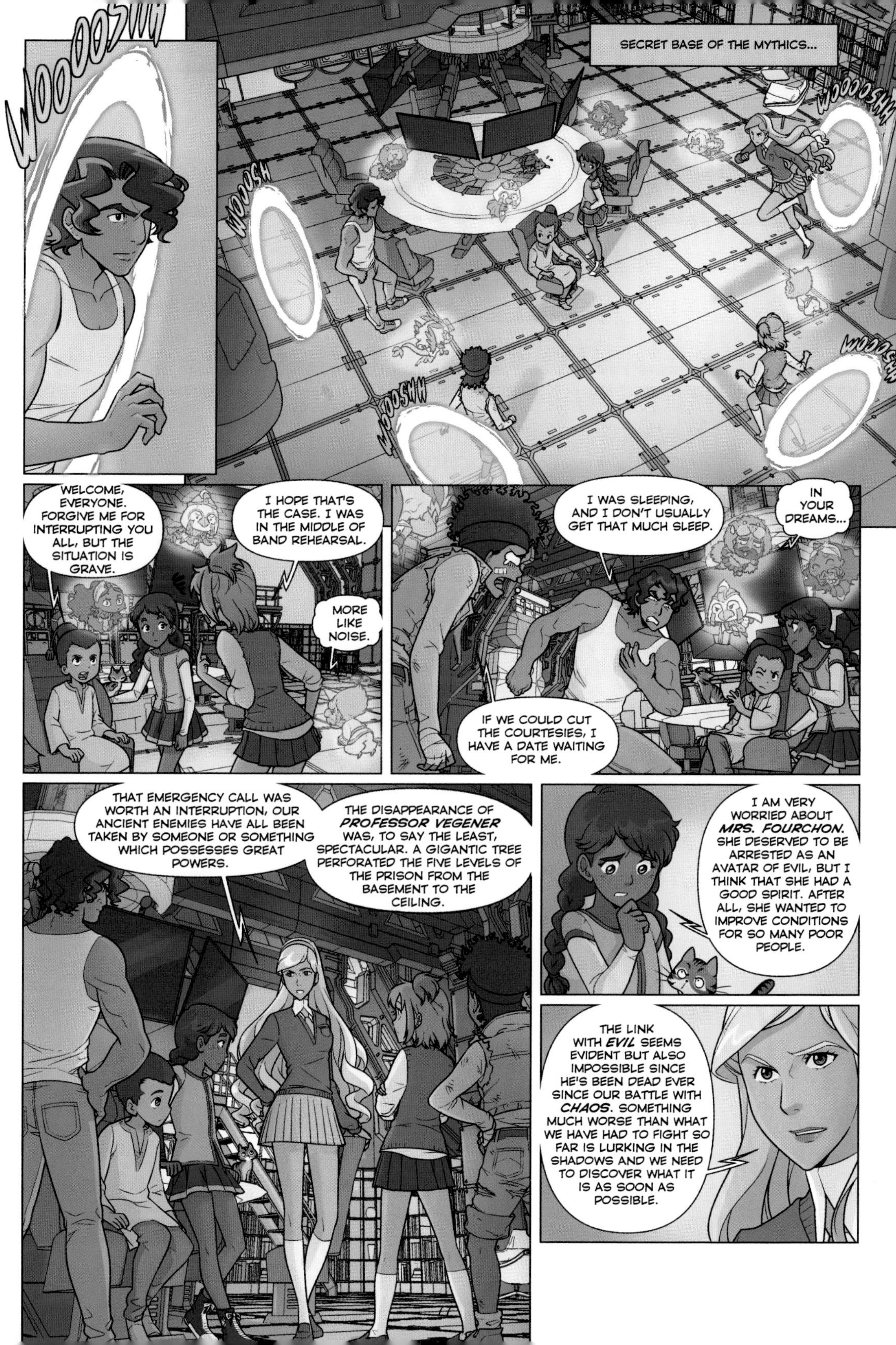
WOOOOSHH
SECRET BASE OF THE MYTHICS...
WOOOOSH
WOOOSH
WOOOOSH
WOOOSHH
WELCOME, EVERYONE. FORGIVE ME FOR INTERRUPTING YOU ALL, BUT THE SITUATION IS GRAVE.
I HOPE THAT'S THE CASE. I WAS IN THE MIDDLE OF BAND REHEARSAL.
MORE LIKE NOISE.
I WAS SLEEPING, AND I DON'T USUALLY GET THAT MUCH SLEEP.
IN YOUR DREAMS...
IF WE COULD CUT THE COURTESIES, I HAVE A DATE WAITING FOR ME.
THAT EMERGENCY CALL WAS WORTH AN INTERRUPTION, OUR ANCIENT ENEMIES HAVE ALL BEEN TAKEN BY SOMEONE OR SOMETHING WHICH POSSESSES GREAT POWERS.
THE DISAPPEARANCE OF PROFESSOR VEGENER WAS, TO SAY THE LEAST, SPECTACULAR. A GIGANTIC TREE PERFORATED THE FIVE LEVELS OF THE PRISON FROM THE BASEMENT TO THE CEILING.
I AM VERY WORRIED ABOUT MRS. FOURCHON. SHE DESERVED TO BE ARRESTED AS AN AVATAR OF EVIL, BUT I THINK THAT SHE HAD A GOOD SPIRIT. AFTER ALL, SHE WANTED TO IMPROVE CONDITIONS FOR SO MANY POOR PEOPLE.
THE LINK WITH EVIL SEEMS EVIDENT BUT ALSO IMPOSSIBLE SINCE HE'S BEEN DEAD EVER SINCE OUR BATTLE WITH CHAOS. SOMETHING MUCH WORSE THAN WHAT WE HAVE HAD TO FIGHT SO FAR IS LURKING IN THE SHADOWS AND WE NEED TO DISCOVER WHAT IT IS AS SOON AS POSSIBLE.

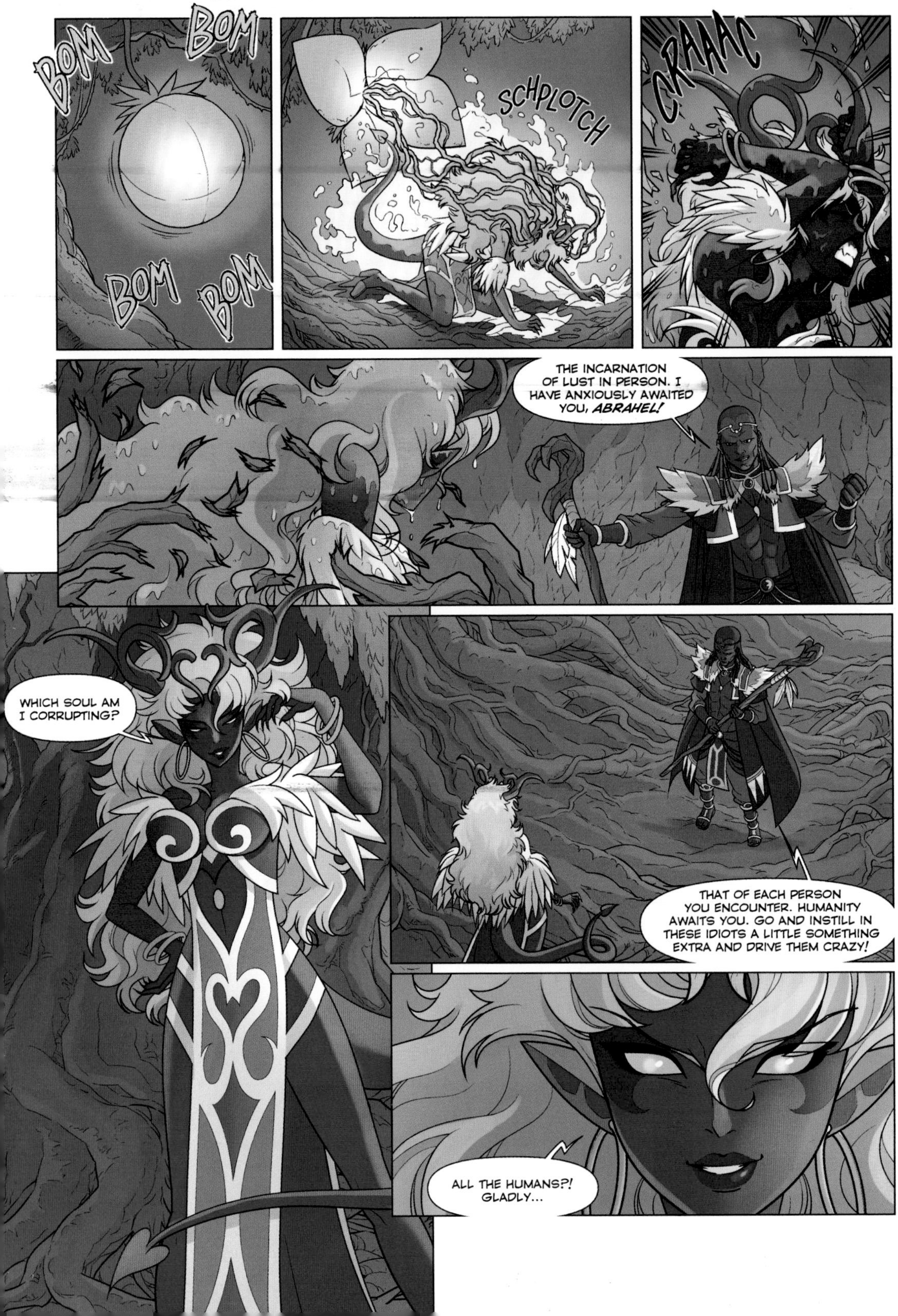
BOM
BOM
BOM
BOM
SCHPLOTCH
CRAAAC
THE INCARNATION OF LUST IN PERSON. I HAVE ANXIOUSLY AWAITED YOU, *ABRAHEL!*
WHICH SOUL AM I CORRUPTING?
THAT OF EACH PERSON YOU ENCOUNTER. HUMANITY AWAITS YOU. GO AND INSTILL IN THESE IDIOTS A LITTLE SOMETHING EXTRA AND DRIVE THEM CRAZY!
ALL THE HUMANS?! GLADLY...

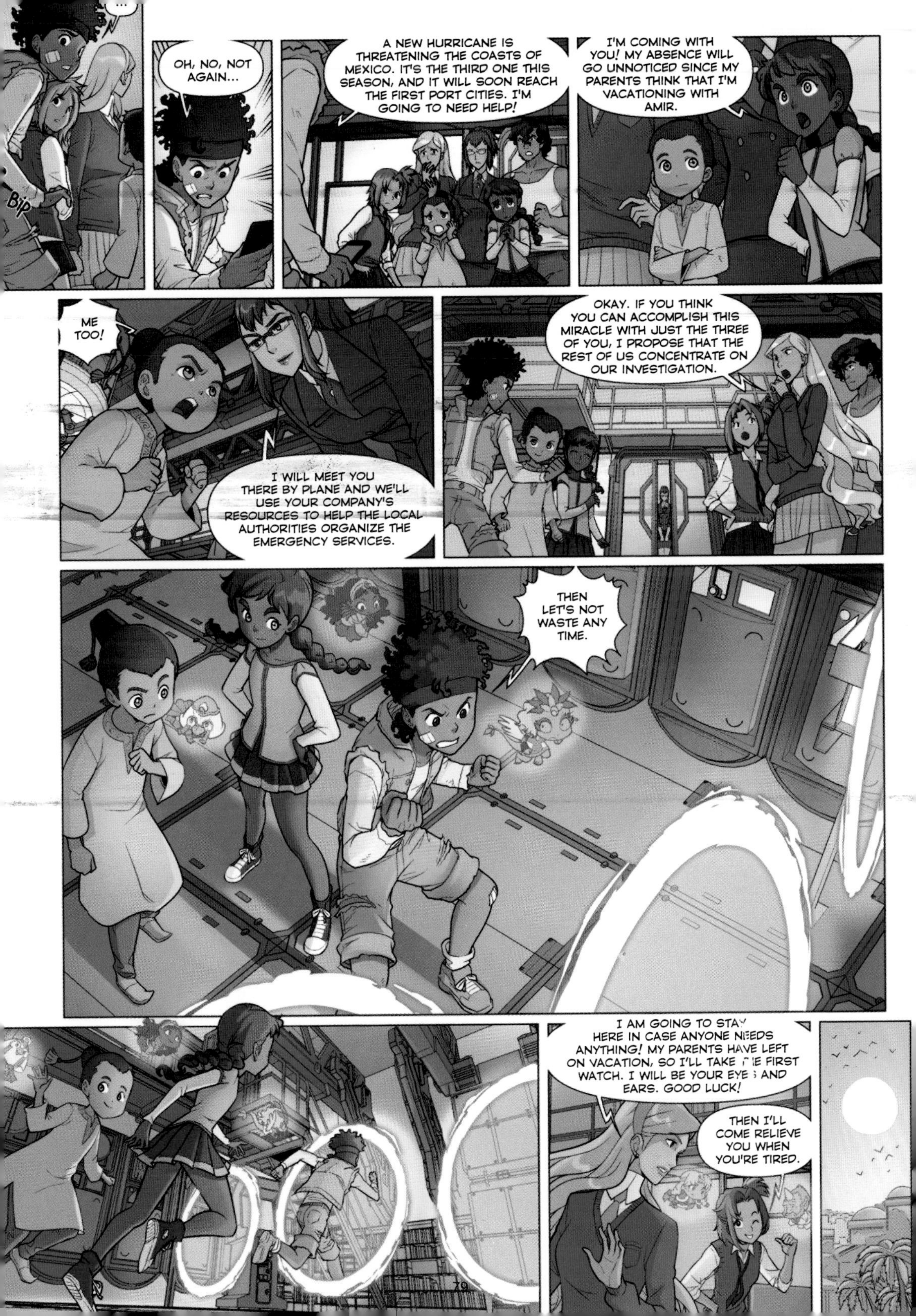
...
Bip
OH, NO, NOT AGAIN...
A NEW HURRICANE IS THREATENING THE COASTS OF MEXICO. IT'S THE THIRD ONE THIS SEASON, AND IT WILL SOON REACH THE FIRST PORT CITIES. I'M GOING TO NEED HELP!
I'M COMING WITH YOU! MY ABSENCE WILL GO UNNOTICED SINCE MY PARENTS THINK THAT I'M VACATIONING WITH AMIR.
ME TOO!
I WILL MEET YOU THERE BY PLANE AND WE'LL USE YOUR COMPANY'S RESOURCES TO HELP THE LOCAL AUTHORITIES ORGANIZE THE EMERGENCY SERVICES.
OKAY. IF YOU THINK YOU CAN ACCOMPLISH THIS MIRACLE WITH JUST THE THREE OF YOU, I PROPOSE THAT THE REST OF US CONCENTRATE ON OUR INVESTIGATION.
THEN LET'S NOT WASTE ANY TIME.
I AM GOING TO STAY HERE IN CASE ANYONE NEEDS ANYTHING! MY PARENTS HAVE LEFT ON VACATION, SO I'LL TAKE THE FIRST WATCH. I WILL BE YOUR EYES AND EARS. GOOD LUCK!
THEN I'LL COME RELIEVE YOU WHEN YOU'RE TIRED.

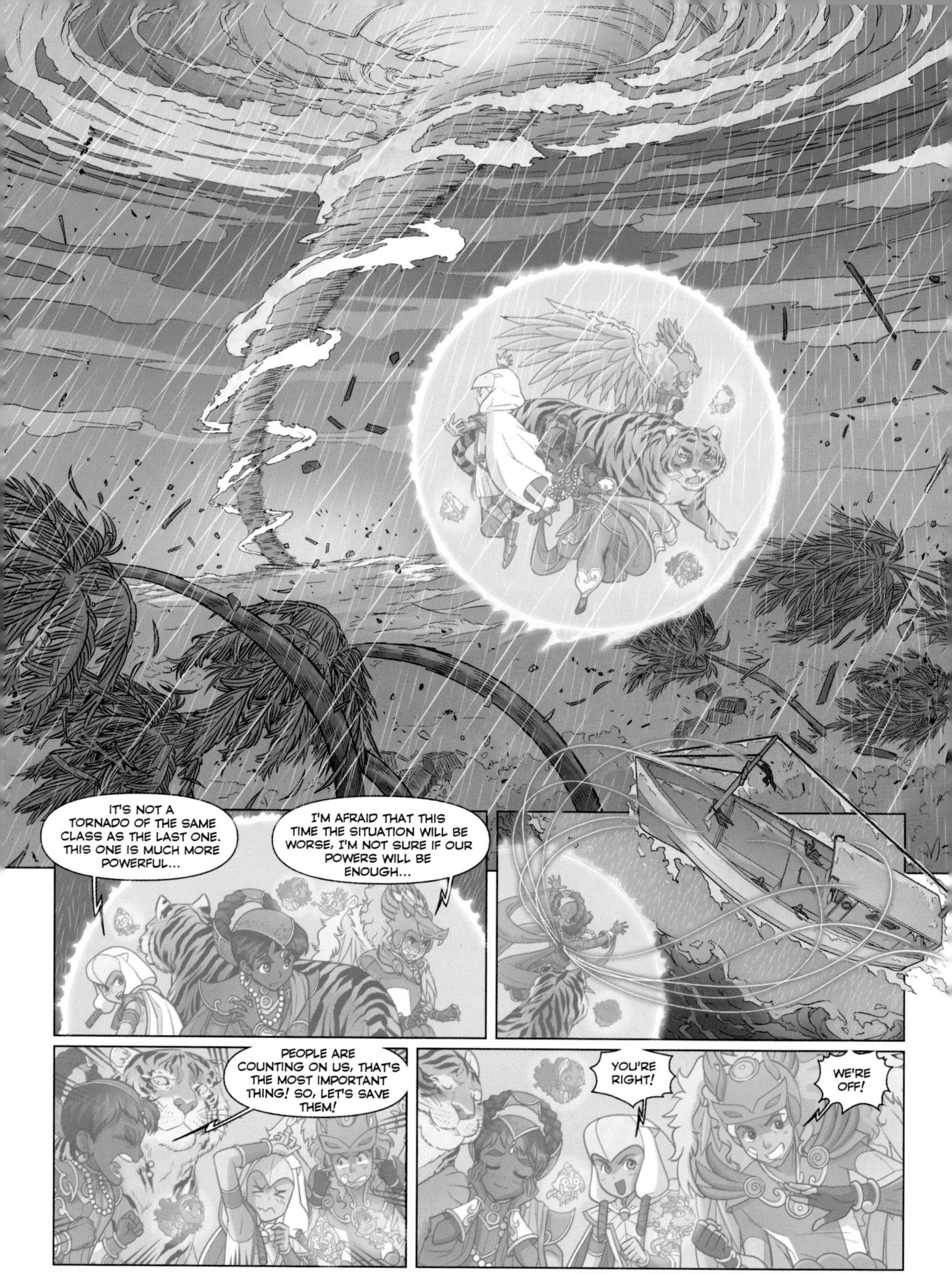
IT'S NOT A TORNADO OF THE SAME CLASS AS THE LAST ONE. THIS ONE IS MUCH MORE POWERFUL...
I'M AFRAID THAT THIS TIME THE SITUATION WILL BE WORSE, I'M NOT SURE IF OUR POWERS WILL BE ENOUGH...
PEOPLE ARE COUNTING ON US, THAT'S THE MOST IMPORTANT THING! SO, LET'S SAVE THEM!
YOU'RE RIGHT!
WE'RE OFF!

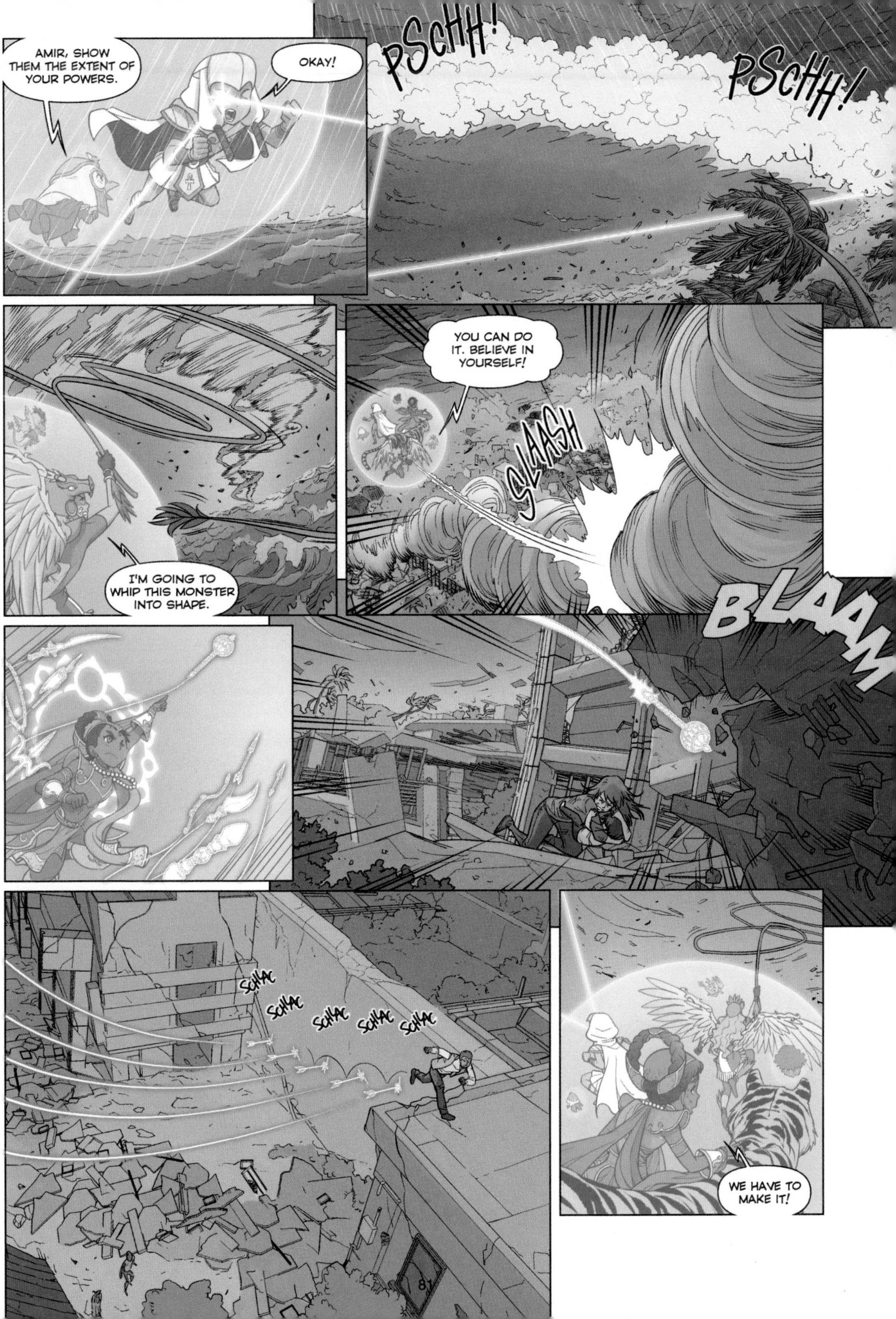
AMIR, SHOW THEM THE EXTENT OF YOUR POWERS.
OKAY!
PSCHH!
PSCHH!
YOU CAN DO IT. BELIEVE IN YOURSELF!
SLAASH
I'M GOING TO WHIP THIS MONSTER INTO SHAPE.
BLAAM
SCHAC
SCHAC
SCHAC
SCHAC
SCHAC
WE HAVE TO MAKE IT!

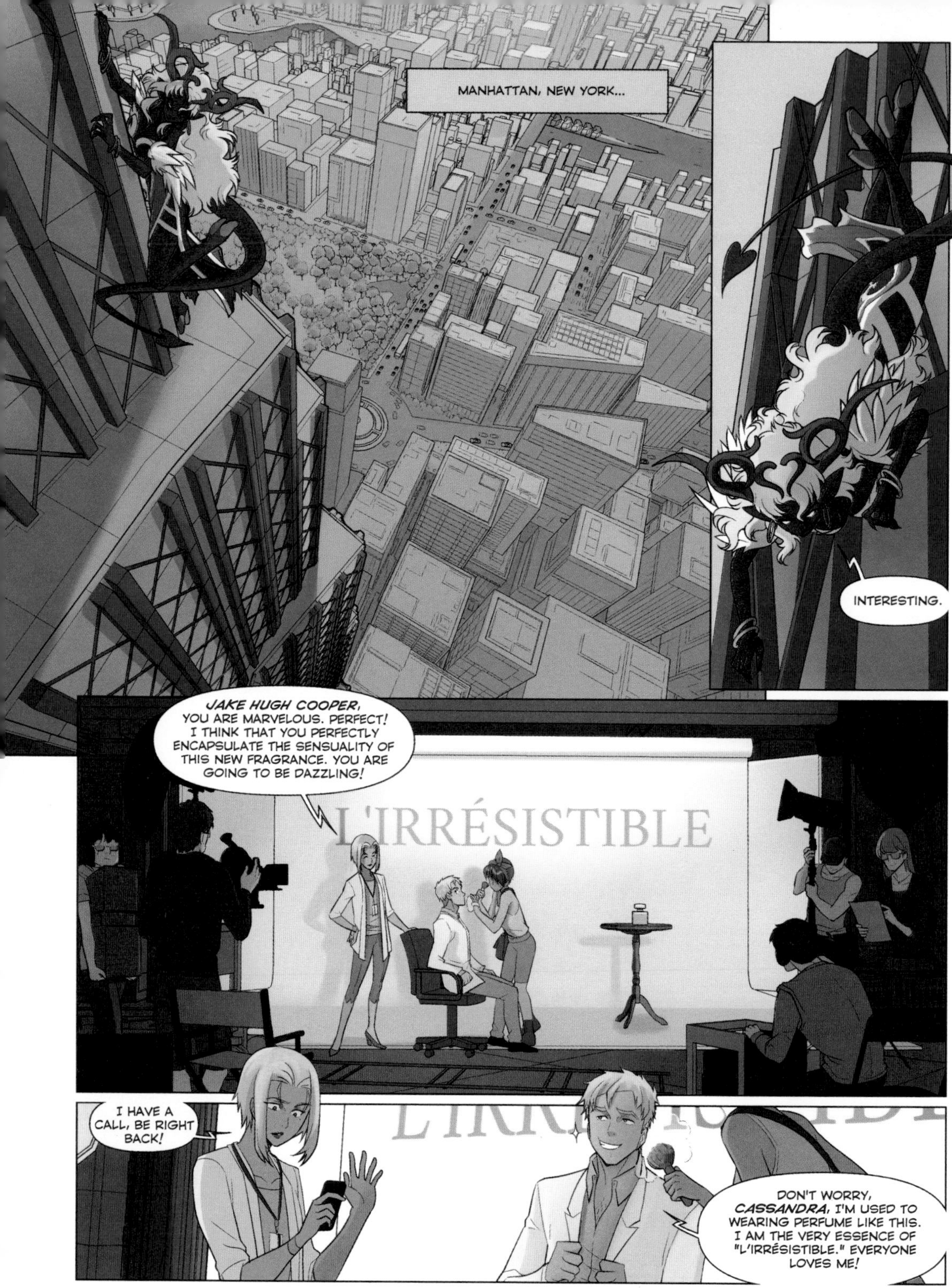
MANHATTAN, NEW YORK...
INTERESTING.
JAKE HUGH COOPER, YOU ARE MARVELOUS. PERFECT! I THINK THAT YOU PERFECTLY ENCAPSULATE THE SENSUALITY OF THIS NEW FRAGRANCE. YOU ARE GOING TO BE DAZZLING!
L'IRRÉSISTIBLE
I HAVE A CALL, BE RIGHT BACK!
DON'T WORRY, CASSANDRA, I'M USED TO WEARING PERFUME LIKE THIS. I AM THE VERY ESSENCE OF "L'IRRÉSISTIBLE." EVERYONE LOVES ME!

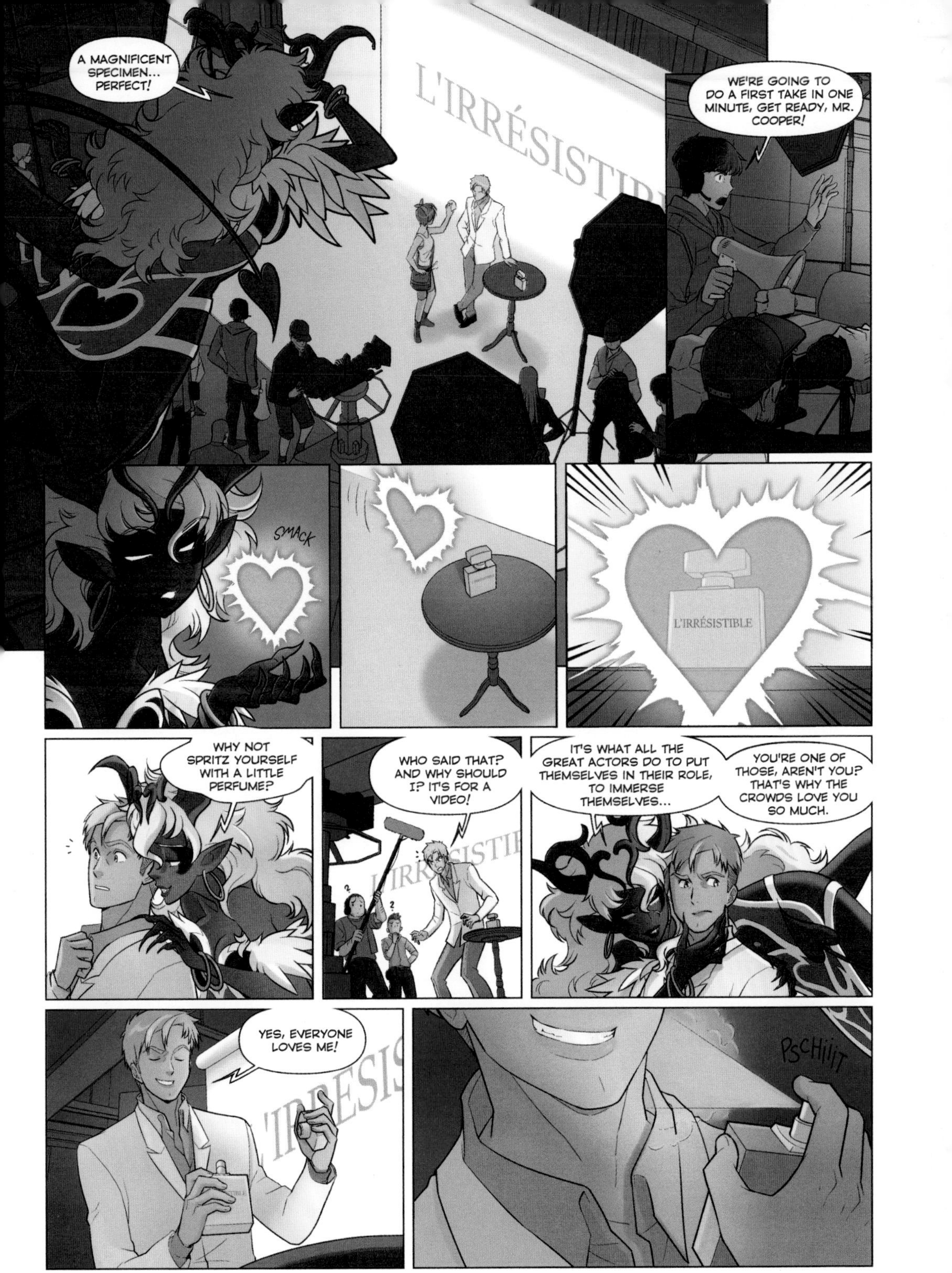
A MAGNIFICENT SPECIMEN... PERFECT!
L'IRRÉSISTIBLE
WE'RE GOING TO DO A FIRST TAKE IN ONE MINUTE, GET READY, MR. COOPER!
SMACK
L'IRRÉSISTIBLE
WHY NOT SPRITZ YOURSELF WITH A LITTLE PERFUME?
WHO SAID THAT? AND WHY SHOULD I? IT'S FOR A VIDEO!
IT'S WHAT ALL THE GREAT ACTORS DO TO PUT THEMSELVES IN THEIR ROLE, TO IMMERSE THEMSELVES...
YOU'RE ONE OF THOSE, AREN'T YOU? THAT'S WHY THE CROWDS LOVE YOU SO MUCH.
YES, EVERYONE LOVES ME!
PSCHIIIT

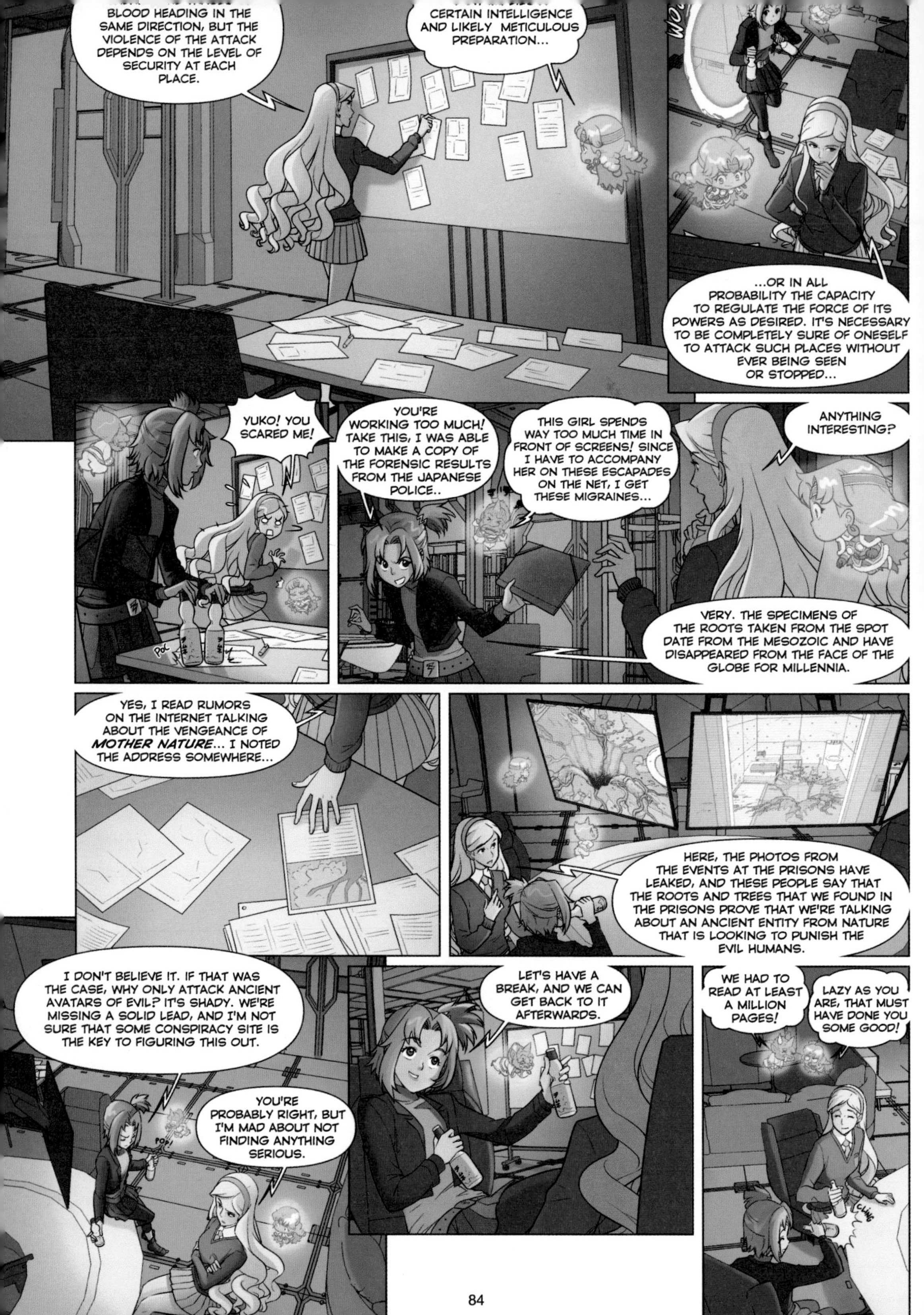
BLOOD HEADING IN THE SAME DIRECTION, BUT THE VIOLENCE OF THE ATTACK DEPENDS ON THE LEVEL OF SECURITY AT EACH PLACE.
CERTAIN INTELLIGENCE AND LIKELY METICULOUS PREPARATION...
...OR IN ALL PROBABILITY THE CAPACITY TO REGULATE THE FORCE OF ITS POWERS AS DESIRED. IT'S NECESSARY TO BE COMPLETELY SURE OF ONESELF TO ATTACK SUCH PLACES WITHOUT EVER BEING SEEN OR STOPPED...
YUKO! YOU SCARED ME!
POC
YOU'RE WORKING TOO MUCH! TAKE THIS, I WAS ABLE TO MAKE A COPY OF THE FORENSIC RESULTS FROM THE JAPANESE POLICE..
THIS GIRL SPENDS WAY TOO MUCH TIME IN FRONT OF SCREENS! SINCE I HAVE TO ACCOMPANY HER ON THESE ESCAPADES ON THE NET, I GET THESE MIGRAINES...
ANYTHING INTERESTING?
VERY. THE SPECIMENS OF THE ROOTS TAKEN FROM THE SPOT DATE FROM THE MESOZOIC AND HAVE DISAPPEARED FROM THE FACE OF THE GLOBE FOR MILLENNIA.
YES, I READ RUMORS ON THE INTERNET TALKING ABOUT THE VENGEANCE OF *MOTHER NATURE*... I NOTED THE ADDRESS SOMEWHERE...
HERE, THE PHOTOS FROM THE EVENTS AT THE PRISONS HAVE LEAKED, AND THESE PEOPLE SAY THAT THE ROOTS AND TREES THAT WE FOUND IN THE PRISONS PROVE THAT WE'RE TALKING ABOUT AN ANCIENT ENTITY FROM NATURE THAT IS LOOKING TO PUNISH THE EVIL HUMANS.
I DON'T BELIEVE IT. IF THAT WAS THE CASE, WHY ONLY ATTACK ANCIENT AVATARS OF EVIL? IT'S SHADY. WE'RE MISSING A SOLID LEAD, AND I'M NOT SURE THAT SOME CONSPIRACY SITE IS THE KEY TO FIGURING THIS OUT.
YOU'RE PROBABLY RIGHT, BUT I'M MAD ABOUT NOT FINDING ANYTHING SERIOUS.
POP!
LET'S HAVE A BREAK, AND WE CAN GET BACK TO IT AFTERWARDS.
WE HAD TO READ AT LEAST A MILLION PAGES!
LAZY AS YOU ARE, THAT MUST HAVE DONE YOU SOME GOOD!
CLING

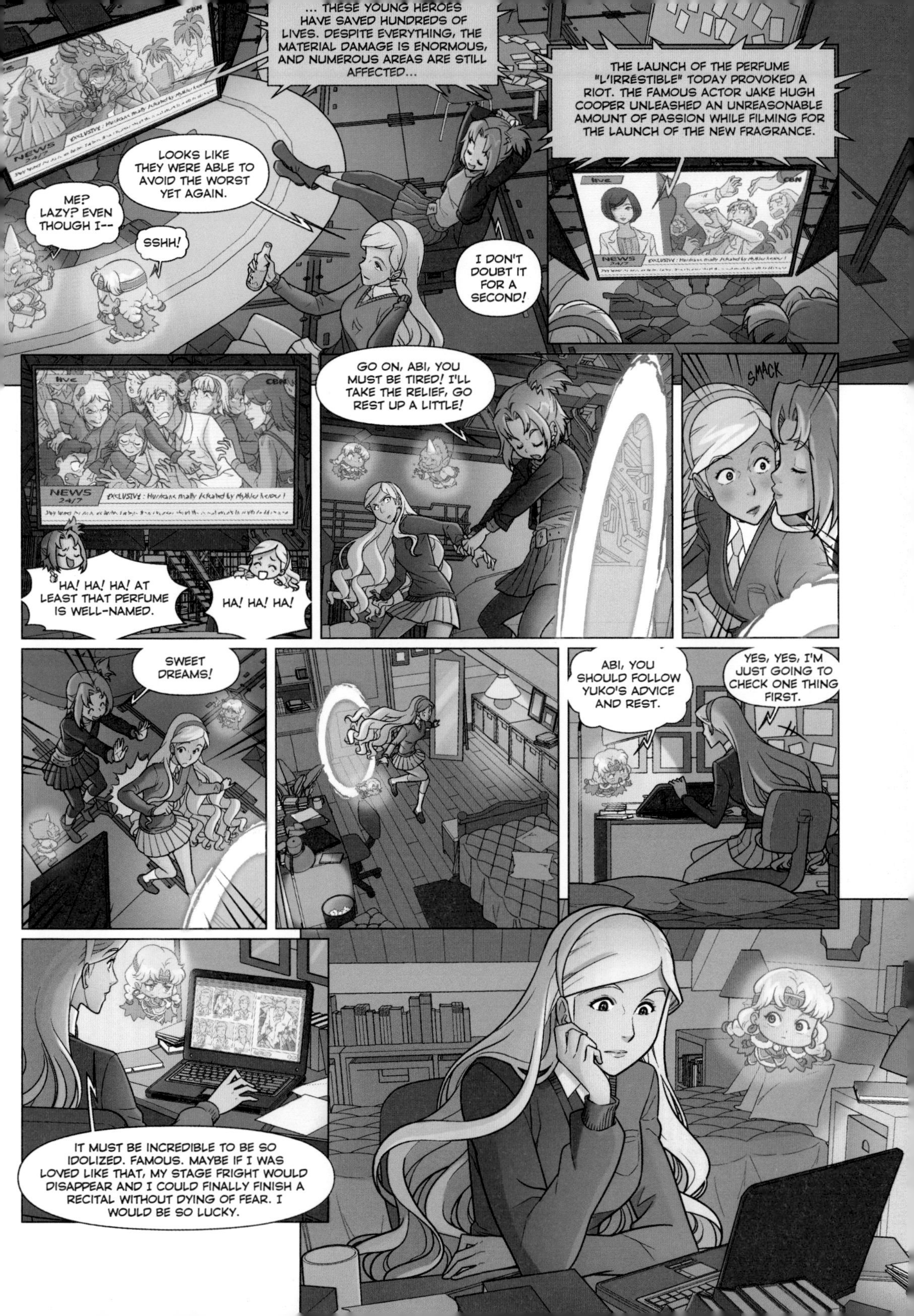

... THESE YOUNG HEROES HAVE SAVED HUNDREDS OF LIVES. DESPITE EVERYTHING, THE MATERIAL DAMAGE IS ENORMOUS, AND NUMEROUS AREAS ARE STILL AFFECTED...
LOOKS LIKE THEY WERE ABLE TO AVOID THE WORST YET AGAIN.
ME? LAZY? EVEN THOUGH I--
SSHH!
I DON'T DOUBT IT FOR A SECOND!
THE LAUNCH OF THE PERFUME "L'IRRESTIBLE" TODAY PROVOKED A RIOT. THE FAMOUS ACTOR JAKE HUGH COOPER UNLEASHED AN UNREASONABLE AMOUNT OF PASSION WHILE FILMING FOR THE LAUNCH OF THE NEW FRAGRANCE.
HA! HA! HA! AT LEAST THAT PERFUME IS WELL-NAMED.
HA! HA! HA!
GO ON, ABI, YOU MUST BE TIRED! I'LL TAKE THE RELIEF, GO REST UP A LITTLE!
SMACK
SWEET DREAMS!
ABI, YOU SHOULD FOLLOW YUKO'S ADVICE AND REST.
YES, YES, I'M JUST GOING TO CHECK ONE THING FIRST.
IT MUST BE INCREDIBLE TO BE SO IDOLIZED. FAMOUS. MAYBE IF I WAS LOVED LIKE THAT, MY STAGE FRIGHT WOULD DISAPPEAR AND I COULD FINALLY FINISH A RECITAL WITHOUT DYING OF FEAR. I WOULD BE SO LUCKY.

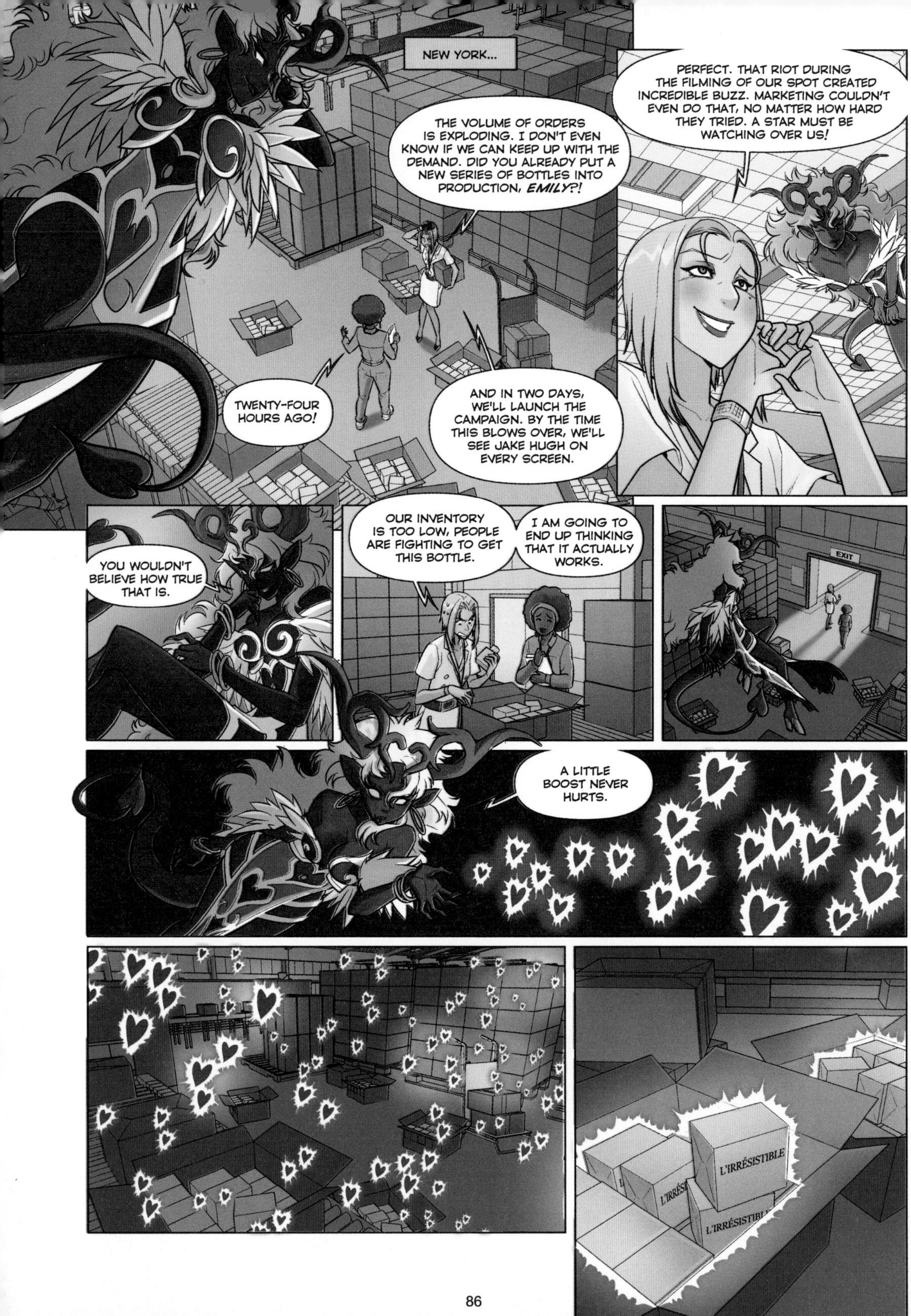

NEW YORK...
THE VOLUME OF ORDERS IS EXPLODING. I DON'T EVEN KNOW IF WE CAN KEEP UP WITH THE DEMAND. DID YOU ALREADY PUT A NEW SERIES OF BOTTLES INTO PRODUCTION, EMILY?!
TWENTY-FOUR HOURS AGO!
AND IN TWO DAYS, WE'LL LAUNCH THE CAMPAIGN. BY THE TIME THIS BLOWS OVER, WE'LL SEE JAKE HUGH ON EVERY SCREEN.
PERFECT. THAT RIOT DURING THE FILMING OF OUR SPOT CREATED INCREDIBLE BUZZ. MARKETING COULDN'T EVEN DO THAT, NO MATTER HOW HARD THEY TRIED. A STAR MUST BE WATCHING OVER US!
YOU WOULDN'T BELIEVE HOW TRUE THAT IS.
OUR INVENTORY IS TOO LOW, PEOPLE ARE FIGHTING TO GET THIS BOTTLE.
I AM GOING TO END UP THINKING THAT IT ACTUALLY WORKS.
EXIT
A LITTLE BOOST NEVER HURTS.
L'IRRÉSISTIBLE
L'IRRÉSISTIBLE

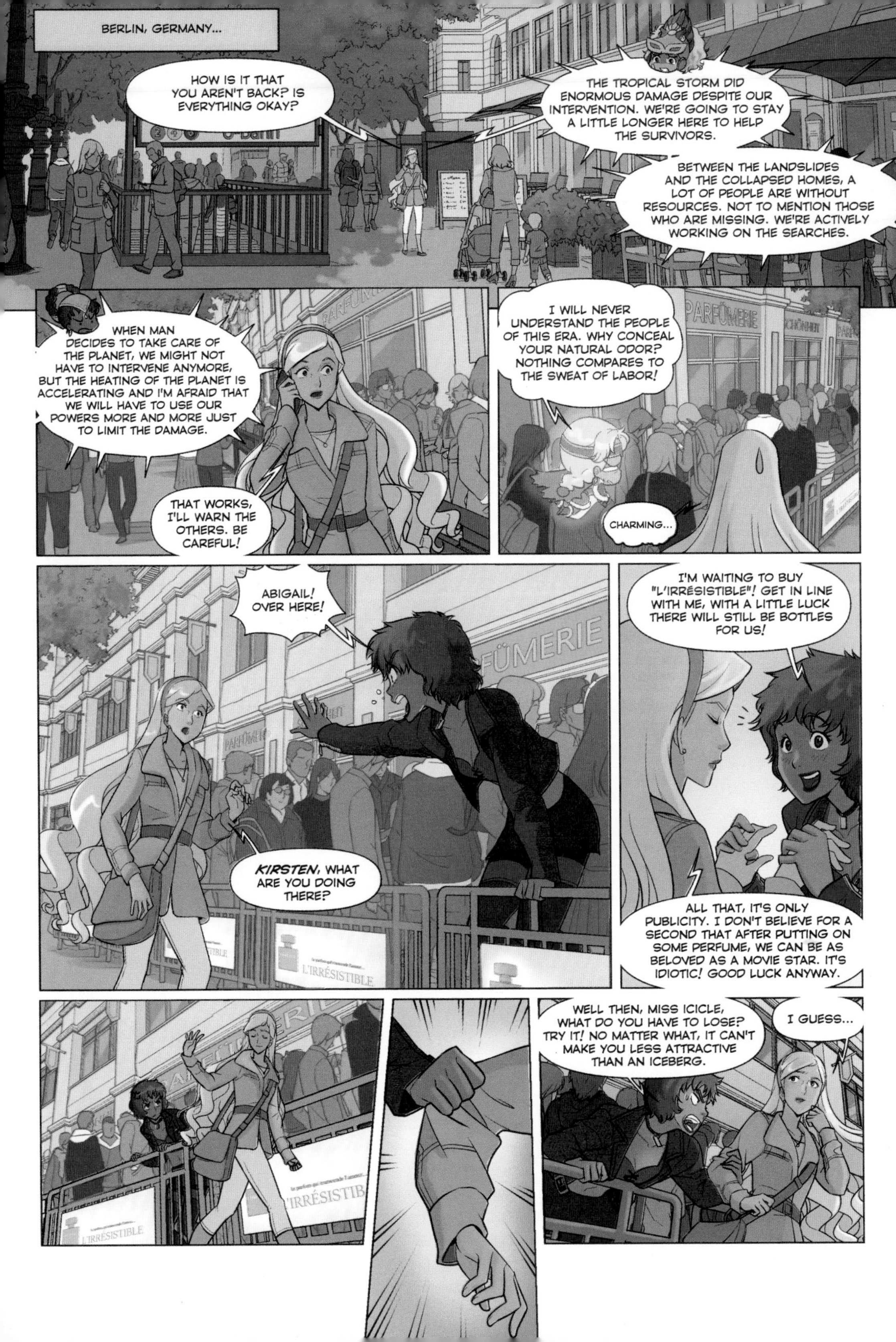
BERLIN, GERMANY...
HOW IS IT THAT YOU AREN'T BACK? IS EVERYTHING OKAY?
THE TROPICAL STORM DID ENORMOUS DAMAGE DESPITE OUR INTERVENTION. WE'RE GOING TO STAY A LITTLE LONGER HERE TO HELP THE SURVIVORS.
BETWEEN THE LANDSLIDES AND THE COLLAPSED HOMES, A LOT OF PEOPLE ARE WITHOUT RESOURCES. NOT TO MENTION THOSE WHO ARE MISSING. WE'RE ACTIVELY WORKING ON THE SEARCHES.
WHEN MAN DECIDES TO TAKE CARE OF THE PLANET, WE MIGHT NOT HAVE TO INTERVENE ANYMORE, BUT THE HEATING OF THE PLANET IS ACCELERATING AND I'M AFRAID THAT WE WILL HAVE TO USE OUR POWERS MORE AND MORE JUST TO LIMIT THE DAMAGE.
THAT WORKS, I'LL WARN THE OTHERS. BE CAREFUL!
PARFÜMERIE
I WILL NEVER UNDERSTAND THE PEOPLE OF THIS ERA. WHY CONCEAL YOUR NATURAL ODOR? NOTHING COMPARES TO THE SWEAT OF LABOR!
CHARMING...
ABIGAIL! OVER HERE!
KIRSTEN, WHAT ARE YOU DOING THERE?
L'IRRÉSISTIBLE
I'M WAITING TO BUY "L'IRRÉSISTIBLE"! GET IN LINE WITH ME, WITH A LITTLE LUCK THERE WILL STILL BE BOTTLES FOR US!
ALL THAT, IT'S ONLY PUBLICITY. I DON'T BELIEVE FOR A SECOND THAT AFTER PUTTING ON SOME PERFUME, WE CAN BE AS BELOVED AS A MOVIE STAR. IT'S IDIOTIC! GOOD LUCK ANYWAY.
WELL THEN, MISS ICICLE, WHAT DO YOU HAVE TO LOSE? TRY IT! NO MATTER WHAT, IT CAN'T MAKE YOU LESS ATTRACTIVE THAN AN ICEBERG.
I GUESS...

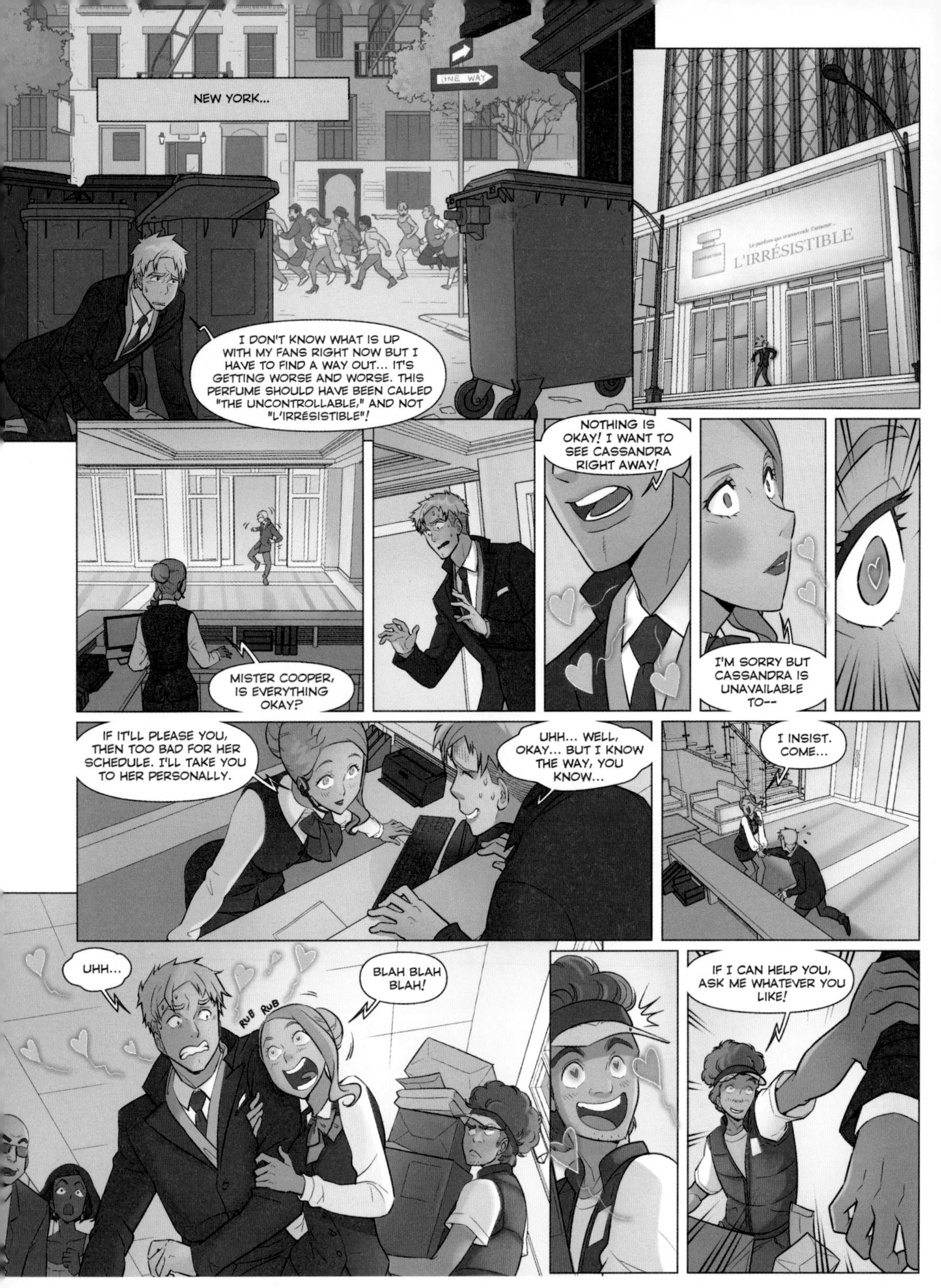

NEW YORK...
ONE WAY
I DON'T KNOW WHAT IS UP WITH MY FANS RIGHT NOW BUT I HAVE TO FIND A WAY OUT... IT'S GETTING WORSE AND WORSE. THIS PERFUME SHOULD HAVE BEEN CALLED "THE UNCONTROLLABLE," AND NOT "L'IRRÉSISTIBLE"!
L'IRRÉSISTIBLE
MISTER COOPER, IS EVERYTHING OKAY?
NOTHING IS OKAY! I WANT TO SEE CASSANDRA RIGHT AWAY!
I'M SORRY BUT CASSANDRA IS UNAVAILABLE TO--
IF IT'LL PLEASE YOU, THEN TOO BAD FOR HER SCHEDULE. I'LL TAKE YOU TO HER PERSONALLY.
UHH... WELL, OKAY... BUT I KNOW THE WAY, YOU KNOW...
I INSIST. COME...
UHH...
RUB RUB
BLAH BLAH BLAH!
IF I CAN HELP YOU, ASK ME WHATEVER YOU LIKE!

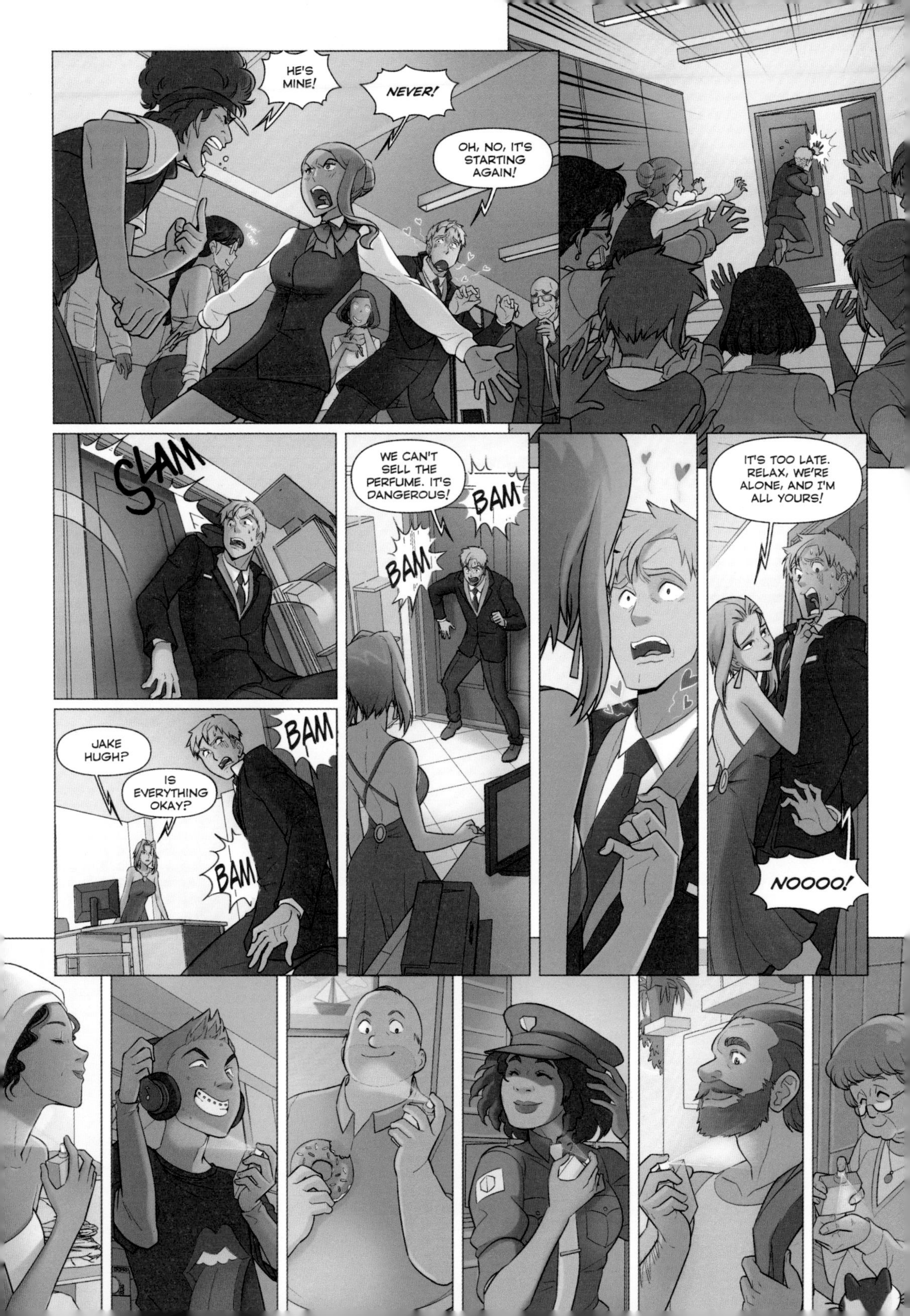
HE'S MINE!
NEVER!
OH, NO, IT'S STARTING AGAIN!
SLAM
WE CAN'T SELL THE PERFUME. IT'S DANGEROUS!
BAM
BAM
IT'S TOO LATE. RELAX, WE'RE ALONE, AND I'M ALL YOURS!
NOOOO!
BAM
JAKE HUGH?
IS EVERYTHING OKAY?
BAM

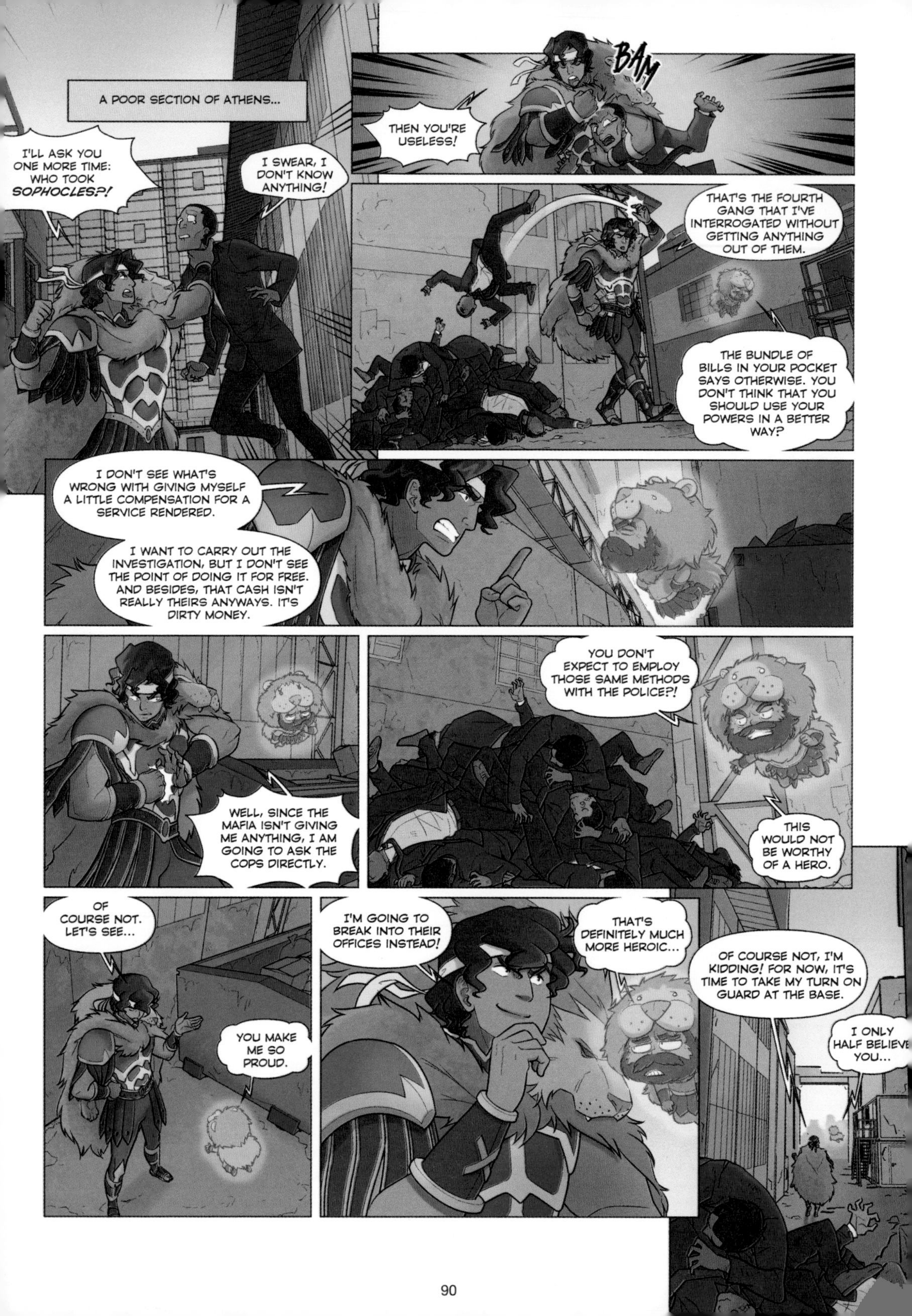

A POOR SECTION OF ATHENS...
I'LL ASK YOU ONE MORE TIME: WHO TOOK SOPHOCLES?!
I SWEAR, I DON'T KNOW ANYTHING!
BAM
THEN YOU'RE USELESS!
THAT'S THE FOURTH GANG THAT I'VE INTERROGATED WITHOUT GETTING ANYTHING OUT OF THEM.
THE BUNDLE OF BILLS IN YOUR POCKET SAYS OTHERWISE. YOU DON'T THINK THAT YOU SHOULD USE YOUR POWERS IN A BETTER WAY?
I DON'T SEE WHAT'S WRONG WITH GIVING MYSELF A LITTLE COMPENSATION FOR A SERVICE RENDERED.
I WANT TO CARRY OUT THE INVESTIGATION, BUT I DON'T SEE THE POINT OF DOING IT FOR FREE. AND BESIDES, THAT CASH ISN'T REALLY THEIRS ANYWAYS. IT'S DIRTY MONEY.
WELL, SINCE THE MAFIA ISN'T GIVING ME ANYTHING, I AM GOING TO ASK THE COPS DIRECTLY.
YOU DON'T EXPECT TO EMPLOY THOSE SAME METHODS WITH THE POLICE?!
THIS WOULD NOT BE WORTHY OF A HERO.
OF COURSE NOT. LET'S SEE...
YOU MAKE ME SO PROUD.
I'M GOING TO BREAK INTO THEIR OFFICES INSTEAD!
THAT'S DEFINITELY MUCH MORE HEROIC...
OF COURSE NOT, I'M KIDDING! FOR NOW, IT'S TIME TO TAKE MY TURN ON GUARD AT THE BASE.
I ONLY HALF BELIEVE YOU...

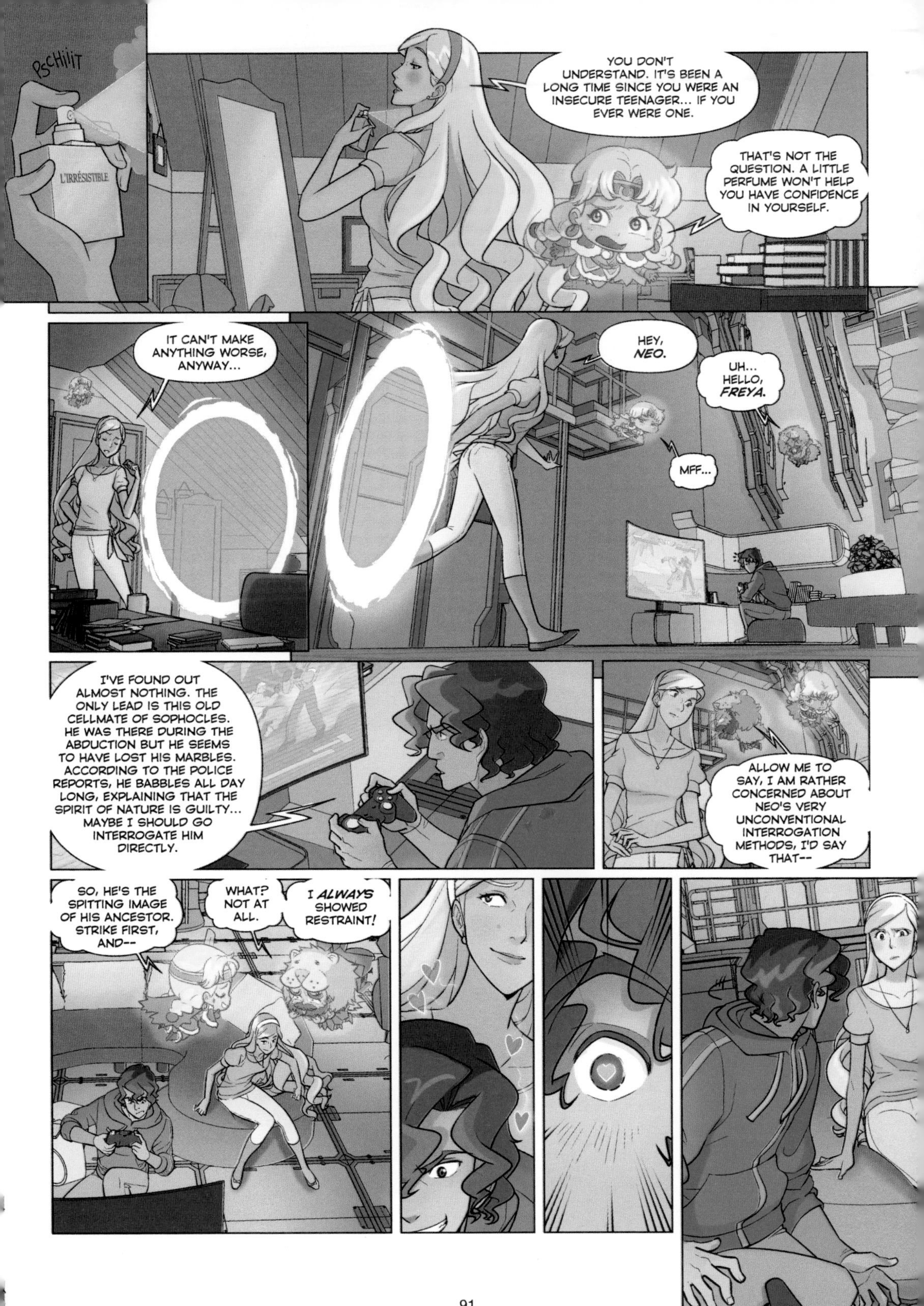
PSCHIIIT
L'IRRÉSISTIBLE
YOU DON'T UNDERSTAND. IT'S BEEN A LONG TIME SINCE YOU WERE AN INSECURE TEENAGER... IF YOU EVER WERE ONE.
THAT'S NOT THE QUESTION. A LITTLE PERFUME WON'T HELP YOU HAVE CONFIDENCE IN YOURSELF.
IT CAN'T MAKE ANYTHING WORSE, ANYWAY...
HEY, *NEO*.
UH... HELLO, *FREYA*.
MFF...
I'VE FOUND OUT ALMOST NOTHING. THE ONLY LEAD IS THIS OLD CELLMATE OF SOPHOCLES. HE WAS THERE DURING THE ABDUCTION BUT HE SEEMS TO HAVE LOST HIS MARBLES. ACCORDING TO THE POLICE REPORTS, HE BABBLES ALL DAY LONG, EXPLAINING THAT THE SPIRIT OF NATURE IS GUILTY... MAYBE I SHOULD GO INTERROGATE HIM DIRECTLY.
ALLOW ME TO SAY, I AM RATHER CONCERNED ABOUT NEO'S VERY UNCONVENTIONAL INTERROGATION METHODS, I'D SAY THAT--
SO, HE'S THE SPITTING IMAGE OF HIS ANCESTOR. STRIKE FIRST, AND--
WHAT? NOT AT ALL.
I *ALWAYS* SHOWED RESTRAINT!

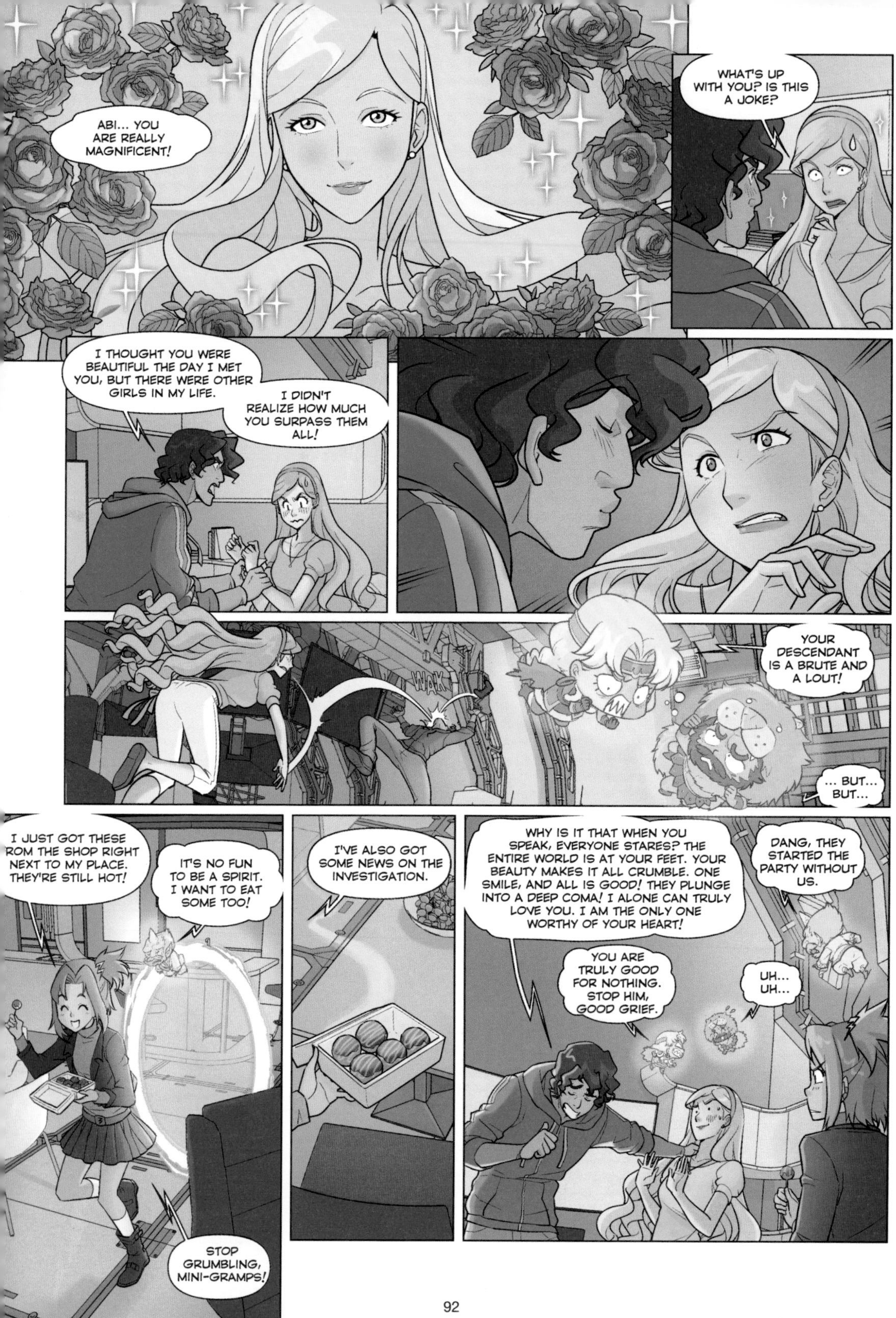
ABI... YOU ARE REALLY MAGNIFICENT!
WHAT'S UP WITH YOU? IS THIS A JOKE?
I THOUGHT YOU WERE BEAUTIFUL THE DAY I MET YOU, BUT THERE WERE OTHER GIRLS IN MY LIFE.
I DIDN'T REALIZE HOW MUCH YOU SURPASS THEM ALL!
WAK
YOUR DESCENDANT IS A BRUTE AND A LOUT!
... BUT... BUT...
I JUST GOT THESE ROM THE SHOP RIGHT NEXT TO MY PLACE. THEY'RE STILL HOT!
IT'S NO FUN TO BE A SPIRIT. I WANT TO EAT SOME TOO!
STOP GRUMBLING, MINI-GRAMPS!
I'VE ALSO GOT SOME NEWS ON THE INVESTIGATION.
WHY IS IT THAT WHEN YOU SPEAK, EVERYONE STARES? THE ENTIRE WORLD IS AT YOUR FEET. YOUR BEAUTY MAKES IT ALL CRUMBLE. ONE SMILE, AND ALL IS GOOD! THEY PLUNGE INTO A DEEP COMA! I ALONE CAN TRULY LOVE YOU. I AM THE ONLY ONE WORTHY OF YOUR HEART!
DANG, THEY STARTED THE PARTY WITHOUT US.
YOU ARE TRULY GOOD FOR NOTHING. STOP HIM, GOOD GRIEF.
UH... UH...

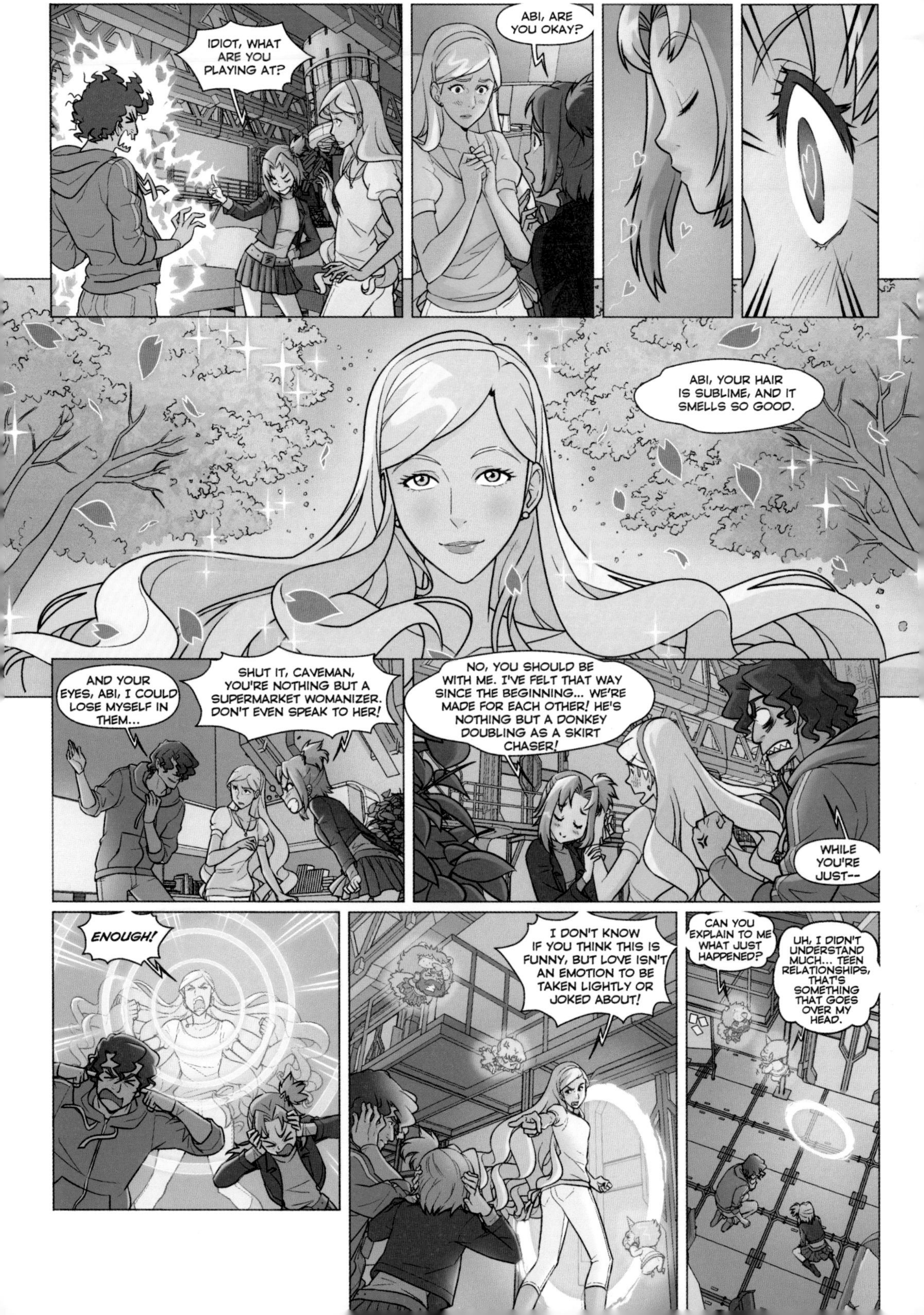
IDIOT, WHAT ARE YOU PLAYING AT?
ABI, ARE YOU OKAY?
ABI, YOUR HAIR IS SUBLIME, AND IT SMELLS SO GOOD.
AND YOUR EYES, ABI, I COULD LOSE MYSELF IN THEM...
SHUT IT, CAVEMAN, YOU'RE NOTHING BUT A SUPERMARKET WOMANIZER. DON'T EVEN SPEAK TO HER!
NO, YOU SHOULD BE WITH ME. I'VE FELT THAT WAY SINCE THE BEGINNING... WE'RE MADE FOR EACH OTHER! HE'S NOTHING BUT A DONKEY DOUBLING AS A SKIRT CHASER!
WHILE YOU'RE JUST--
ENOUGH!
I DON'T KNOW IF YOU THINK THIS IS FUNNY, BUT LOVE ISN'T AN EMOTION TO BE TAKEN LIGHTLY OR JOKED ABOUT!
CAN YOU EXPLAIN TO ME WHAT JUST HAPPENED?
UH, I DIDN'T UNDERSTAND MUCH... TEEN RELATIONSHIPS, THAT'S SOMETHING THAT GOES OVER MY HEAD.

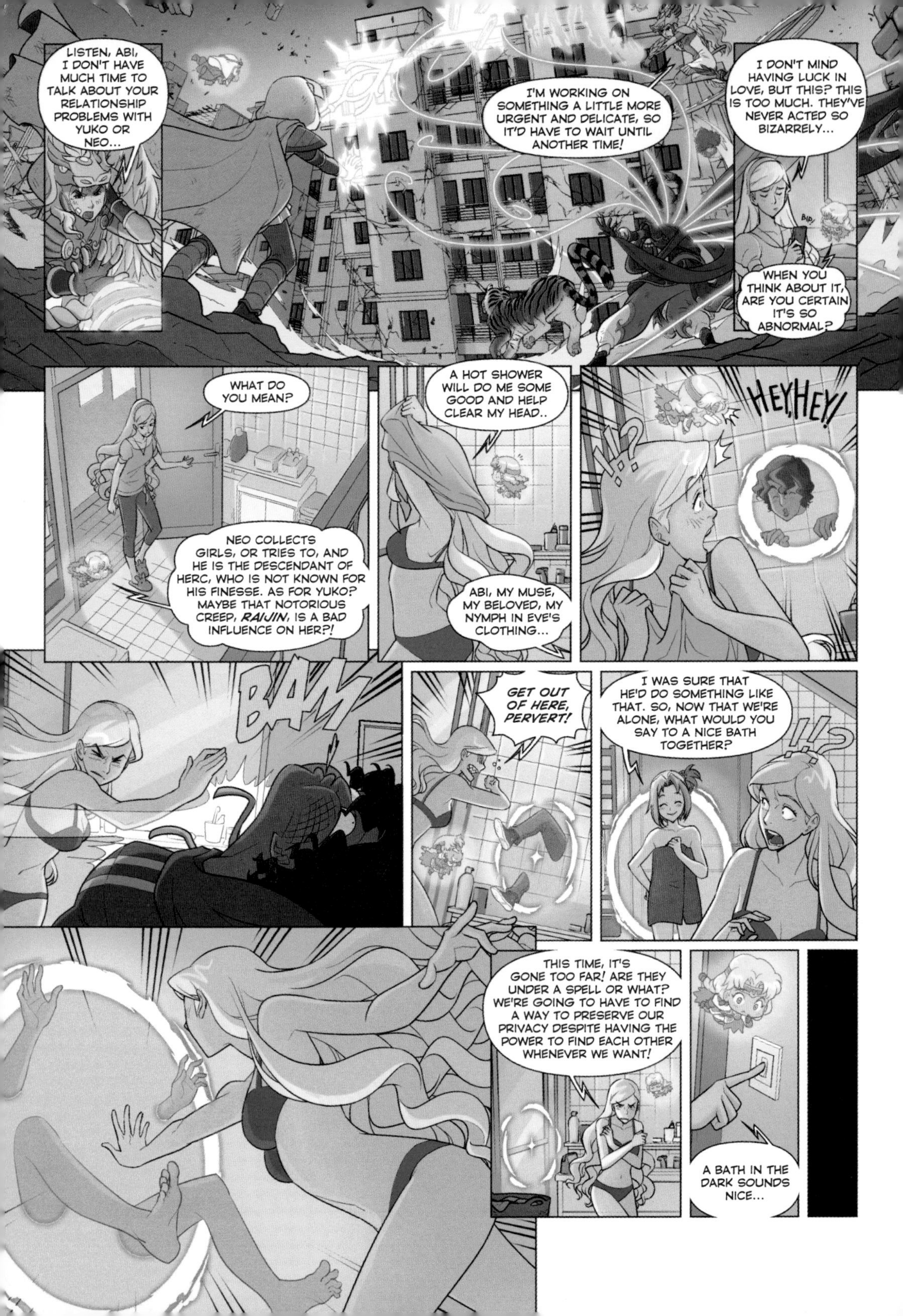
LISTEN, ABI, I DON'T HAVE MUCH TIME TO TALK ABOUT YOUR RELATIONSHIP PROBLEMS WITH YUKO OR NEO...
I'M WORKING ON SOMETHING A LITTLE MORE URGENT AND DELICATE, SO IT'D HAVE TO WAIT UNTIL ANOTHER TIME!
I DON'T MIND HAVING LUCK IN LOVE, BUT THIS? THIS IS TOO MUCH. THEY'VE NEVER ACTED SO BIZARRELY...
WHEN YOU THINK ABOUT IT, ARE YOU CERTAIN IT'S SO ABNORMAL?
WHAT DO YOU MEAN?
NEO COLLECTS GIRLS, OR TRIES TO, AND HE IS THE DESCENDANT OF HERC, WHO IS NOT KNOWN FOR HIS FINESSE. AS FOR YUKO? MAYBE THAT NOTORIOUS CREEP, RAIJIN, IS A BAD INFLUENCE ON HER?!
A HOT SHOWER WILL DO ME SOME GOOD AND HELP CLEAR MY HEAD..
ABI, MY MUSE, MY BELOVED, MY NYMPH IN EVE'S CLOTHING...
HEY, HEY!
BAM
GET OUT OF HERE, PERVERT!
I WAS SURE THAT HE'D DO SOMETHING LIKE THAT. SO, NOW THAT WE'RE ALONE, WHAT WOULD YOU SAY TO A NICE BATH TOGETHER?
THIS TIME, IT'S GONE TOO FAR! ARE THEY UNDER A SPELL OR WHAT? WE'RE GOING TO HAVE TO FIND A WAY TO PRESERVE OUR PRIVACY DESPITE HAVING THE POWER TO FIND EACH OTHER WHENEVER WE WANT!
A BATH IN THE DARK SOUNDS NICE...

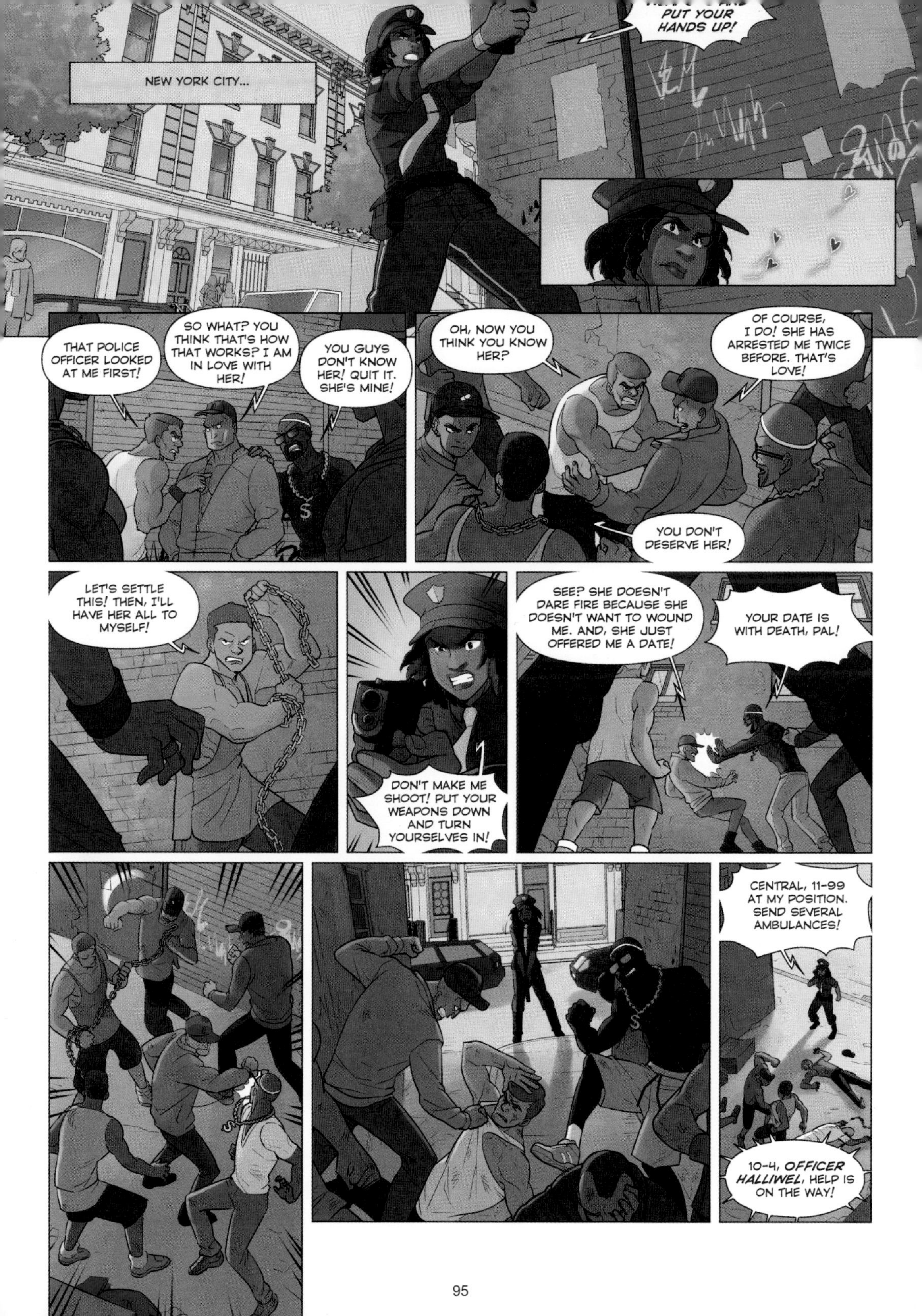

NEW YORK CITY...
PUT YOUR HANDS UP!
THAT POLICE OFFICER LOOKED AT ME FIRST!
SO WHAT? YOU THINK THAT'S HOW THAT WORKS? I AM IN LOVE WITH HER!
YOU GUYS DON'T KNOW HER! QUIT IT. SHE'S MINE!
OH, NOW YOU THINK YOU KNOW HER?
OF COURSE, I DO! SHE HAS ARRESTED ME TWICE BEFORE. THAT'S LOVE!
YOU DON'T DESERVE HER!
LET'S SETTLE THIS! THEN, I'LL HAVE HER ALL TO MYSELF!
DON'T MAKE ME SHOOT! PUT YOUR WEAPONS DOWN AND TURN YOURSELVES IN!
SEE? SHE DOESN'T DARE FIRE BECAUSE SHE DOESN'T WANT TO WOUND ME. AND, SHE JUST OFFERED ME A DATE!
YOUR DATE IS WITH DEATH, PAL!
CENTRAL, 11-99 AT MY POSITION. SEND SEVERAL AMBULANCES!
10-4, OFFICER HALLIWEL, HELP IS ON THE WAY!

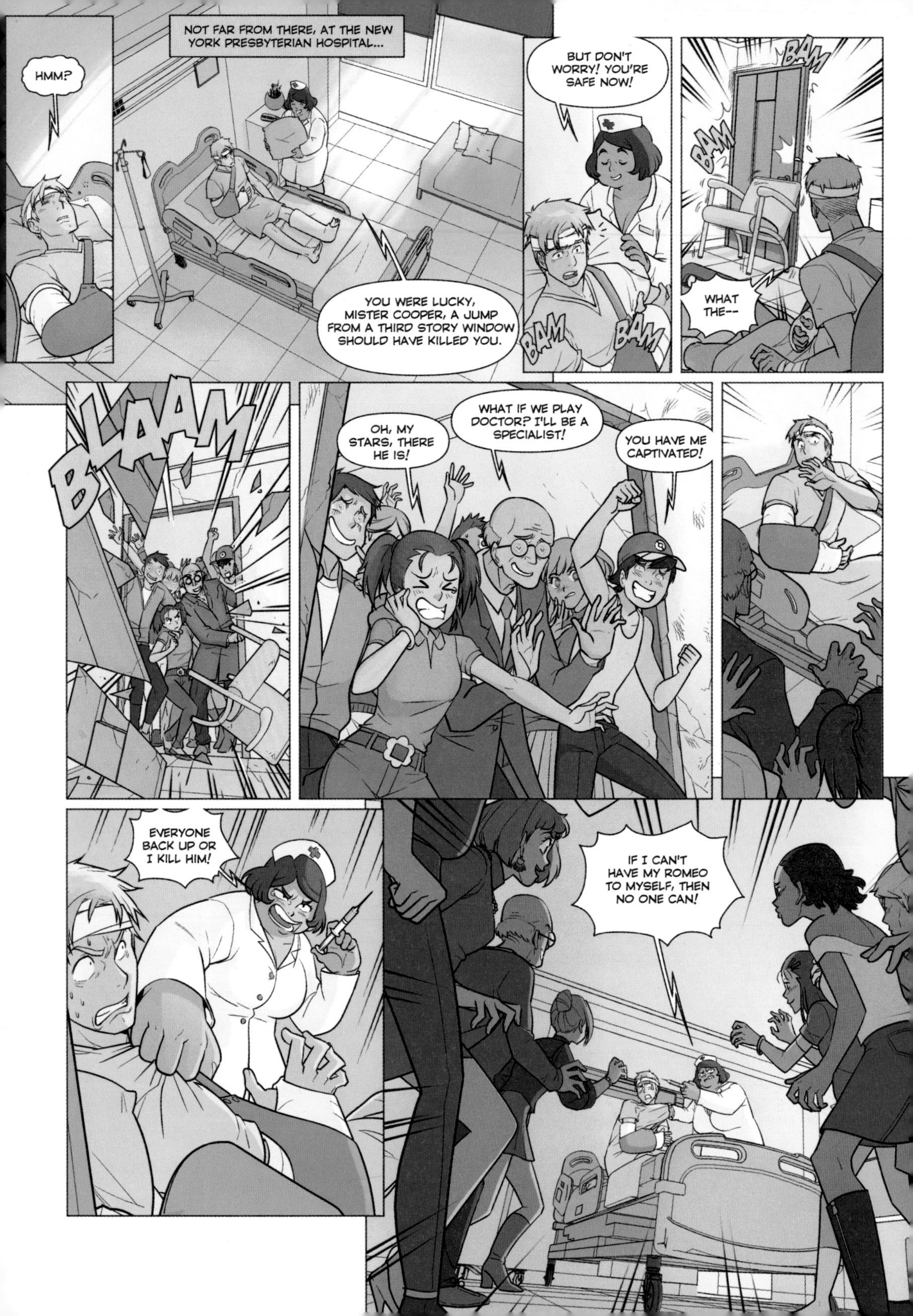

HMM?
NOT FAR FROM THERE, AT THE NEW YORK PRESBYTERIAN HOSPITAL...
YOU WERE LUCKY, MISTER COOPER, A JUMP FROM A THIRD STORY WINDOW SHOULD HAVE KILLED YOU.
BUT DON'T WORRY! YOU'RE SAFE NOW!
BAM
BAM
BAM
BAM
BAM
WHAT THE--
BLAAM
OH, MY STARS, THERE HE IS!
WHAT IF WE PLAY DOCTOR? I'LL BE A SPECIALIST!
YOU HAVE ME CAPTIVATED!
EVERYONE BACK UP OR I KILL HIM!
IF I CAN'T HAVE MY ROMEO TO MYSELF, THEN NO ONE CAN!

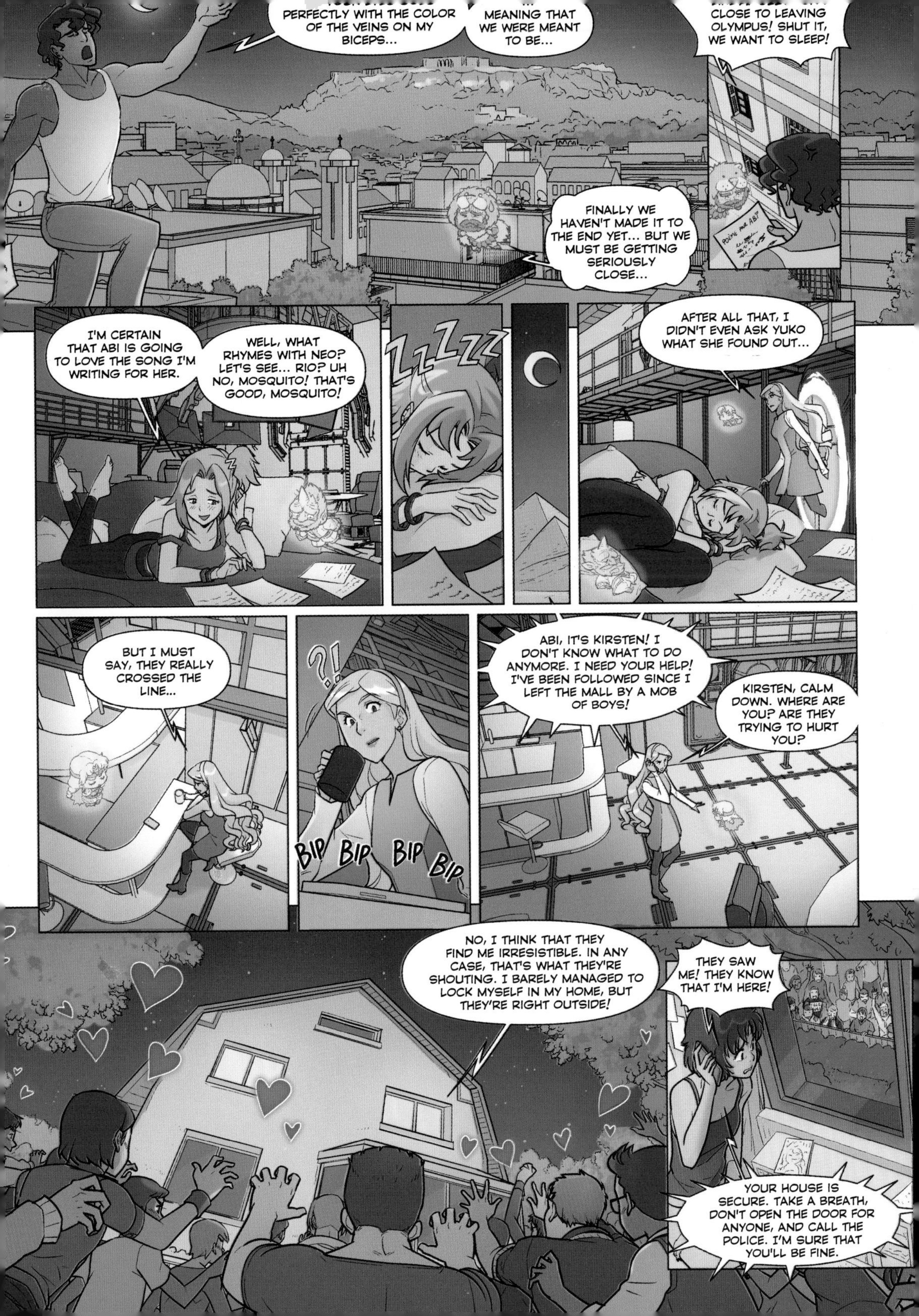
PERFECTLY WITH THE COLOR OF THE VEINS ON MY BICEPS...
MEANING THAT WE WERE MEANT TO BE...
CLOSE TO LEAVING OLYMPUS! SHUT IT, WE WANT TO SLEEP!
FINALLY WE HAVEN'T MADE IT TO THE END YET... BUT WE MUST BE GETTING SERIOUSLY CLOSE...
I'M CERTAIN THAT ABI IS GOING TO LOVE THE SONG I'M WRITING FOR HER.
WELL, WHAT RHYMES WITH NEO? LET'S SEE... RIO? UH NO, MOSQUITO! THAT'S GOOD, MOSQUITO!
ZZZZZZ
AFTER ALL THAT, I DIDN'T EVEN ASK YUKO WHAT SHE FOUND OUT...
BUT I MUST SAY, THEY REALLY CROSSED THE LINE...
?!
BIP BIP BIP BIP
ABI, IT'S KIRSTEN! I DON'T KNOW WHAT TO DO ANYMORE. I NEED YOUR HELP! I'VE BEEN FOLLOWED SINCE I LEFT THE MALL BY A MOB OF BOYS!
KIRSTEN, CALM DOWN. WHERE ARE YOU? ARE THEY TRYING TO HURT YOU?
NO, I THINK THAT THEY FIND ME IRRESISTIBLE. IN ANY CASE, THAT'S WHAT THEY'RE SHOUTING. I BARELY MANAGED TO LOCK MYSELF IN MY HOME, BUT THEY'RE RIGHT OUTSIDE!
THEY SAW ME! THEY KNOW THAT I'M HERE!
YOUR HOUSE IS SECURE. TAKE A BREATH, DON'T OPEN THE DOOR FOR ANYONE, AND CALL THE POLICE. I'M SURE THAT YOU'LL BE FINE.

DID YOU HEAR THAT?

IT SEEMS TO ME THAT THE WORD SHE USED WAS "IRRESISTIBLE"...

YES, THE PERFUME IS SURELY AT THE BOTTOM OF ALL THIS.

I'M GOING TO DO A SEARCH...

IT SEEMS YOU AREN'T THE ONLY ONE WHO BOUGHT A BOTTLE OF PERFUME...

EXCEPT THAT NOW THINGS ARE GETTING WORSE, THE PAPERS ARE TALKING ABOUT NUMEROUS WOUNDED.

TAP TAP

TAP

TAP

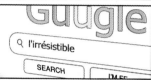

Guugle

🔍 l'irrésistible

SEARCH

I'M FE

I'M HAVING TROUBLE FINDING ANYTHING ELSE ON THIS PERFUME OTHER THAN TMD GOSSIP. WE'RE GOING TO NEED YUKO, I'M GOING TO WAKE HER.

YUKO, WAKE UP...

WHEN YOU'RE THE ONE WAKING ME, I FEEL LIKE SLEEPING BEAUTY. WHAT MIGHT I DO FOR THE LOVE OF MY LIFE?

UH... RIGHT...

I SUSPECT THE PERFUME "L'IRRÉSISTIBLE" IS THE CAUSE OF THIS WAVE OF RIOTS ALL ACROSS THE GLOBE, BUT I NEED HELP TO LEARN MORE ABOUT IT. COULD YOU DO THAT FOR ME?

ANYTHING FOR YOU!

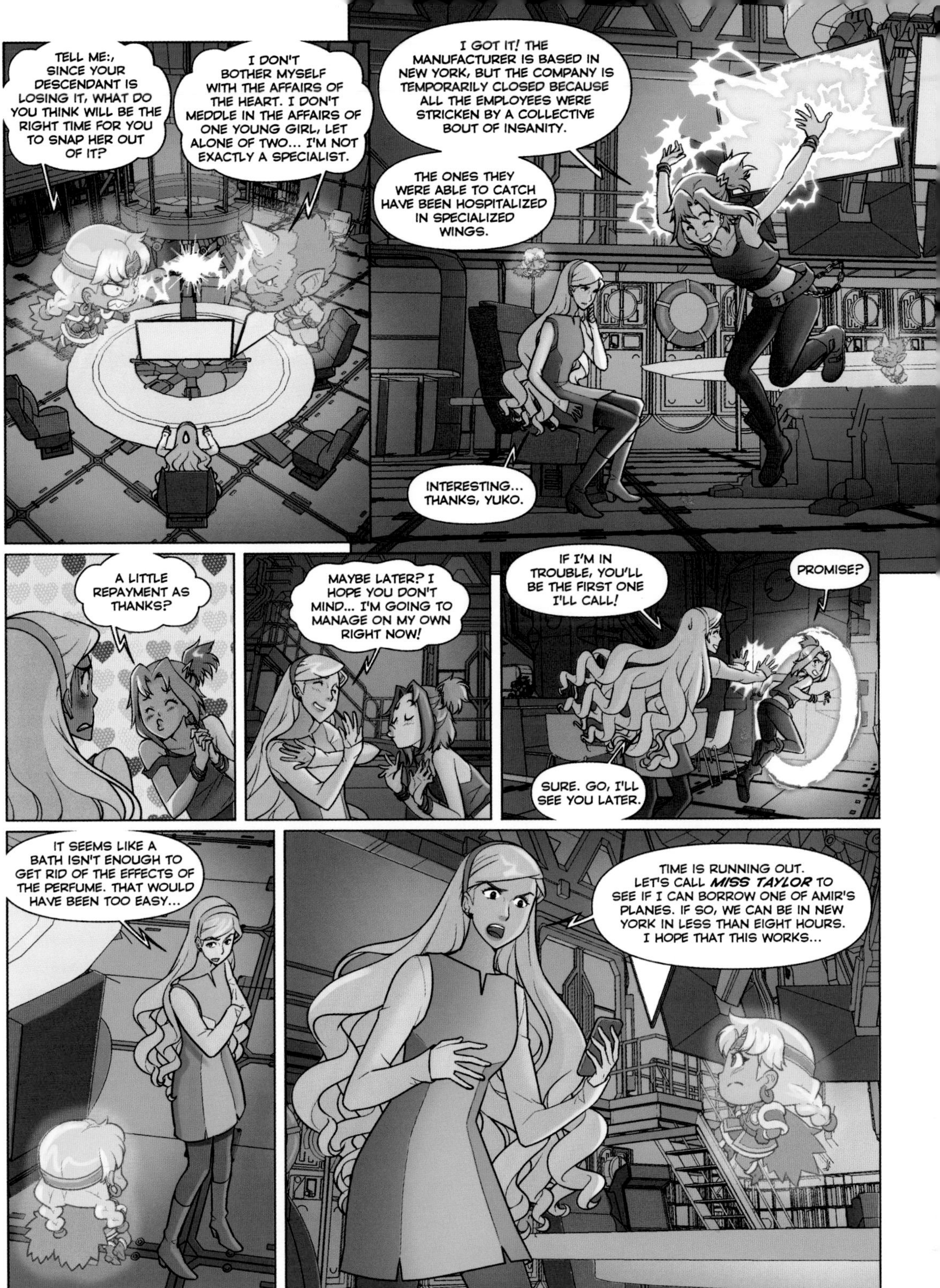
TELL ME:, SINCE YOUR DESCENDANT IS LOSING IT, WHAT DO YOU THINK WILL BE THE RIGHT TIME FOR YOU TO SNAP HER OUT OF IT?
I DON'T BOTHER MYSELF WITH THE AFFAIRS OF THE HEART. I DON'T MEDDLE IN THE AFFAIRS OF ONE YOUNG GIRL, LET ALONE OF TWO... I'M NOT EXACTLY A SPECIALIST.
I GOT IT! THE MANUFACTURER IS BASED IN NEW YORK, BUT THE COMPANY IS TEMPORARILY CLOSED BECAUSE ALL THE EMPLOYEES WERE STRICKEN BY A COLLECTIVE BOUT OF INSANITY.
THE ONES THEY WERE ABLE TO CATCH HAVE BEEN HOSPITALIZED IN SPECIALIZED WINGS.
INTERESTING... THANKS, YUKO.
A LITTLE REPAYMENT AS THANKS?
MAYBE LATER? I HOPE YOU DON'T MIND... I'M GOING TO MANAGE ON MY OWN RIGHT NOW!
IF I'M IN TROUBLE, YOU'LL BE THE FIRST ONE I'LL CALL!
PROMISE?
SURE. GO, I'LL SEE YOU LATER.
IT SEEMS LIKE A BATH ISN'T ENOUGH TO GET RID OF THE EFFECTS OF THE PERFUME. THAT WOULD HAVE BEEN TOO EASY...
TIME IS RUNNING OUT. LET'S CALL MISS TAYLOR TO SEE IF I CAN BORROW ONE OF AMIR'S PLANES. IF SO, WE CAN BE IN NEW YORK IN LESS THAN EIGHT HOURS. I HOPE THAT THIS WORKS...

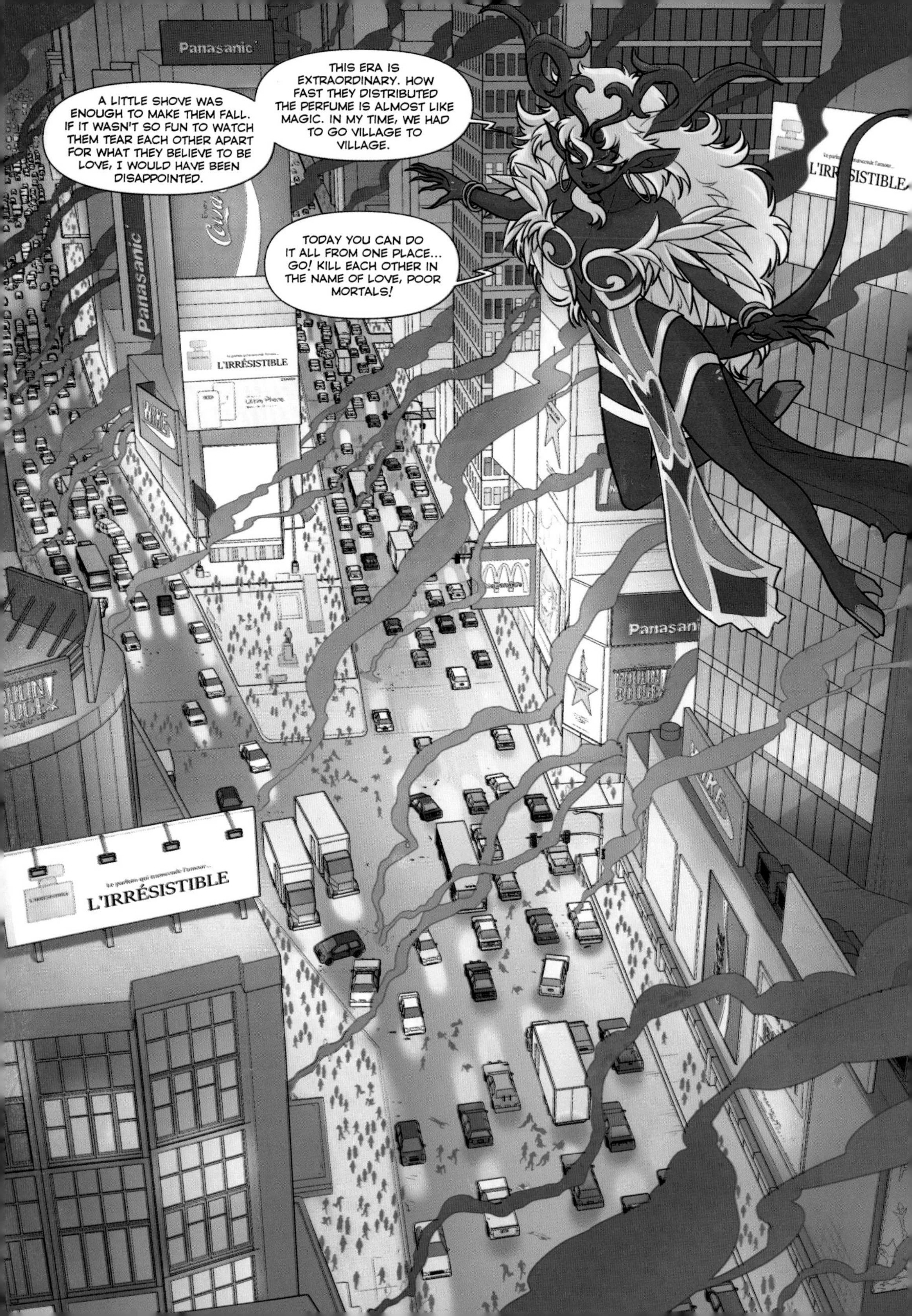
A LITTLE SHOVE WAS ENOUGH TO MAKE THEM FALL. IF IT WASN'T SO FUN TO WATCH THEM TEAR EACH OTHER APART FOR WHAT THEY BELIEVE TO BE LOVE, I WOULD HAVE BEEN DISAPPOINTED.
THIS ERA IS EXTRAORDINARY. HOW FAST THEY DISTRIBUTED THE PERFUME IS ALMOST LIKE MAGIC. IN MY TIME, WE HAD TO GO VILLAGE TO VILLAGE.
TODAY YOU CAN DO IT ALL FROM ONE PLACE... GO! KILL EACH OTHER IN THE NAME OF LOVE, POOR MORTALS!
Panasanic
Panasanic
L'IRRÉSISTIBLE
Ultim Phone
Panasanic
L'IRRÉSISTIBLE

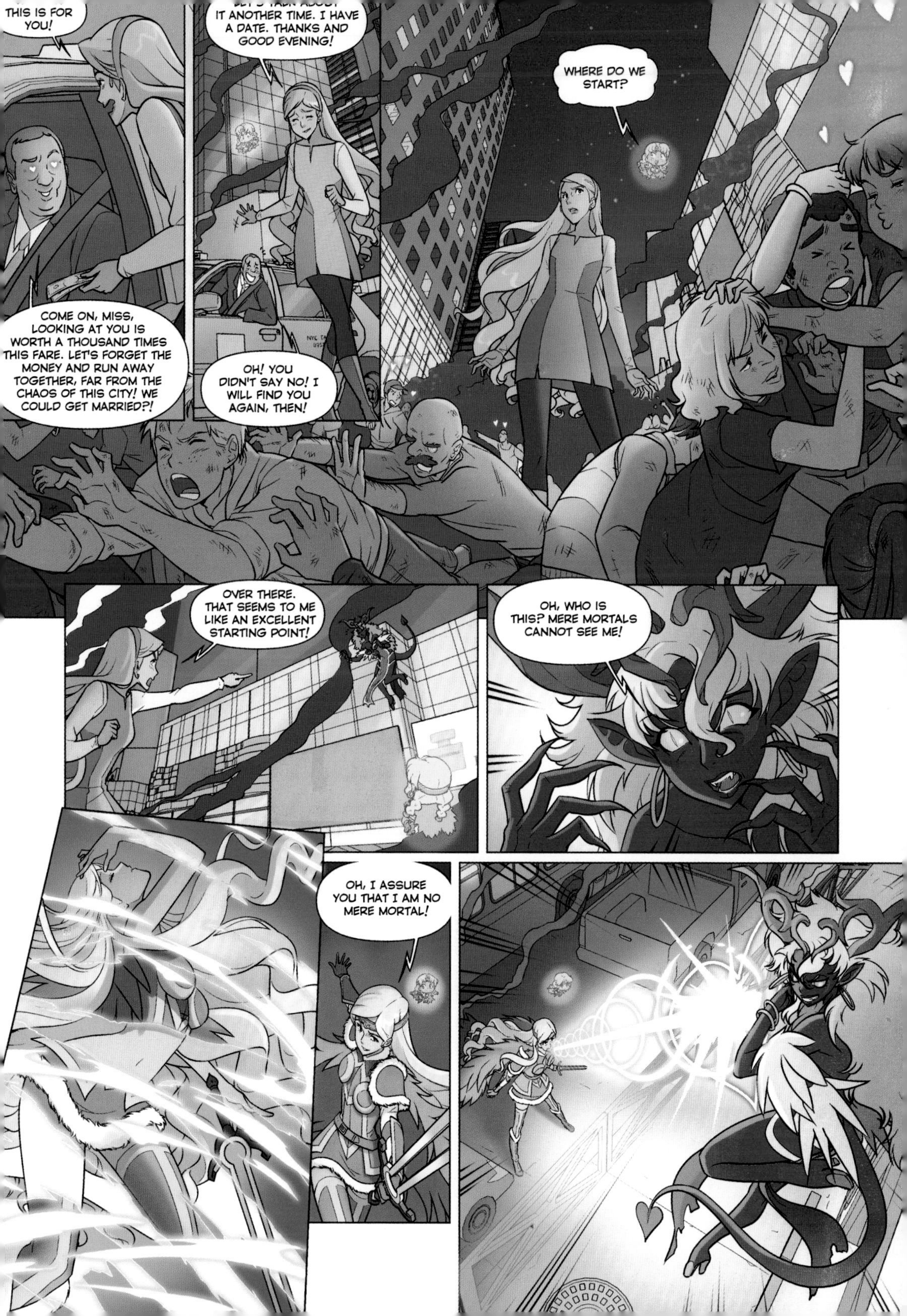
THIS IS FOR YOU!
COME ON, MISS, LOOKING AT YOU IS WORTH A THOUSAND TIMES THIS FARE. LET'S FORGET THE MONEY AND RUN AWAY TOGETHER, FAR FROM THE CHAOS OF THIS CITY! WE COULD GET MARRIED?!
IT ANOTHER TIME. I HAVE A DATE. THANKS AND GOOD EVENING!
OH! YOU DIDN'T SAY NO! I WILL FIND YOU AGAIN, THEN!
WHERE DO WE START?
OVER THERE. THAT SEEMS TO ME LIKE AN EXCELLENT STARTING POINT!
OH, WHO IS THIS? MERE MORTALS CANNOT SEE ME!
OH, I ASSURE YOU THAT I AM NO MERE MORTAL!

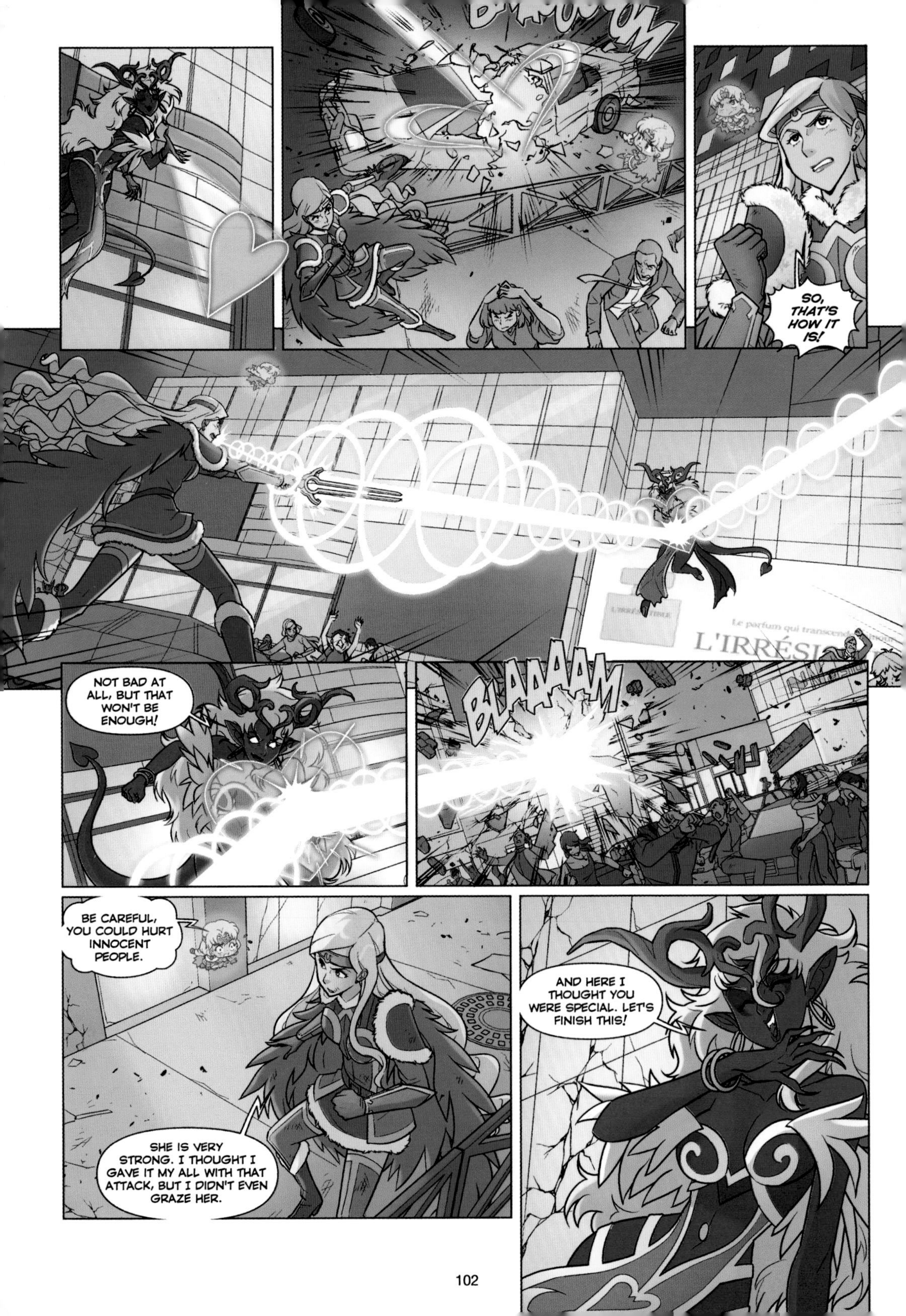
SO, THAT'S HOW IT IS!
NOT BAD AT ALL, BUT THAT WON'T BE ENOUGH!
BLAAAAM
BE CAREFUL, YOU COULD HURT INNOCENT PEOPLE.
SHE IS VERY STRONG. I THOUGHT I GAVE IT MY ALL WITH THAT ATTACK, BUT I DIDN'T EVEN GRAZE HER.
AND HERE I THOUGHT YOU WERE SPECIAL. LET'S FINISH THIS!

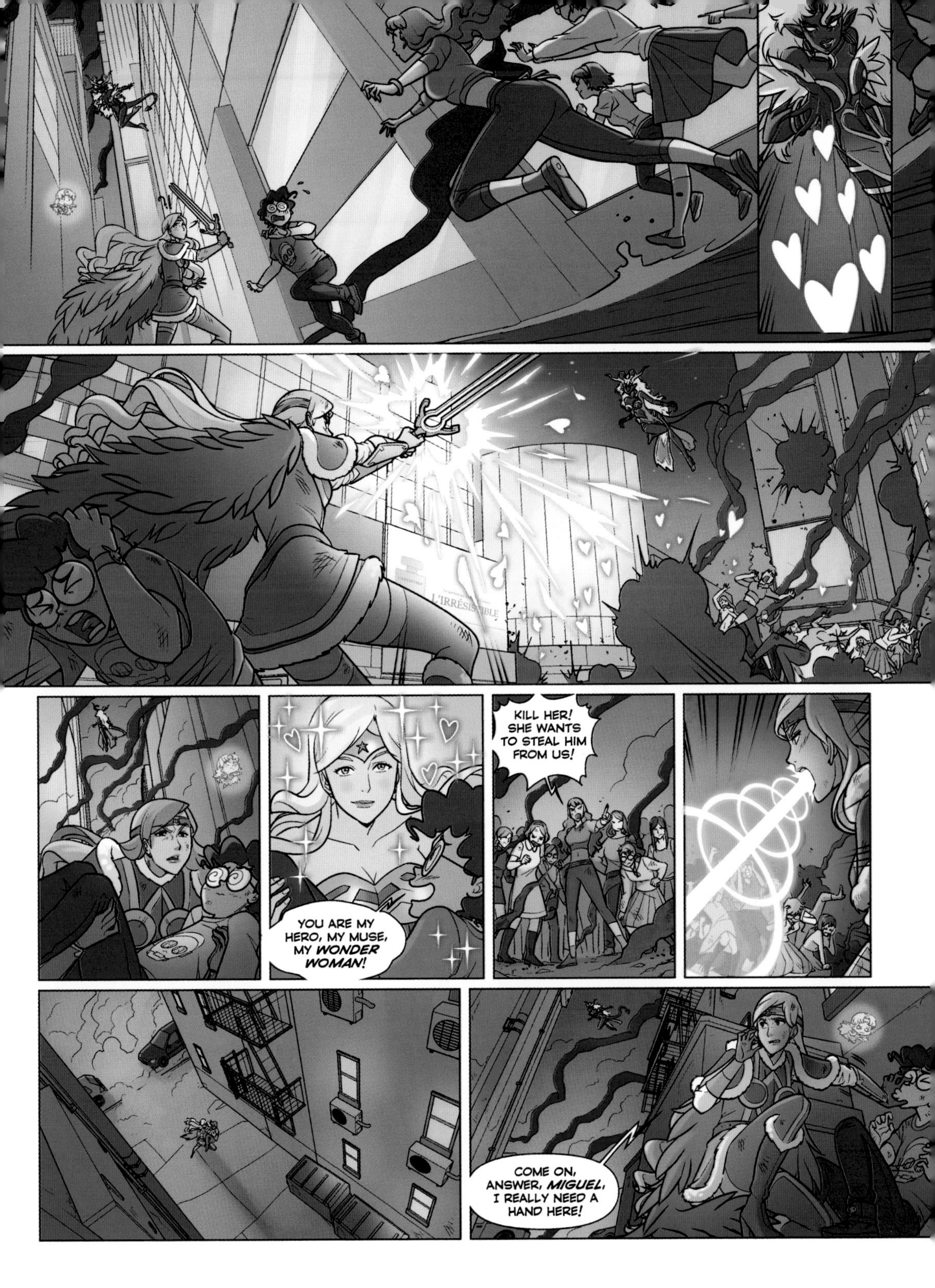

YOU ARE MY HERO, MY MUSE, MY *WONDER WOMAN*!
KILL HER! SHE WANTS TO STEAL HIM FROM US!
COME ON, ANSWER, *MIGUEL*, I REALLY NEED A HAND HERE!

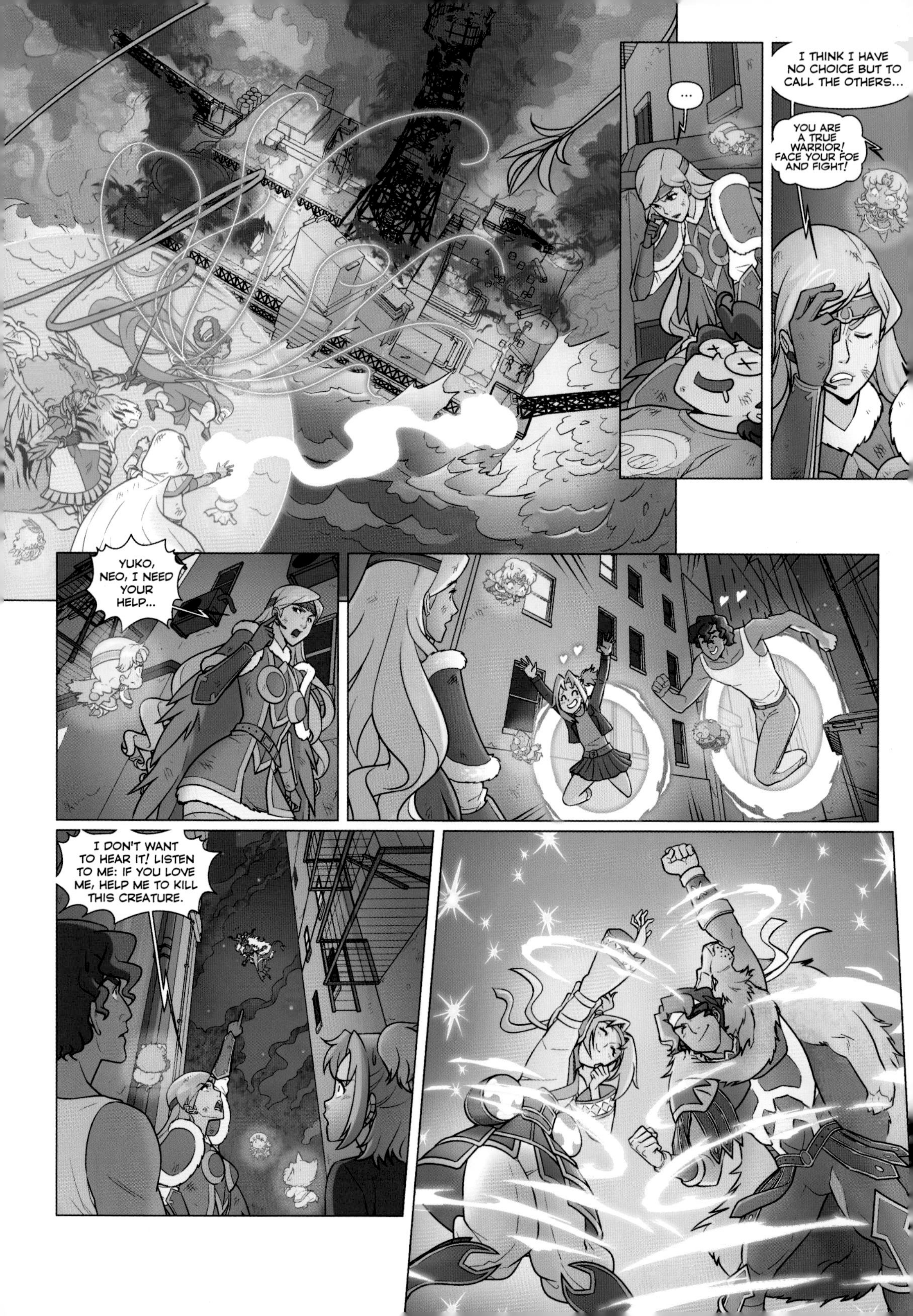
...
I THINK I HAVE NO CHOICE BUT TO CALL THE OTHERS...
YOU ARE A TRUE WARRIOR! FACE YOUR FOE AND FIGHT!
YUKO, NEO, I NEED YOUR HELP...
I DON'T WANT TO HEAR IT! LISTEN TO ME: IF YOU LOVE ME, HELP ME TO KILL THIS CREATURE.

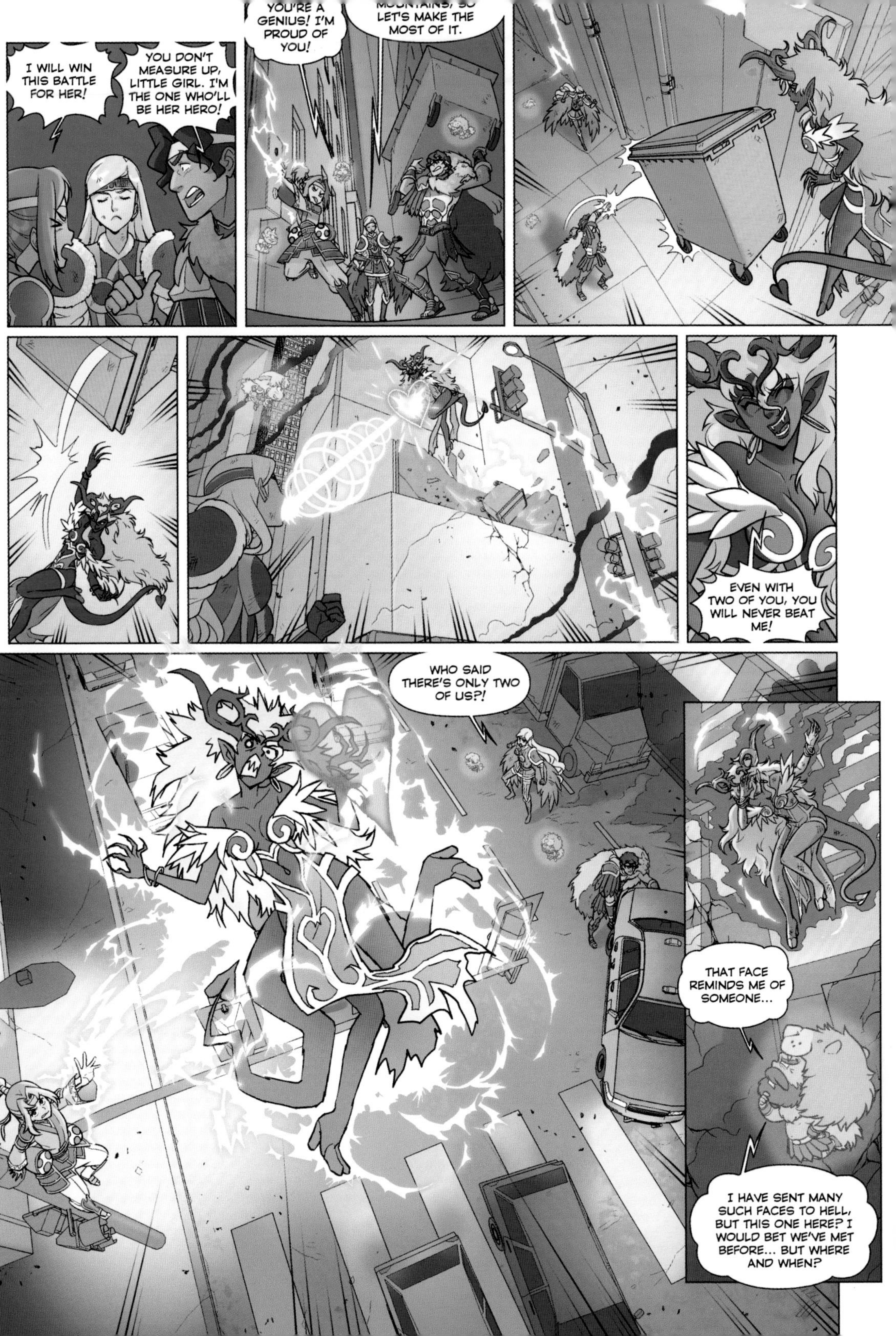

I WILL WIN THIS BATTLE FOR HER!
YOU DON'T MEASURE UP, LITTLE GIRL. I'M THE ONE WHO'LL BE HER HERO!
YOU'RE A GENIUS! I'M PROUD OF YOU!
LET'S MAKE THE MOST OF IT.
EVEN WITH TWO OF YOU, YOU WILL NEVER BEAT ME!
WHO SAID THERE'S ONLY TWO OF US?!
THAT FACE REMINDS ME OF SOMEONE...
I HAVE SENT MANY SUCH FACES TO HELL, BUT THIS ONE HERE? I WOULD BET WE'VE MET BEFORE... BUT WHERE AND WHEN?

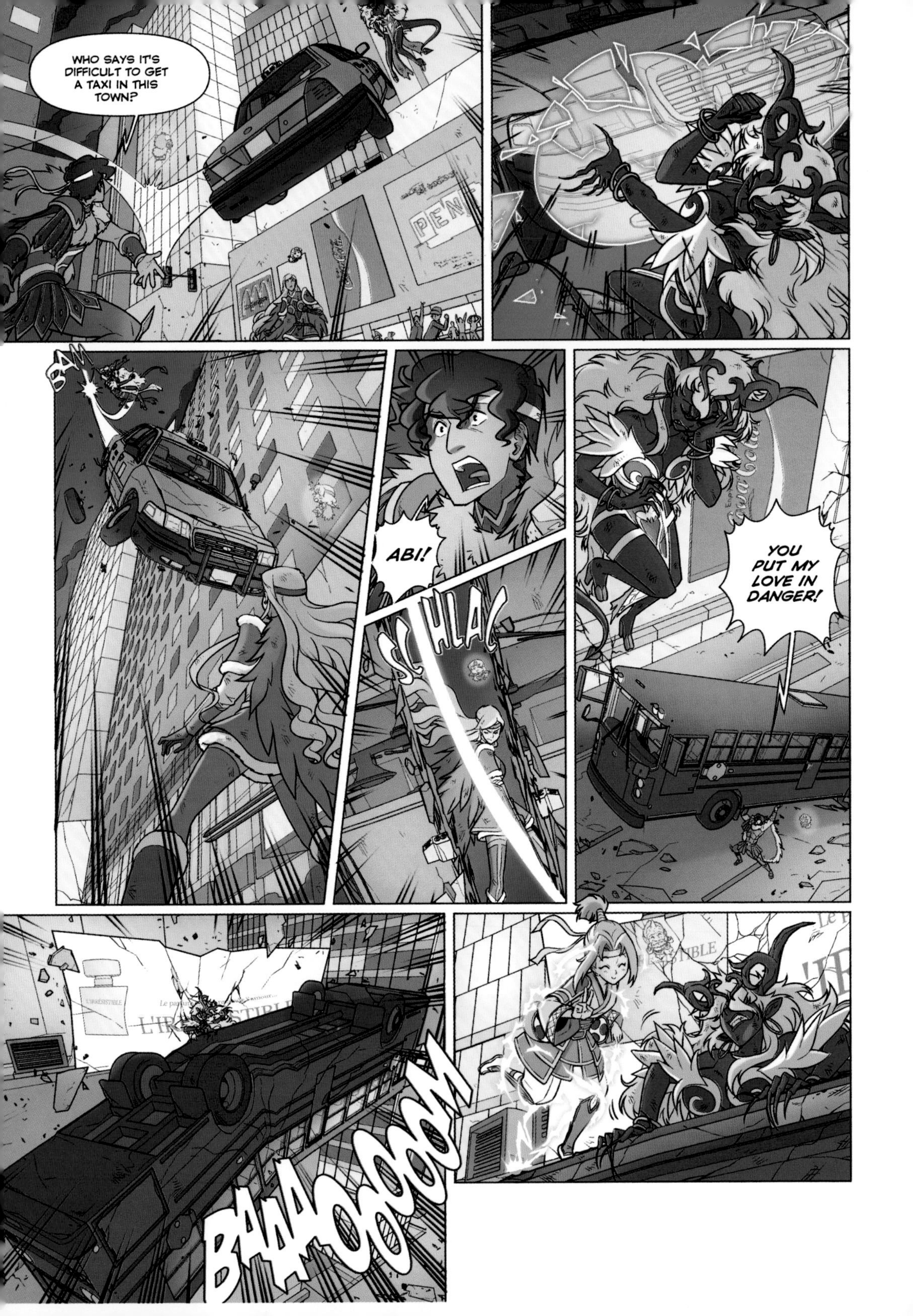
WHO SAYS IT'S DIFFICULT TO GET A TAXI IN THIS TOWN?
BAM
ABI!
SCHLAC
YOU PUT MY LOVE IN DANGER!
L'IRRÉSISTIBLE
BAAAOOOOM

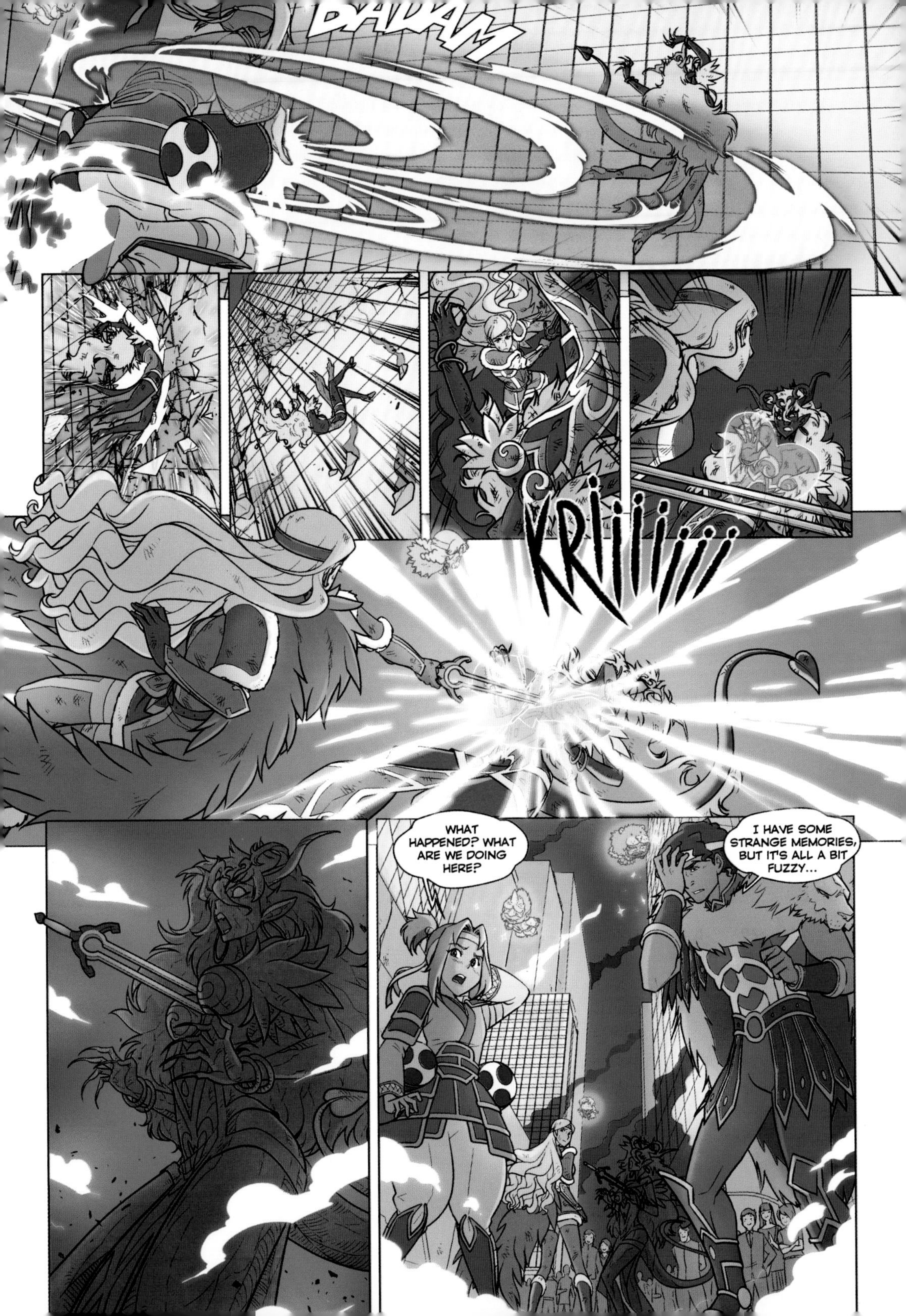
BADAM
KRIIIIIIII
WHAT HAPPENED? WHAT ARE WE DOING HERE?
I HAVE SOME STRANGE MEMORIES, BUT IT'S ALL A BIT FUZZY...

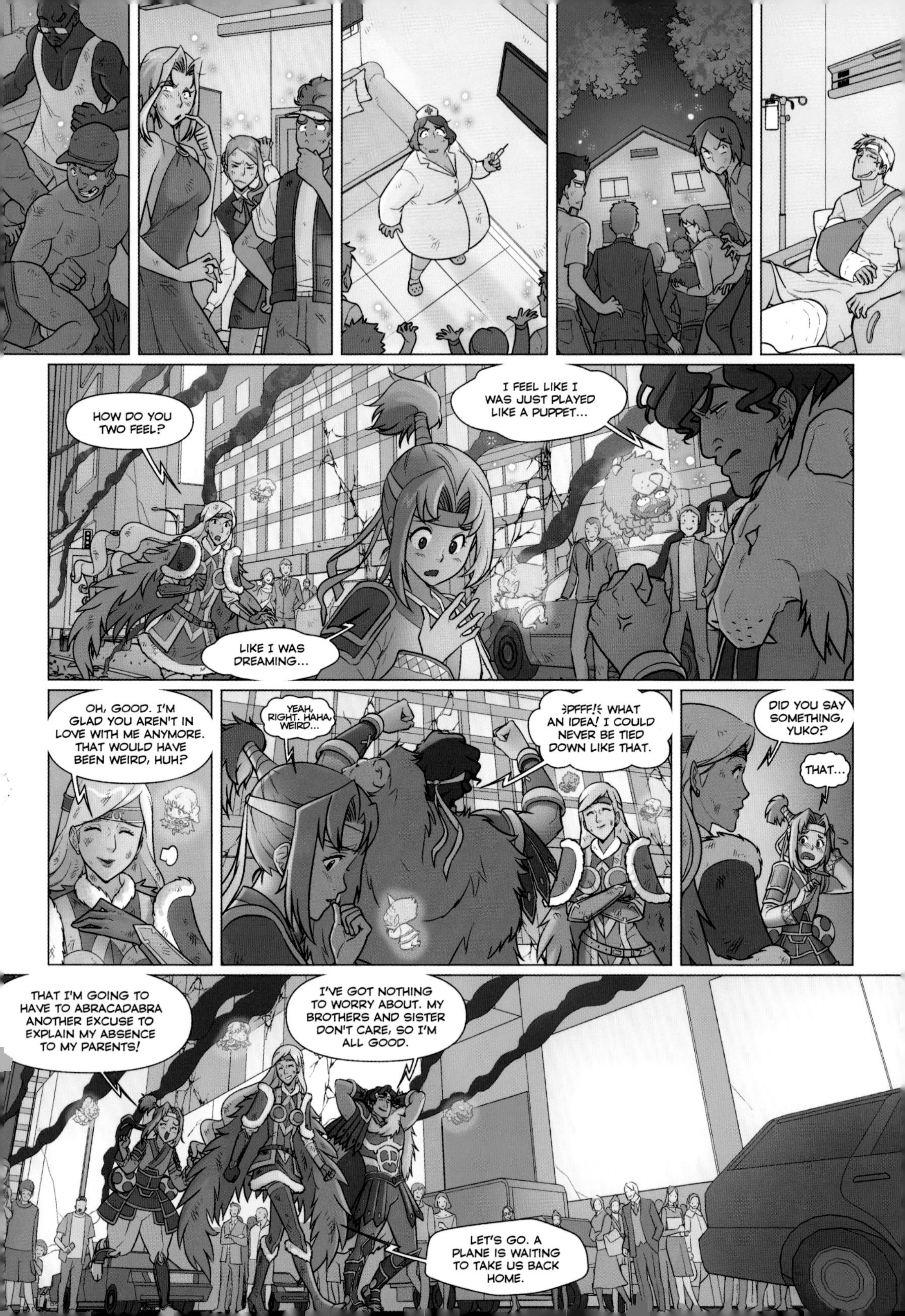
HOW DO YOU TWO FEEL?
I FEEL LIKE I WAS JUST PLAYED LIKE A PUPPET...
LIKE I WAS DREAMING...
OH, GOOD. I'M GLAD YOU AREN'T IN LOVE WITH ME ANYMORE. THAT WOULD HAVE BEEN WEIRD, HUH?
YEAH, RIGHT. HAHA, WEIRD...
PFFF! WHAT AN IDEA! I COULD NEVER BE TIED DOWN LIKE THAT.
DID YOU SAY SOMETHING, YUKO?
THAT...
THAT I'M GOING TO HAVE TO ABRACADABRA ANOTHER EXCUSE TO EXPLAIN MY ABSENCE TO MY PARENTS!
I'VE GOT NOTHING TO WORRY ABOUT. MY BROTHERS AND SISTER DON'T CARE, SO I'M ALL GOOD.
LET'S GO. A PLANE IS WAITING TO TAKE US BACK HOME.

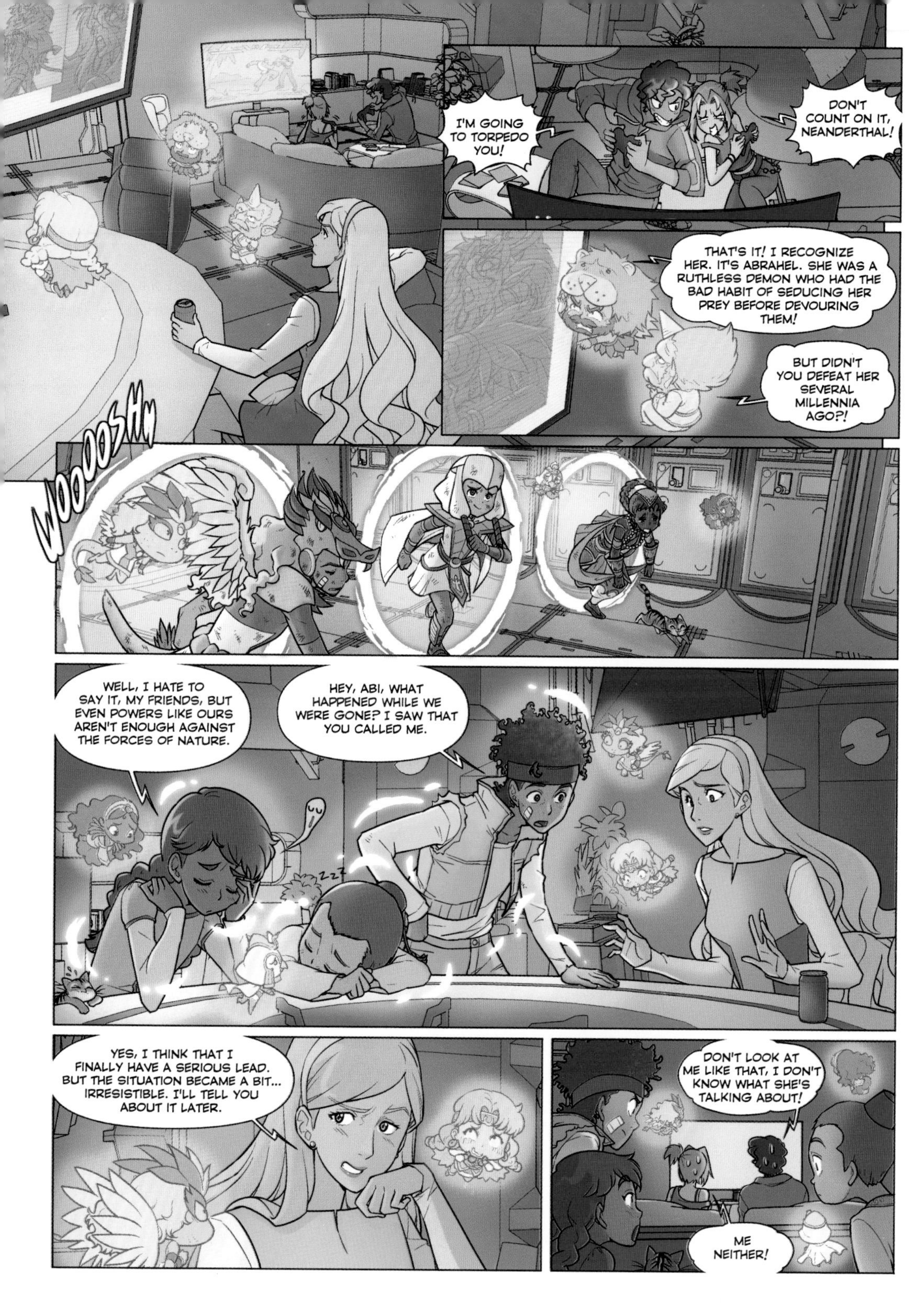
I'M GOING TO TORPEDO YOU!
DON'T COUNT ON IT, NEANDERTHAL!
THAT'S IT! I RECOGNIZE HER. IT'S ABRAHEL. SHE WAS A RUTHLESS DEMON WHO HAD THE BAD HABIT OF SEDUCING HER PREY BEFORE DEVOURING THEM!
BUT DIDN'T YOU DEFEAT HER SEVERAL MILLENNIA AGO?!
WOOOOSHH
WELL, I HATE TO SAY IT, MY FRIENDS, BUT EVEN POWERS LIKE OURS AREN'T ENOUGH AGAINST THE FORCES OF NATURE.
HEY, ABI, WHAT HAPPENED WHILE WE WERE GONE? I SAW THAT YOU CALLED ME.
YES, I THINK THAT I FINALLY HAVE A SERIOUS LEAD. BUT THE SITUATION BECAME A BIT... IRRESISTIBLE. I'LL TELL YOU ABOUT IT LATER.
DON'T LOOK AT ME LIKE THAT, I DON'T KNOW WHAT SHE'S TALKING ABOUT!
ME NEITHER!

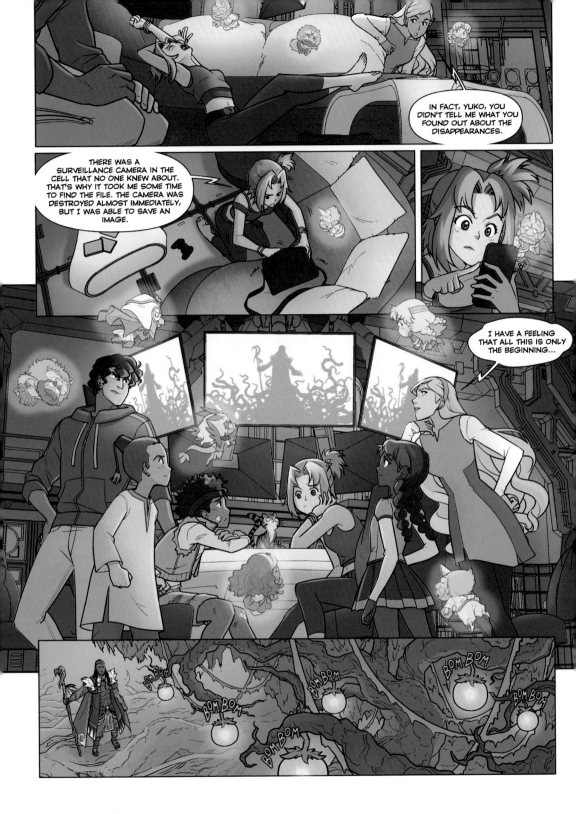

IN FACT, YUKO, YOU DIDN'T TELL ME WHAT YOU FOUND OUT ABOUT THE DISAPPEARANCES.

THERE WAS A SURVEILLANCE CAMERA IN THE CELL THAT NO ONE KNEW ABOUT. THAT'S WHY IT TOOK ME SOME TIME TO FIND THE FILE. THE CAMERA WAS DESTROYED ALMOST IMMEDIATELY, BUT I WAS ABLE TO SAVE AN IMAGE.

I HAVE A FEELING THAT ALL THIS IS ONLY THE BEGINNING...

BOM BOM

BOM BOM

BOM BOM

BOM BOM

BOM BOM

THE MYTHICS

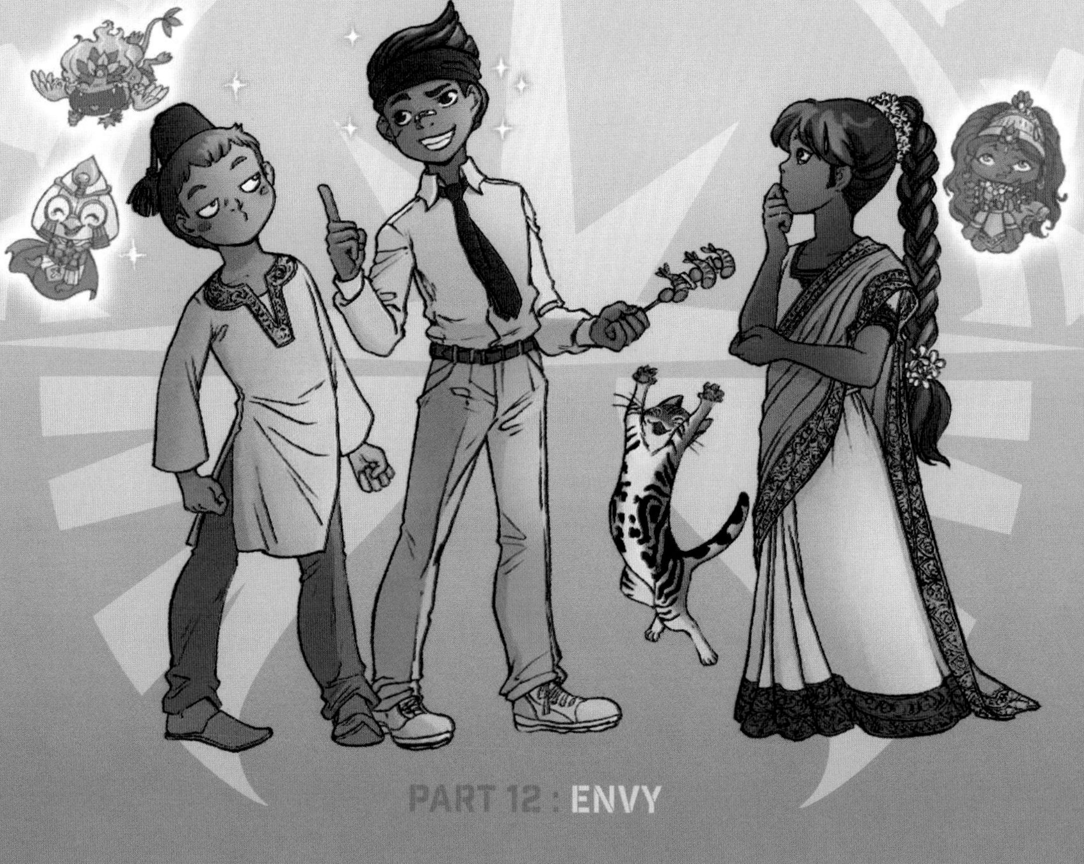

PART 12 : ENVY

Story
PHILIPPE OGAKI
WITH HELP FROM RÉMI GUÉRIN

Art
ALICE PICARD

Color
MAGALI PAILLAT

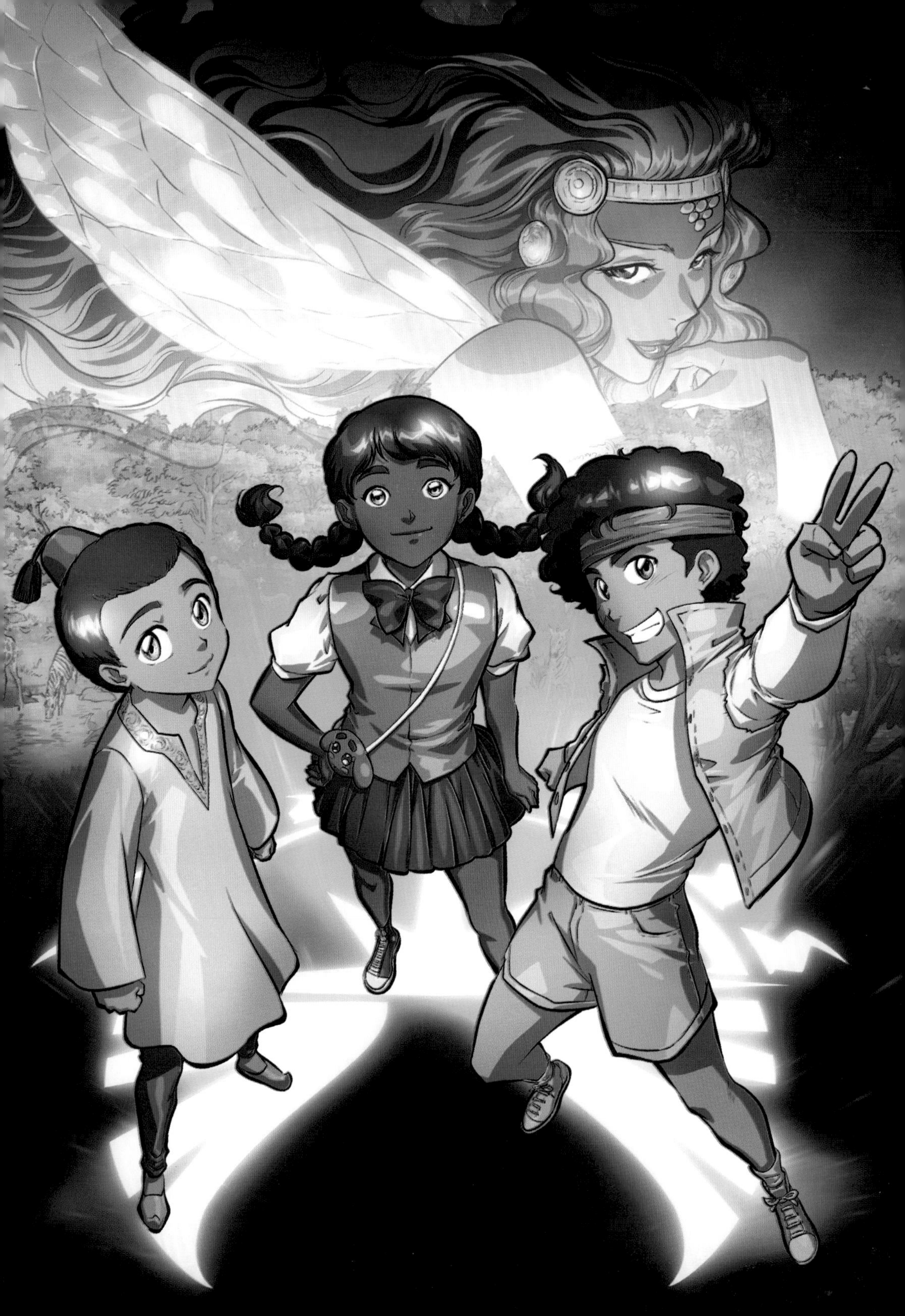

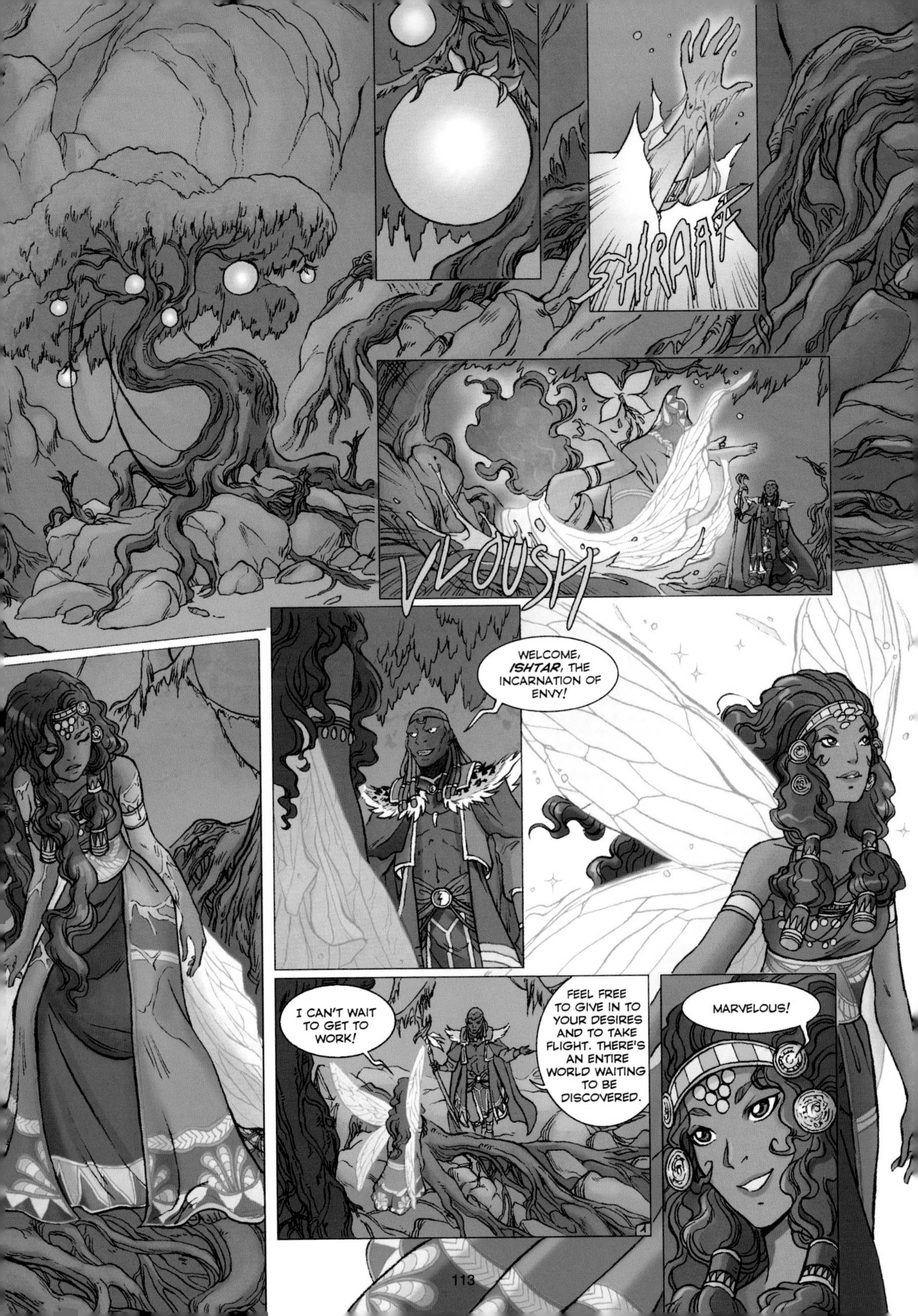
SHRAAA
VLOUSH
WELCOME, ISHTAR, THE INCARNATION OF ENVY!
I CAN'T WAIT TO GET TO WORK!
FEEL FREE TO GIVE IN TO YOUR DESIRES AND TO TAKE FLIGHT. THERE'S AN ENTIRE WORLD WAITING TO BE DISCOVERED.
MARVELOUS!

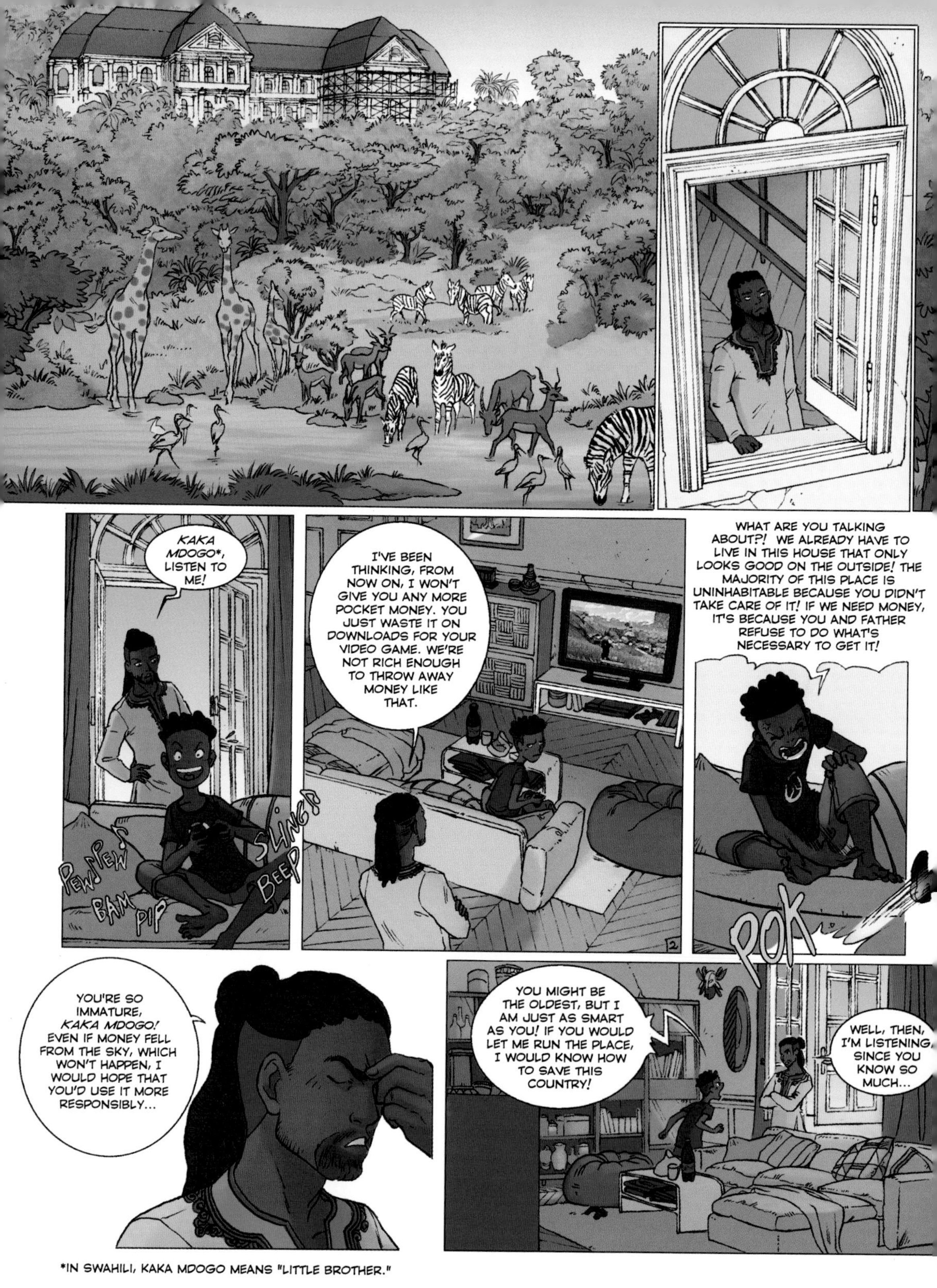

KAKA MDOGO*, LISTEN TO ME!
PEW PEW
BAM
PIP
SLING
BEEP
I'VE BEEN THINKING, FROM NOW ON, I WON'T GIVE YOU ANY MORE POCKET MONEY. YOU JUST WASTE IT ON DOWNLOADS FOR YOUR VIDEO GAME. WE'RE NOT RICH ENOUGH TO THROW AWAY MONEY LIKE THAT.
WHAT ARE YOU TALKING ABOUT?! WE ALREADY HAVE TO LIVE IN THIS HOUSE THAT ONLY LOOKS GOOD ON THE OUTSIDE! THE MAJORITY OF THIS PLACE IS UNINHABITABLE BECAUSE YOU DIDN'T TAKE CARE OF IT! IF WE NEED MONEY, IT'S BECAUSE YOU AND FATHER REFUSE TO DO WHAT'S NECESSARY TO GET IT!
POK
YOU'RE SO IMMATURE, KAKA MDOGO! EVEN IF MONEY FELL FROM THE SKY, WHICH WON'T HAPPEN, I WOULD HOPE THAT YOU'D USE IT MORE RESPONSIBLY...
YOU MIGHT BE THE OLDEST, BUT I AM JUST AS SMART AS YOU! IF YOU WOULD LET ME RUN THE PLACE, I WOULD KNOW HOW TO SAVE THIS COUNTRY!
WELL, THEN, I'M LISTENING, SINCE YOU KNOW SO MUCH...

*IN SWAHILI, KAKA MDOGO MEANS "LITTLE BROTHER."

ALL WE HAVE TO DO IS SELL THE WATER FROM OUR RIVERS. EVERYONE NEEDS WATER, AND WE HAVE SO MUCH JUST SITTING THERE! WE COULD MAKE A FORTUNE! LET ME PRESENT MY PLAN. I'M OLD ENOUGH TO ACCOMPANY YOU TO THE COUNCIL OF MINISTERS. I COULD SAVE THE COUNTRY! ME!

KILA JAMBO NA WAKATI WAKE,* FOR THE THOUSANDTH TIME, RULING A COUNTRY IS NOT A GAME. YOU NEED A LITTLE MORE TIME AND EXPERIENCE THAN YOU SEEM TO WANT TO GIVE IT! YOU STILL HAVE TO GROW AND LEARN.

WELL, YOU TAKE YOURSELF TOO SERIOUSLY!

THE DELEGATION IS ARRIVING, MISTER PRIME MINISTER. THEY'RE WAITING IN THE BOARDROOM.

I'LL BE RIGHT THERE. AS FOR OUR CONVERSATION, SEMMI, WE WILL FINISH IT WHEN I GET BACK!

YOU, THERE, MAKE SURE WE ARE NOT DISTURBED. AS FOR YOU, PLEASE TAKE MY BROTHER BACK TO HIS ROOM AND MAKE SURE HE DOES NOT LEAVE. HE SHOULD BE RIGHT BEHIND US, HIDING BEHIND ONE OF THE COLUMNS.

I HATE YOU! IF ONLY YOU'D GIVE ME A CHANCE TO PROVE MYSELF!

HATA UKINICHUKIA LA KWELI NITAKWAMBIA**.

KEEP TALKING!

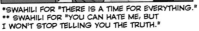

*SWAHILI FOR "THERE IS A TIME FOR EVERYTHING."
** SWAHILI FOR "YOU CAN HATE ME, BUT I WON'T STOP TELLING YOU THE TRUTH."

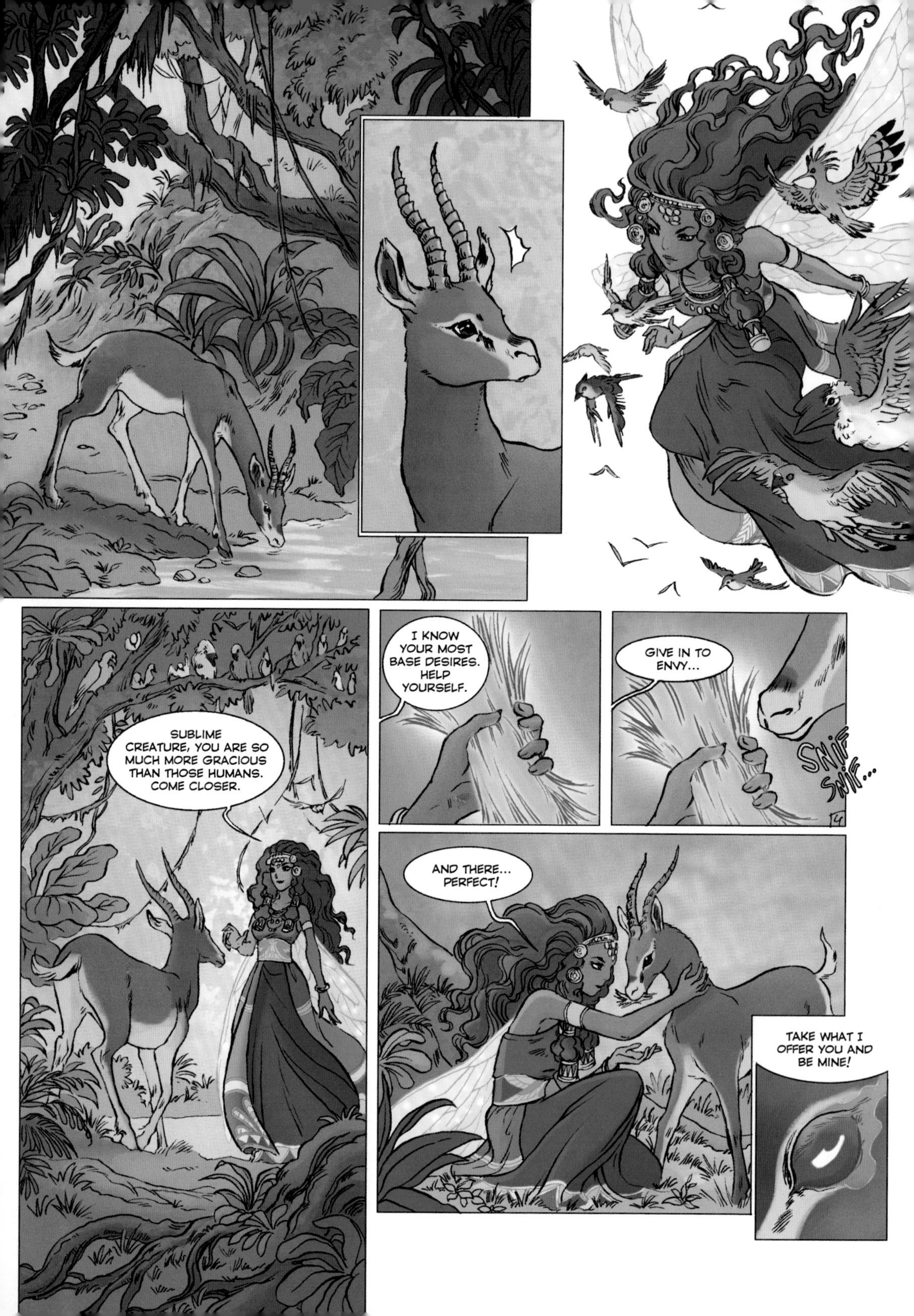
SUBLIME CREATURE, YOU ARE SO MUCH MORE GRACIOUS THAN THOSE HUMANS. COME CLOSER.
I KNOW YOUR MOST BASE DESIRES. HELP YOURSELF.
GIVE IN TO ENVY...
SNIF SNIF...
AND THERE... PERFECT!
TAKE WHAT I OFFER YOU AND BE MINE!

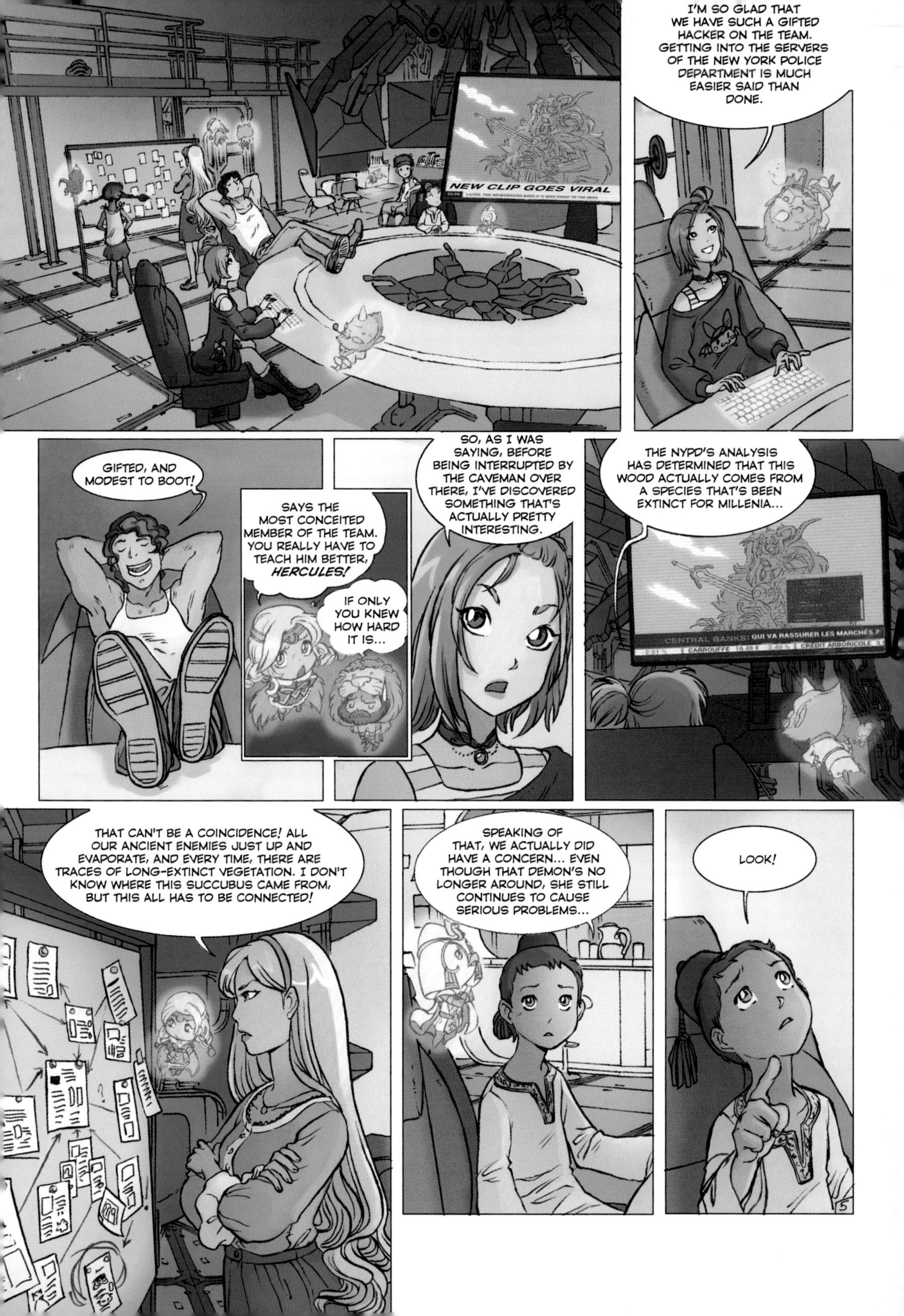

NEW CLIP GOES VIRAL
I'M SO GLAD THAT WE HAVE SUCH A GIFTED HACKER ON THE TEAM. GETTING INTO THE SERVERS OF THE NEW YORK POLICE DEPARTMENT IS MUCH EASIER SAID THAN DONE.
GIFTED, AND MODEST TO BOOT!
SAYS THE MOST CONCEITED MEMBER OF THE TEAM. YOU REALLY HAVE TO TEACH HIM BETTER, ***HERCULES!***
IF ONLY YOU KNEW HOW HARD IT IS...
SO, AS I WAS SAYING, BEFORE BEING INTERRUPTED BY THE CAVEMAN OVER THERE, I'VE DISCOVERED SOMETHING THAT'S ACTUALLY PRETTY INTERESTING.
THE NYPD'S ANALYSIS HAS DETERMINED THAT THIS WOOD ACTUALLY COMES FROM A SPECIES THAT'S BEEN EXTINCT FOR MILLENIA...
CENTRAL BANKS: QUI VA RASSURER LES MARCHÉS ?
CARROUFFE
CRÉDIT ARBORICOLE
THAT CAN'T BE A COINCIDENCE! ALL OUR ANCIENT ENEMIES JUST UP AND EVAPORATE, AND EVERY TIME, THERE ARE TRACES OF LONG-EXTINCT VEGETATION. I DON'T KNOW WHERE THIS SUCCUBUS CAME FROM, BUT THIS ALL HAS TO BE CONNECTED!
SPEAKING OF THAT, WE ACTUALLY DID HAVE A CONCERN... EVEN THOUGH THAT DEMON'S NO LONGER AROUND, SHE STILL CONTINUES TO CAUSE SERIOUS PROBLEMS...
LOOK!
5

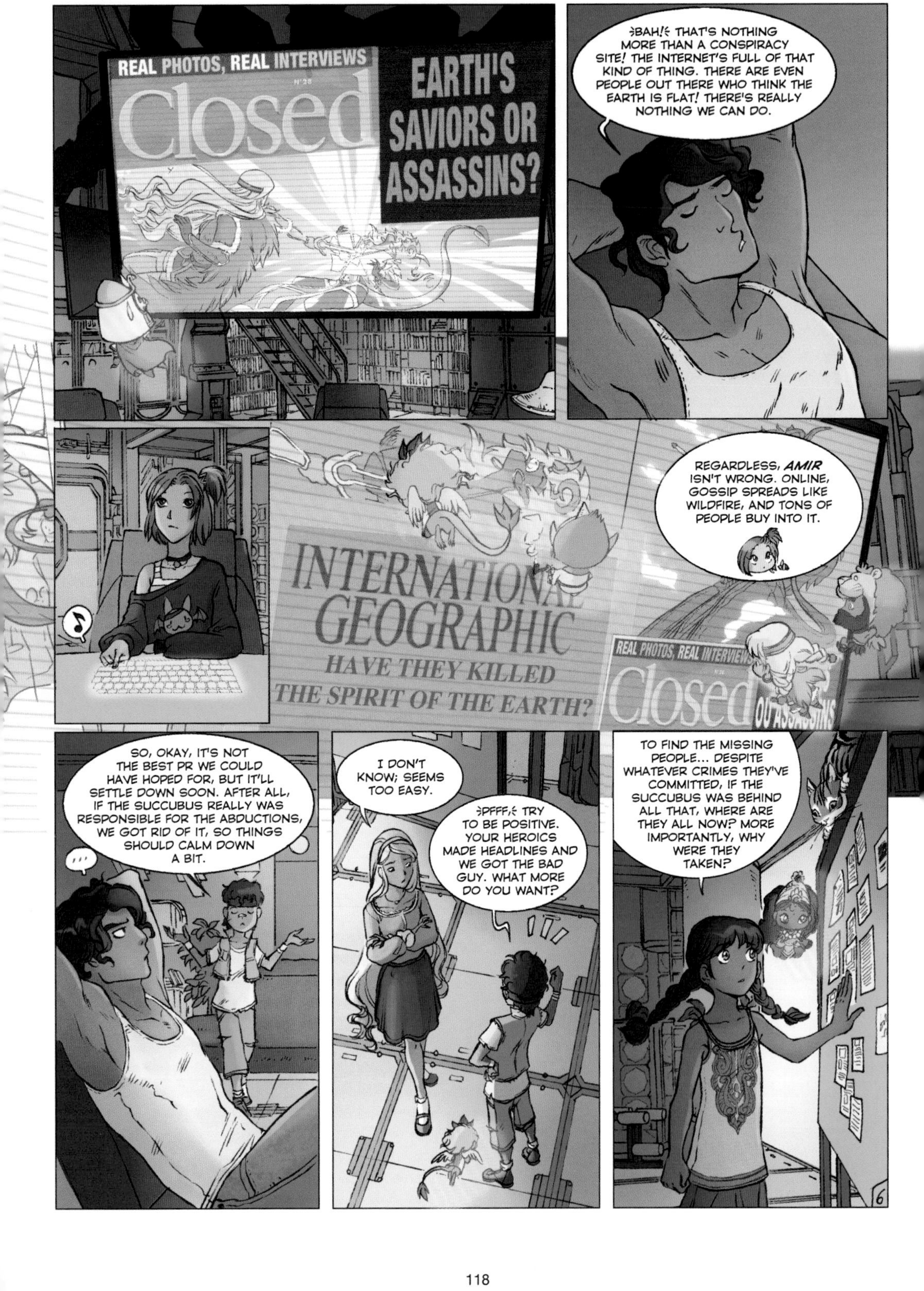
REAL PHOTOS, REAL INTERVIEWS
Closed
EARTH'S SAVIORS OR ASSASSINS?
BAH! THAT'S NOTHING MORE THAN A CONSPIRACY SITE! THE INTERNET'S FULL OF THAT KIND OF THING. THERE ARE EVEN PEOPLE OUT THERE WHO THINK THE EARTH IS FLAT! THERE'S REALLY NOTHING WE CAN DO.
INTERNATIONAL GEOGRAPHIC
HAVE THEY KILLED THE SPIRIT OF THE EARTH?
REAL PHOTOS, REAL INTERVIEWS
Closed
OU ASSASSINS
REGARDLESS, **AMIR** ISN'T WRONG. ONLINE, GOSSIP SPREADS LIKE WILDFIRE, AND TONS OF PEOPLE BUY INTO IT.
SO, OKAY, IT'S NOT THE BEST PR WE COULD HAVE HOPED FOR, BUT IT'LL SETTLE DOWN SOON. AFTER ALL, IF THE SUCCUBUS REALLY WAS RESPONSIBLE FOR THE ABDUCTIONS, WE GOT RID OF IT, SO THINGS SHOULD CALM DOWN A BIT.
I DON'T KNOW; SEEMS TOO EASY.
PFFF, TRY TO BE POSITIVE. YOUR HEROICS MADE HEADLINES AND WE GOT THE BAD GUY. WHAT MORE DO YOU WANT?
TO FIND THE MISSING PEOPLE... DESPITE WHATEVER CRIMES THEY'VE COMMITTED, IF THE SUCCUBUS WAS BEHIND ALL THAT, WHERE ARE THEY ALL NOW? MORE IMPORTANTLY, WHY WERE THEY TAKEN?
6

MISTER AMIR, I HOPE THAT I'M NOT INTERRUPTING YOUR MEETING. I THOUGHT THAT YOU WOULD BE ALONE. IF YOU WOULD PREFER, I CAN COME BACK LATER.

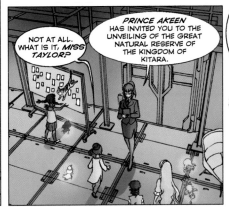

NOT AT ALL. WHAT IS IT, *MISS TAYLOR?*

PRINCE AKEEN HAS INVITED YOU TO THE UNVEILING OF THE GREAT NATURAL RESERVE OF THE KINGDOM OF KITARA.

PRINCE AKEEN, HUH? I HAVEN'T SEEN HIM IN YEARS. HE WAS MY TUTOR FOR A YEAR BEFORE HE WAS CALLED BACK TO GOVERN ALONGSIDE HIS FATHER. MY TIME SPENT STUDYING WITH HIM ARE AMONG MY HAPPIEST MEMORIES!

CURIOUS AND STUDIOUS! IT'S UNBELIEVABLE THAT THIS LITTLE GUY IS YOUR DESCENDANT, *HORUS.*

NOT AT ALL, MA'AM! I ALREADY KNEW EVERYTHING, AFTER ALL, SO I DIDN'T NEED TO WASTE MY TIME PUTTING IT ON PAPYRUS.

AMIR, DO YOU THINK THAT I COULD COME WITH YOU? I WOULD LOVE TO VISIT THE RESERVE. I'VE HEARD ABOUT THE EFFORTS OF THE KINGDOM TO PROTECT ITS WILDLIFE. AND, I'M SURE THAT *SHAHRUK* WOULD LOVE TO BE ABLE TO PLAY IN THE OPEN AIR!

OF COURSE! AND, YOU'LL GET TO SEE FIRSTHAND HOW GREAT THEY ARE. THESE ARE SOME EXTRAORDINARY PEOPLE!

MEOW!

AFTER ALL OF THIS BATTLING, I COULD ALSO USE A LITTLE BREAK. ESPECIALLY IN A PALACE...

YOU'VE GOT A POINT, *MIGUEL!* WHY DON'T YOU ALL COME?!

COUNT ME OUT! BOWING DOWN TO A BUNCH OF ARROGANT RICH GUYS REALLY ISN'T MY THING. BESIDES, I'VE GOT TWO OR THREE DATES JUST WAITING TO SEE ME AGAIN!

SURE, IN YOUR DREAMS...

IF I GO AWAY AGAIN, I CAN SAY GOODBYE TO MY SECRET IDENTITY. I'M SURE THAT MY IDIOT BROTHER'S ALREADY SUSPICIOUS...

WELL, YOU DON'T HOLD BACK FROM SHOCKING HIM WHENEVER HE GETS ON YOUR NERVES..

HE DESERVES IT! IT'S LIKE HE THINKS IT'S FUN TO RUIN MY LIFE! AND BESIDES, I'M PRETTY DISCREET ABOUT IT!

AS FOR ME, I WON'T REST UNTIL WE'VE CLOSED THIS CASE. I'LL CONTINUE SEARCHING FOR ALL THOSE MISSING PEOPLE!

YOU KNOW, *ABI,* THERE'S MORE TO LIFE THAN JUST WORK. YOU SHOULD TRY RELAXING A BIT!

YOU JUST TAKE MY BREAK FOR ME. I'M SURE YOU'LL BE GREAT AT IT! WHILE YOU'RE AT IT, I'LL TAKE CARE OF SAVING THE WORLD!

SURE! IF YOU SUCCEED, GIVE ME A CALL SO I CAN SAVE FACE!

MISS TAYLOR, LET HIM KNOW THAT WE GLADLY ACCEPT HIS INVITATION!

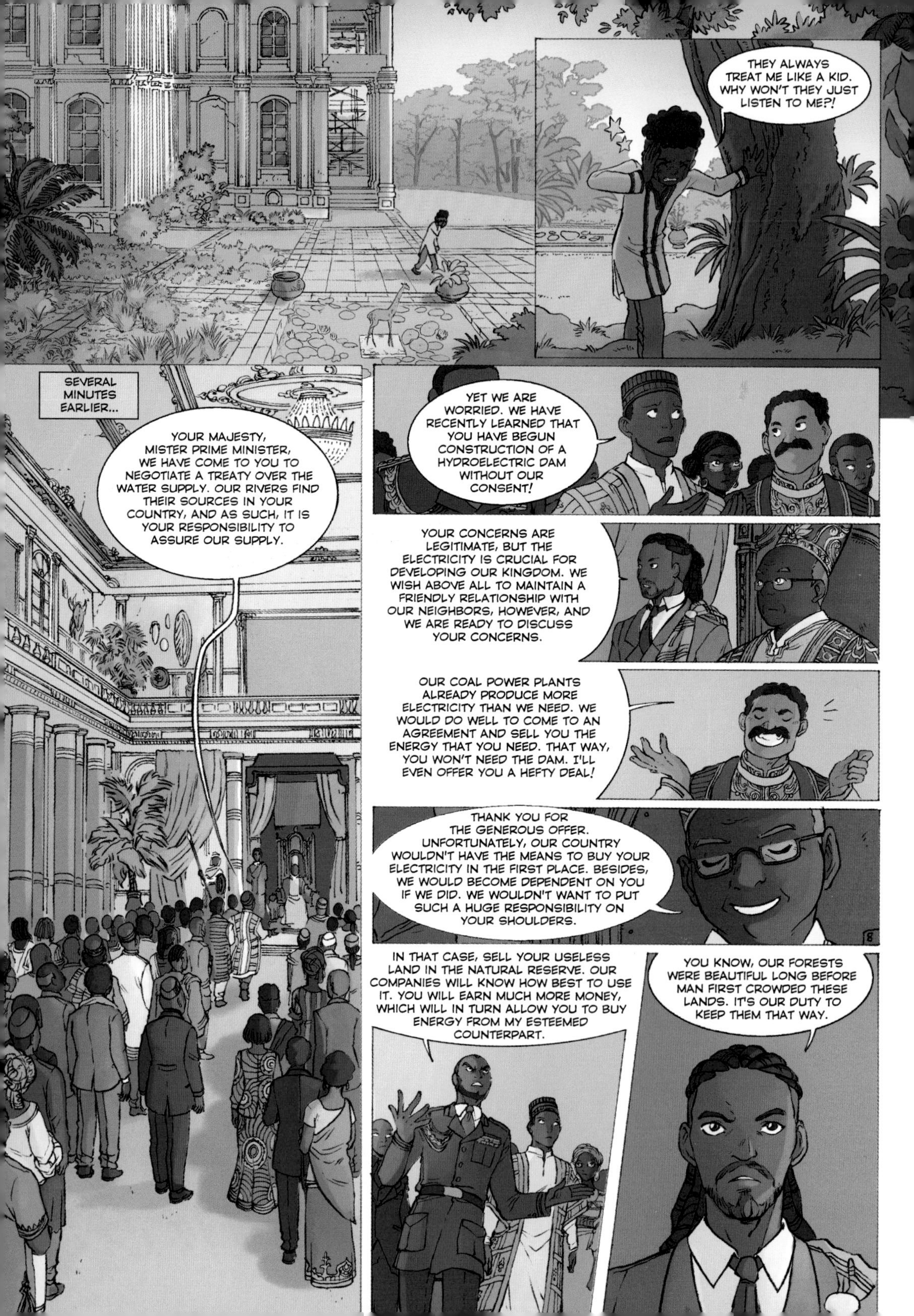
THEY ALWAYS TREAT ME LIKE A KID. WHY WON'T THEY JUST LISTEN TO ME?!
SEVERAL MINUTES EARLIER...
YOUR MAJESTY, MISTER PRIME MINISTER, WE HAVE COME TO YOU TO NEGOTIATE A TREATY OVER THE WATER SUPPLY. OUR RIVERS FIND THEIR SOURCES IN YOUR COUNTRY, AND AS SUCH, IT IS YOUR RESPONSIBILITY TO ASSURE OUR SUPPLY.
YET WE ARE WORRIED. WE HAVE RECENTLY LEARNED THAT YOU HAVE BEGUN CONSTRUCTION OF A HYDROELECTRIC DAM WITHOUT OUR CONSENT!
YOUR CONCERNS ARE LEGITIMATE, BUT THE ELECTRICITY IS CRUCIAL FOR DEVELOPING OUR KINGDOM. WE WISH ABOVE ALL TO MAINTAIN A FRIENDLY RELATIONSHIP WITH OUR NEIGHBORS, HOWEVER, AND WE ARE READY TO DISCUSS YOUR CONCERNS.
OUR COAL POWER PLANTS ALREADY PRODUCE MORE ELECTRICITY THAN WE NEED. WE WOULD DO WELL TO COME TO AN AGREEMENT AND SELL YOU THE ENERGY THAT YOU NEED. THAT WAY, YOU WON'T NEED THE DAM. I'LL EVEN OFFER YOU A HEFTY DEAL!
THANK YOU FOR THE GENEROUS OFFER. UNFORTUNATELY, OUR COUNTRY WOULDN'T HAVE THE MEANS TO BUY YOUR ELECTRICITY IN THE FIRST PLACE. BESIDES, WE WOULD BECOME DEPENDENT ON YOU IF WE DID. WE WOULDN'T WANT TO PUT SUCH A HUGE RESPONSIBILITY ON YOUR SHOULDERS.
IN THAT CASE, SELL YOUR USELESS LAND IN THE NATURAL RESERVE. OUR COMPANIES WILL KNOW HOW BEST TO USE IT. YOU WILL EARN MUCH MORE MONEY, WHICH WILL IN TURN ALLOW YOU TO BUY ENERGY FROM MY ESTEEMED COUNTERPART.
YOU KNOW, OUR FORESTS WERE BEAUTIFUL LONG BEFORE MAN FIRST CROWDED THESE LANDS. IT'S OUR DUTY TO KEEP THEM THAT WAY.

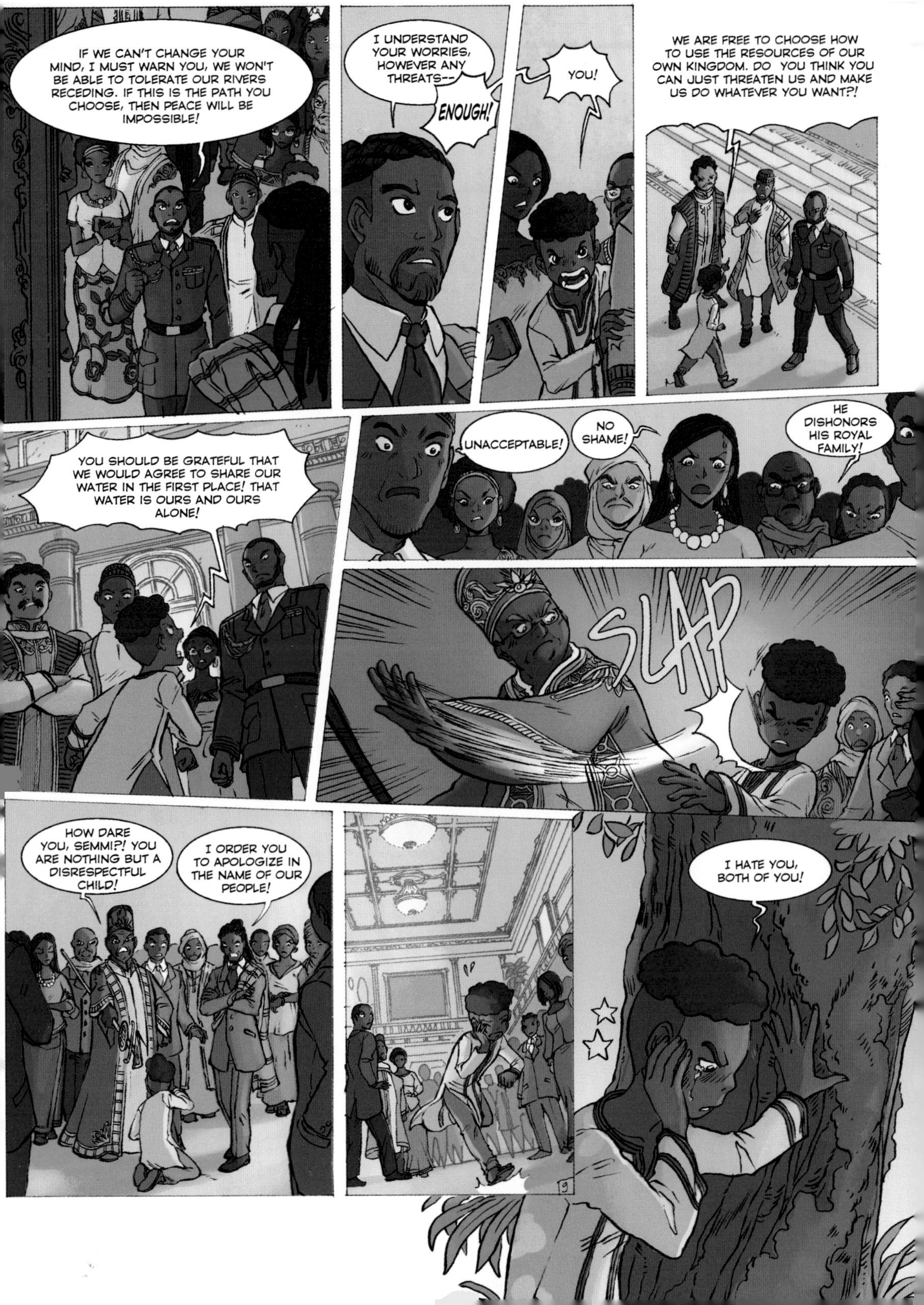
IF WE CAN'T CHANGE YOUR MIND, I MUST WARN YOU, WE WON'T BE ABLE TO TOLERATE OUR RIVERS RECEDING. IF THIS IS THE PATH YOU CHOOSE, THEN PEACE WILL BE IMPOSSIBLE!
I UNDERSTAND YOUR WORRIES, HOWEVER ANY THREATS--
ENOUGH!
YOU!
WE ARE FREE TO CHOOSE HOW TO USE THE RESOURCES OF OUR OWN KINGDOM. DO YOU THINK YOU CAN JUST THREATEN US AND MAKE US DO WHATEVER YOU WANT?!
YOU SHOULD BE GRATEFUL THAT WE WOULD AGREE TO SHARE OUR WATER IN THE FIRST PLACE! THAT WATER IS OURS AND OURS ALONE!
UNACCEPTABLE!
NO SHAME!
HE DISHONORS HIS ROYAL FAMILY!
SLAP
HOW DARE YOU, SEMMI?! YOU ARE NOTHING BUT A DISRESPECTFUL CHILD!
I ORDER YOU TO APOLOGIZE IN THE NAME OF OUR PEOPLE!
I HATE YOU, BOTH OF YOU!

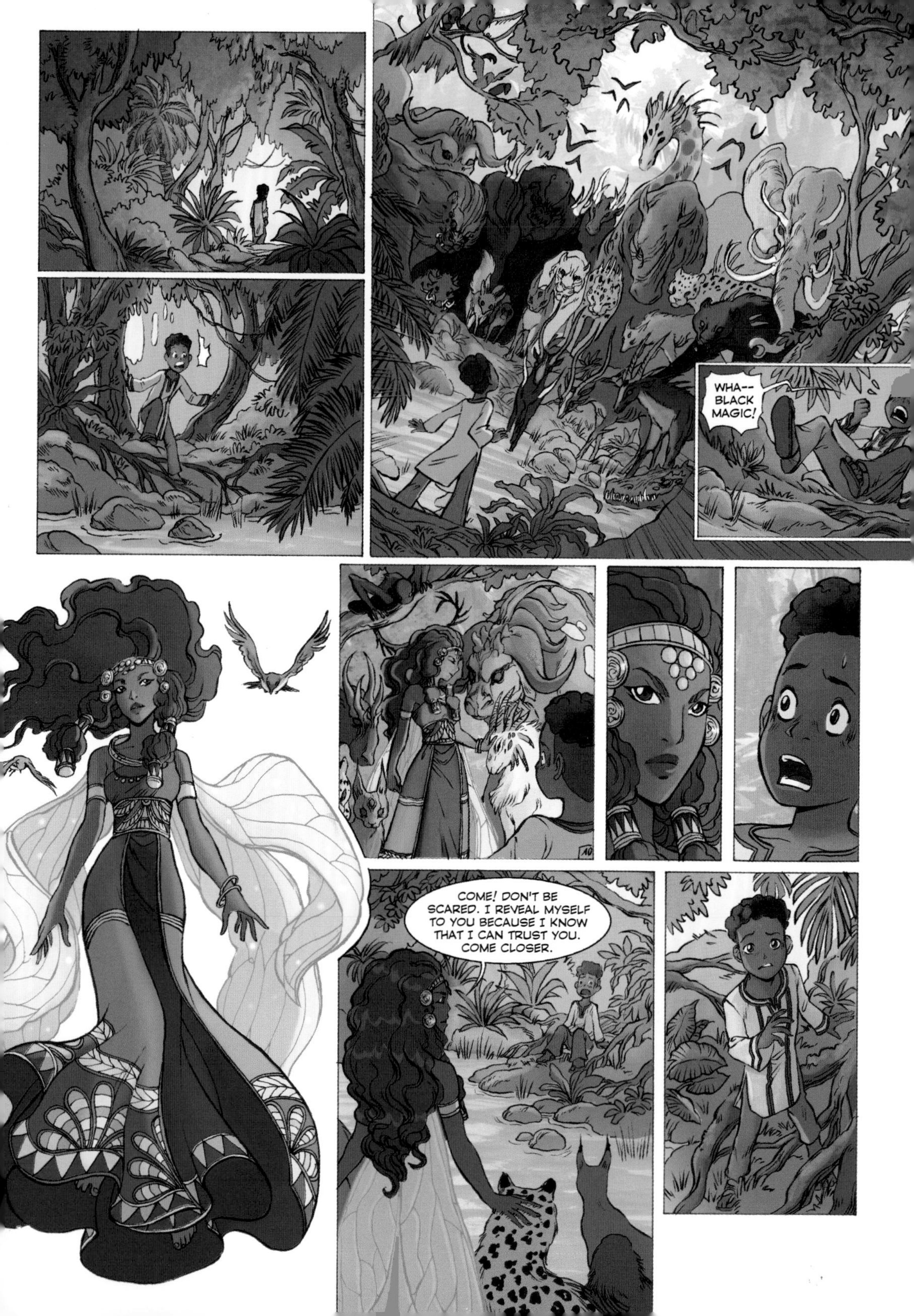
WHA--
BLACK
MAGIC!
COME! DON'T BE
SCARED. I REVEAL MYSELF
TO YOU BECAUSE I KNOW
THAT I CAN TRUST YOU.
COME CLOSER.

 YOU... YOU ARE ON PRIVATE LAND. YOU CAN'T BE HERE! WHOEVER YOU ARE, GET OUT!

 AND HOW DO YOU EXPECT TO MAKE ME?

 I COULD CALL THE ROYAL GUARDS. THEY FOLLOW MY ORDERS!

THREATENING ME IS NOT WISE. MANY LIKE YOU HAVE TRIED. NONE OF THEM HAVE LIVED TO REGRET IT. HAS NO ONE EVER TAUGHT YOU TO KNOW YOUR PLACE?!

 I SEE SADNESS AND ANGER BEHIND THE VEIL OF FEAR THAT CLOUDS YOUR EYES.

 THERE IS POTENTIAL, YES... THIS COULD BE INTERESTING. I COULD GIVE YOU ALL YOU'VE EVER WANTED, YOUNG PRINCE. ALL YOU HAVE TO DO IS BE COMPLETELY MINE...

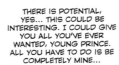

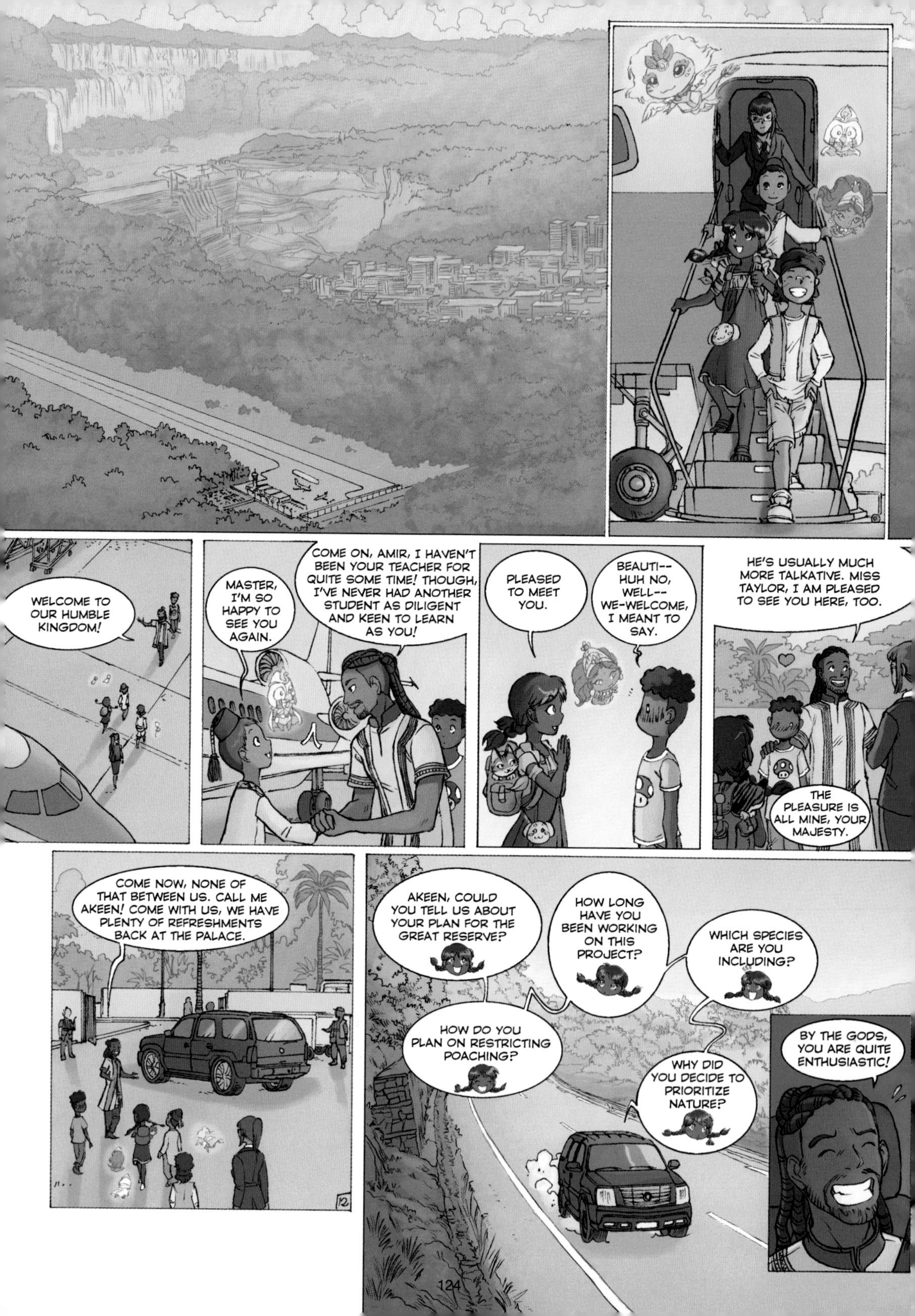

WELCOME TO OUR HUMBLE KINGDOM!
MASTER, I'M SO HAPPY TO SEE YOU AGAIN.
COME ON, AMIR, I HAVEN'T BEEN YOUR TEACHER FOR QUITE SOME TIME! THOUGH, I'VE NEVER HAD ANOTHER STUDENT AS DILIGENT AND KEEN TO LEARN AS YOU!
PLEASED TO MEET YOU.
BEAUTI-- HUH NO, WELL-- WE-WELCOME, I MEANT TO SAY.
HE'S USUALLY MUCH MORE TALKATIVE. MISS TAYLOR, I AM PLEASED TO SEE YOU HERE, TOO.
THE PLEASURE IS ALL MINE, YOUR MAJESTY.
COME NOW, NONE OF THAT BETWEEN US. CALL ME AKEEN! COME WITH US, WE HAVE PLENTY OF REFRESHMENTS BACK AT THE PALACE.
AKEEN, COULD YOU TELL US ABOUT YOUR PLAN FOR THE GREAT RESERVE?
HOW DO YOU PLAN ON RESTRICTING POACHING?
HOW LONG HAVE YOU BEEN WORKING ON THIS PROJECT?
WHICH SPECIES ARE YOU INCLUDING?
WHY DID YOU DECIDE TO PRIORITIZE NATURE?
BY THE GODS, YOU ARE QUITE ENTHUSIASTIC!

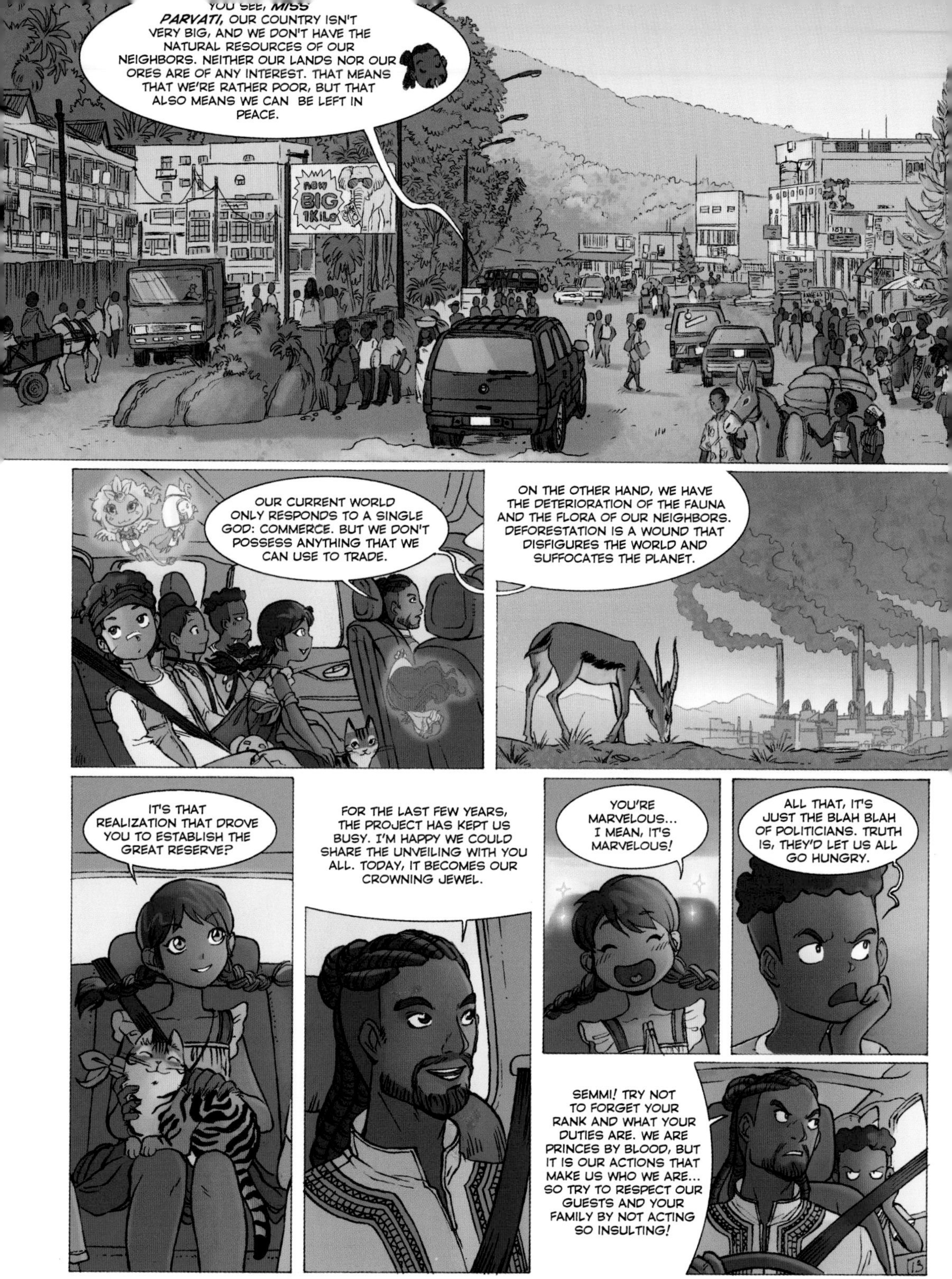
YOU SEE, MISS PARVATI, OUR COUNTRY ISN'T VERY BIG, AND WE DON'T HAVE THE NATURAL RESOURCES OF OUR NEIGHBORS. NEITHER OUR LANDS NOR OUR ORES ARE OF ANY INTEREST. THAT MEANS THAT WE'RE RATHER POOR, BUT THAT ALSO MEANS WE CAN BE LEFT IN PEACE.
NEW BIG 1KILO
OUR CURRENT WORLD ONLY RESPONDS TO A SINGLE GOD: COMMERCE. BUT WE DON'T POSSESS ANYTHING THAT WE CAN USE TO TRADE.
ON THE OTHER HAND, WE HAVE THE DETERIORATION OF THE FAUNA AND THE FLORA OF OUR NEIGHBORS. DEFORESTATION IS A WOUND THAT DISFIGURES THE WORLD AND SUFFOCATES THE PLANET.
IT'S THAT REALIZATION THAT DROVE YOU TO ESTABLISH THE GREAT RESERVE?
FOR THE LAST FEW YEARS, THE PROJECT HAS KEPT US BUSY. I'M HAPPY WE COULD SHARE THE UNVEILING WITH YOU ALL. TODAY, IT BECOMES OUR CROWNING JEWEL.
YOU'RE MARVELOUS... I MEAN, IT'S MARVELOUS!
ALL THAT, IT'S JUST THE BLAH BLAH OF POLITICIANS. TRUTH IS, THEY'D LET US ALL GO HUNGRY.
SEMMI! TRY NOT TO FORGET YOUR RANK AND WHAT YOUR DUTIES ARE. WE ARE PRINCES BY BLOOD, BUT IT IS OUR ACTIONS THAT MAKE US WHO WE ARE... SO TRY TO RESPECT OUR GUESTS AND YOUR FAMILY BY NOT ACTING SO INSULTING!
13

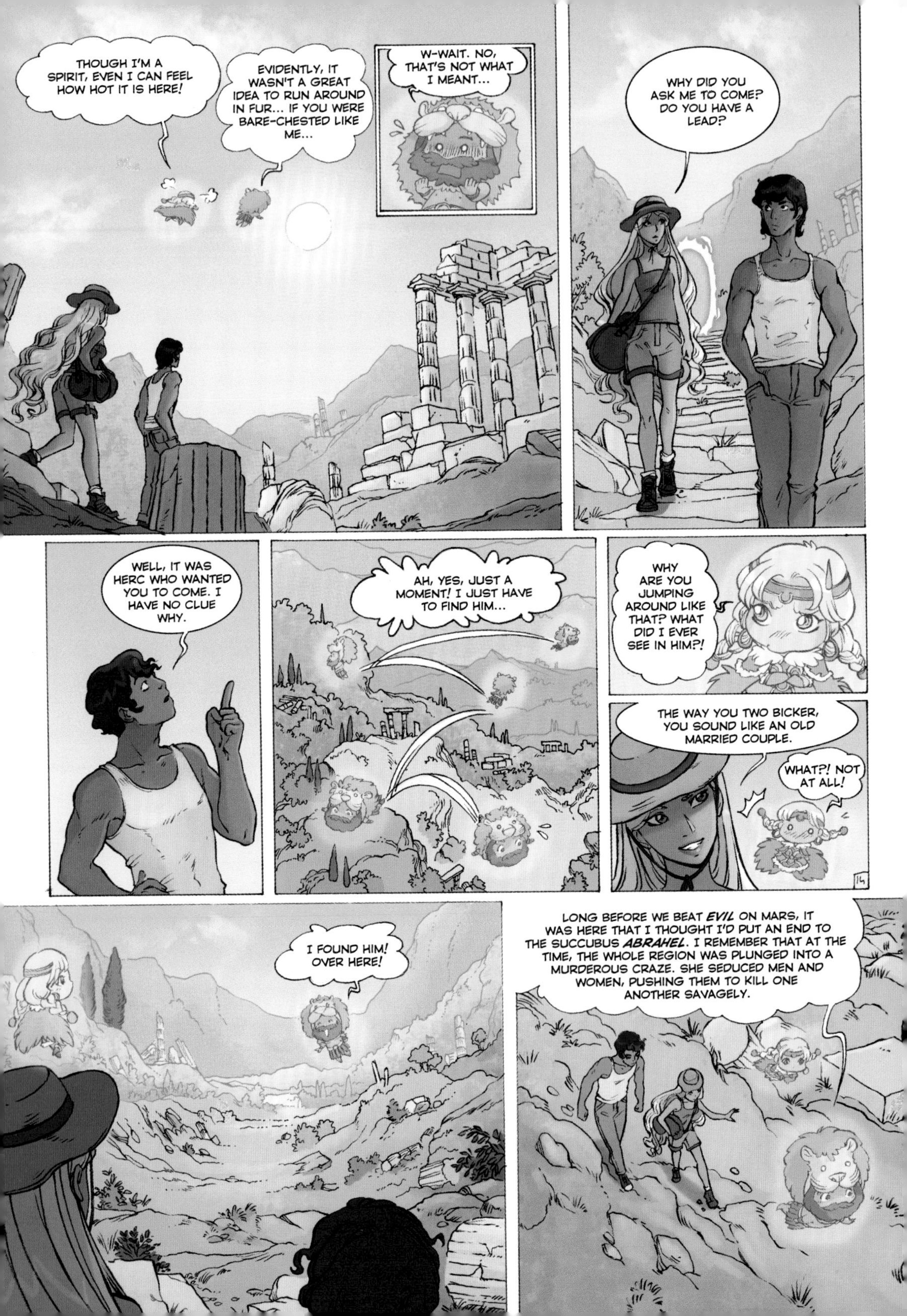
THOUGH I'M A SPIRIT, EVEN I CAN FEEL HOW HOT IT IS HERE!
EVIDENTLY, IT WASN'T A GREAT IDEA TO RUN AROUND IN FUR... IF YOU WERE BARE-CHESTED LIKE ME...
W-WAIT. NO, THAT'S NOT WHAT I MEANT...
WHY DID YOU ASK ME TO COME? DO YOU HAVE A LEAD?
WELL, IT WAS HERC WHO WANTED YOU TO COME. I HAVE NO CLUE WHY.
AH, YES, JUST A MOMENT! I JUST HAVE TO FIND HIM...
WHY ARE YOU JUMPING AROUND LIKE THAT? WHAT DID I EVER SEE IN HIM?!
THE WAY YOU TWO BICKER, YOU SOUND LIKE AN OLD MARRIED COUPLE.
WHAT?! NOT AT ALL!
I FOUND HIM! OVER HERE!
LONG BEFORE WE BEAT EVIL ON MARS, IT WAS HERE THAT I THOUGHT I'D PUT AN END TO THE SUCCUBUS ABRAHEL. I REMEMBER THAT AT THE TIME, THE WHOLE REGION WAS PLUNGED INTO A MURDEROUS CRAZE. SHE SEDUCED MEN AND WOMEN, PUSHING THEM TO KILL ONE ANOTHER SAVAGELY.

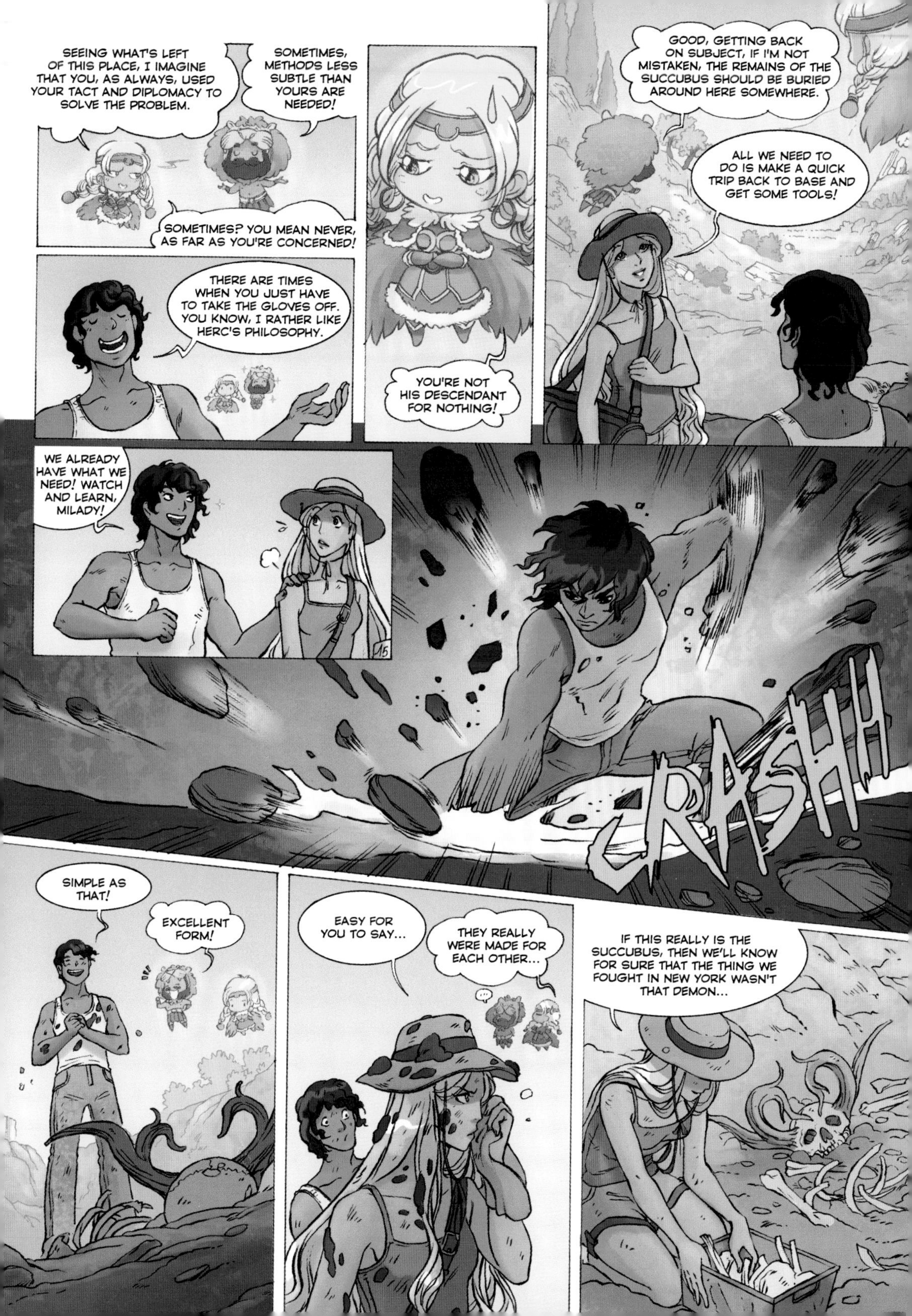
SEEING WHAT'S LEFT OF THIS PLACE, I IMAGINE THAT YOU, AS ALWAYS, USED YOUR TACT AND DIPLOMACY TO SOLVE THE PROBLEM.
SOMETIMES, METHODS LESS SUBTLE THAN YOURS ARE NEEDED!
SOMETIMES? YOU MEAN NEVER, AS FAR AS YOU'RE CONCERNED!
THERE ARE TIMES WHEN YOU JUST HAVE TO TAKE THE GLOVES OFF. YOU KNOW, I RATHER LIKE HERC'S PHILOSOPHY.
YOU'RE NOT HIS DESCENDANT FOR NOTHING!
GOOD, GETTING BACK ON SUBJECT, IF I'M NOT MISTAKEN, THE REMAINS OF THE SUCCUBUS SHOULD BE BURIED AROUND HERE SOMEWHERE.
ALL WE NEED TO DO IS MAKE A QUICK TRIP BACK TO BASE AND GET SOME TOOLS!
WE ALREADY HAVE WHAT WE NEED! WATCH AND LEARN, MILADY!
15
CRASH!!
SIMPLE AS THAT!
EXCELLENT FORM!
EASY FOR YOU TO SAY...
THEY REALLY WERE MADE FOR EACH OTHER...
...
IF THIS REALLY IS THE SUCCUBUS, THEN WE'LL KNOW FOR SURE THAT THE THING WE FOUGHT IN NEW YORK WASN'T THAT DEMON...

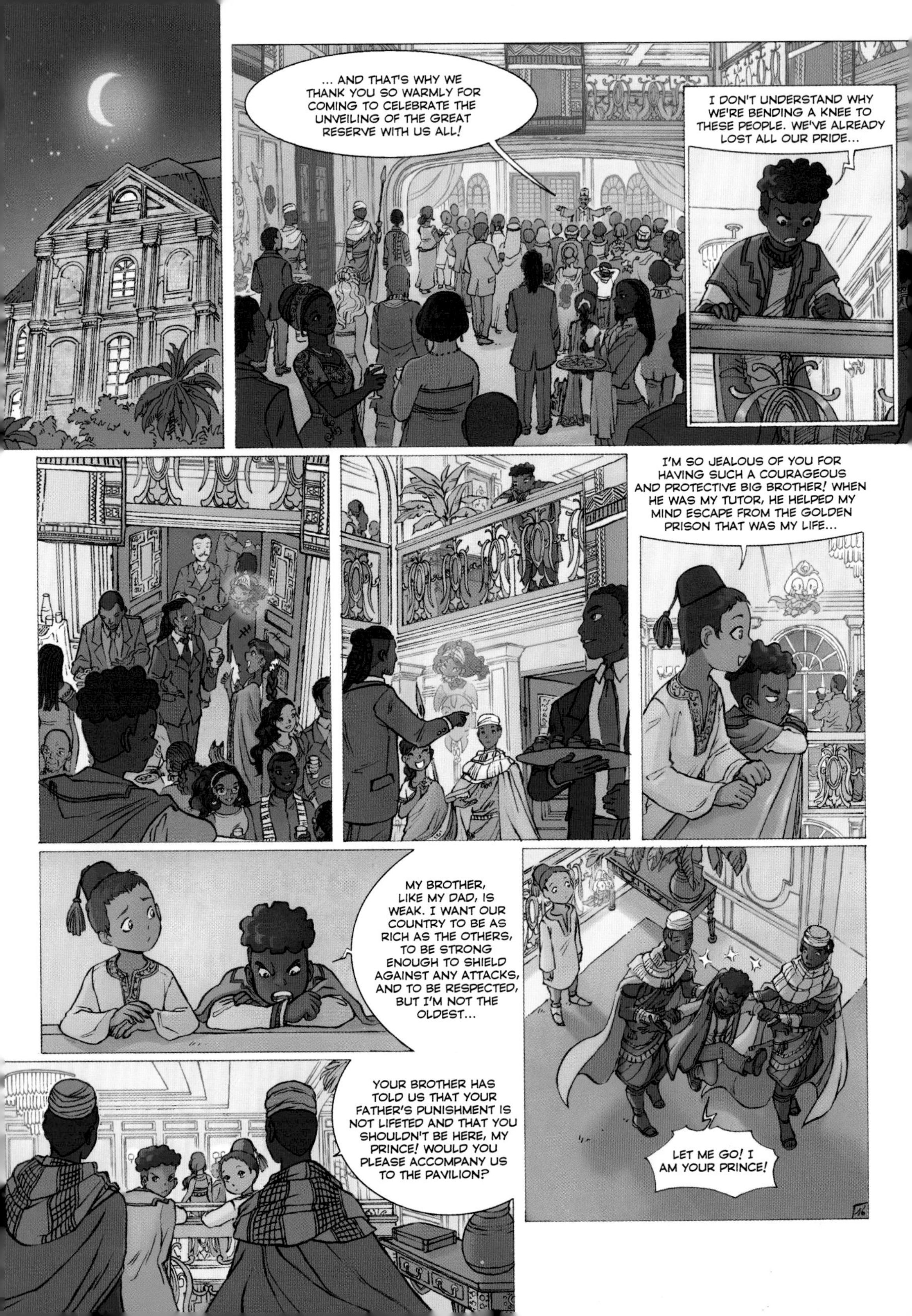

... AND THAT'S WHY WE THANK YOU SO WARMLY FOR COMING TO CELEBRATE THE UNVEILING OF THE GREAT RESERVE WITH US ALL!
I DON'T UNDERSTAND WHY WE'RE BENDING A KNEE TO THESE PEOPLE. WE'VE ALREADY LOST ALL OUR PRIDE...
I'M SO JEALOUS OF YOU FOR HAVING SUCH A COURAGEOUS AND PROTECTIVE BIG BROTHER! WHEN HE WAS MY TUTOR, HE HELPED MY MIND ESCAPE FROM THE GOLDEN PRISON THAT WAS MY LIFE...
MY BROTHER, LIKE MY DAD, IS WEAK. I WANT OUR COUNTRY TO BE AS RICH AS THE OTHERS, TO BE STRONG ENOUGH TO SHIELD AGAINST ANY ATTACKS, AND TO BE RESPECTED, BUT I'M NOT THE OLDEST...
YOUR BROTHER HAS TOLD US THAT YOUR FATHER'S PUNISHMENT IS NOT LIFETED AND THAT YOU SHOULDN'T BE HERE, MY PRINCE! WOULD YOU PLEASE ACCOMPANY US TO THE PAVILION?
LET ME GO! I AM YOUR PRINCE!

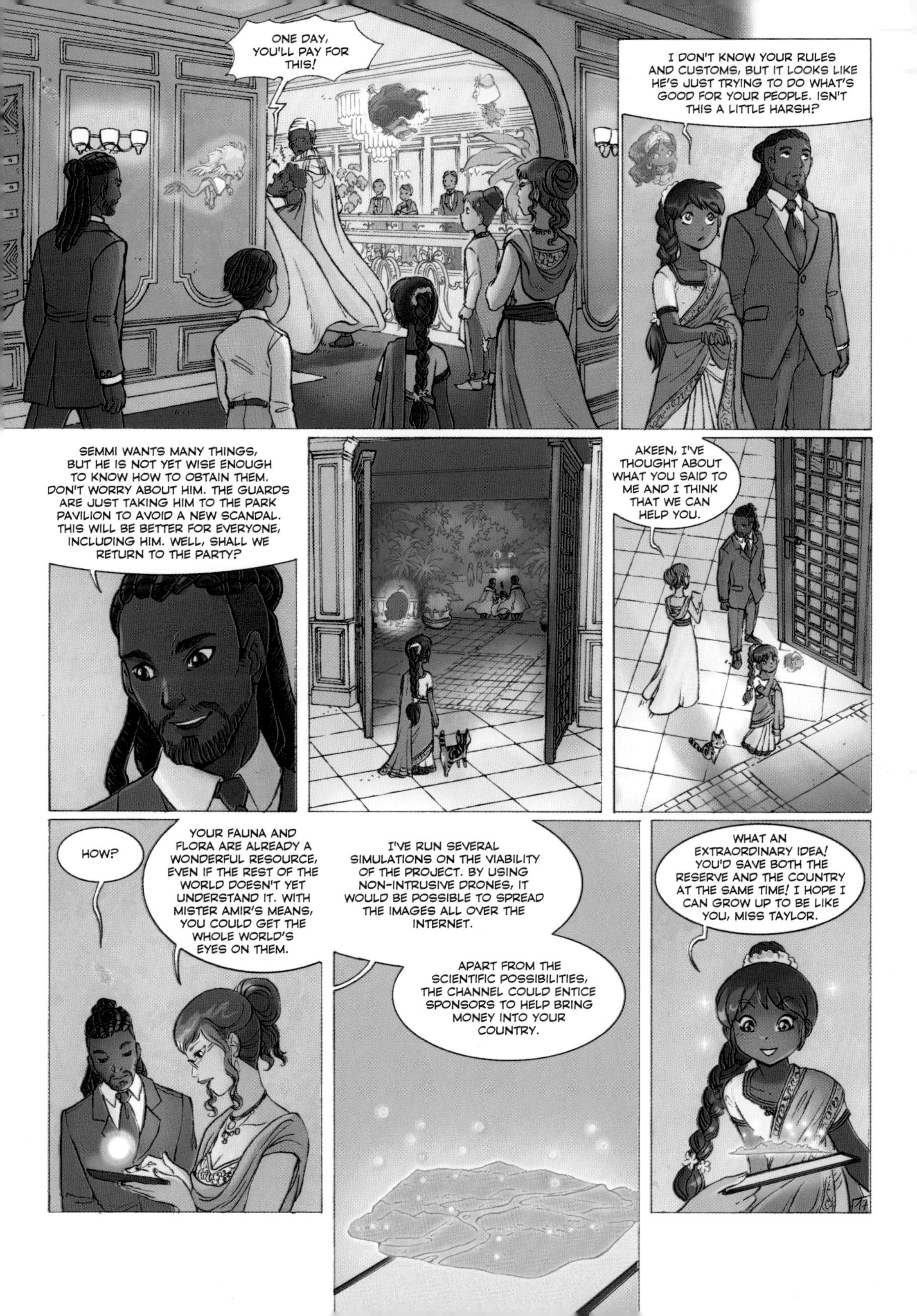
ONE DAY, YOU'LL PAY FOR THIS!
I DON'T KNOW YOUR RULES AND CUSTOMS, BUT IT LOOKS LIKE HE'S JUST TRYING TO DO WHAT'S GOOD FOR YOUR PEOPLE. ISN'T THIS A LITTLE HARSH?
SEMMI WANTS MANY THINGS, BUT HE IS NOT YET WISE ENOUGH TO KNOW HOW TO OBTAIN THEM. DON'T WORRY ABOUT HIM. THE GUARDS ARE JUST TAKING HIM TO THE PARK PAVILION TO AVOID A NEW SCANDAL. THIS WILL BE BETTER FOR EVERYONE, INCLUDING HIM. WELL, SHALL WE RETURN TO THE PARTY?
AKEEN, I'VE THOUGHT ABOUT WHAT YOU SAID TO ME AND I THINK THAT WE CAN HELP YOU.
HOW?
YOUR FAUNA AND FLORA ARE ALREADY A WONDERFUL RESOURCE, EVEN IF THE REST OF THE WORLD DOESN'T YET UNDERSTAND IT. WITH MISTER AMIR'S MEANS, YOU COULD GET THE WHOLE WORLD'S EYES ON THEM.
I'VE RUN SEVERAL SIMULATIONS ON THE VIABILITY OF THE PROJECT. BY USING NON-INTRUSIVE DRONES, IT WOULD BE POSSIBLE TO SPREAD THE IMAGES ALL OVER THE INTERNET.
APART FROM THE SCIENTIFIC POSSIBILITIES, THE CHANNEL COULD ENTICE SPONSORS TO HELP BRING MONEY INTO YOUR COUNTRY.
WHAT AN EXTRAORDINARY IDEA! YOU'D SAVE BOTH THE RESERVE AND THE COUNTRY AT THE SAME TIME! I HOPE I CAN GROW UP TO BE LIKE YOU, MISS TAYLOR.

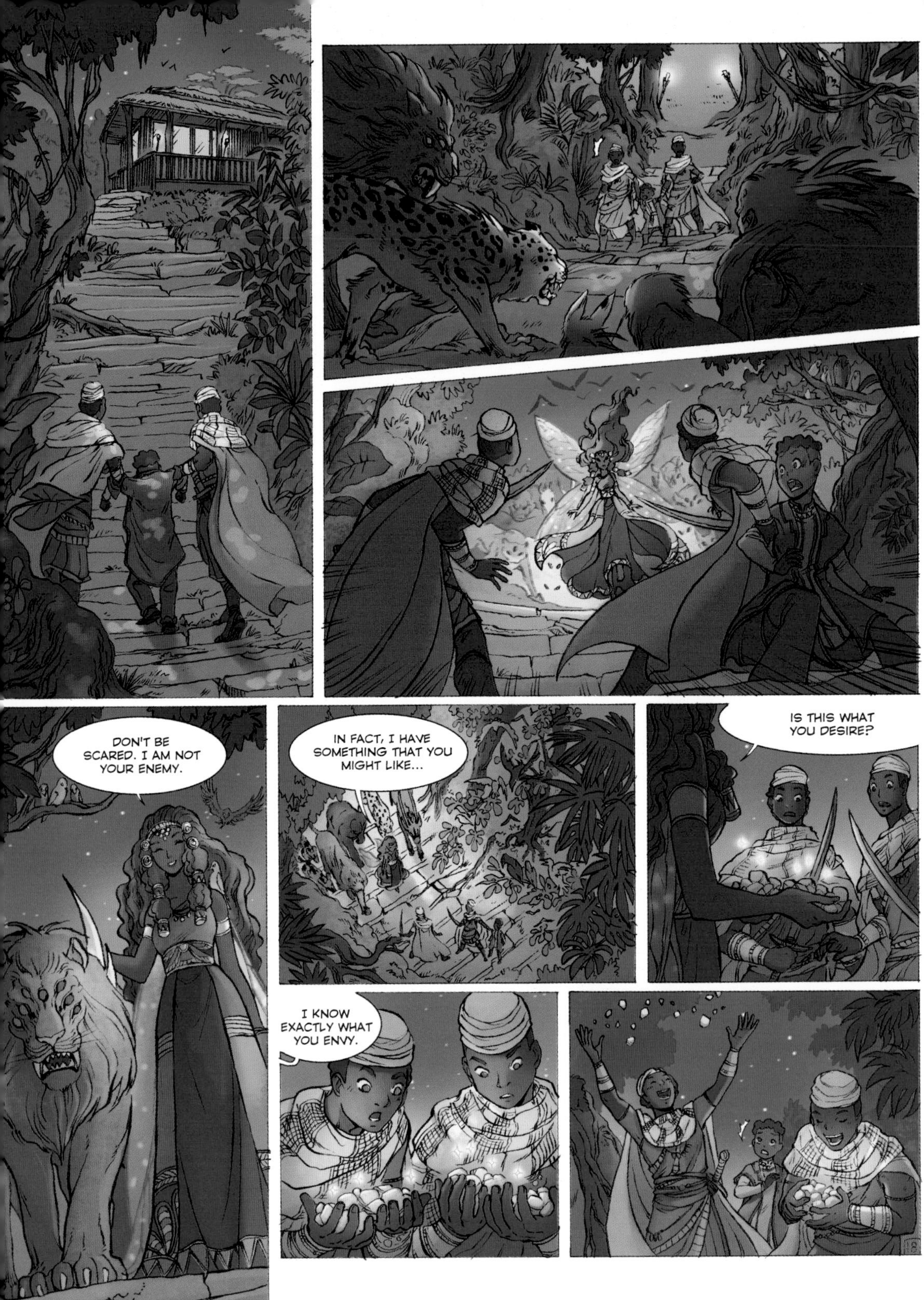
DON'T BE SCARED. I AM NOT YOUR ENEMY.
IN FACT, I HAVE SOMETHING THAT YOU MIGHT LIKE...
IS THIS WHAT YOU DESIRE?
I KNOW EXACTLY WHAT YOU ENVY.

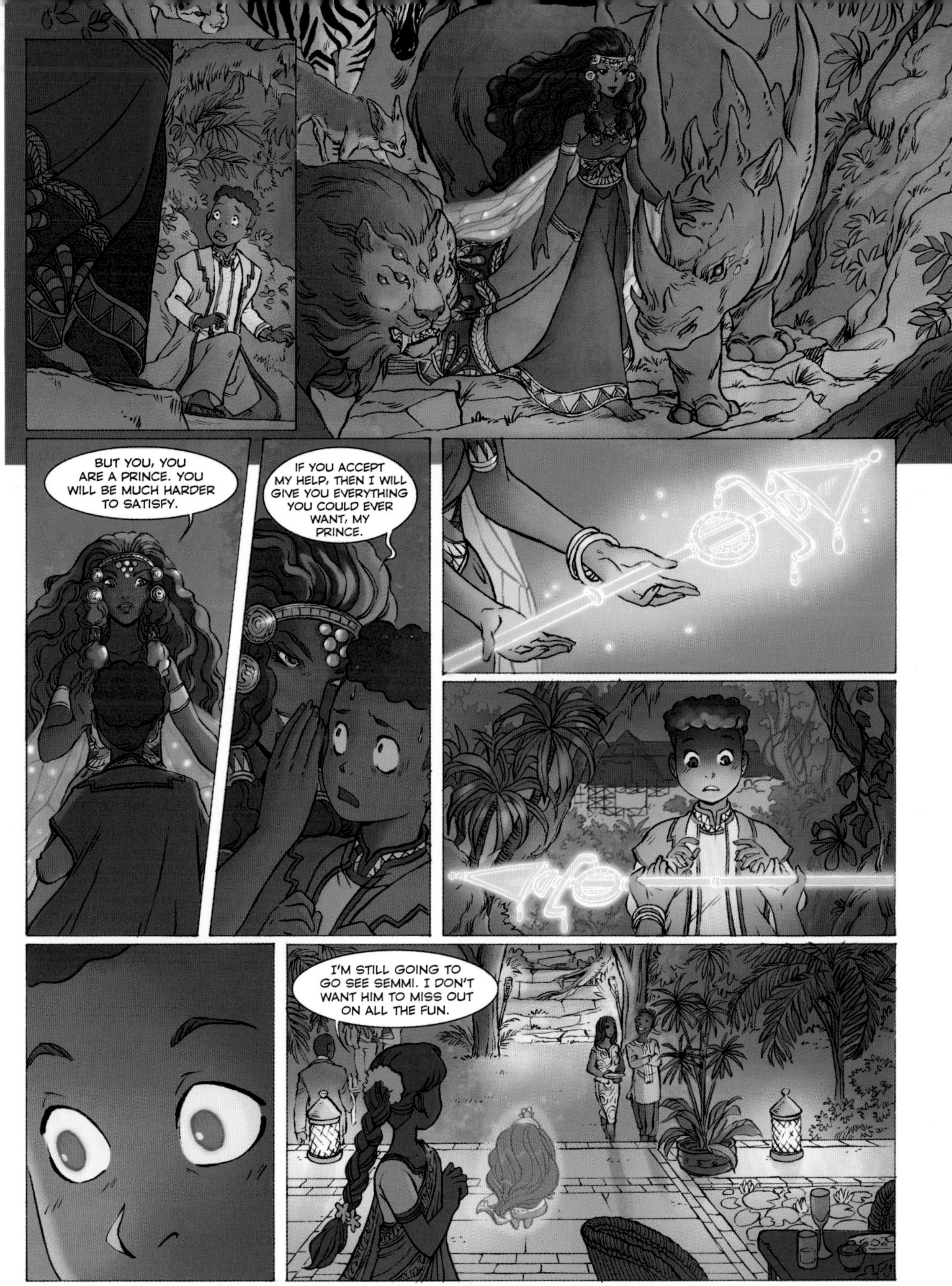

BUT YOU, YOU ARE A PRINCE. YOU WILL BE MUCH HARDER TO SATISFY.
IF YOU ACCEPT MY HELP, THEN I WILL GIVE YOU EVERYTHING YOU COULD EVER WANT, MY PRINCE.
I'M STILL GOING TO GO SEE SEMMI. I DON'T WANT HIM TO MISS OUT ON ALL THE FUN.

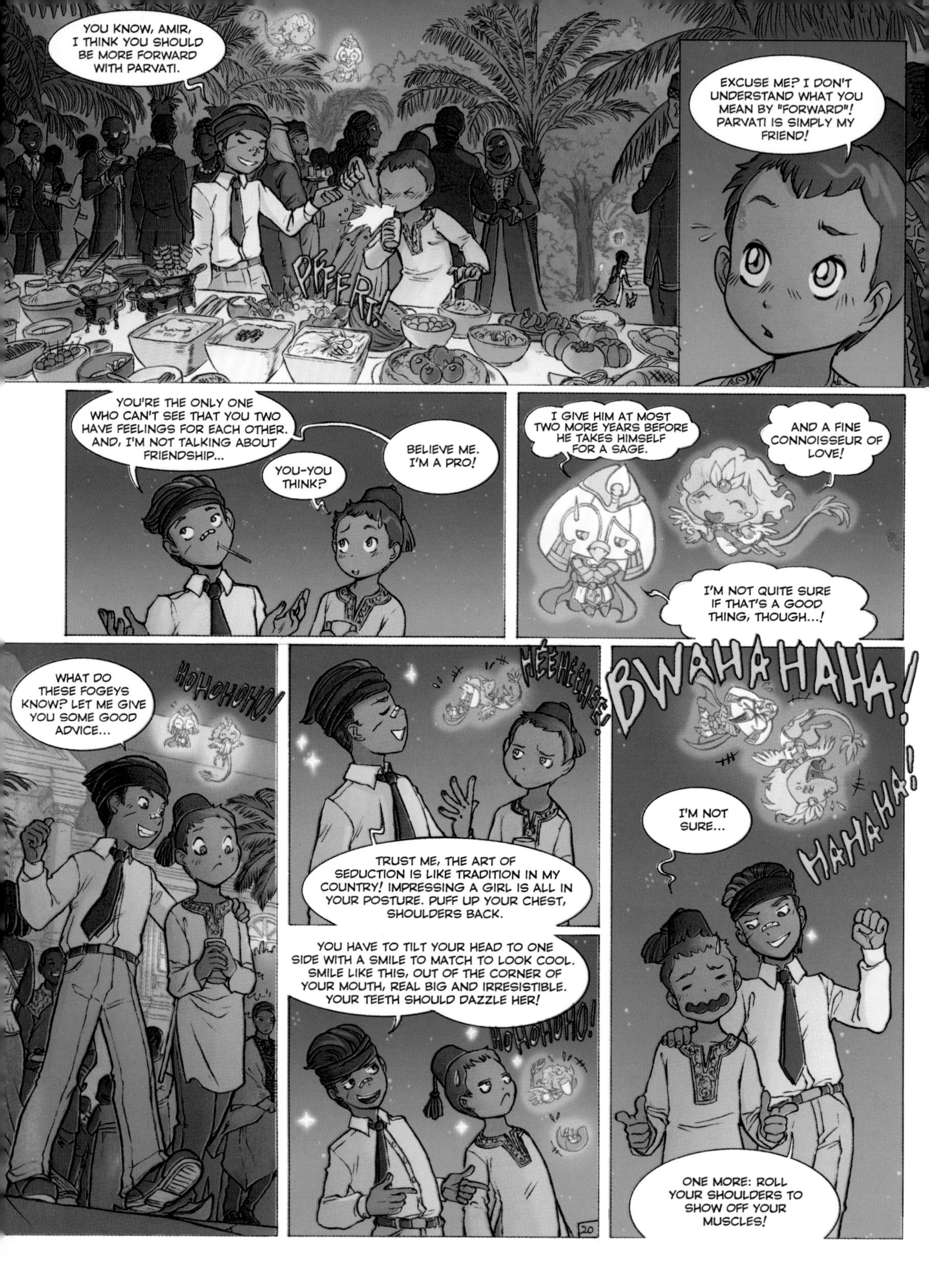

YOU KNOW, AMIR, I THINK YOU SHOULD BE MORE FORWARD WITH PARVATI.
PFFFRT!
EXCUSE ME? I DON'T UNDERSTAND WHAT YOU MEAN BY "FORWARD"! PARVATI IS SIMPLY MY FRIEND!
YOU'RE THE ONLY ONE WHO CAN'T SEE THAT YOU TWO HAVE FEELINGS FOR EACH OTHER. AND, I'M NOT TALKING ABOUT FRIENDSHIP...
YOU-YOU THINK?
BELIEVE ME. I'M A PRO!
I GIVE HIM AT MOST TWO MORE YEARS BEFORE HE TAKES HIMSELF FOR A SAGE.
AND A FINE CONNOISSEUR OF LOVE!
I'M NOT QUITE SURE IF THAT'S A GOOD THING, THOUGH...!
WHAT DO THESE FOGEYS KNOW? LET ME GIVE YOU SOME GOOD ADVICE...
HOHOHOHO!
HÉEHEEHÉE!
TRUST ME, THE ART OF SEDUCTION IS LIKE TRADITION IN MY COUNTRY! IMPRESSING A GIRL IS ALL IN YOUR POSTURE. PUFF UP YOUR CHEST, SHOULDERS BACK.
YOU HAVE TO TILT YOUR HEAD TO ONE SIDE WITH A SMILE TO MATCH TO LOOK COOL. SMILE LIKE THIS, OUT OF THE CORNER OF YOUR MOUTH, REAL BIG AND IRRESISTIBLE. YOUR TEETH SHOULD DAZZLE HER!
HOHOHOHO!
20
BWAHAHAHAHA!
HAHAHA!
I'M NOT SURE...
ONE MORE: ROLL YOUR SHOULDERS TO SHOW OFF YOUR MUSCLES!

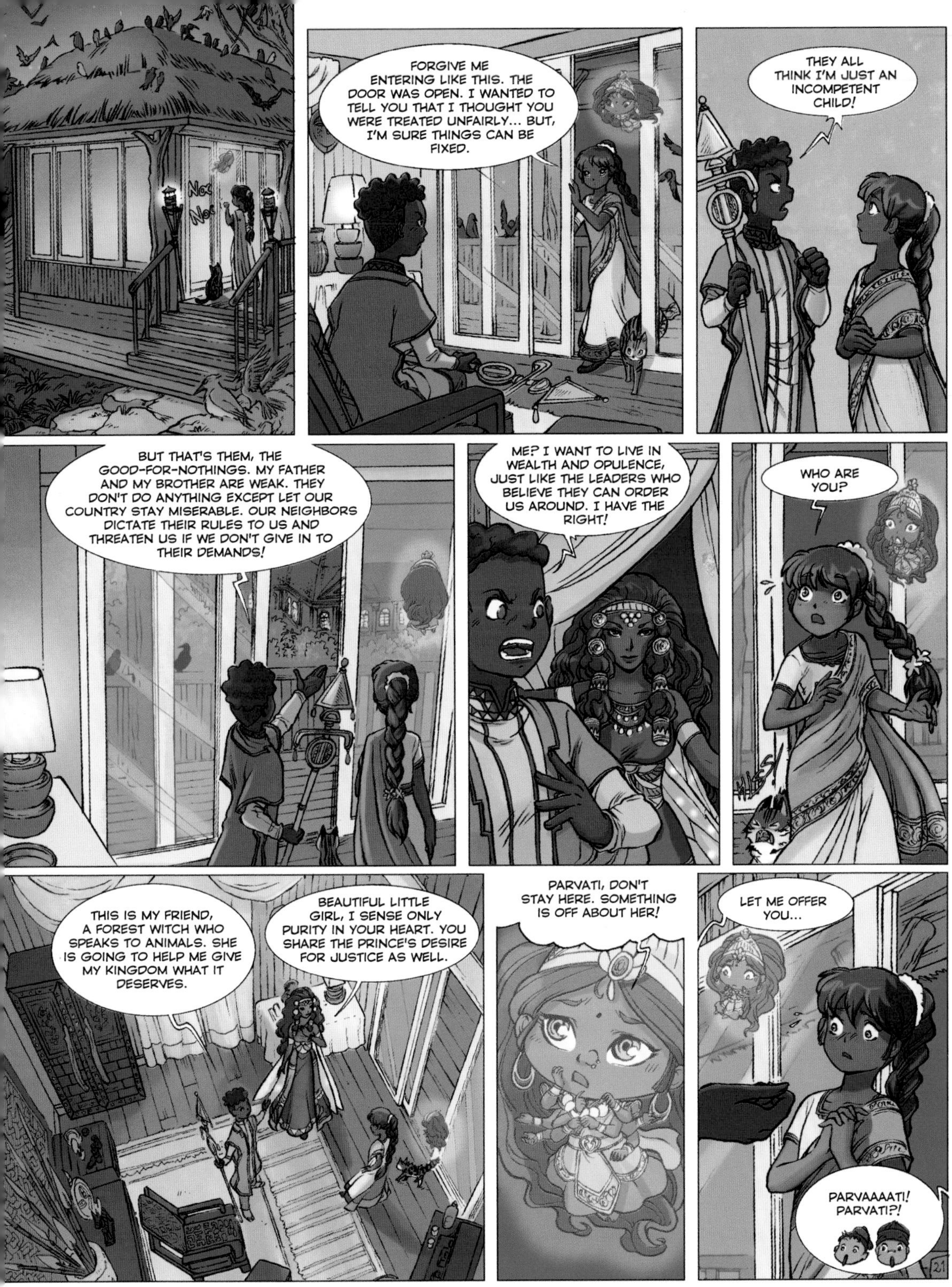
Noc
Noc
FORGIVE ME ENTERING LIKE THIS. THE DOOR WAS OPEN. I WANTED TO TELL YOU THAT I THOUGHT YOU WERE TREATED UNFAIRLY... BUT, I'M SURE THINGS CAN BE FIXED.
THEY ALL THINK I'M JUST AN INCOMPETENT CHILD!
BUT THAT'S THEM, THE GOOD-FOR-NOTHINGS. MY FATHER AND MY BROTHER ARE WEAK. THEY DON'T DO ANYTHING EXCEPT LET OUR COUNTRY STAY MISERABLE. OUR NEIGHBORS DICTATE THEIR RULES TO US AND THREATEN US IF WE DON'T GIVE IN TO THEIR DEMANDS!
ME? I WANT TO LIVE IN WEALTH AND OPULENCE, JUST LIKE THE LEADERS WHO BELIEVE THEY CAN ORDER US AROUND. I HAVE THE RIGHT!
WHO ARE YOU?
THIS IS MY FRIEND, A FOREST WITCH WHO SPEAKS TO ANIMALS. SHE IS GOING TO HELP ME GIVE MY KINGDOM WHAT IT DESERVES.
BEAUTIFUL LITTLE GIRL, I SENSE ONLY PURITY IN YOUR HEART. YOU SHARE THE PRINCE'S DESIRE FOR JUSTICE AS WELL.
PARVATI, DON'T STAY HERE. SOMETHING IS OFF ABOUT HER!
LET ME OFFER YOU...
PARVAAAATI! PARVATI?!
21

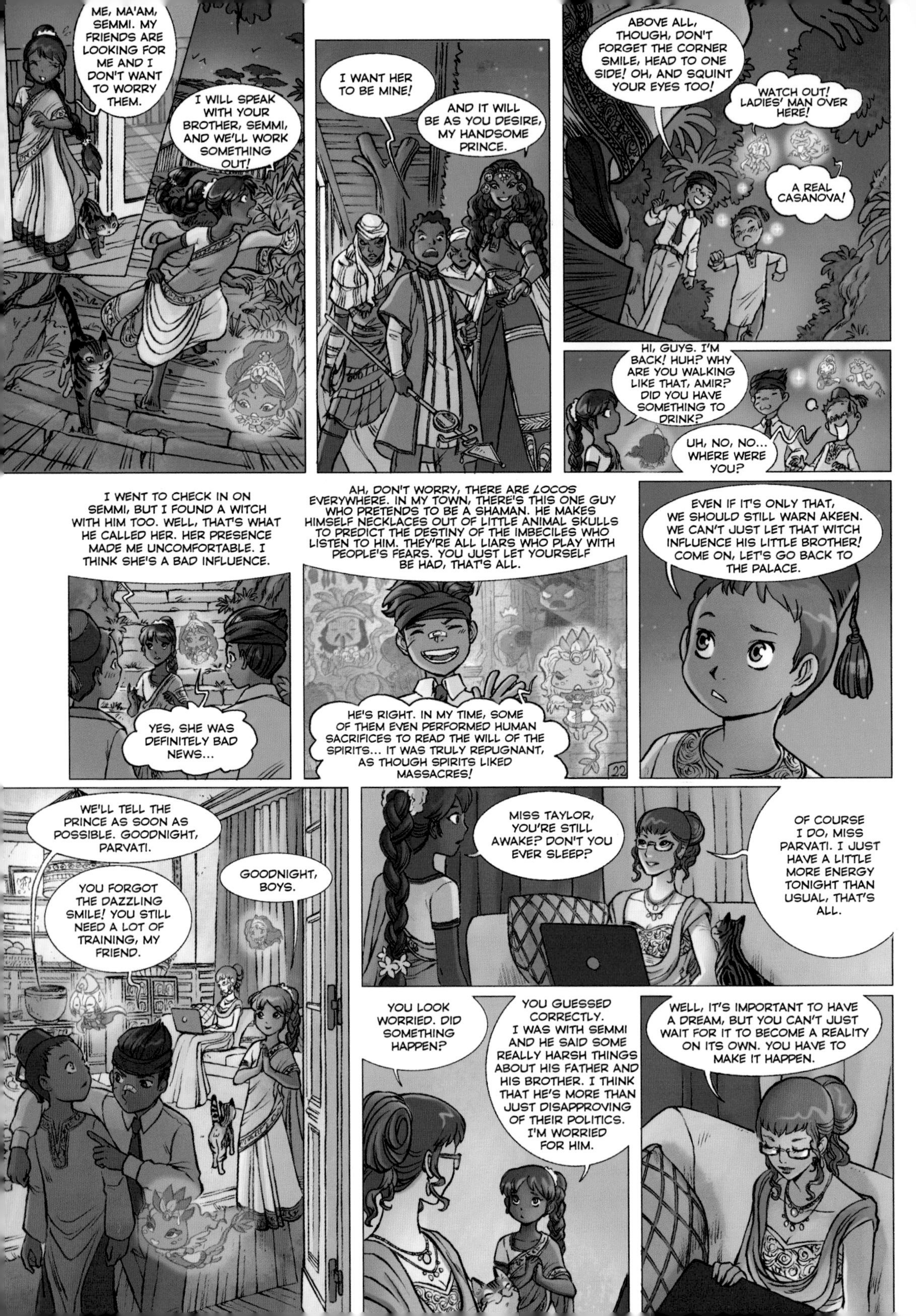

ME, MA'AM, SEMMI. MY FRIENDS ARE LOOKING FOR ME AND I DON'T WANT TO WORRY THEM.
I WILL SPEAK WITH YOUR BROTHER, SEMMI, AND WE'LL WORK SOMETHING OUT!
I WANT HER TO BE MINE!
AND IT WILL BE AS YOU DESIRE, MY HANDSOME PRINCE.
ABOVE ALL, THOUGH, DON'T FORGET THE CORNER SMILE, HEAD TO ONE SIDE! OH, AND SQUINT YOUR EYES TOO!
WATCH OUT! LADIES' MAN OVER HERE!
A REAL CASANOVA!
HI, GUYS. I'M BACK! HUH? WHY ARE YOU WALKING LIKE THAT, AMIR? DID YOU HAVE SOMETHING TO DRINK?
UH, NO, NO... WHERE WERE YOU?
I WENT TO CHECK IN ON SEMMI, BUT I FOUND A WITCH WITH HIM TOO. WELL, THAT'S WHAT HE CALLED HER. HER PRESENCE MADE ME UNCOMFORTABLE. I THINK SHE'S A BAD INFLUENCE.
YES, SHE WAS DEFINITELY BAD NEWS...
AH, DON'T WORRY, THERE ARE LOCOS EVERYWHERE. IN MY TOWN, THERE'S THIS ONE GUY WHO PRETENDS TO BE A SHAMAN. HE MAKES HIMSELF NECKLACES OUT OF LITTLE ANIMAL SKULLS TO PREDICT THE DESTINY OF THE IMBECILES WHO LISTEN TO HIM. THEY'RE ALL LIARS WHO PLAY WITH PEOPLE'S FEARS. YOU JUST LET YOURSELF BE HAD, THAT'S ALL.
HE'S RIGHT. IN MY TIME, SOME OF THEM EVEN PERFORMED HUMAN SACRIFICES TO READ THE WILL OF THE SPIRITS... IT WAS TRULY REPUGNANT, AS THOUGH SPIRITS LIKED MASSACRES!
22
EVEN IF IT'S ONLY THAT, WE SHOULD STILL WARN AKEEN. WE CAN'T JUST LET THAT WITCH INFLUENCE HIS LITTLE BROTHER! COME ON, LET'S GO BACK TO THE PALACE.
WE'LL TELL THE PRINCE AS SOON AS POSSIBLE. GOODNIGHT, PARVATI.
YOU FORGOT THE DAZZLING SMILE! YOU STILL NEED A LOT OF TRAINING, MY FRIEND.
GOODNIGHT, BOYS.
MISS TAYLOR, YOU'RE STILL AWAKE? DON'T YOU EVER SLEEP?
OF COURSE I DO, MISS PARVATI. I JUST HAVE A LITTLE MORE ENERGY TONIGHT THAN USUAL, THAT'S ALL.
YOU LOOK WORRIED. DID SOMETHING HAPPEN?
YOU GUESSED CORRECTLY. I WAS WITH SEMMI AND HE SAID SOME REALLY HARSH THINGS ABOUT HIS FATHER AND HIS BROTHER. I THINK THAT HE'S MORE THAN JUST DISAPPROVING OF THEIR POLITICS. I'M WORRIED FOR HIM.
WELL, IT'S IMPORTANT TO HAVE A DREAM, BUT YOU CAN'T JUST WAIT FOR IT TO BECOME A REALITY ON ITS OWN. YOU HAVE TO MAKE IT HAPPEN.

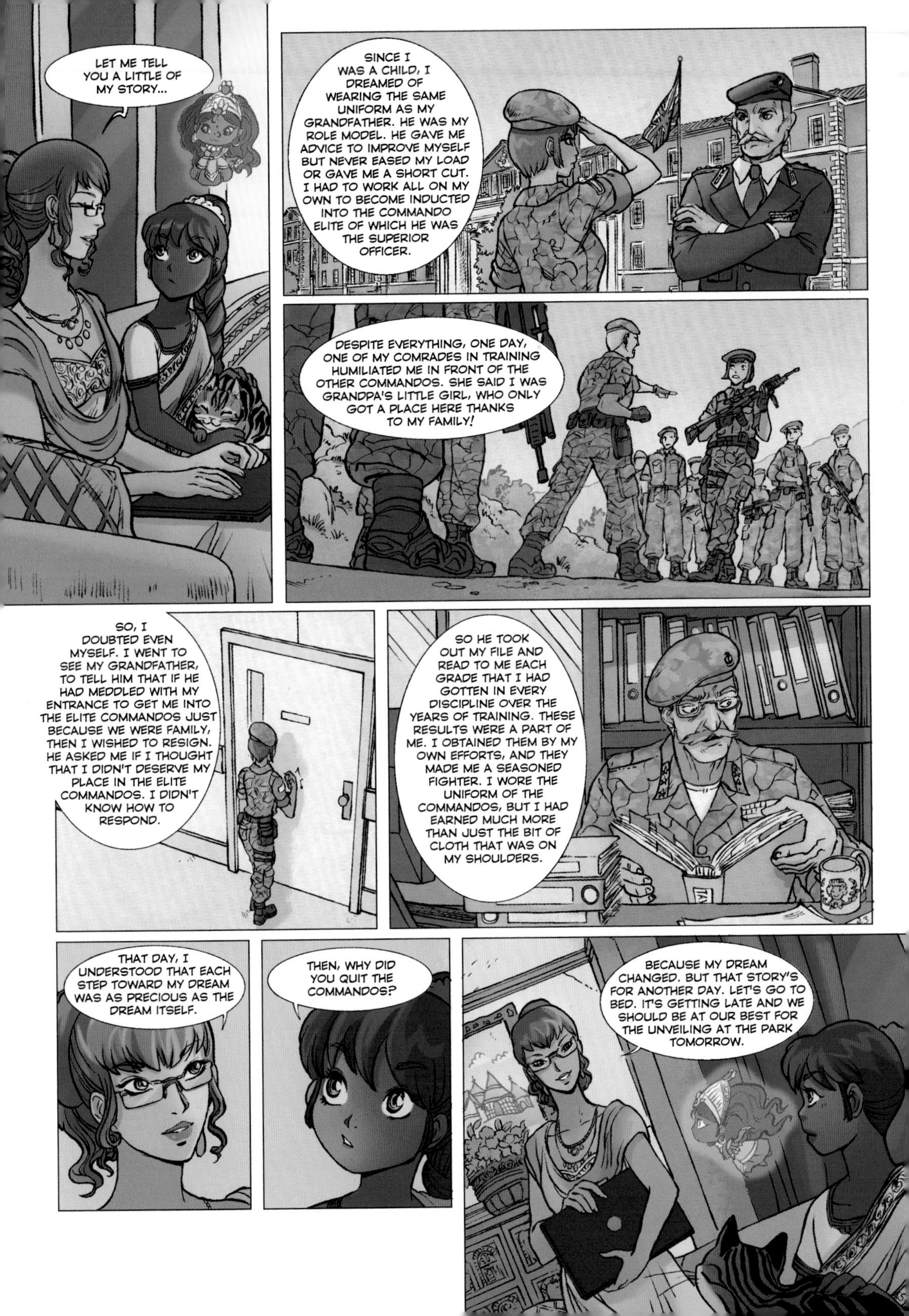
LET ME TELL YOU A LITTLE OF MY STORY...
SINCE I WAS A CHILD, I DREAMED OF WEARING THE SAME UNIFORM AS MY GRANDFATHER. HE WAS MY ROLE MODEL. HE GAVE ME ADVICE TO IMPROVE MYSELF BUT NEVER EASED MY LOAD OR GAVE ME A SHORT CUT. I HAD TO WORK ALL ON MY OWN TO BECOME INDUCTED INTO THE COMMANDO ELITE OF WHICH HE WAS THE SUPERIOR OFFICER.
DESPITE EVERYTHING, ONE DAY, ONE OF MY COMRADES IN TRAINING HUMILIATED ME IN FRONT OF THE OTHER COMMANDOS. SHE SAID I WAS GRANDPA'S LITTLE GIRL, WHO ONLY GOT A PLACE HERE THANKS TO MY FAMILY!
SO, I DOUBTED EVEN MYSELF. I WENT TO SEE MY GRANDFATHER, TO TELL HIM THAT IF HE HAD MEDDLED WITH MY ENTRANCE TO GET ME INTO THE ELITE COMMANDOS JUST BECAUSE WE WERE FAMILY, THEN I WISHED TO RESIGN. HE ASKED ME IF I THOUGHT THAT I DIDN'T DESERVE MY PLACE IN THE ELITE COMMANDOS. I DIDN'T KNOW HOW TO RESPOND.
SO HE TOOK OUT MY FILE AND READ TO ME EACH GRADE THAT I HAD GOTTEN IN EVERY DISCIPLINE OVER THE YEARS OF TRAINING. THESE RESULTS WERE A PART OF ME. I OBTAINED THEM BY MY OWN EFFORTS, AND THEY MADE ME A SEASONED FIGHTER. I WORE THE UNIFORM OF THE COMMANDOS, BUT I HAD EARNED MUCH MORE THAN JUST THE BIT OF CLOTH THAT WAS ON MY SHOULDERS.
THAT DAY, I UNDERSTOOD THAT EACH STEP TOWARD MY DREAM WAS AS PRECIOUS AS THE DREAM ITSELF.
THEN, WHY DID YOU QUIT THE COMMANDOS?
BECAUSE MY DREAM CHANGED. BUT THAT STORY'S FOR ANOTHER DAY. LET'S GO TO BED. IT'S GETTING LATE AND WE SHOULD BE AT OUR BEST FOR THE UNVEILING AT THE PARK TOMORROW.

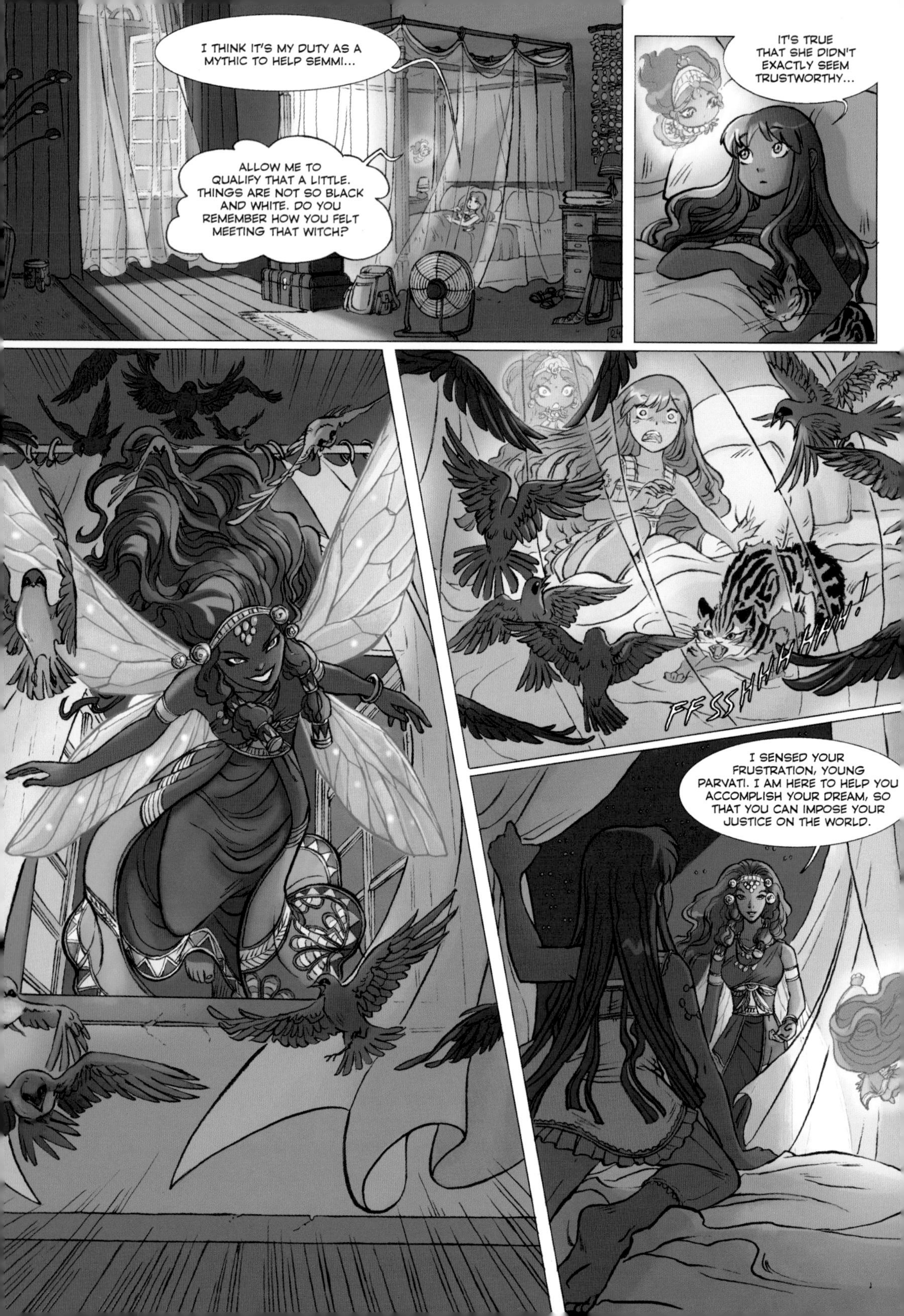
I THINK IT'S MY DUTY AS A MYTHIC TO HELP SEMMI...
ALLOW ME TO QUALIFY THAT A LITTLE. THINGS ARE NOT SO BLACK AND WHITE. DO YOU REMEMBER HOW YOU FELT MEETING THAT WITCH?
IT'S TRUE THAT SHE DIDN'T EXACTLY SEEM TRUSTWORTHY...
FFSSHHHHHHH!
I SENSED YOUR FRUSTRATION, YOUNG PARVATI. I AM HERE TO HELP YOU ACCOMPLISH YOUR DREAM, SO THAT YOU CAN IMPOSE YOUR JUSTICE ON THE WORLD.

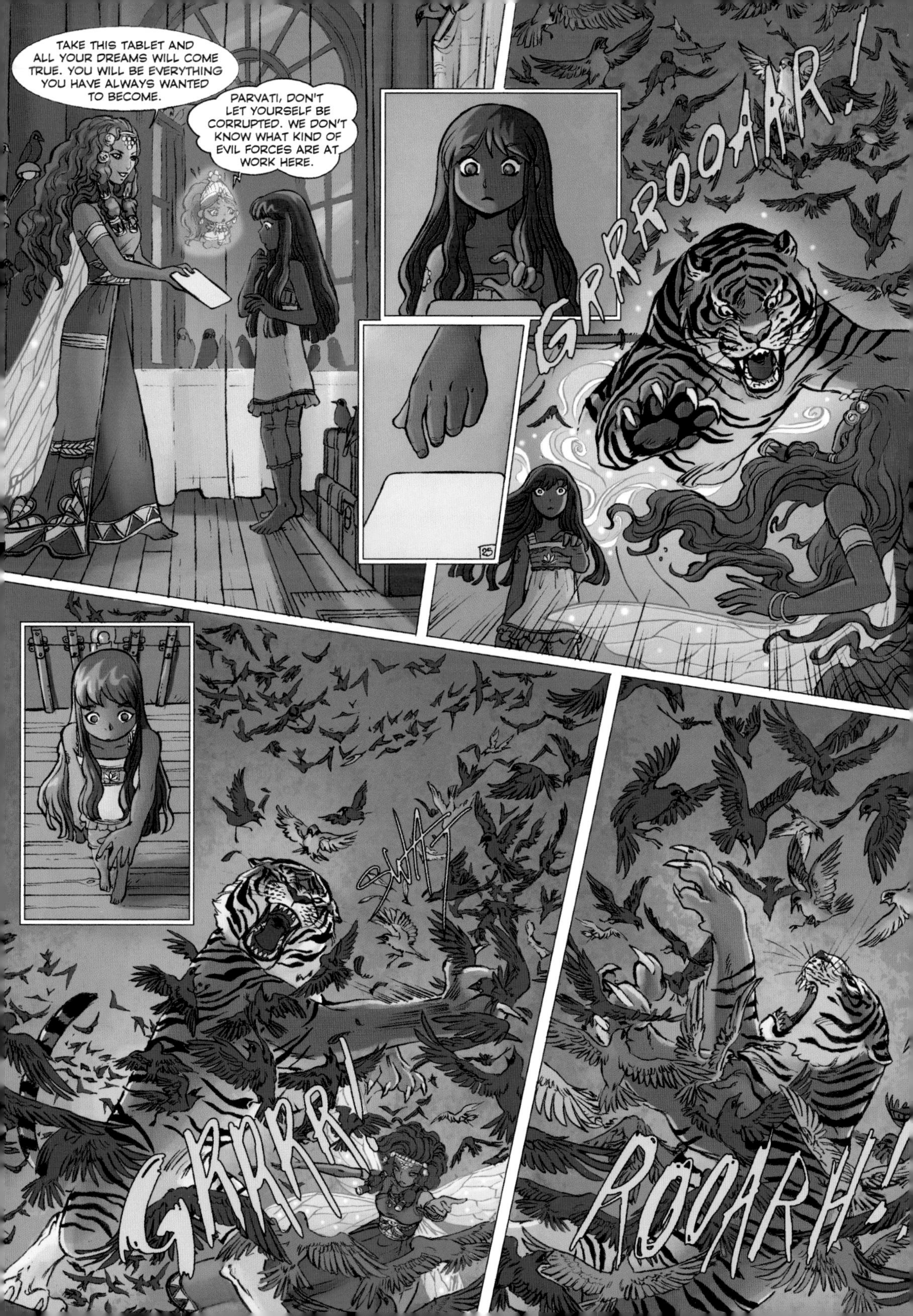
TAKE THIS TABLET AND ALL YOUR DREAMS WILL COME TRUE. YOU WILL BE EVERYTHING YOU HAVE ALWAYS WANTED TO BECOME.
PARVATI, DON'T LET YOURSELF BE CORRUPTED. WE DON'T KNOW WHAT KIND OF EVIL FORCES ARE AT WORK HERE.
GRRROOAAR!
GRRRR!
ROOARH!

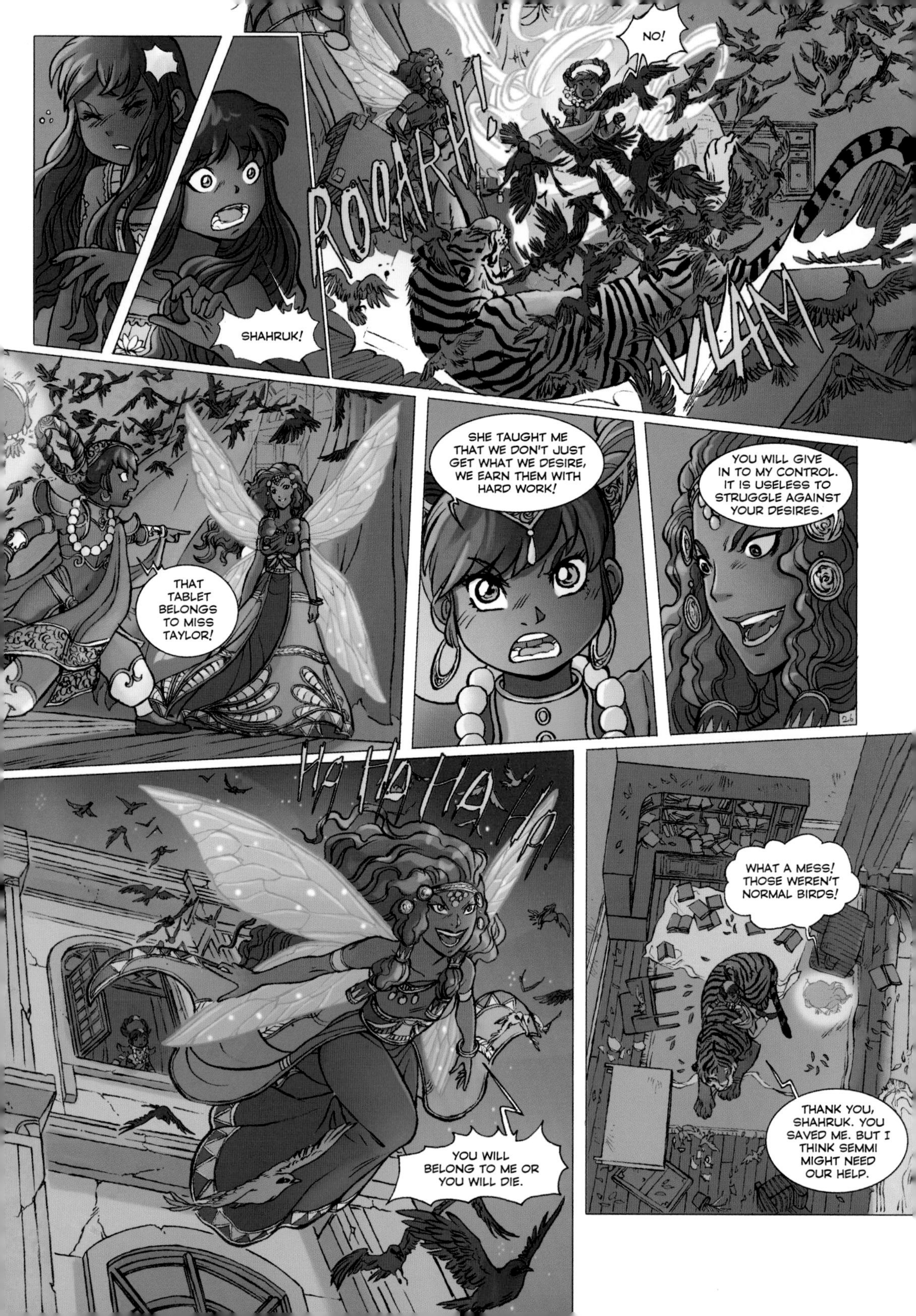
SHAHRUK!
NO!
ROOARH!
VLAM
THAT TABLET BELONGS TO MISS TAYLOR!
SHE TAUGHT ME THAT WE DON'T JUST GET WHAT WE DESIRE, WE EARN THEM WITH HARD WORK!
YOU WILL GIVE IN TO MY CONTROL. IT IS USELESS TO STRUGGLE AGAINST YOUR DESIRES.
HA HA HA HA HA!
YOU WILL BELONG TO ME OR YOU WILL DIE.
WHAT A MESS! THOSE WEREN'T NORMAL BIRDS!
THANK YOU, SHAHRUK. YOU SAVED ME. BUT I THINK SEMMI MIGHT NEED OUR HELP.

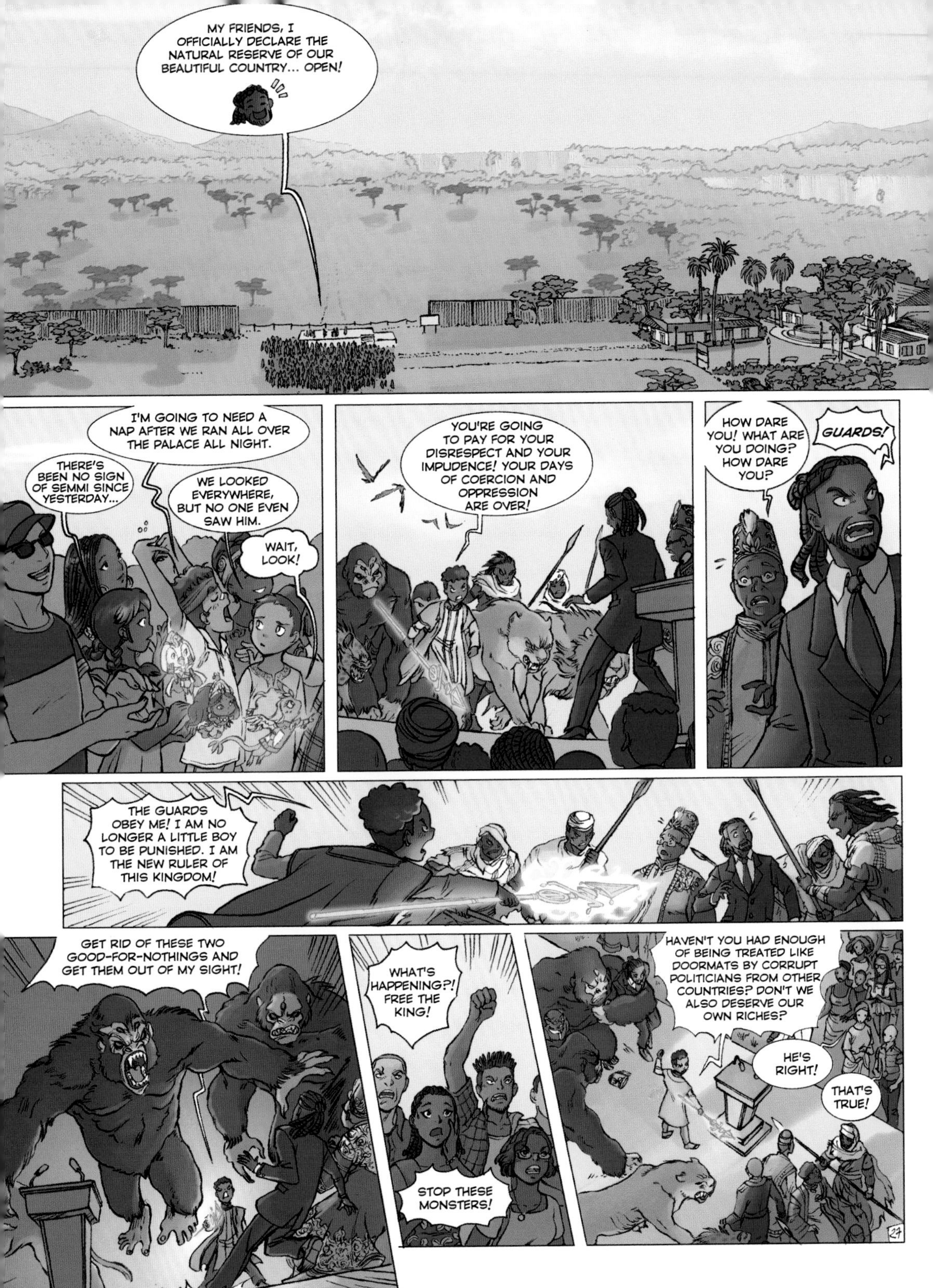
MY FRIENDS, I OFFICIALLY DECLARE THE NATURAL RESERVE OF OUR BEAUTIFUL COUNTRY... OPEN!
I'M GOING TO NEED A NAP AFTER WE RAN ALL OVER THE PALACE ALL NIGHT.
THERE'S BEEN NO SIGN OF SEMMI SINCE YESTERDAY...
WE LOOKED EVERYWHERE, BUT NO ONE EVEN SAW HIM.
WAIT, LOOK!
YOU'RE GOING TO PAY FOR YOUR DISRESPECT AND YOUR IMPUDENCE! YOUR DAYS OF COERCION AND OPPRESSION ARE OVER!
HOW DARE YOU! WHAT ARE YOU DOING? HOW DARE YOU?
GUARDS!
THE GUARDS OBEY ME! I AM NO LONGER A LITTLE BOY TO BE PUNISHED. I AM THE NEW RULER OF THIS KINGDOM!
GET RID OF THESE TWO GOOD-FOR-NOTHINGS AND GET THEM OUT OF MY SIGHT!
WHAT'S HAPPENING?! FREE THE KING!
STOP THESE MONSTERS!
HAVEN'T YOU HAD ENOUGH OF BEING TREATED LIKE DOORMATS BY CORRUPT POLITICIANS FROM OTHER COUNTRIES? DON'T WE ALSO DESERVE OUR OWN RICHES?
HE'S RIGHT!
THAT'S TRUE!
27

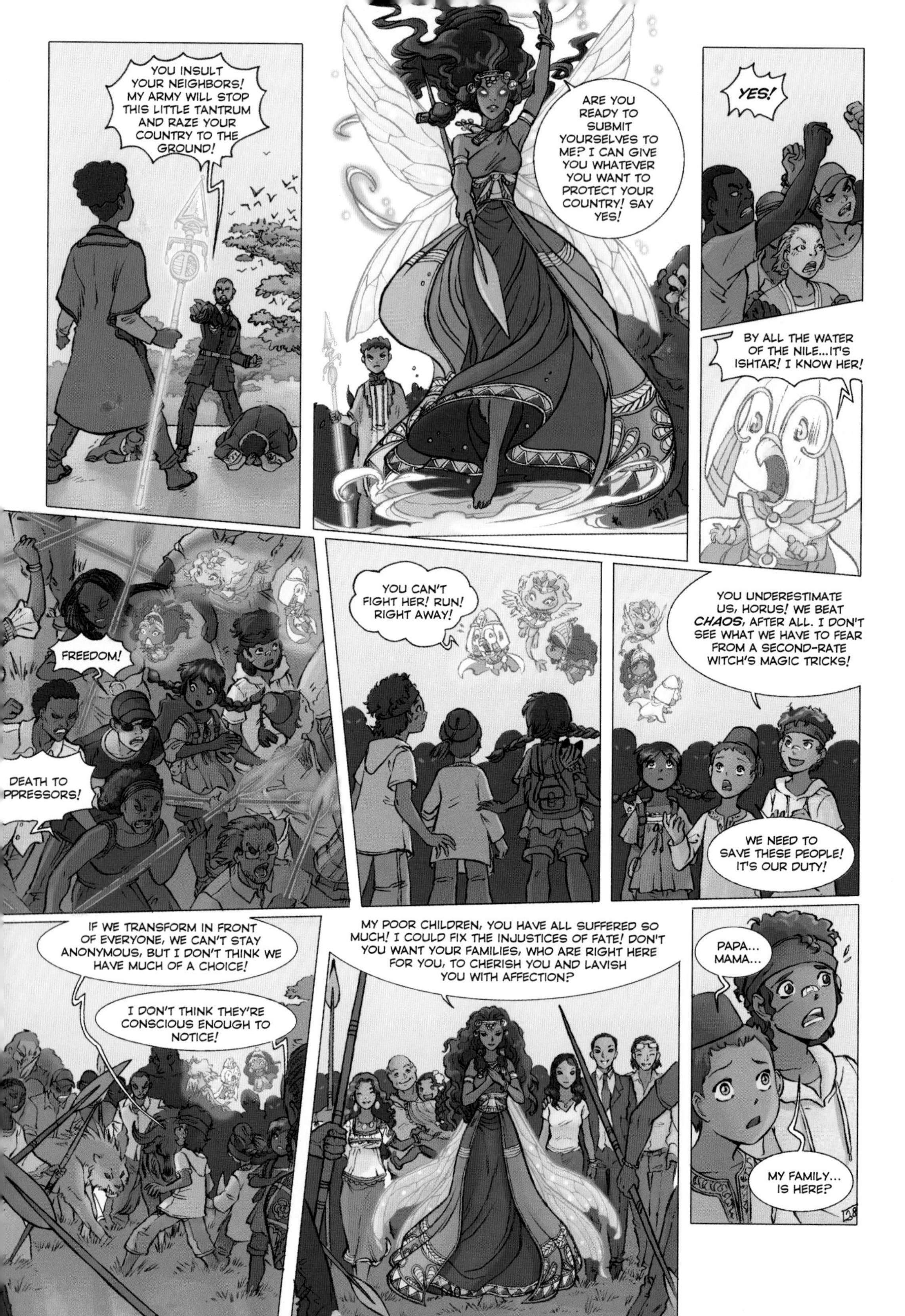

YOU INSULT YOUR NEIGHBORS! MY ARMY WILL STOP THIS LITTLE TANTRUM AND RAZE YOUR COUNTRY TO THE GROUND!
ARE YOU READY TO SUBMIT YOURSELVES TO ME? I CAN GIVE YOU WHATEVER YOU WANT TO PROTECT YOUR COUNTRY! SAY YES!
YES!
BY ALL THE WATER OF THE NILE...IT'S ISHTAR! I KNOW HER!
FREEDOM!
DEATH TO
PPRESSORS!
YOU CAN'T FIGHT HER! RUN! RIGHT AWAY!
YOU UNDERESTIMATE US, HORUS! WE BEAT CHAOS, AFTER ALL. I DON'T SEE WHAT WE HAVE TO FEAR FROM A SECOND-RATE WITCH'S MAGIC TRICKS!
WE NEED TO SAVE THESE PEOPLE! IT'S OUR DUTY!
IF WE TRANSFORM IN FRONT OF EVERYONE, WE CAN'T STAY ANONYMOUS, BUT I DON'T THINK WE HAVE MUCH OF A CHOICE!
I DON'T THINK THEY'RE CONSCIOUS ENOUGH TO NOTICE!
MY POOR CHILDREN, YOU HAVE ALL SUFFERED SO MUCH! I COULD FIX THE INJUSTICES OF FATE! DON'T YOU WANT YOUR FAMILIES, WHO ARE RIGHT HERE FOR YOU, TO CHERISH YOU AND LAVISH YOU WITH AFFECTION?
PAPA... MAMA...
MY FAMILY... IS HERE?

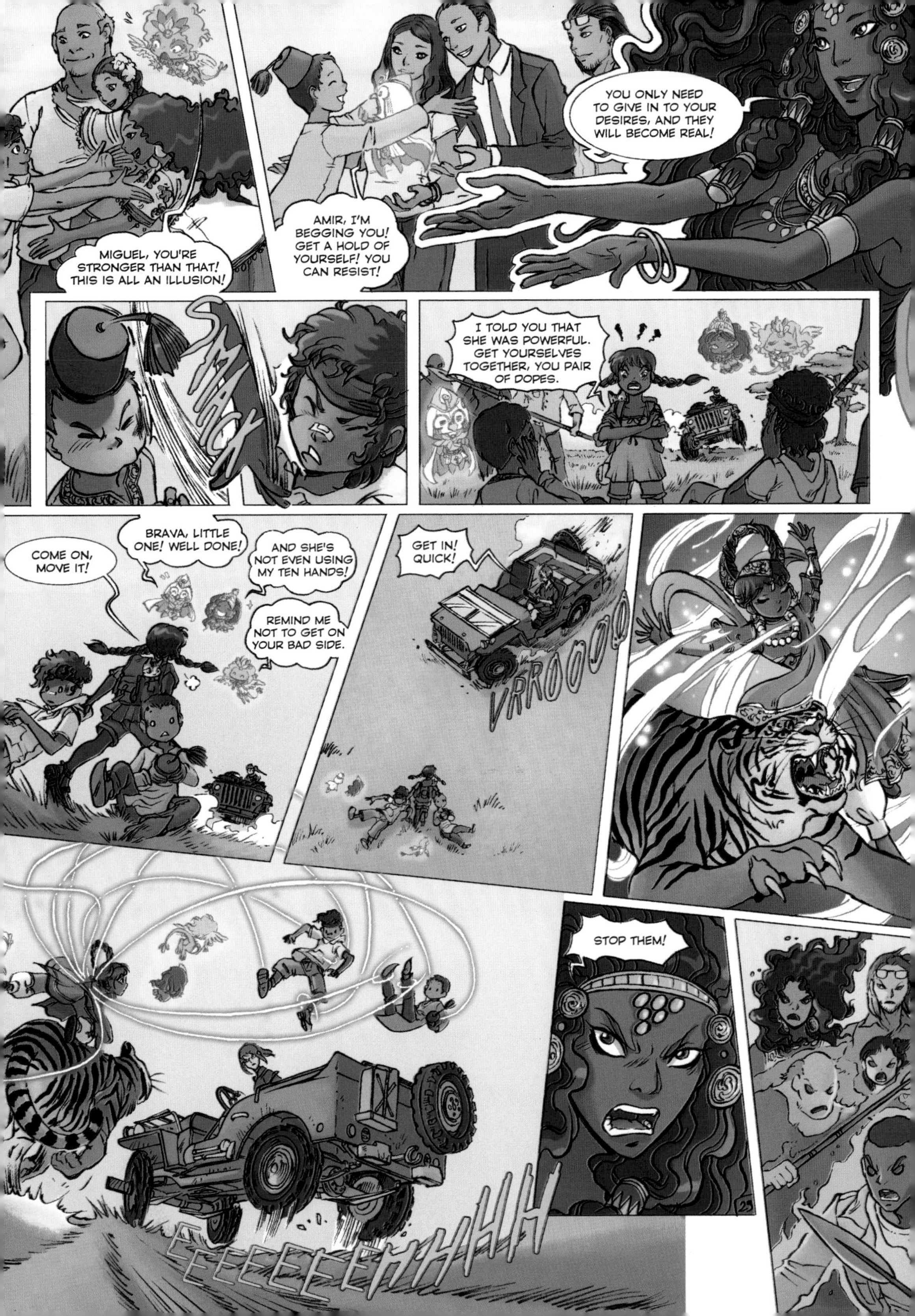
MIGUEL, YOU'RE STRONGER THAN THAT! THIS IS ALL AN ILLUSION!
AMIR, I'M BEGGING YOU! GET A HOLD OF YOURSELF! YOU CAN RESIST!
YOU ONLY NEED TO GIVE IN TO YOUR DESIRES, AND THEY WILL BECOME REAL!
SMACK
I TOLD YOU THAT SHE WAS POWERFUL. GET YOURSELVES TOGETHER, YOU PAIR OF DOPES.
COME ON, MOVE IT!
BRAVA, LITTLE ONE! WELL DONE!
AND SHE'S NOT EVEN USING MY TEN HANDS!
REMIND ME NOT TO GET ON YOUR BAD SIDE.
GET IN! QUICK!
VRROOOOO
EEEEEEEHHHHH
STOP THEM!
25

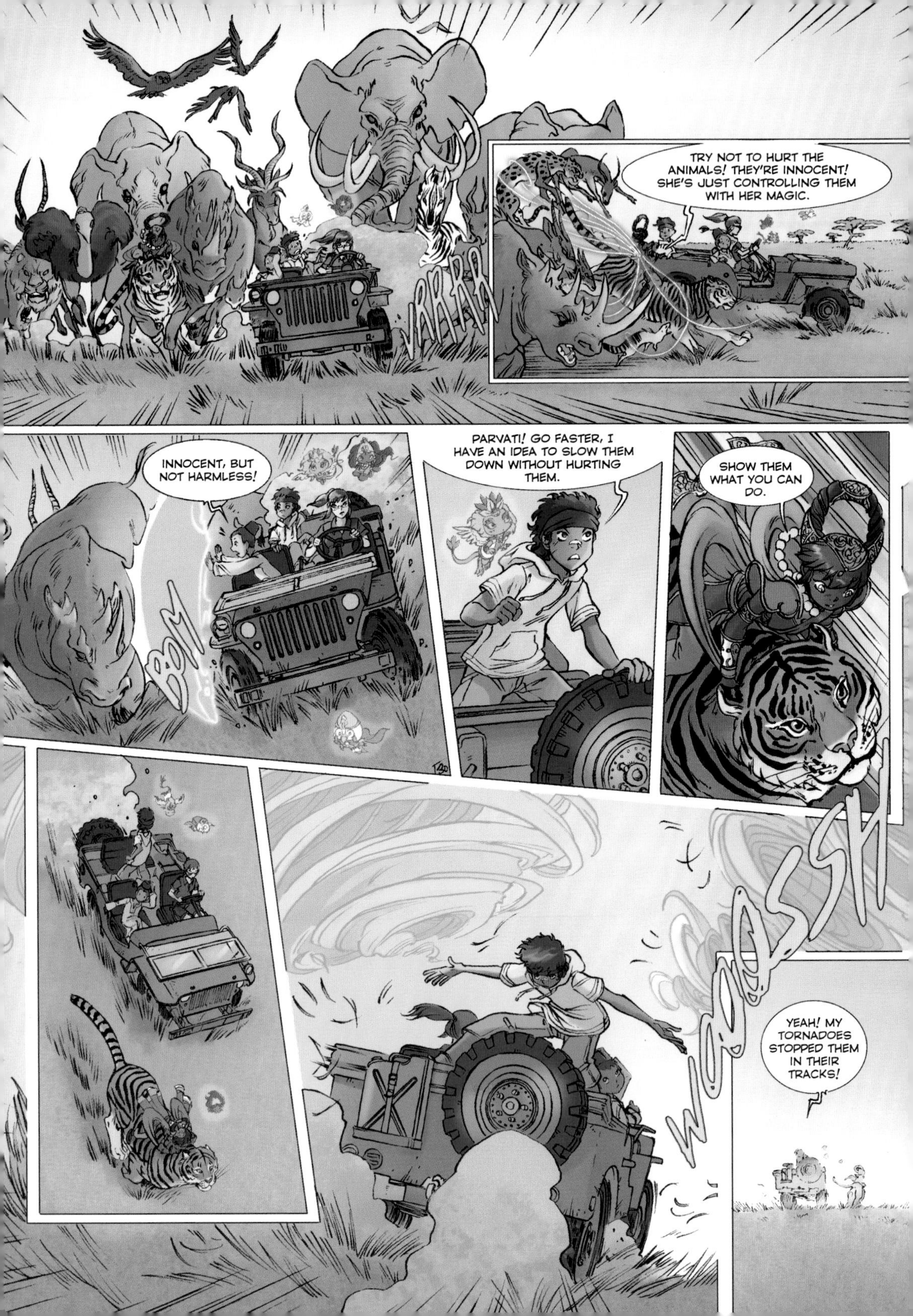
VRRRR
TRY NOT TO HURT THE ANIMALS! THEY'RE INNOCENT! SHE'S JUST CONTROLLING THEM WITH HER MAGIC.
INNOCENT, BUT NOT HARMLESS!
BOM
PARVATI! GO FASTER, I HAVE AN IDEA TO SLOW THEM DOWN WITHOUT HURTING THEM.
SHOW THEM WHAT YOU CAN DO.
WOOOSH
YEAH! MY TORNADOES STOPPED THEM IN THEIR TRACKS!

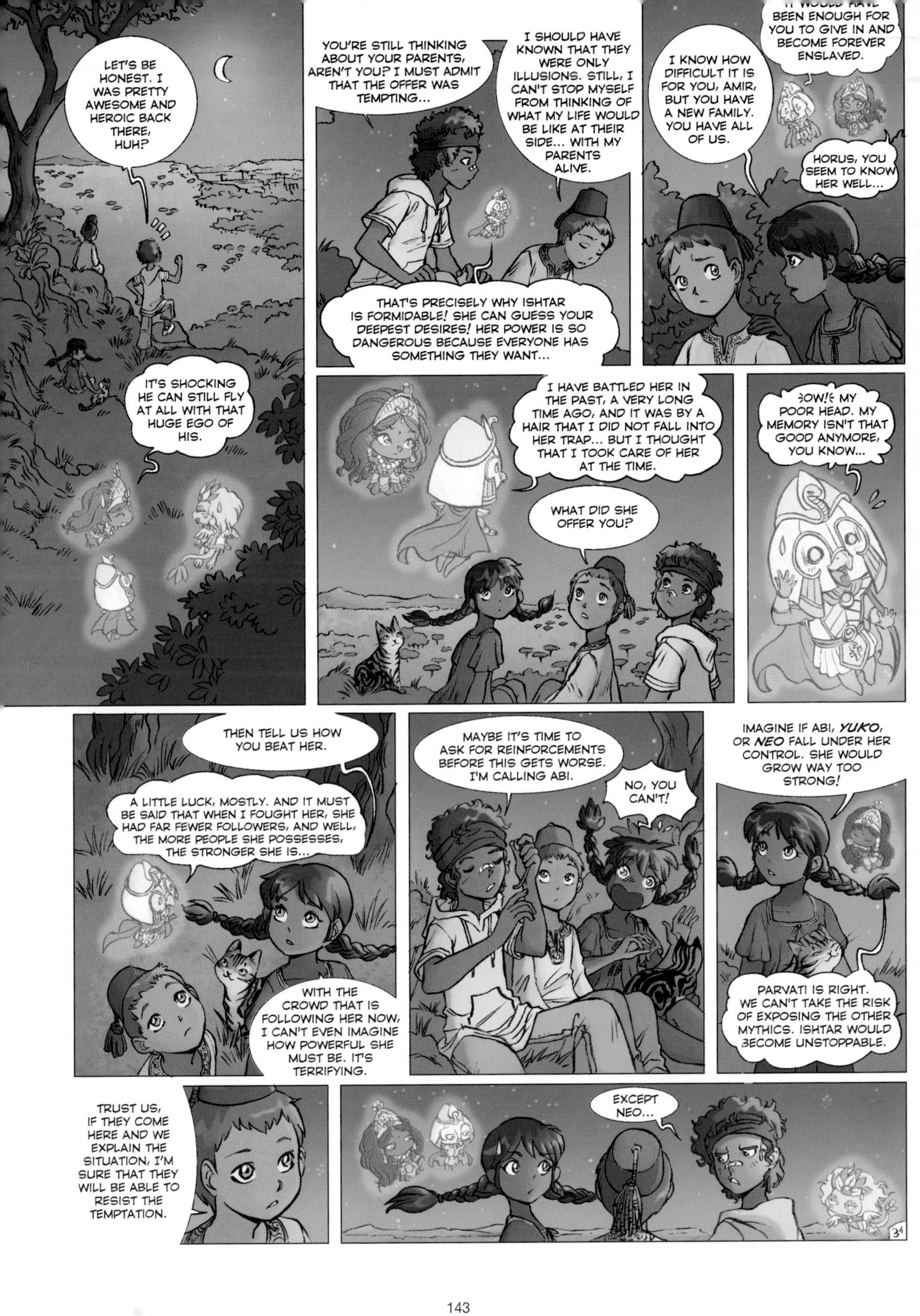

LET'S BE HONEST. I WAS PRETTY AWESOME AND HEROIC BACK THERE, HUH?
IT'S SHOCKING HE CAN STILL FLY AT ALL WITH THAT HUGE EGO OF HIS.
YOU'RE STILL THINKING ABOUT YOUR PARENTS, AREN'T YOU? I MUST ADMIT THAT THE OFFER WAS TEMPTING...
I SHOULD HAVE KNOWN THAT THEY WERE ONLY ILLUSIONS. STILL, I CAN'T STOP MYSELF FROM THINKING OF WHAT MY LIFE WOULD BE LIKE AT THEIR SIDE... WITH MY PARENTS ALIVE.
THAT'S PRECISELY WHY ISHTAR IS FORMIDABLE! SHE CAN GUESS YOUR DEEPEST DESIRES! HER POWER IS SO DANGEROUS BECAUSE EVERYONE HAS SOMETHING THEY WANT...
BEEN ENOUGH FOR YOU TO GIVE IN AND BECOME FOREVER ENSLAVED.
I KNOW HOW DIFFICULT IT IS FOR YOU, AMIR, BUT YOU HAVE A NEW FAMILY. YOU HAVE ALL OF US.
HORUS, YOU SEEM TO KNOW HER WELL...
I HAVE BATTLED HER IN THE PAST, A VERY LONG TIME AGO, AND IT WAS BY A HAIR THAT I DID NOT FALL INTO HER TRAP... BUT I THOUGHT THAT I TOOK CARE OF HER AT THE TIME.
WHAT DID SHE OFFER YOU?
OW!! MY POOR HEAD. MY MEMORY ISN'T THAT GOOD ANYMORE, YOU KNOW...
THEN TELL US HOW YOU BEAT HER.
A LITTLE LUCK, MOSTLY. AND IT MUST BE SAID THAT WHEN I FOUGHT HER, SHE HAD FAR FEWER FOLLOWERS, AND WELL, THE MORE PEOPLE SHE POSSESSES, THE STRONGER SHE IS...
WITH THE CROWD THAT IS FOLLOWING HER NOW, I CAN'T EVEN IMAGINE HOW POWERFUL SHE MUST BE. IT'S TERRIFYING.
MAYBE IT'S TIME TO ASK FOR REINFORCEMENTS BEFORE THIS GETS WORSE. I'M CALLING ABI.
NO, YOU CAN'T!
IMAGINE IF ABI, *YUKO*, OR *NEO* FALL UNDER HER CONTROL. SHE WOULD GROW WAY TOO STRONG!
PARVATI IS RIGHT. WE CAN'T TAKE THE RISK OF EXPOSING THE OTHER MYTHICS. ISHTAR WOULD BECOME UNSTOPPABLE.
TRUST US, IF THEY COME HERE AND WE EXPLAIN THE SITUATION, I'M SURE THAT THEY WILL BE ABLE TO RESIST THE TEMPTATION.
EXCEPT NEO...
31

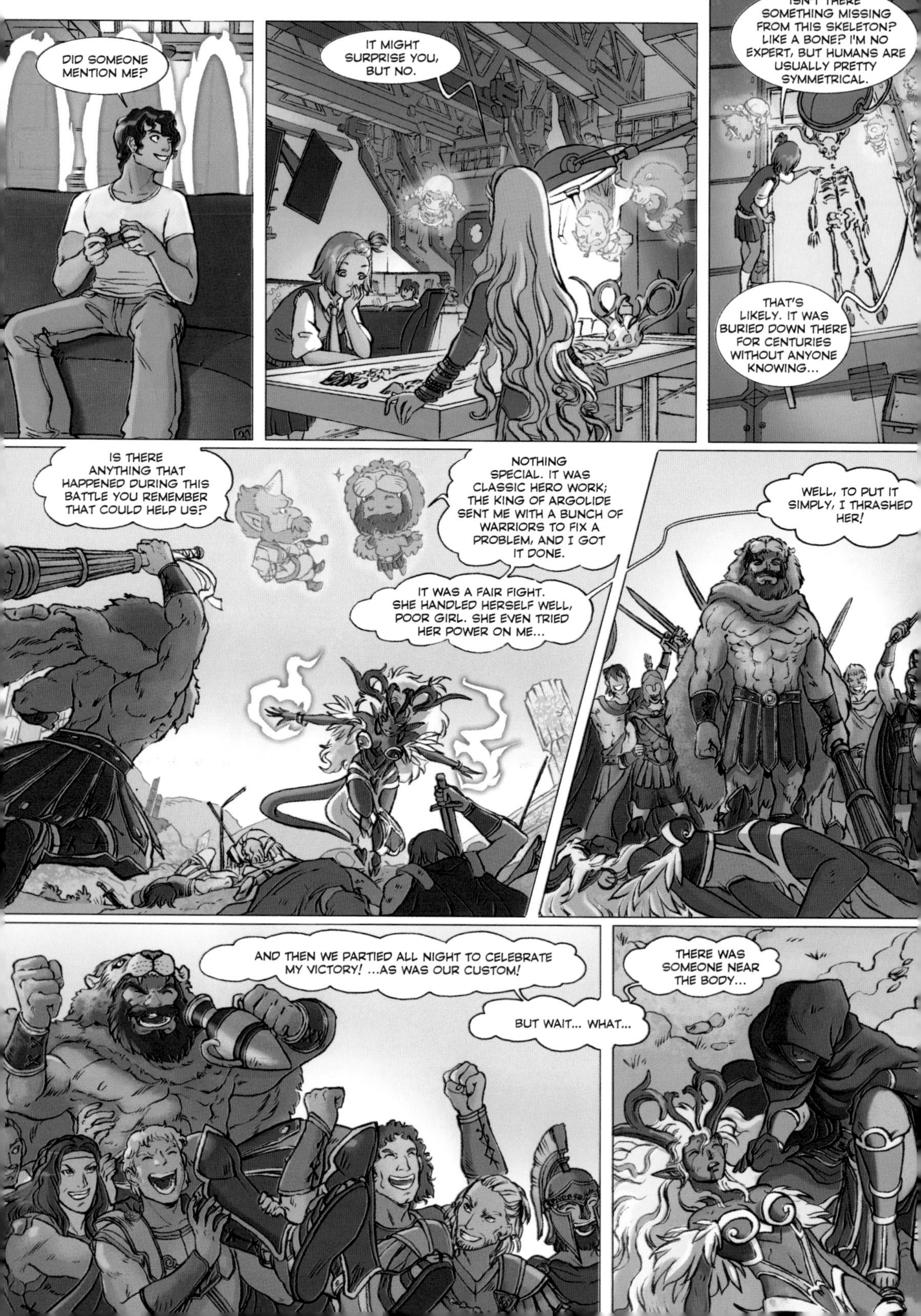
DID SOMEONE MENTION ME?
IT MIGHT SURPRISE YOU, BUT NO.
ISN'T THERE SOMETHING MISSING FROM THIS SKELETON? LIKE A BONE? I'M NO EXPERT, BUT HUMANS ARE USUALLY PRETTY SYMMETRICAL.
THAT'S LIKELY. IT WAS BURIED DOWN THERE FOR CENTURIES WITHOUT ANYONE KNOWING...
IS THERE ANYTHING THAT HAPPENED DURING THIS BATTLE YOU REMEMBER THAT COULD HELP US?
NOTHING SPECIAL. IT WAS CLASSIC HERO WORK; THE KING OF ARGOLIDE SENT ME WITH A BUNCH OF WARRIORS TO FIX A PROBLEM, AND I GOT IT DONE.
IT WAS A FAIR FIGHT. SHE HANDLED HERSELF WELL, POOR GIRL. SHE EVEN TRIED HER POWER ON ME...
WELL, TO PUT IT SIMPLY, I THRASHED HER!
AND THEN WE PARTIED ALL NIGHT TO CELEBRATE MY VICTORY! ...AS WAS OUR CUSTOM!
BUT WAIT... WHAT...
THERE WAS SOMEONE NEAR THE BODY...

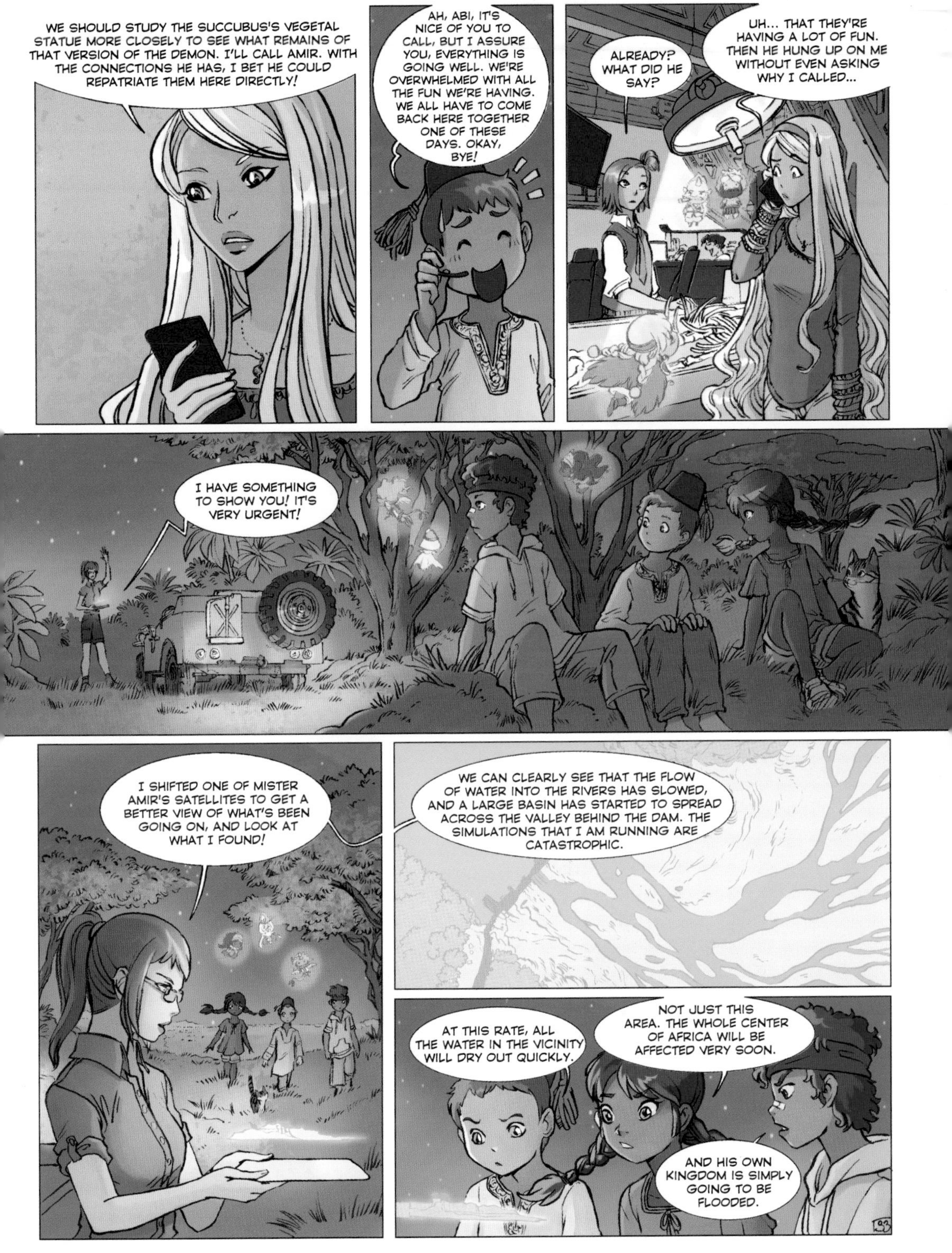
WE SHOULD STUDY THE SUCCUBUS'S VEGETAL STATUE MORE CLOSELY TO SEE WHAT REMAINS OF THAT VERSION OF THE DEMON. I'LL CALL AMIR. WITH THE CONNECTIONS HE HAS, I BET HE COULD REPATRIATE THEM HERE DIRECTLY!
AH, ABI, IT'S NICE OF YOU TO CALL, BUT I ASSURE YOU, EVERYTHING IS GOING WELL. WE'RE OVERWHELMED WITH ALL THE FUN WE'RE HAVING. WE ALL HAVE TO COME BACK HERE TOGETHER ONE OF THESE DAYS. OKAY, BYE!
ALREADY? WHAT DID HE SAY?
UH... THAT THEY'RE HAVING A LOT OF FUN. THEN HE HUNG UP ON ME WITHOUT EVEN ASKING WHY I CALLED...
I HAVE SOMETHING TO SHOW YOU! IT'S VERY URGENT!
I SHIFTED ONE OF MISTER AMIR'S SATELLITES TO GET A BETTER VIEW OF WHAT'S BEEN GOING ON, AND LOOK AT WHAT I FOUND!
WE CAN CLEARLY SEE THAT THE FLOW OF WATER INTO THE RIVERS HAS SLOWED, AND A LARGE BASIN HAS STARTED TO SPREAD ACROSS THE VALLEY BEHIND THE DAM. THE SIMULATIONS THAT I AM RUNNING ARE CATASTROPHIC.
AT THIS RATE, ALL THE WATER IN THE VICINITY WILL DRY OUT QUICKLY.
NOT JUST THIS AREA. THE WHOLE CENTER OF AFRICA WILL BE AFFECTED VERY SOON.
AND HIS OWN KINGDOM IS SIMPLY GOING TO BE FLOODED.

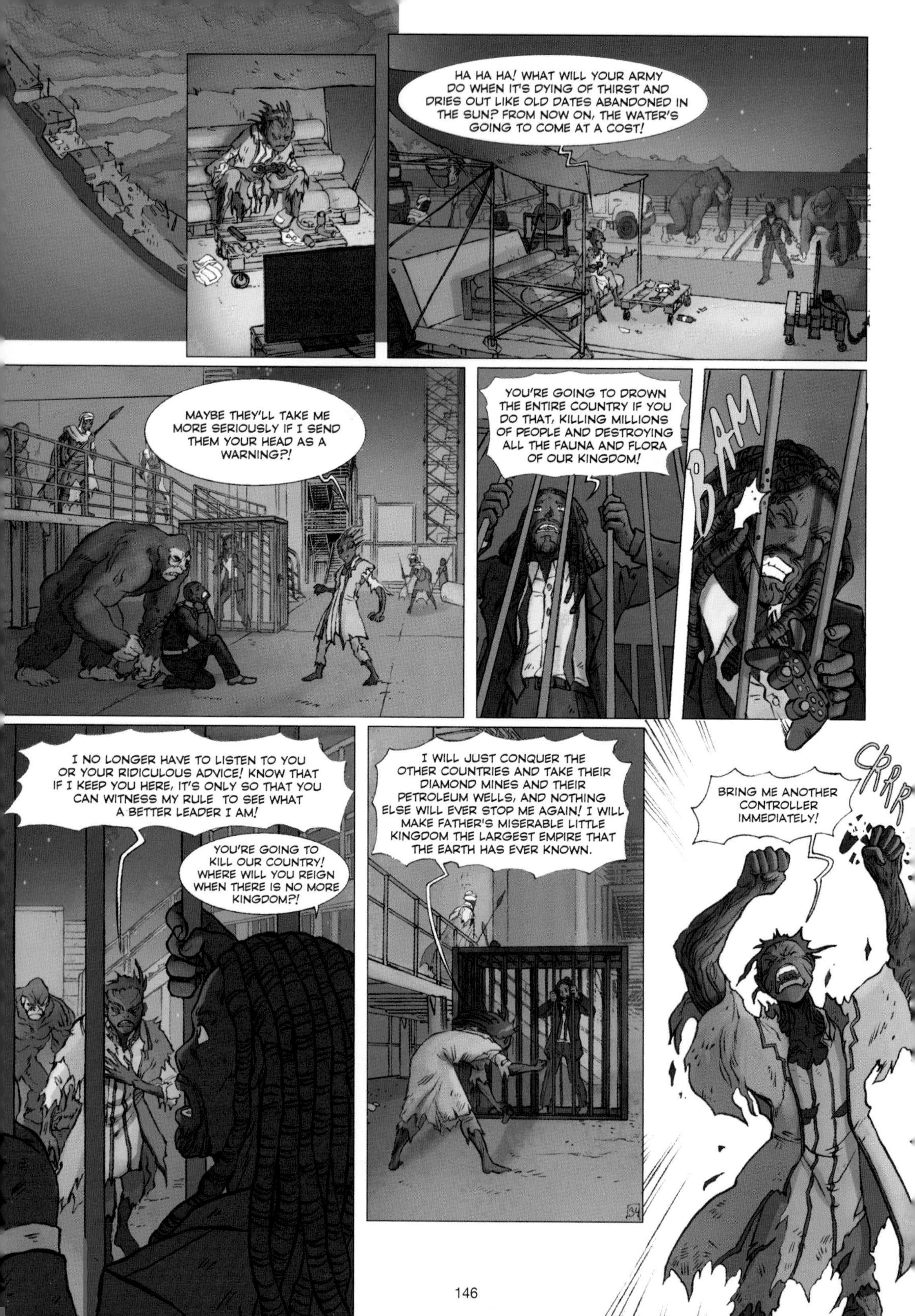
HA HA HA! WHAT WILL YOUR ARMY DO WHEN IT'S DYING OF THIRST AND DRIES OUT LIKE OLD DATES ABANDONED IN THE SUN? FROM NOW ON, THE WATER'S GOING TO COME AT A COST!
MAYBE THEY'LL TAKE ME MORE SERIOUSLY IF I SEND THEM YOUR HEAD AS A WARNING?!
YOU'RE GOING TO DROWN THE ENTIRE COUNTRY IF YOU DO THAT, KILLING MILLIONS OF PEOPLE AND DESTROYING ALL THE FAUNA AND FLORA OF OUR KINGDOM!
BAM
I NO LONGER HAVE TO LISTEN TO YOU OR YOUR RIDICULOUS ADVICE! KNOW THAT IF I KEEP YOU HERE, IT'S ONLY SO THAT YOU CAN WITNESS MY RULE TO SEE WHAT A BETTER LEADER I AM!
YOU'RE GOING TO KILL OUR COUNTRY! WHERE WILL YOU REIGN WHEN THERE IS NO MORE KINGDOM?!
I WILL JUST CONQUER THE OTHER COUNTRIES AND TAKE THEIR DIAMOND MINES AND THEIR PETROLEUM WELLS, AND NOTHING ELSE WILL EVER STOP ME AGAIN! I WILL MAKE FATHER'S MISERABLE LITTLE KINGDOM THE LARGEST EMPIRE THAT THE EARTH HAS EVER KNOWN.
34
CRRR
BRING ME ANOTHER CONTROLLER IMMEDIATELY!

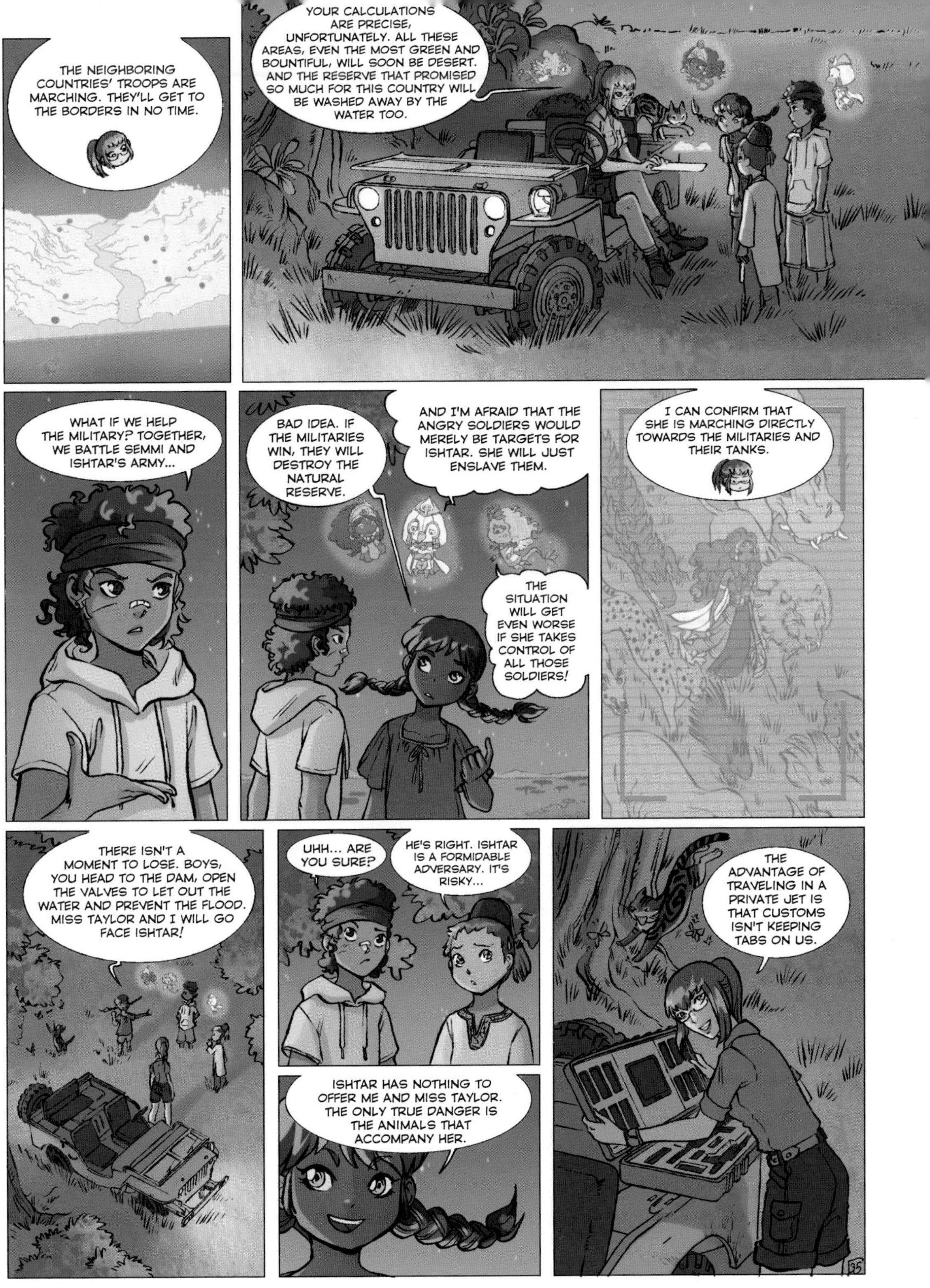
THE NEIGHBORING COUNTRIES' TROOPS ARE MARCHING. THEY'LL GET TO THE BORDERS IN NO TIME.
YOUR CALCULATIONS ARE PRECISE, UNFORTUNATELY. ALL THESE AREAS, EVEN THE MOST GREEN AND BOUNTIFUL, WILL SOON BE DESERT. AND THE RESERVE THAT PROMISED SO MUCH FOR THIS COUNTRY WILL BE WASHED AWAY BY THE WATER TOO.
WHAT IF WE HELP THE MILITARY? TOGETHER, WE BATTLE SEMMI AND ISHTAR'S ARMY...
BAD IDEA. IF THE MILITARIES WIN, THEY WILL DESTROY THE NATURAL RESERVE.
AND I'M AFRAID THAT THE ANGRY SOLDIERS WOULD MERELY BE TARGETS FOR ISHTAR. SHE WILL JUST ENSLAVE THEM.
THE SITUATION WILL GET EVEN WORSE IF SHE TAKES CONTROL OF ALL THOSE SOLDIERS!
I CAN CONFIRM THAT SHE IS MARCHING DIRECTLY TOWARDS THE MILITARIES AND THEIR TANKS.
THERE ISN'T A MOMENT TO LOSE. BOYS, YOU HEAD TO THE DAM, OPEN THE VALVES TO LET OUT THE WATER AND PREVENT THE FLOOD. MISS TAYLOR AND I WILL GO FACE ISHTAR!
UHH... ARE YOU SURE?
HE'S RIGHT. ISHTAR IS A FORMIDABLE ADVERSARY. IT'S RISKY...
ISHTAR HAS NOTHING TO OFFER ME AND MISS TAYLOR. THE ONLY TRUE DANGER IS THE ANIMALS THAT ACCOMPANY HER.
THE ADVANTAGE OF TRAVELING IN A PRIVATE JET IS THAT CUSTOMS ISN'T KEEPING TABS ON US.
35

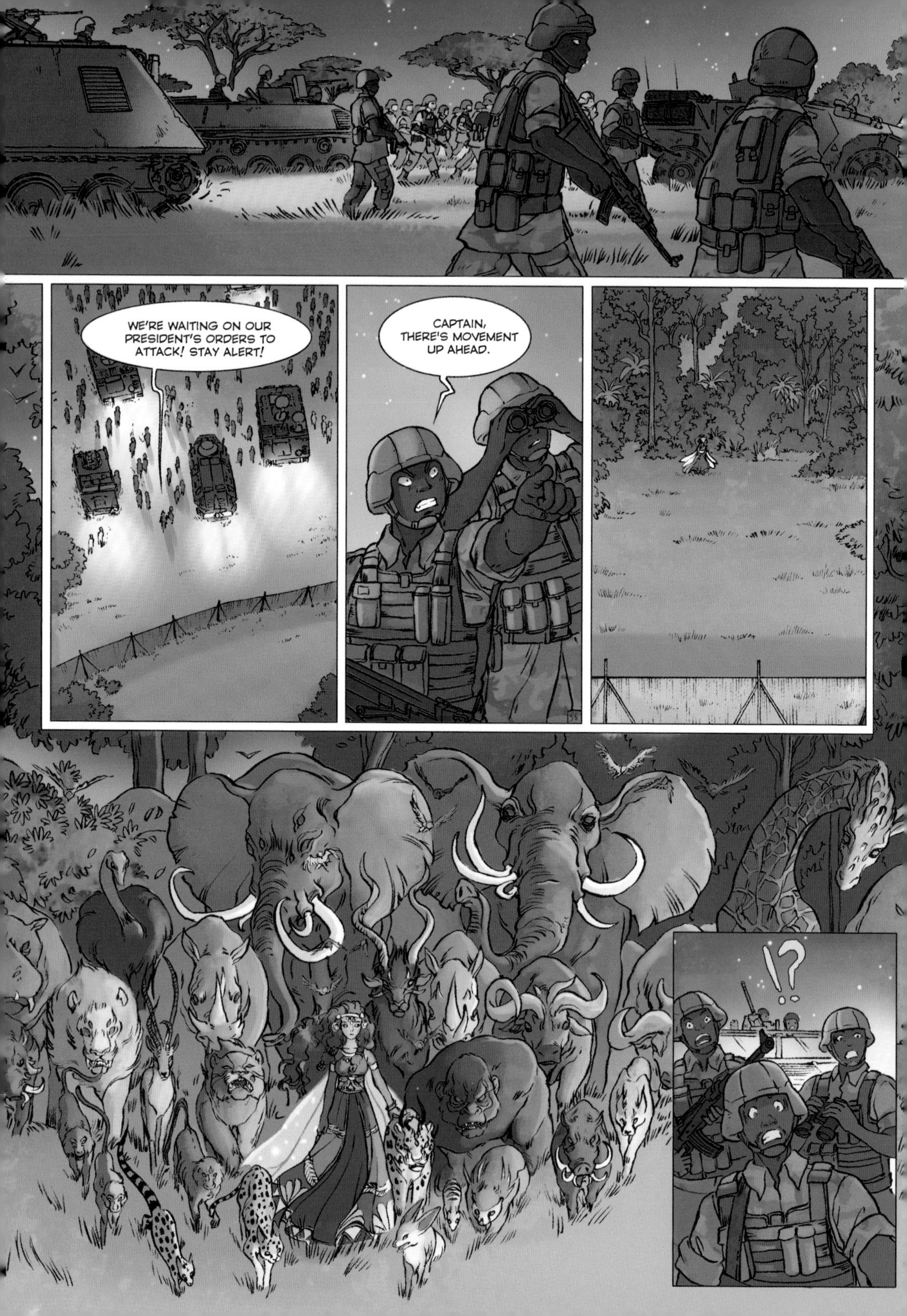
WE'RE WAITING ON OUR PRESIDENT'S ORDERS TO ATTACK! STAY ALERT!
CAPTAIN, THERE'S MOVEMENT UP AHEAD.
!?

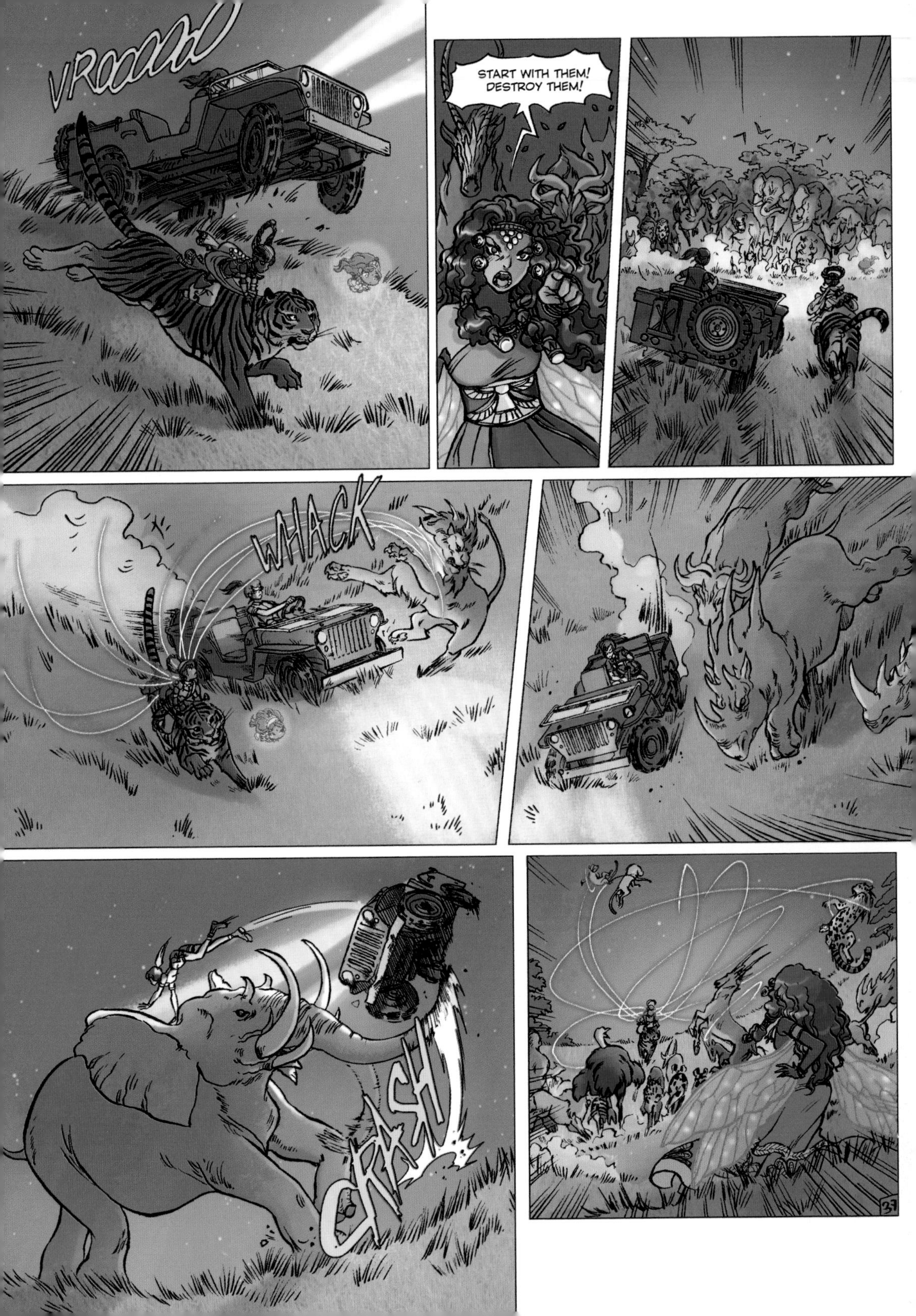
START WITH THEM! DESTROY THEM!
WHACK
CRASH

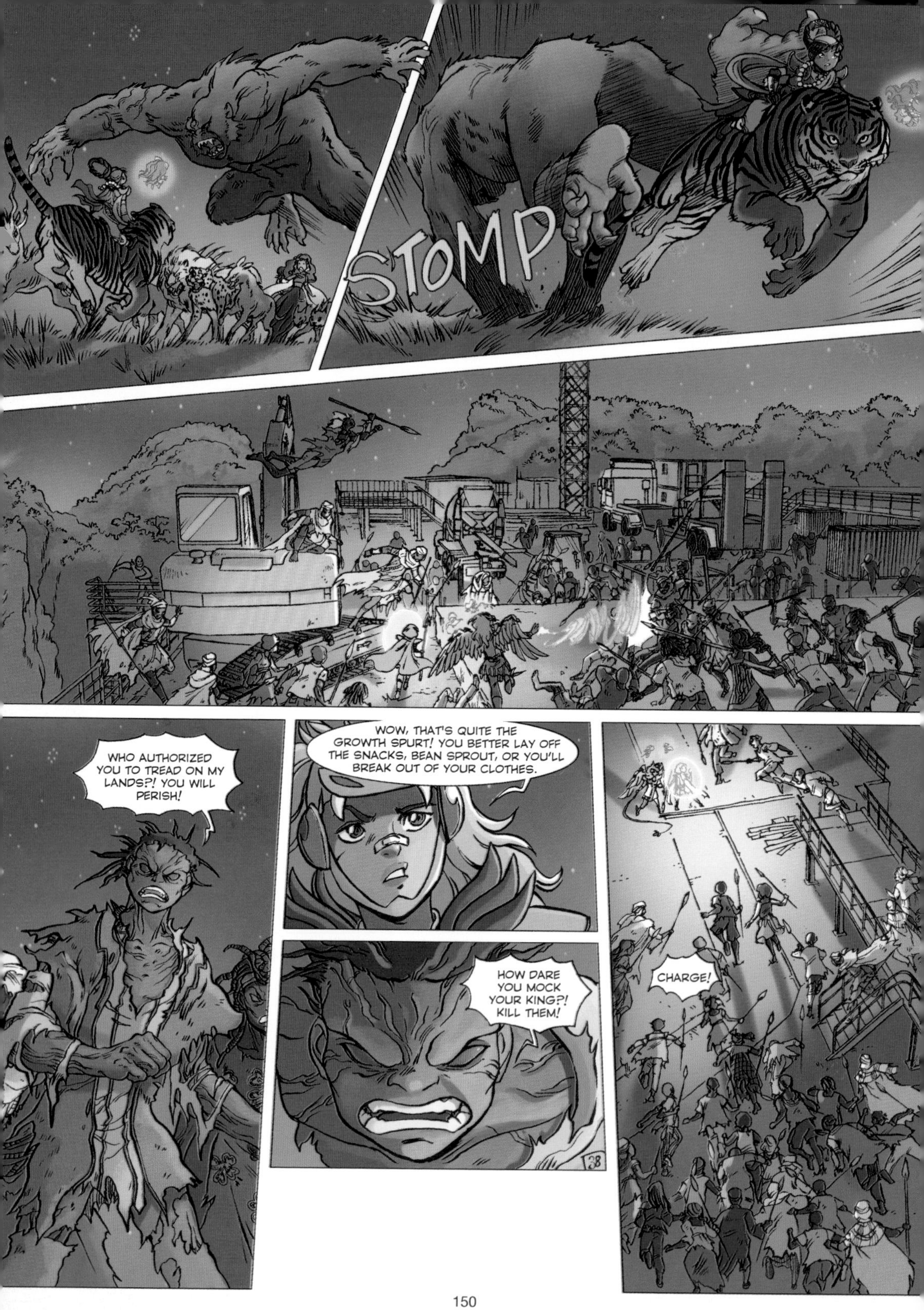
STOMP
WHO AUTHORIZED YOU TO TREAD ON MY LANDS?! YOU WILL PERISH!
WOW, THAT'S QUITE THE GROWTH SPURT! YOU BETTER LAY OFF THE SNACKS, BEAN SPROUT, OR YOU'LL BREAK OUT OF YOUR CLOTHES.
HOW DARE YOU MOCK YOUR KING?! KILL THEM!
CHARGE!

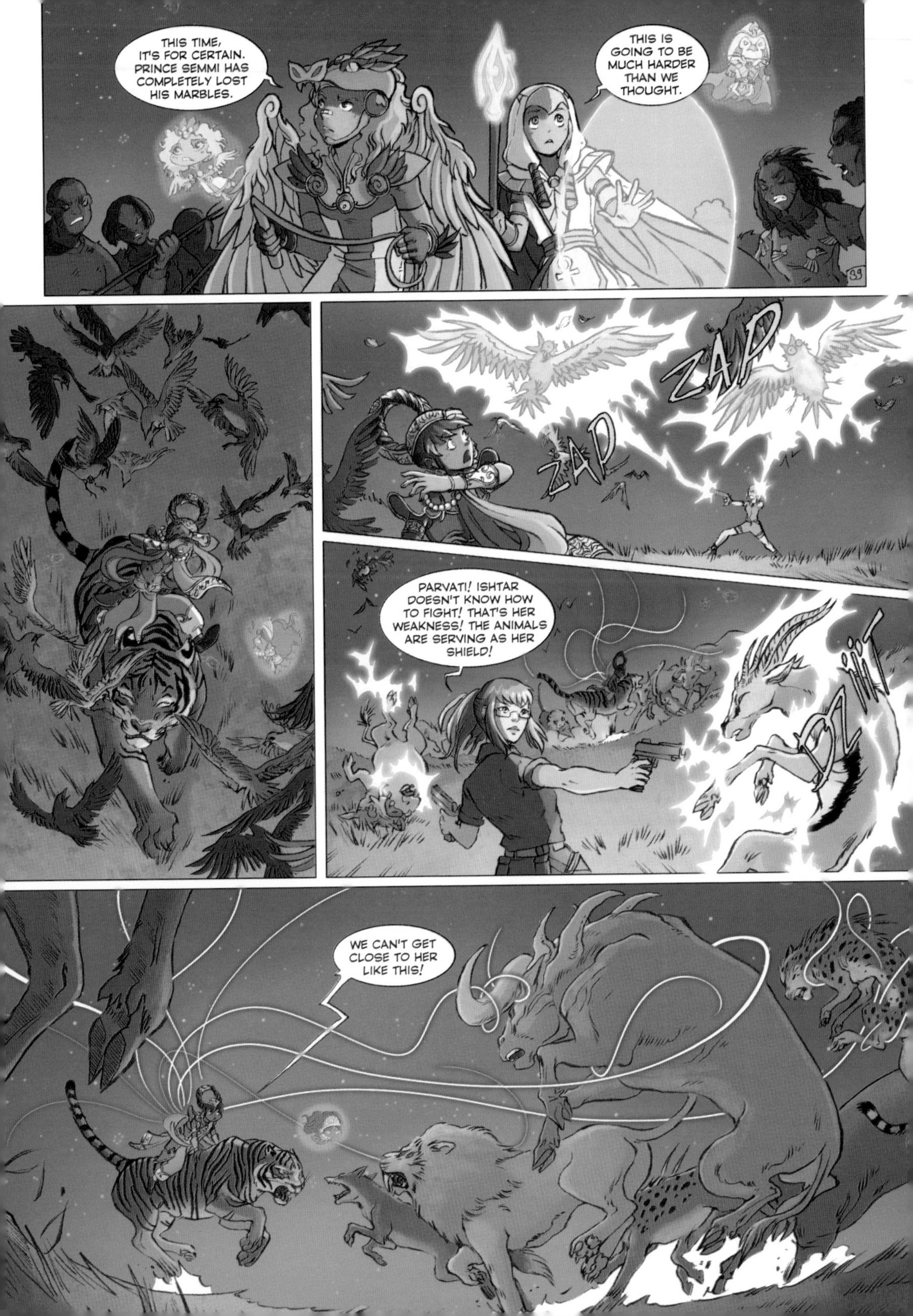
THIS TIME, IT'S FOR CERTAIN. PRINCE SEMMI HAS COMPLETELY LOST HIS MARBLES.
THIS IS GOING TO BE MUCH HARDER THAN WE THOUGHT.
ZAP
ZAP
ZAP
PARVATI! ISHTAR DOESN'T KNOW HOW TO FIGHT! THAT'S HER WEAKNESS! THE ANIMALS ARE SERVING AS HER SHIELD!
WE CAN'T GET CLOSE TO HER LIKE THIS!

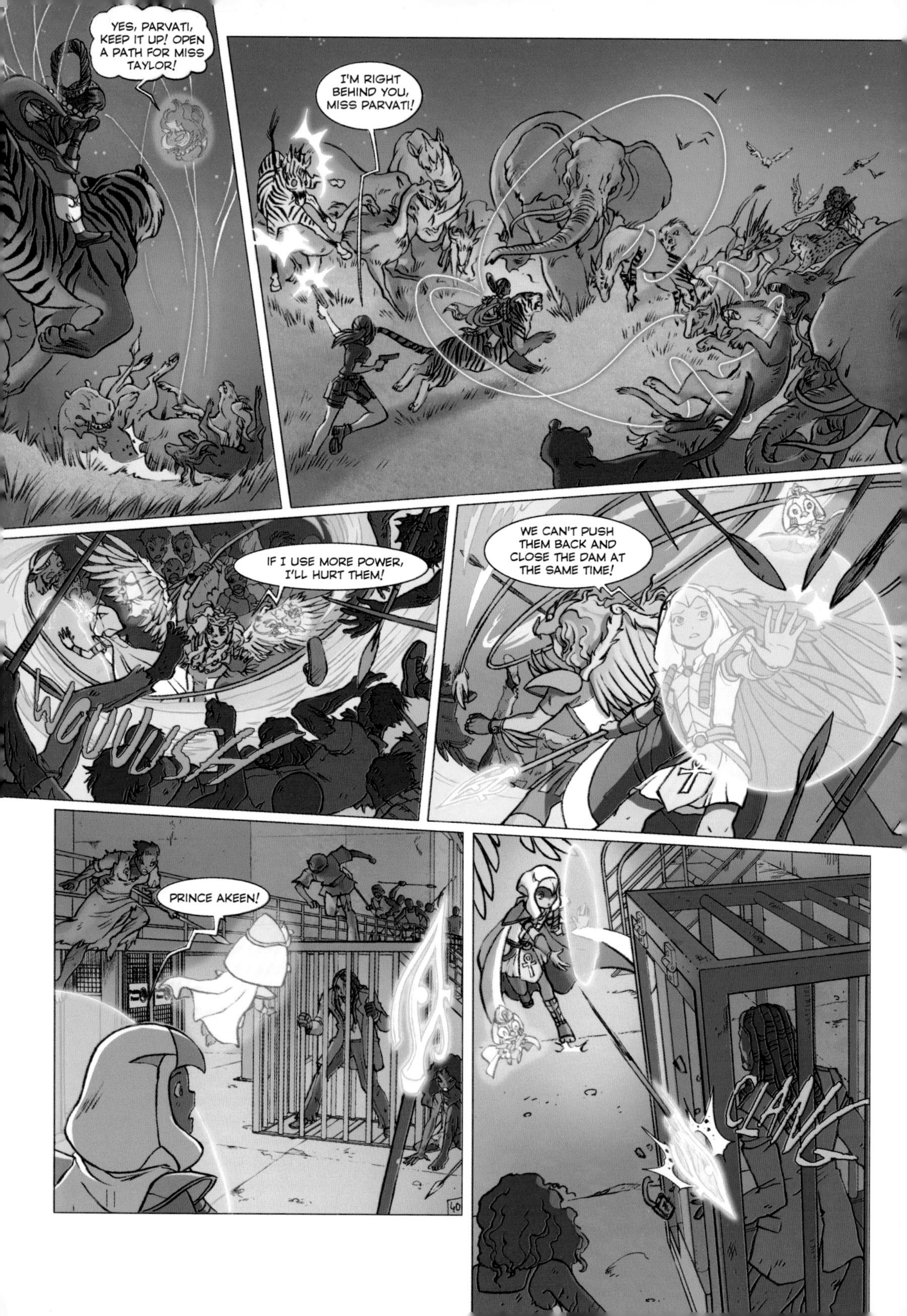
YES, PARVATI, KEEP IT UP! OPEN A PATH FOR MISS TAYLOR!
I'M RIGHT BEHIND YOU, MISS PARVATI!
IF I USE MORE POWER, I'LL HURT THEM!
WOOUUSH
WE CAN'T PUSH THEM BACK AND CLOSE THE DAM AT THE SAME TIME!
PRINCE AKEEN!
40
CLANG

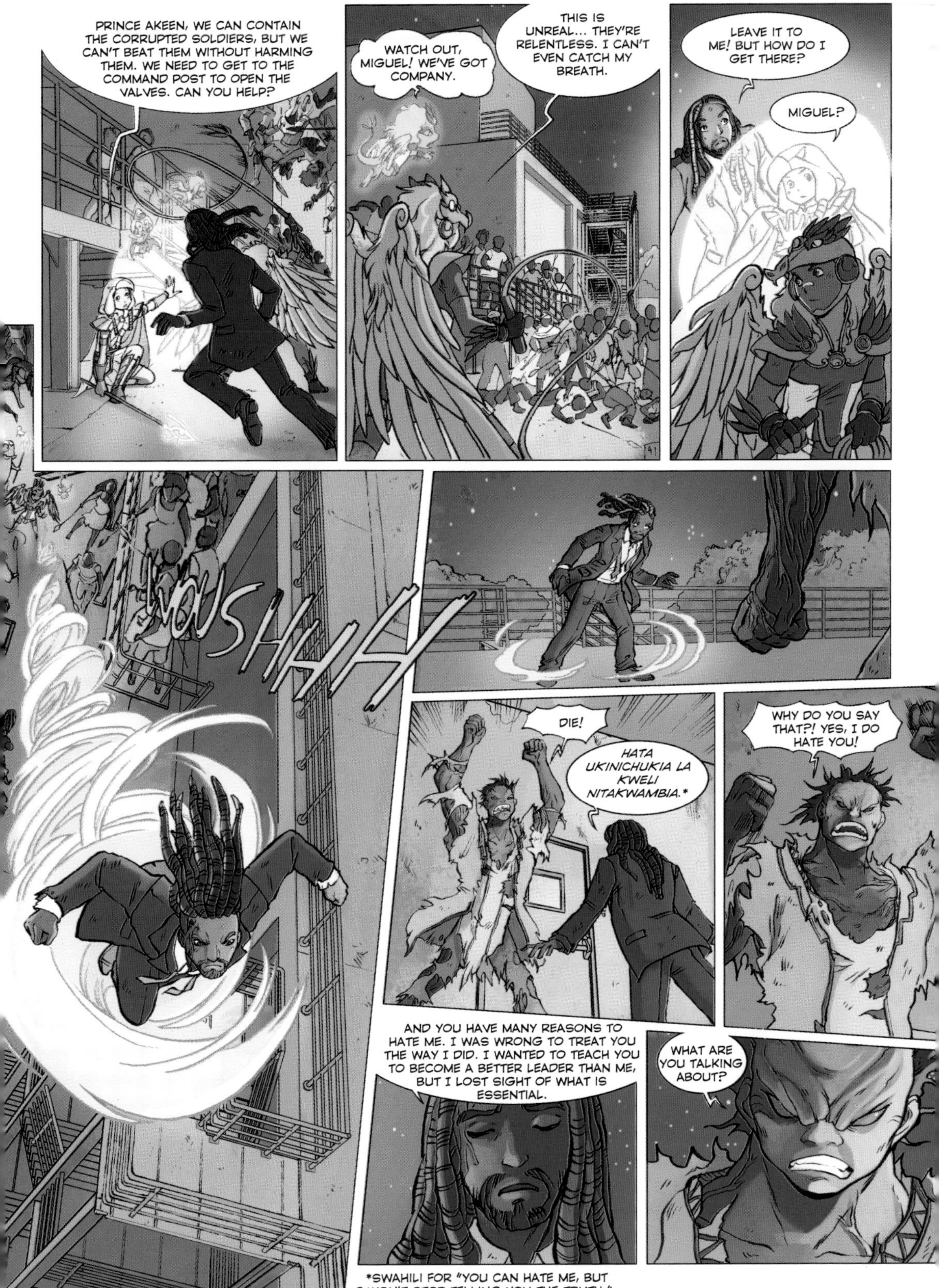
PRINCE AKEEN, WE CAN CONTAIN THE CORRUPTED SOLDIERS, BUT WE CAN'T BEAT THEM WITHOUT HARMING THEM. WE NEED TO GET TO THE COMMAND POST TO OPEN THE VALVES. CAN YOU HELP?
WATCH OUT, MIGUEL! WE'VE GOT COMPANY.
THIS IS UNREAL... THEY'RE RELENTLESS. I CAN'T EVEN CATCH MY BREATH.
LEAVE IT TO ME! BUT HOW DO I GET THERE?
MIGUEL?
WOUSHHH
DIE!
HATA UKINICHUKIA LA KWELI NITAKWAMBIA.*
WHY DO YOU SAY THAT?! YES, I DO HATE YOU!
AND YOU HAVE MANY REASONS TO HATE ME. I WAS WRONG TO TREAT YOU THE WAY I DID. I WANTED TO TEACH YOU TO BECOME A BETTER LEADER THAN ME, BUT I LOST SIGHT OF WHAT IS ESSENTIAL.
WHAT ARE YOU TALKING ABOUT?
*SWAHILI FOR "YOU CAN HATE ME, BUT I WON'T STOP TELLING YOU THE TRUTH."

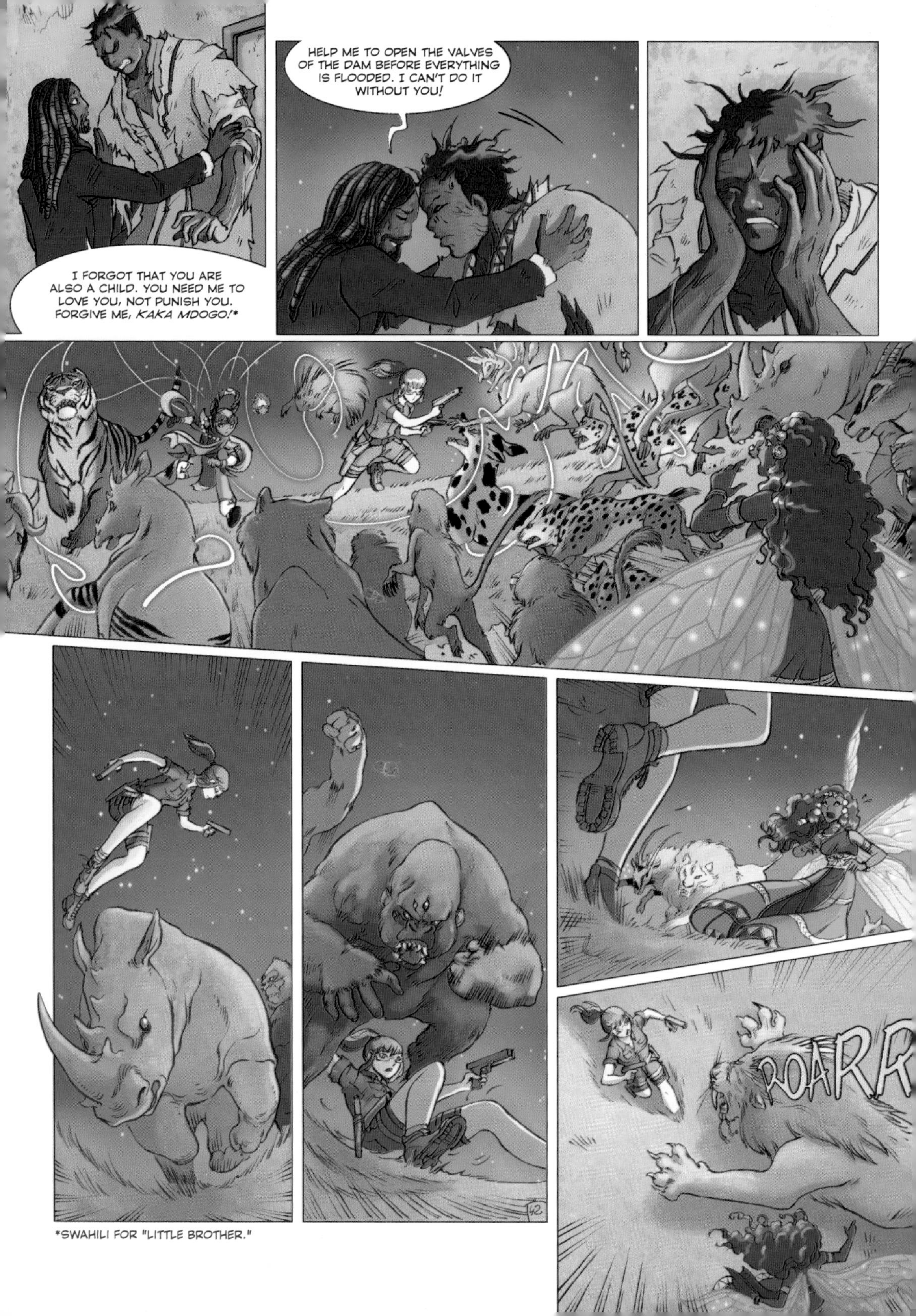
I FORGOT THAT YOU ARE ALSO A CHILD. YOU NEED ME TO LOVE YOU, NOT PUNISH YOU. FORGIVE ME, *KAKA MDOGO!**
HELP ME TO OPEN THE VALVES OF THE DAM BEFORE EVERYTHING IS FLOODED. I CAN'T DO IT WITHOUT YOU!
ROARR
42

*SWAHILI FOR "LITTLE BROTHER."

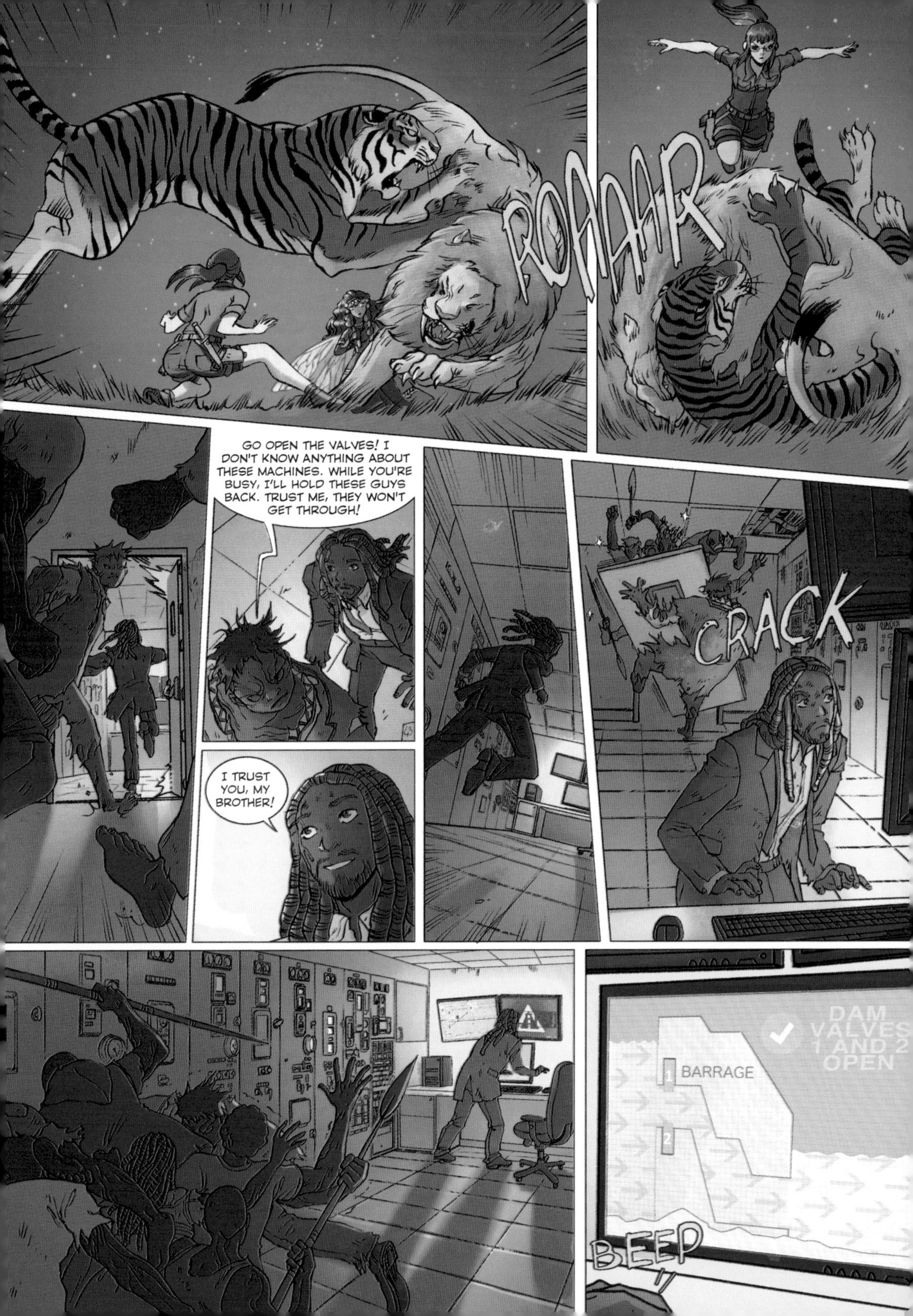
ROAAAR
GO OPEN THE VALVES! I DON'T KNOW ANYTHING ABOUT THESE MACHINES. WHILE YOU'RE BUSY, I'LL HOLD THESE GUYS BACK. TRUST ME, THEY WON'T GET THROUGH!
I TRUST YOU, MY BROTHER!
CRACK
DAM VALVES 1 AND 2 OPEN
BARRAGE
1
2
BEEP

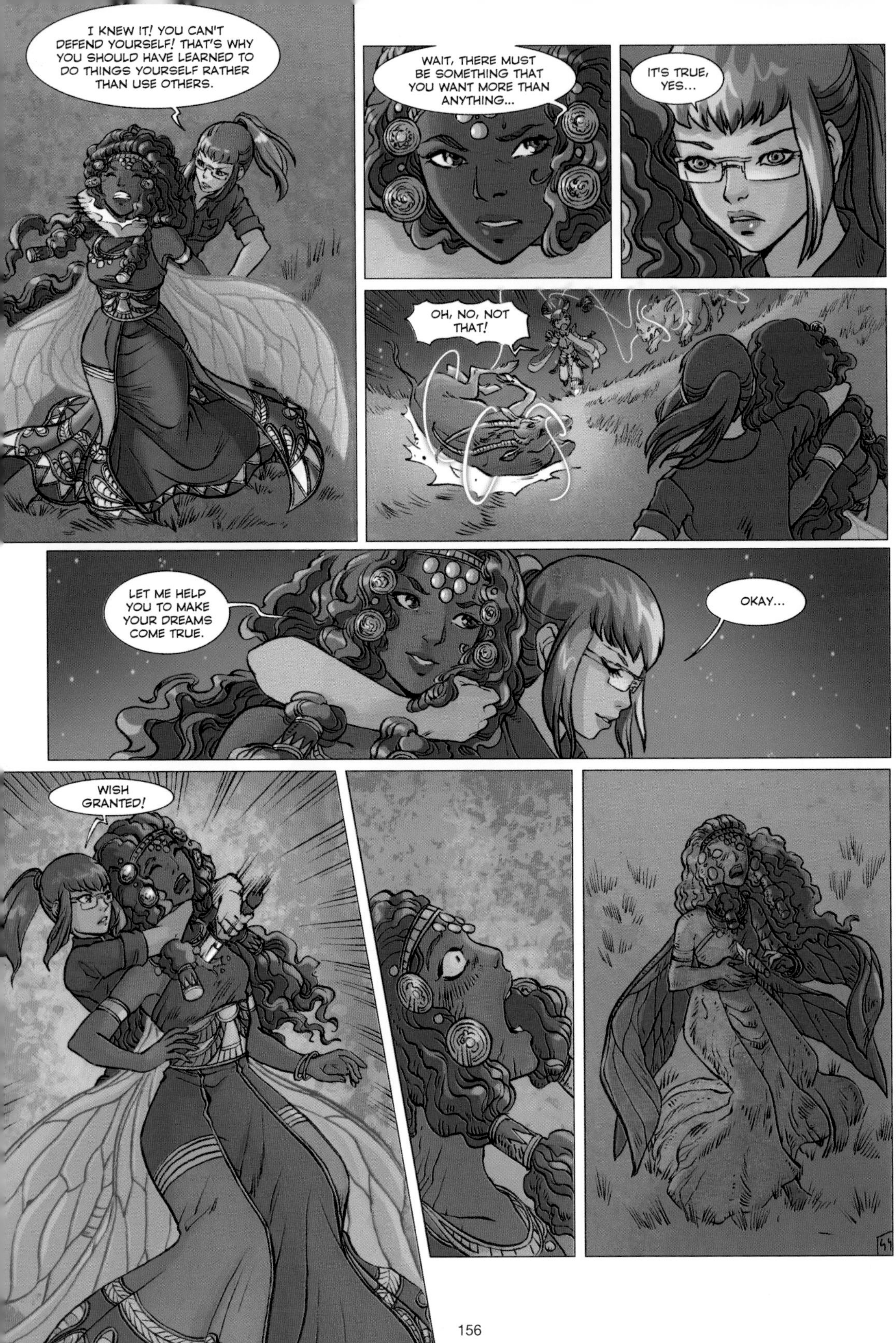
I KNEW IT! YOU CAN'T DEFEND YOURSELF! THAT'S WHY YOU SHOULD HAVE LEARNED TO DO THINGS YOURSELF RATHER THAN USE OTHERS.
WAIT, THERE MUST BE SOMETHING THAT YOU WANT MORE THAN ANYTHING...
IT'S TRUE, YES...
OH, NO, NOT THAT!
LET ME HELP YOU TO MAKE YOUR DREAMS COME TRUE.
OKAY...
WISH GRANTED!

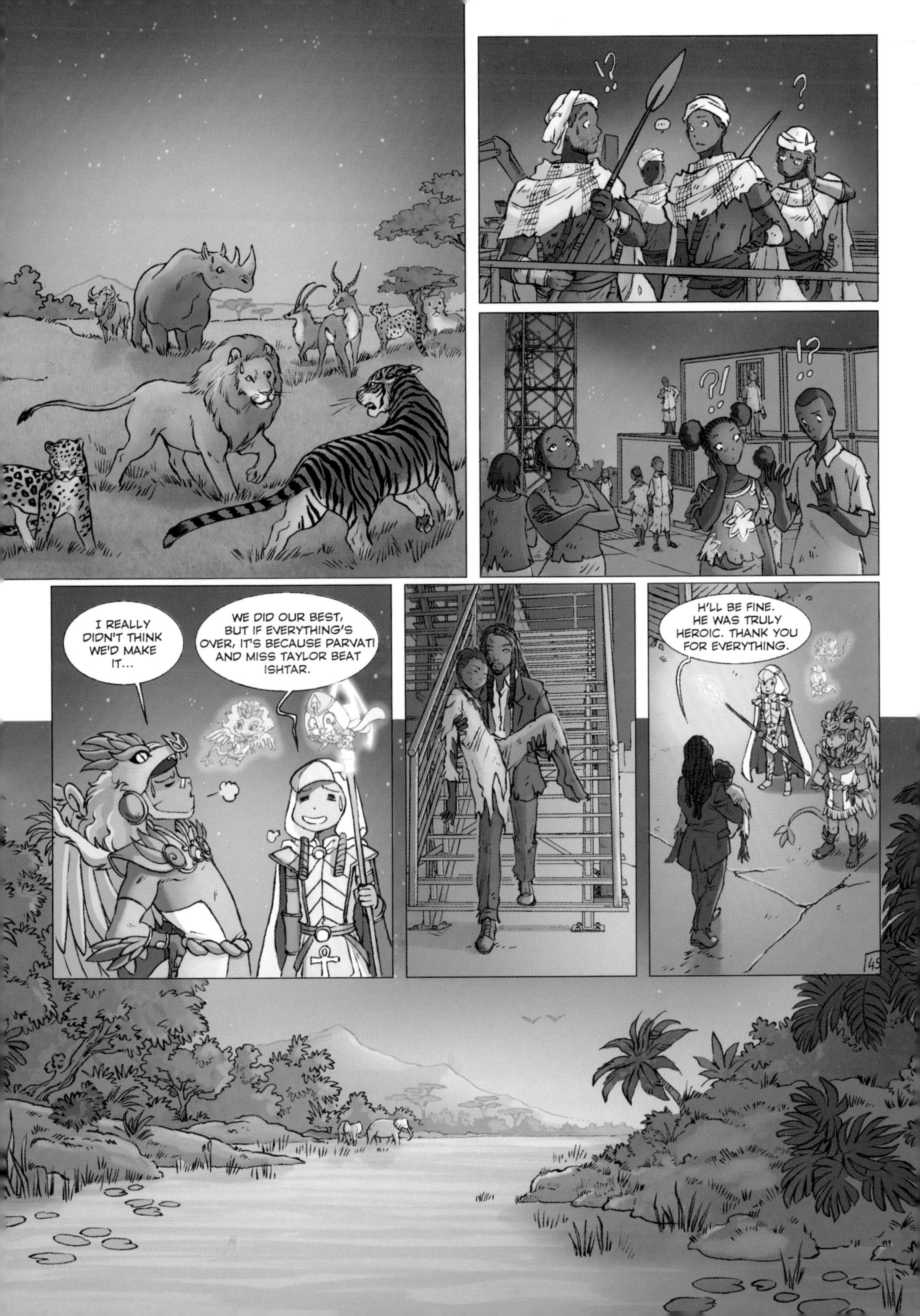
!?
...
?
?!
!?
I REALLY DIDN'T THINK WE'D MAKE IT...
WE DID OUR BEST, BUT IF EVERYTHING'S OVER, IT'S BECAUSE PARVATI AND MISS TAYLOR BEAT ISHTAR.
H'LL BE FINE. HE WAS TRULY HEROIC. THANK YOU FOR EVERYTHING.
45

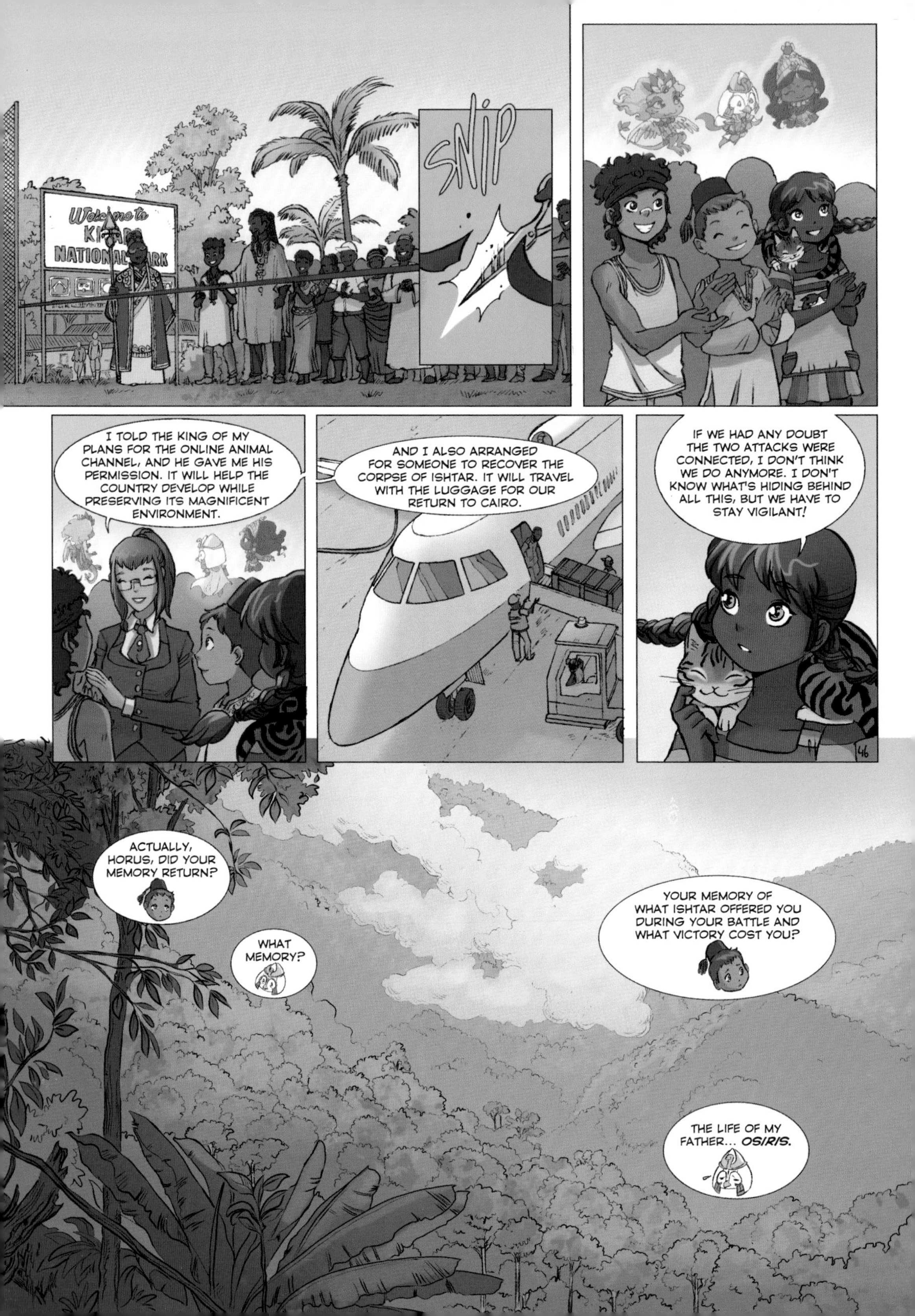
Welcome to
SNIP
I TOLD THE KING OF MY PLANS FOR THE ONLINE ANIMAL CHANNEL, AND HE GAVE ME HIS PERMISSION. IT WILL HELP THE COUNTRY DEVELOP WHILE PRESERVING ITS MAGNIFICENT ENVIRONMENT.
AND I ALSO ARRANGED FOR SOMEONE TO RECOVER THE CORPSE OF ISHTAR. IT WILL TRAVEL WITH THE LUGGAGE FOR OUR RETURN TO CAIRO.
IF WE HAD ANY DOUBT THE TWO ATTACKS WERE CONNECTED, I DON'T THINK WE DO ANYMORE. I DON'T KNOW WHAT'S HIDING BEHIND ALL THIS, BUT WE HAVE TO STAY VIGILANT!
ACTUALLY, HORUS, DID YOUR MEMORY RETURN?
WHAT MEMORY?
YOUR MEMORY OF WHAT ISHTAR OFFERED YOU DURING YOUR BATTLE AND WHAT VICTORY COST YOU?
THE LIFE OF MY FATHER... *OSIRIS.*

WATCH OUT FOR PAPERCUTZ

Welcome to the frenzied, frightening fourth volume of THE MYTHICS, "Global Chaos," by the all-star creative crew consisting of Patrick Sobral, Patricia Lyfoung, Philippe Ogaki, Jenny, Dara, Alice Picard, and Magali Paillat, brought to you by Papercutz — the locally chaotic chums dedicated to publishing great graphic novels for all ages. I'm Jim Salicrup, the Editor-in-Chief and MYTHICS-lover (and not because the pages of this graphic novel him been doused with *L'irrésistible*!), here to reflect on this volume's fascinating stories…

Obviously, the inspiration for THE MYTHICS in general comes from actual myths. Just about every culture has its own mythology — stories of ancient gods that not only had exciting exploits, but also explained various parts of real life or provided answers to life's big questions. Myths would tell us where we (humanity) came from and where we'll ultimately go. These ancient gods often provided everything we needed to survive on Earth — from the sun to the weather and just about everything else. Myths weren't just stories, to many people they were totally true. As humanity began to figure a lot of stuff out, suddenly these mythological characters started to seem somewhat silly. Certainly, the simplistic explanations the myths provided couldn't be taken as seriously once people knew the scientific answers for lots of stuff. Facts were wiping out fictions.

Yet people from all cultures still loved stories, especially stories that they could relate to. Stories with heroic characters bringing justice to those who have been wronged or unfairly exploited. Stories of romantic relationships. Stories involving the struggles of the rich and the poor. Or everything you'll find in William Shakespeare's world-famous plays. Even stories with larger-than-life imaginary characters found great acceptance over the years. From Frankenstein's monster and Count Dracula to Sherlock Holmes and Tarzan of the Apes. It wasn't long after comicbooks were created that tales of superheroes began to fill-up their four-color pages. Astute observers could easily see that comicbook superheroes were greatly inspired by the myths. One classic character would even shout out "SHAZAM!" to become the original Captain Marvel — SHAZAM standing for Solomon, Hercules, Atlas, Zeus, Achilles, and Mercury. Comicbook superheroes were often described as "modern mythology." And now you can see how popular those comicbook superheroes have become as they've transformed into the stars of countless blockbuster movies and hit television shows.

With THE MYTHICS it's all come full circle. While there have been plenty of myth-inspired superheroes, *Thor* and *Wonder Woman* for example, THE MYTHICS are especially interesting as they are a super team of several different mythologies. Which makes sense since the world has become far more connected than ever before. After all, we're an American graphic novel publisher publishing a graphic novel series created in France by a multi-cultural crew of creators and printed in India, but also available digitally anywhere in the world.

Yet the stories are still about things that affect us all. Lust and Envy have been aspects of the human personality since there have been humans. While everyone may want to be loved, there are certain ways to go about finding love and giving love — mostly involving respect for others. Likewise, being envious could lead to all sorts of problems. Most "con artists," the term for people who will cheat others out of money or other things of value, find victims who will give almost anything for what they want. The lessons these stories tell us is that there are no shortcuts to either finding love or anything else you may desire. That even goes for the next thrilling volume of THE MYTHICS. Just be patient — we're working on translating, editing, and putting it all together for you! In the meantime, you can go to papercutz.com and find out about other great Papercutz graphic novels such as THE SCHOOL FOR EXTRATERRESTRIAL GIRLS, LOLA'S SUPER CLUB, THE ONLY LIVING GIRL, ASTRO MOUSE AND LIGHT BULB, and even GILLBERT for more great tales of mythological proportions!

Thanks,

Jim

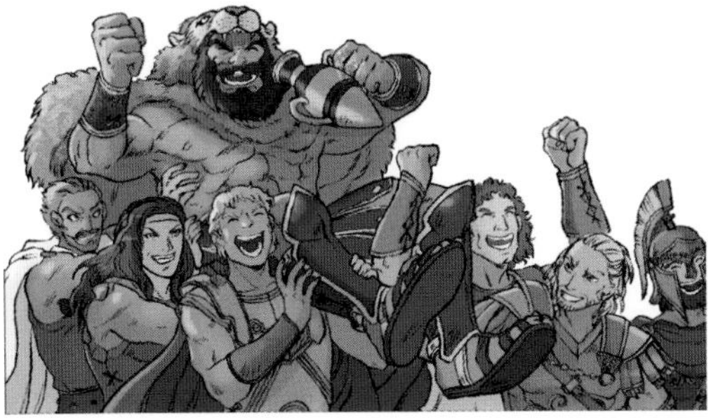

STAY IN TOUCH!

EMAIL:	salicrup@papercutz.com
WEB:	www.papercutz.com
TWITTER:	@papercutzgn
INSTAGRAM:	@papercutzgn
FACEBOOK:	PAPERCUTZGRAPHICNOVELS
FANMAIL:	Papercutz, 160 Broadway, Suite 700, East Wing, New York, NY 10038

Go to papercutz.com and sign up for the free Papercutz e-newsletter!